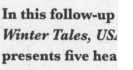

In this follow-up ~~~~~~~~~~~~~~~~ **tion**
Winter Tales, USA ~~~~~~~~~~~~~~ **sz**
presents five hea~~~~~~~~~~~~~~ —
stories set during the holiday season.

In the title novella, it's the UnHoly Trinity's first Christmas in New Orleans. Mistress Nora decides she, Søren, and Kingsley need to celebrate with a very special gift-giving game—not a boring White Elephant exchange, but a Black & Blue Elephant exchange where the gifts hurt as much to receive as they do to give. And Nora already knows exactly what she wants...

This collection also includes the Original Sinners novellas *A Winter Symphony* and *A Midwinter Night's Dream*, as well as the short stories "A Christmas Maggie" and "A Beautiful Thing."

PRAISE FOR TIFFANY REISZ

"Daring, sophisticated, and literary... Exactly what good erotica should be." — **Kitty Thomas on *The Siren***

"Kinky, well-written, hot as hell." — **Little Red Reading Hood on *The Red: An Erotic Fantasy***

"Impossible to stop reading." — **Heroes & Heartbreakers on *The Bourbon Thief***

"Stunning... Transcends genres and will leave readers absolutely breathless." — ***RT Book Reviews* on the Original Sinners series**

"I worship at the altar of Tiffany Reisz!" — ***New York Times* bestselling author Lorelei James**

"Sensual, smart, and hilarious." — ***Library Journal* on *One Hot December***

"*The Bourbon Thief* isn't just good, it's exceptional. The story captured my imagination; the characters captured my heart." — **Literati Literature Lovers**

"I loved the Original Sinners series... Her prose is quite beautiful, and she can weave a wonderful tight story." — ***New York Times* and *USA Today* bestseller Jennifer Probst**

WRAPPED IN BLACK

WRAPPED IN BLACK

Wrapped In Black

Tiffany Reisz

8TH CIRCLE PRESS
LOUISVILLE, KY

CONTENTS

AUTHOR'S NOTE

The stories in Wrapped In Black *are part of the ongoing Original Sinners series.*

Readers new to the series should start with the first book, The Siren. *Those looking to avoid spoilers should read at least through the fourth book,* The Mistress, *prior to reading this collection.*

A complete reading order can be found at TiffanyReisz.com.

A BEAUTIFUL THING

AUTHOR'S NOTE

This story takes place three months before the events of The Siren.

While he was in Bethany, reclining at the table in the home of Simon the Leper, a woman came with an alabaster jar of very expensive perfume, made of pure nard. She broke the jar and poured the perfume on his head. Some of those present were saying indignantly to one another, "Why this waste of perfume? It could have been sold for more than a year's wages and the money given to the poor." And they rebuked her harshly.

"Leave her alone," said Jesus. "Why are you bothering her? She has done a beautiful thing to me."

MARK 14:3-6

NORA DROVE to the music store at the other end of town and ignored her ringing phone the entire way. Maybe if she didn't answer it, Kingsley would forget about why he was calling her. December 12th meant Christmas was all of thirteen days away. She had shit to do that didn't involve beating up the mayor's younger brother.

She pulled into Theremin's as her phone bleated at her once more. With a growl, she pulled it out of her coat pocket.

"King, new rule," she answered. "No kink at Christmas." She got out of her car and slammed the door behind her.

"Forty-thousand dollars," Kingsley said.

Nora paused a moment to pick her jaw up off the sidewalk. "Okay, maybe kink at Christmas. What's the job?"

"One week in Vegas. All expenses paid."

Nora leaned back against her car hood and crossed her booted legs at the ankle. She held her coat tight around her neck. The temperature had dropped ten degrees since morning. By nightfall, it would snow. She could smell it on the air.

"Couple?" she asked.

"Only him."

"Fetishes?"

"Feet. Pain. Blood."

Nora sighed. She'd have to have her entire collection of needles professionally sterilized. Again. "Sounds pretty basic. What's the catch?"

For forty-thousand dollars, there had to be a catch.

"No catch," he said. "Not really."

"King, don't bullshit a bullshitter. What's the catch?"

"His name is Victor Moretti."

"Motherfucker."

"Is that *oui* or *non*?" Kingsley asked, his throaty laugh sending the temperature back up ten degrees.

"It's hell no. Moretti? He's mob. You know I don't play with the mob."

"Victor is only one of the Moretti sons," Kingsley said. "He's never been convicted of any crime."

"You've never been convicted of any crime either. That's not saying much."

"He's not in the family business. If he was, he wouldn't have moved across the country to get away from it."

"To Vegas, where mobsters go to retire. King, he's the son of a fucking crime boss. Those people are the reason my dad was buried closed-casket, remember? You know my number one rule," Nora said as she headed toward the entrance of the Theremin's. "'Any job except the mob.' Tell him no, but be nice about it."

Nora hung up on Kingsley as she entered the store. She'd ordered a new guitar case for Wesley, and it had come in finally. She wanted to get it early since he'd be leaving her right after finals on the fifteenth to spend Christmas in Kentucky with his parents. So far, she didn't really have any plans for Christmas. Maybe she'd fly off to Jamaica for a week and spend it on the beach. Maybe she'd go to Paris and find a handsome stranger to seduce. She used to spend her Christmases at Kingsley's. After saying Christmas morning mass, Søren would have lunch with his sister Claire in Manhattan and then spend the rest of the day hiding out with her and Kingsley at the townhouse. They'd exchange presents and eat and drink too much. But then she'd left Søren, and Christmas hadn't been the same since then. She'd almost asked Wesley to stay with her, but knew that sweet boy would do it just so she wouldn't be alone. She couldn't ask him to miss Christmas with his parents. The crazy kid actually liked his family. What a concept.

Jews. That was the answer. She needed more Jewish people in her life. There. Now she had her New Year's resolution:

Make more Jewish friends. Then she'd have people to party with while the rest of the world did the Christmas thing. Perfect plan. Jews, Muslims, Buddhists, and maybe some atheists. She'd get right on that.

The owner went into the back to get the guitar case. While Nora waited, she wandered. In a side room, she stopped short when she laid eyes on the most beautiful grand piano she'd ever seen. Solid black finish with gleaming golden guts on the inside.

Of course the inside of a piano wasn't called the guts, though. What was it called? Søren would know.

"Nice, isn't it?" The store owner had returned with the guitar case. "Imperial Bösendorfer. Fully refurbished. One owner. The wife of a Presbyterian minister."

"Presbyterian?" she repeated. "Damn Calvinists."

"Excuse me?" he said, clearly not understanding her.

"Never mind." Søren was the only man she knew who, when asked what his pet peeves were, would answer *Calvinism*. "It's amazing. How much is it?"

"It's actually very reasonable. It's on consignment and the family can't wait to get rid of it. Forty-five. Delivery and tuning included."

Nora's knees buckled at the figure. "Forty-five thousand?"

"I know," the owner said, shaking his head. "It's a steal. A new one would run you eighty."

"Little out of my price range, I'm afraid." She had enough money for the piano, but just barely. She also had a mortgage, a roommate to feed, and the dream of giving up work with Kingsley to write full-time. If she dropped forty-five thousand dollars on a piano, she and Wes would be eating ramen noodles for the next year. Either that or she'd better get a big fucking book deal real fucking fast.

"You should play it at least. A piano wants to be played."

Nora reached out and touched the keys without depressing them.

"No, I don't play. I have a..." She paused, searching for the right word. "A friend. He plays beautifully. Learned it from his mother and then mostly self-taught. One of those prodigy types."

"Professional?"

"Actually, he's a Jesuit priest. He plays with the symphony sometimes if they need him. He has a Steinway, but, well, it's kind of broken."

"Such a shame."

"Just the sustain pedal. Long story. Do you play?" Nora asked. She was dying to hear the sound of the Bösendorfer. Some of her happiest memories involved Søren and pianos.

"Not much anymore. But I have my own personal pianist I keep around here. Isaiah?" He called out the name, and a boy of about twelve came running from the other room.

"I'm here!" Isaiah announced, his voice so loud the keys of the piano vibrated.

"Isaiah takes lessons here," the owner explained. "His family's apartment's not big enough for a piano. I let him come practice here whenever he likes."

"Nice to meet you." Nora held out her hand and Isaiah only stared at it. "Don't be scared. I know strange white ladies are terrifying, but I won't bite you. Probably not, anyway."

The boy grinned broadly and held out his hand. She shook it with vigor.

"Good handshake," she said. "Strong hands make for a better pianist. Will you play something for me?"

"Yes, ma'am," he said with gusto as he threw himself down onto the piano bench. He cracked his neck and knuckles and wiggled his fingers over the keys. "Any requests?"

"Play a Christmas song," Nora suggested. "Any one you like."

"I like 'em all. But I just learned this one."

He inhaled and closed his eyes. When he opened them again, the blustery boy had transformed into a professional musician. He brought his fingers down onto the keys. The familiar haunting strains of "O Holy Night" filled the store.

The piece brought back a thousand memories. How she loved this song...how much it moved her every time she heard it...how she couldn't hear it without wanting to fall onto her knees and adore the God who had created men and music.

How old had she been? Twenty-four? Twenty-five? One night in early December, she'd gone to the rectory at midnight and found Søren at the piano playing this very piece...

HE KNEW she was coming to him that night, and he knew the song was her favorite. As he played, she came to him and sat on the floor next to the piano bench, resting her head by his thigh. As the last notes rang out and died, he had laid a hand gently on the side of her head. Without a word he bade her to stand. He didn't need words to give her orders. She could read his face, his eyes, his body language like a book. He snapped his fingers, and she reached under her skirt to pull off her panties. Søren lowered the fallboard to cover the keys as she straddled his lap and leaned back against the piano. They kissed, tongues and lips mingling, for what felt like an hour. She ran her fingers through his blond hair. He slid his hands up and down her thighs.

"Please, sir," she whispered against his neck.

"Please what?"

She growled in playful frustration. He hadn't hurt her yet. They'd done nothing but kiss. As long as he didn't hurt her, he could kiss her and tease her and taunt her and touch her forever without needing to fuck her. It wasn't until he inflicted pain on her that he grew aroused enough that he had to have her. But she...she had to have him, and right now.

"Please...I need you inside me, sir."

"Keep begging. It's under consideration."

He kissed her earlobe, her neck. He opened her blouse and kissed the swell of her breasts. And so she begged him as instructed. *Please, sir... Please... I'll do anything, submit to anything, give you anything, accept anything... Use me, abuse me, bruise me,* she begged him in a poem of desperation.

When his teeth bit into the soft flesh of her shoulder, she knew it would happen. She gasped in pain as his previously gentle fingers dug into her hips hard enough she flinched.

The flinch did it. Seconds later, the piano bench sat toppled on the floor. Nora—then still "Eleanor"—lay on her stomach on the floor halfway under the piano. She braced herself with slow deep breaths and wasn't shocked when Søren pulled her shirt off and pushed her skirt to her waist. He landed the first brutal blow on the back of her thighs. She didn't look at what instrument of torture Søren wielded on her. Cane or crop or switch from a tree, it didn't matter. They all hurt like fuck.

Good. The greater the pain now, the greater the pleasure after.

After a dozen or more brutal blows to the back of her body, Søren dropped a crop onto the floor. It hit the hardwood with a softer sort of thud instead of a rattle of rattan. She braced herself for more pain. He might flog her next or whip her. She closed her eyes and let go of herself and any fears. No reason to be afraid. Søren loved her. He'd hurt her, but he would never harm her. He took more pleasure from inflicting pain than she took from an orgasm. She gave up her body to him, gave it up like a gift. And like a present, wrapped and given, he tore her open.

Søren straddled her thighs and gripped the back of her neck. Scalding candle wax landed on the center of her spine. Another drop hit a few inches higher. With Søren on top of her and holding her down, she couldn't flinch. She reached out for something, anything to grasp, and wrapped her fingers around the sustain pedal. She focused on the metal in her hand, its coolness and smoothness. The burning wax coated her spine and sent pain shooting through her entire body. It ended, finally it ended, and Søren pushed her onto her back. Her inflamed skin slapped the hardwood and she cried out in agony.

The agony was short-lived as Søren kissed her again, kissed her mouth, her neck, and spent as much time kissing her breasts as he had brutalizing her back. The moans that came from her were borne of pleasure, the deepest pleasure, the sort of pleasure that came only after suffering pain. The pain threw the pleasure into such sharp relief that sex without pain seemed illogical to her. Why even bother with someone so muted? So dampened?

So boring.

When Søren pushed her thighs wide open and brought his head between her legs, she felt anything but bored. His fingers dug deep into her and ground against her most sensitive spots while his tongue and lips against her clitoris brought her to the edge of orgasm and left her hanging there with knots of need coiling in her stomach and her hand still gripping the sustain pedal to steady herself.

Søren rose up and covered her with his body. He entered her hard and fast, and she came after the first few thrusts. After her climax, she relaxed and simply let him have her. She loved the pressure of him inside her, filling her up, moving within her, and the ragged but controlled tenor of his breathing.

After he came inside her, he slowly pulled out and dragged

her into his arms. She panted against his chest as he stroked her hair and kissed her forehead.

"Did you enjoy that?" he asked as she lay across his lap.

"So fucking much. Only..."

"What?"

She eyed the piano and saw the sustain pedal hanging at a somewhat off-angle. "I think I broke your piano."

THE SONG ENDED, and the final notes of "O Holy Night" played by young Isaiah shivered up Nora's spine.

"Thank you," she said to the boy. "You're very talented. I hope you never quit playing."

He shrugged. "Don't know. I'm on the basketball team at school. My dad, he wants me to quit piano and only play basketball. He thinks my sister should take the piano lessons. She doesn't like it, though. Just me."

"Why does he think your sister should take piano lessons and not you?"

"Says music is for girls. Mom tells him he's crazy and that it's good for me to know music so I can play in church."

"Music's for girls?" She looked up at the store owner and winked at him. "I'll have you know the strongest, smartest, toughest, and most intimidating man I know also plays piano. What do you think of that?"

"That true?"

"Very true. And when he plays piano every woman in the room falls in love with him. Girls love musicians."

"That's true," said the store owner. "My wife said she didn't even notice I existed until she heard me playing saxophone."

Isaiah seemed to think it over. "Maybe I'll keep playing," he said. "Maybe I'll keep playing basketball, too. You know, double my chances with the ladies, right?"

"I like the way you think, kid." Nora chucked him under the chin. He scrambled off the piano bench and headed back to the other room of the store. "It's an amazing piano," she told the owner. "I love the sound. Richer than a Steinway."

"It's got beautiful bass notes. Holds the sound better. There's no piano like the Bösendorfer. They call them the Rolls Royce of pianos. If you change your mind, let me know. Like I said, price includes delivery."

The store owner left her alone with the piano. Nora touched the top and felt the ghost of a thousand concertos lurking in the polished wood.

Nora fished her phone out of her pocket.

"To what do I owe the pleasure?" Kingsley asked when he answered.

"Call Moretti back. Tell him I'll do it."

Kingsley said nothing and Nora rolled her eyes. Typical dominant trick—stop speaking to force the other to fill the silence.

"I'm at a music store," she explained.

Silence.

"It's December."

Silence.

"Did you know they call Bösendorfer pianos the Rolls Royce of pianos?"

Silence.

"It's almost Christmas. And it's almost his birthday, King."

Silence. And then...

"I'll tell him fifty or nothing," Kingsley said. "And I know him. He'll pay fifty. You can keep my cut this time."

"I knew you still loved him."

"I could say the same to you," Kingsley said.

The past year had been a cold war between her and Søren, between Kingsley and Søren. She didn't know what had started the war, but she knew she wanted to finish it. Maybe this would help. Even if it didn't, she had to give Søren the piano. She didn't know why, except for the reason Kingsley had named: She still loved Søren.

"I'll front you the money. Buy him the piano," Kingsley said.

"*Joyeux Noël*, King," Nora whispered.

"Merry Christmas, Elle."

She hung up the phone and called out for the store owner. "You said you deliver?"

"We deliver," he said, stepping back into the room with a broad smile crossing his wizened face.

"Sacred Heart Catholic Church in Wakefield. It goes to the rectory, not the church. You'll have to drive up to it around the block. It's tucked back in a little wooded area. You should be writing all this down. And it'll need to be delivered on December 21st. Do it after six, otherwise he'll be at the church working."

"Quite a Christmas gift you're giving," he said as he wrote down the details.

"Well..." She kissed her fingertips and touched the top of the piano in a benediction. "It's really for Christmas *and* his birthday."

THAT FRIDAY, Nora boarded a plane for Vegas. A limo picked her up at the airport and took her to a sprawling mansion in Summerlin outside the Vegas city limits. Some sort of servant attempted to take her toy bag from her, but she waved him away as she entered the home. A man of about forty with a dark tan, a face that had once been handsome, and desperate eyes met her in the sunroom.

"Mistress Nora." He took her hand and kissed it. "It's an honor to have you in my home."

"Fuck your honor. You can do better than that," she said without a smile. "Floor."

He dropped to his feet and kissed the toe of her dirty boot.

"You know, Vic," she said as she pulled a riding crop out of her toy bag, "I really hate you mob guys. Bunch of fucking rich bullies. You act like royalty and you're all just lowlife thugs in expensive suits." Victor didn't disagree with her. He was too busy worshipping her feet with his tongue. "I hate the mob so much that I'm probably going to do some shit to you this week that you're not going to like. It'll be immoral, indecent, and very likely illegal. And you won't even get to fuck me. Not once. And then you know what I'm going to do?"

"What, Mistress?" he asked, looking up at her from the floor with groveling eyes.

"I'm going to leave this shit-hole house of yours and forget you ever existed. Now take off your clothes."

NORA MADE it back to New York on December 20th. She spent a sleepless night in her bed wondering if she'd done the right thing fucking around with a mob guy. Victor hadn't been that bad. He, like her, had been an unwitting accomplice to the mafia far more than a willing participant. Victor hadn't chosen to be born of a crime boss and claimed to hate his father's world.

"Yeah, you hate the sinner," she said as she carved a shallow dollar sign into his back with a razor blade, "but you love that sinner's money, don't you?"

"I couldn't give it away, could I?" he asked as if she'd

suggested he should put the money into a rocket ship and aim it at the sun. "Who would do that?"

"I know a guy who did." Søren had inherited a vast fortune from his monster father and kept not a penny for himself. "I'd let you meet him, but you don't even deserve to tie his shoelaces. Fuck you, Rich Bitch, you don't even deserve to tie mine."

She showed him that night and all week how little he deserved any mercy, compassion, or kindness from her. By the end of the week, he was so in love with her he offered her another fifty grand to stay through Christmas. As she walked out his front door without even a backward glance, she'd told him to shove his dirty money up his ass.

Knowing what a freak he was, he probably did.

The morning after returning, Nora called Theremin's and made sure the piano delivery would take place. They promised it would, and she spent the rest of the day working on her new book. Without Wes around, the house echoed with silence. She played some Christmas music, but it didn't fill up the emptiness in the house. She put on her coat and went for a walk, but the emptiness went with her. It wasn't in the house at all. It was inside her.

At six that evening, she put her coat on, grabbed her keys, and got into her car. She drove to Wakefield and found herself parking across the street from Sacred Heart. The memories pressed in so close she had to shove them away lest she trip over them.

The parking lot was empty, thank God. No one around to recognize her, ask her what she was doing hanging around.

She stepped onto the cobblestone path that led down a tree-lined walkway to the rectory. It had snowed the night before, and a thousand footprints marred the new-fallen powder. The piano movers had come this way as they'd rolled the piano toward the house. She wished she'd been here to see the look on

Søren's face. She'd given the piano anonymously, although she knew he'd know the gift came from her. After all, it was she who'd broken the sustain pedal on his Steinway. She sort of owed him a new piano.

As Nora reached the end of the path, she paused and cocked her head to the side. Through the windows of the rectory, she heard music emanating. She stepped closer and listened harder. Yes, music. Piano music. Søren was already playing his new piano. At the front door, she pressed her ear to the wood. She knew this song. Of course she knew it. She could even hear the lyrics in her head as the notes drifted through the door.

> *A thrill of hope, the weary world rejoices...*
> *For yonder breaks, a new and glorious morn...*
> *Fall on your knees...*

Nora wanted to fall on her knees right then and there. She wanted to fall on her knees at Søren's side and rest her head on the piano bench like she had so many years ago. He played the song because he knew it was her favorite. He played even though he didn't know she could hear him. He played it for the memory of that night and all the Christmases they'd celebrated together in secret, each one more holy than the last.

She raised her hand and let it hover two inches from the door. When she knocked, the music would cease. He'd come to the door, open it and let her in, and he would beat her brutally, the way she liked it, and make love to her all night long.

Tonight was Søren's birthday. If she crossed the threshold tonight, she knew she would give herself to him. And not only for one night, but forever. She would lose Wesley. She would lose the life she'd made for herself. She'd even lose her name.

Infamous, notorious Mistress Nora would turn back into Eleanor again if she returned to Søren.

Maybe he would let her be herself. Maybe he would let her keep her name. Maybe they would find a new way to be together. And maybe magic elves would show up at her house and crown her Queen of the Christmas Fairies.

Nice dream, but Søren had already told her when and if she came back to him, his first order would be to give up her job with Kingsley. She could be with Søren or she could be Mistress Nora. She couldn't be both.

Nora took a step back without knocking. But before leaving, she reached out and drew a heart with her fingertip in the window.

"Merry Christmas, sir," she whispered into the crisp night winter air. "Happy birthday, my love."

When she walked away from the rectory, she didn't take the path. Instead, she crossed the unmarred snowy ground, leaving her small and familiar footprints behind her. At least he would know she had been there.

Sometimes that's all one needed to get through a hard day— someone just being there.

Maybe one of these days she would finally tire of being Mistress Nora, and she would go back to him and fall on her knees at his feet again. Maybe someday she'd give up the new life she'd made for herself and be his once more.

But not tonight. She'd already given him his Christmas and birthday present this year. He wasn't getting anything else from her.

NORA DROVE the forty minutes back to her house. She'd make it through Christmas even if she didn't celebrate

Christmas at all. Once upon a time, Christmas had been a fearful time for the early Christians, which is why they'd hidden their celebration under the mantle of a pagan one. The earliest Christians didn't celebrate Christmas at all, she told herself. She would be like one of them this year. She would skip Christmas, and it would be fine.

When Nora pulled into her driveway, she noticed a light in her window. Hadn't she turned them off when she'd left?

She opened the front door and found a teenage boy sitting in the middle of the living room floor wrapping a present. He was wearing jeans and a red-and-green plaid flannel shirt over a white V-neck tee. With the Christmas lights on the tree so bright and shining, even his sandy hair was glowing red and green.

"Holy shit, Wes. What are you doing here?"

Wes smiled at her, and it felt like summer had snuck in the house while winter had its back turned. "I told Mom and Dad I had to work over break and could only come home for a few days. We did Christmas yesterday. I got back this afternoon."

"But..."

"I know your dad's long gone," he said a little sheepishly. "And you said you and your mom don't get along. You don't do Christmas with your friends like you used to... I just didn't want you to be alone."

"Well. Damn."

"Since I don't want to be a liar, you're gonna have to put me to work," Wes said. "Does your office need cleaned again?"

"You swore you'd never clean my office again after last time."

"Oh yeah," he said, blushing slightly. "That was...traumatic."

"I swear the butt plugs in the bottom drawer aren't for me," she said. "Mine are in my bedroom. The ones in my office are for a client."

"That really doesn't make it better, Nor. And I don't even want to know why you store them next to your spare printer cartridges."

"It's the *bottom* drawer. Of course I store them there. Where do you store your butt plugs?"

"In my butt. Duh."

"Why didn't I think of that?"

Nora knelt on the floor in front of Wesley's mess of wrapping paper, ribbons, tape, and bows.

"So no office cleaning. What can I do for you?" Wes asked, taping the ribbon to the bottom of his box. The wrapped box looked legitimately awful and absolutely adorable. She would teach him how to wrap a present the right way this week.

"You came back from Christmas with your family early to spend it with me. You don't have to do anything else. Nothing. You didn't even have to do that."

"I like giving big Christmas gifts. I can't buy you a new car or a house or anything, not like you need another car or another house. But I can give you me for Christmas. If you want me. You know, my company."

"Right," Nora said. "Your company." She was already picturing their Christmas together. Ice skating. Christmas present shopping. Going to the Nativity play at St. Luke's down the street. He hadn't just given her his company for Christmas. Now that she wasn't going to be alone, he'd given her Christmas for Christmas.

"You have to give me something to do or I'm a liar," he said.

"Telling men what to do is my specialty, kid. Go and get your guitar," she said. "You can sing for your supper. I need some Christmas music."

He brought out his guitar and quickly tuned it. "Any requests?" he asked as he picked out a few stray notes.

"Anything you like."

"Anything?"

"Anything but 'O Holy Night.'"

"Why not?"

"Because it makes me sad."

Wes narrowed his eyes at her and then nodded. He had learned by now that "makes me sad" was code for "makes me think of Søren." That was the last thing either of them wanted tonight.

"No worries." Wes grinned at her and all the sadness went away. "I don't even know how to play that one. How about this?"

Wes leaned back against the couch and stretched out his legs. Nora put a pillow on his shins and laid her head there, curling up like a child. With the tree lights lit and evening draping itself over the house like a black silk sheet and Wes here with her, it finally felt like Christmas. Wes began to play "Silent Night."

Silent night. Holy night. All is calm. All is bright.

And it was beautiful.

Fin.

A CHRISTMAS MAGGIE

AUTHOR'S NOTE

This story occurs after the events of the Original Sinners Pulp Library novella The Auction *starring Daniel and Anya.*

WHEN HE'D HEARD "You're a Mean One, Mr. Grinch" playing on the radio that morning, Daniel had a wonderful, awful idea. Anya looked so delectable in her little slip of silk negligee, he ordered her to stay in it all day long. Now evening, she still wore it...but not entirely without complaint.

"*C'est l'hiver,*" Anya reminded him unnecessarily. Of course it was winter. A foot of snow had piled up outside the windows of his New England estate, trapping them happily inside. "I should be in flannel."

Daniel rolled his eyes at his little spitfire of a *Québécoise* lover. "You wouldn't wear flannel if I bribed you with a million dollars and threatened you with a beating."

Daniel knew his Anya. She barely had a cent to her name, but that didn't stop her from designing and sewing her own clothes—clothes that wouldn't look out of place on the runways of Paris and Milan. Even the negligee she'd shimmied into and out of last night had been one of her own creations.

Smiling, she wrapped her arms around his neck and pressed her slight form against his. God it was good to have a woman in his life again, in his home, in his bed...especially a woman with Anya's tastes.

"Perhaps if you bribed me with a beating...then I would wear flannel for you."

"I like the sound of that." Daniel cupped the back of her thighs and slipped his hands over her bare bottom and up her back. At moments like this he felt the age difference between them most keenly. She'd only just turned twenty-three; he could reach out and touch forty with his eyes closed. His rough hands would never recover from his year of rappelling and mountain climbing in South America. The smoothness of Anya's young skin served as a bitter reminder of how many years separated them. He didn't like to think about what else should and could— and should—separate them.

"I only said 'perhaps,' sir. No promises."

Daniel dipped his head and kissed her. Anytime she called him "sir" in that respectful tone he couldn't resist a kiss. That word empowered him like nothing else. The second a "sir" escaped her lips, he had to drag her to the bed, the floor, the sofa...

But today he pulled back. Too much to do.

"No. None of that." Daniel gave her his most stern stare. "Work. Now."

She flashed him a faux pout. "Yes, sir."

Anya turned her back to him, and he gave her a quick swat to hasten her retreat to the living room. They'd had the tree up with lights on it since December 1st but hadn't decorated it with any ornaments yet. Now Christmas Eve, Anya tore into the boxes Daniel had brought out of storage and started digging through all the glass stars and candy canes and silver and gold garlands.

"So tell me why we had to wait until Christmas Eve to decorate the tree...?" Daniel asked as he opened a box and removed a small sock monkey ornament—a gift from his friend and former lover Eleanor.

Anya shrugged, a move that caused her nightgown to lift up high enough for Daniel to see the pale pink birthmark on the top of her left thigh. His groin tightened at the sight of so much skin illuminated by the Christmas lights.

"*Ma mère*...she always had us wait until Christmas Eve to decorate the tree. Papa had to work so much, he never had a day off until then."

"That's very thoughtful of your mother." Daniel placed the sock monkey ornament high on the tree, front and center. Maggie would have gotten a kick out of such a silly thing on the otherwise traditionally decorated tree. Maggie...where had she come from? Daniel exhaled and tried to away push away thoughts of his late wife. Maggie had been dead for as long as Anya's mother. Time to move on. For both of them.

"She was far kinder to my father than he deserved." Anya pulled a footstool to the tree so she could adjust a string of lights near the top. "She tried to make him a better man by treating him like a king. It didn't work."

"I'm sorry." Daniel reached out and tickled the back of her knee to coax another smile out of her. She responded by hanging a candy cane on his ear.

"Lovely. Thank you." He poked her in the stomach with the candy cane and she flinched harder than he expected her to. But she quickly laughed, tore the candy cane from his hand, and placed it on the tree.

They continued decorating. Anya had a habit of repositioning nearly every ornament he placed on the tree. At first he assumed she was showing off her perfectionist side again, but soon he realized she did it solely to annoy him. And it would have, except the impish grin on her face only made him adore her more.

As Anya climbed back onto the footstool to put the star on top of the tree, Daniel reached into the box and pulled out one last ornament. While she was distracted, Daniel hid the last ornament on one of the bottom boughs. When he looked up from the floor again he could see right up Anya's nightgown.

"Anya, if you were one of Santa's reindeer, you would be Vixen," he said, tracing a line up the back of her leg with his fingertips. He slipped his hand between her thighs and teased her until she moaned softly.

"You ordered me to wear this," she said, her voice breathless and soft. "You didn't tell me to put any panties on."

"And for very good reason." Daniel pulled her off the footstool and dragged her to the floor.

"What is that reason, sir?"

Daniel turned her onto her stomach and over his knee. He flipped up the back of her negligee and exposed her exquisite backside.

"Christmas spankings." He swatted her hard a few times just for the pleasure of hearing that indignant yelp of hers.

"Spankings are for birthdays." She squirmed on his lap.

"It's Jesus's birthday." He gave her one more playful slap on her thigh before turning her onto her back.

"*Maman* said He was actually born in spring," Anya protested as Daniel kissed his way down her stomach. With one hand he pulled the straps of her nightgown down her arms while the other hand yanked it up from the bottom. He could have simply ripped the damn thing off but that would have taken a second longer than he wanted to wait.

"You're arguing theology with me?" Daniel pushed her thighs open wide and found her clitoris with his lips.

Anya gasped in pleasure. "Not anymore, sir."

His mouth was too occupied to tell her to lay back, shut up, and enjoy herself. But his tongue inside her seemed to work better than an order.

Once he had her sufficiently wet and more than sufficiently aroused, Daniel kissed his way up her body to her lips. He let Anya taste herself as he opened his pants and pushed into her. As he sheathed himself deep inside her, she raised her hips, and moaned into his mouth.

When he began to thrust, he couldn't help but laugh as his back tapped the bottom boughs of the tree and sent all the ornaments tinkling and shivering. He lay flat along Anya's body hoping to avoid knocking the tree over in his enthusiasm. Or hers. And her enthusiasm often eclipsed his. She'd come so loudly last week that his ears had rung for hours after.

As he moved in her, Daniel studied her face. She was lost in the moment, lost in the pleasure. Her eyes wore the most beautiful glazed look. A strand of red hair fell across her cheek and he blew it off with a puff of air. She laughed and he whispered an "I love you" in her ear.

"I love you too, sir," she whispered back, arching underneath him. He'd given her one explicit order at the beginning of their relationship—she was always to call him "sir" when he was inside her. This was an order she happily complied with every time.

He held back and waited as long as he could before coming. Everything disappeared when he was inside Anya—his sorrow, his memories, the dreams that still haunted him on the bad nights, which thankfully had become few and far between since bringing her home with him.

Anya clenched around him with a lusty cry. He would have laughed at her vocal acrobatics, but he was too preoccupied with his own orgasm.

He pulled gently out of her and watched her face for any telltale winces or grimaces. The girl had been a virgin before him, and sometimes he left her raw from his thrusts. But now she wore only a smile of angelic bliss.

"Simultaneous orgasm," he said as he rolled onto his side and pulled her back to his chest. "That doesn't happen very often."

"It's a Christmas miracle." Anya pressed into him and sighed.

"I'm not sure if God gives Christmas miracles to sinners like us." He gently bit the back of her shoulder.

"We are not sinners," she protested. Daniel heard a note of hurt in her voice. "We love each other. I'm your..." she paused and searched for the right word.

Daniel grinned into her skin. "*Property* is the word you're looking for. A nice Old Testament concept. I think God would respect that."

"Moi aussi," she said, slipping into French. *Me too.* She did that often when tired or spent. On those rare occasions she didn't fall into French after sex, he knew his job wasn't quite done yet.

They lapsed into contented silence as they stared up at the Christmas tree from where they lay on the carpeted floor. He and Maggie had made love under the tree so many times that he knew this view very well. Maggie had been Christmas crazy. Her first husband had been both an atheist and an asshole and had outlawed Christmas in the house. When she and Daniel had married it had been December. A Christmas-themed wedding. All seven years they spent together, Christmas had meant not only celebrating the season, but commemorating their love.

Anya stretched out her hand and tapped an ornament. "What is this?" she asked, gently removing it from the tree to inspect it closer.

Daniel's stomach dropped, but he kept his voice even and calm. "Maggie gave that to me our first Christmas."

A simple ornament, it consisted of nothing but a bell painted snow white with the words DANIEL AND MAGGIE'S FIRST CHRISTMAS on it and the year they were married.

"It's pretty." Anya's voice held only sincerity, no hurt that he could detect.

"Maggie loved Christmas." He took the ornament from Anya's hand. "She had an older sister named Carol. Maggie said when she was a little girl she drove her parents crazy. She thought it was so unfair Christmas was all about Carol. They sang Christmas Carols. They read Dickens's *A Christmas Carol.* Four-year-old Maggie was so jealous, her parents had to start singing 'Christmas Maggies' just to shut her up."

"Did you read her *A Christmas Maggie?*" Anya asked,

taking the ornament from his hand and placing it back on the tree.

"I did better than that. I found a beautiful leather-bound early edition of *A Christmas Carol* and had a bookbinder friend of mine sew in a new title page that said, *A Christmas Maggie*. She cried when she opened it on our second Christmas together."

Christmases with Maggie had been perfect, every last one of them better than the one before. Until the last one, when they knew it would be their final Christmas together. And even then...

"Do you miss her?" Anya asked the question so softly he barely heard her.

"Of course. She was my wife for seven years." He spoke matter-of-factly, almost brusquely, and only realized the error of his tone when Anya wriggled off the floor and fled the room, tears on her cheeks.

"Dammit." Daniel came to his feet and followed her. She'd run not to the bedroom they shared but to one of the guest rooms. He turned the knob and found the door locked. "Anya, open the door right now. That's an order."

The order was not obeyed. Nor the next one to talk to him, or the one after to please please talk to him.

Daniel rested his forehead against the door and took a deep breath, cursing himself. *Anya, barely twenty-three, virgin before him*, he reminded himself. In other words: emotional, sensitive, scared, fragile. His marriage had always been a touchy subject between them. Anya admitted once that she feared he'd never love her like he'd loved his wife. No amount of reassurance had made that fear completely disappear from her eyes. By saying that of course he still missed Maggie, he'd played right into Anya's deepest fears.

"I'll be downstairs," he called through the door. "I'll be there when you want to come out."

He almost added "I love you" but one bitter spark of anger at her overreaction stopped his tongue.

For the rest of the evening, Daniel straightened the mess they'd made of the living room with the Christmas decorations. He called a few relatives to wish them a Merry Christmas and pretended everything was perfect when they asked about his new girlfriend.

"Together since summer," he told his cousin Matthew in Ontario. "She's not a 'new' girlfriend anymore."

"Lost that new girlfriend smell already, huh?"

"And your mother wonders why you're still single at thirty-three, Matt."

He considered and discarded the idea of calling Maggie's sister. On the phone, their voices sounded almost identical. Hearing Carol on the phone was akin to coming face to face with the ghost of his dead wife. And Maggie had been haunting him far too much already today.

The time crept closer to midnight and Anya still hadn't come downstairs to talk to him. He considered going to bed but didn't want to sleep alone in the room they shared. So instead he sat in the big armchair Maggie had given him as a birthday gift one year. She'd called it his *Masterpiece Theater* throne and said any librarian worth his salt needed a chair that pretentious.

Before he closed his eyes, he reached into his pocket and pulled out a tiny box of Tiffany blue. Opening it, he stared at the princess cut diamond engagement ring. In the low light of the Christmas tree, the diamond sparkled like the Star of Bethlehem. If he didn't close the box soon, wise men and shepherds would start showing up on his doorstep. But he couldn't close it. Not quite yet. Tomorrow morning, Christmas morning, he'd planned on surprising Anya with the ring as her last present—

the ring and a promise to love her and keep her for the rest of his life. But now he wondered if the fight hadn't been a moment of serendipity, saving him from making a huge mistake.

Anya...so much younger than he, so much less experienced and so sensitive. Until their fight this evening, he'd been absolutely certain she was the woman he wanted to spend the rest of his life with, the woman he wanted to raise children with. He didn't even care if they were his children or her younger brothers and sisters, who she called every single day to check on. But now...now he wondered if Anya hadn't been right to be afraid. Did he love her as much as Maggie? And if he didn't, should he marry her anyway?

Sleep slowly stole into the room and crept up on him. The ring fell from his fingers as his eyes closed.

A few minutes or a few hours later, he felt a hand on his knee gently shaking him awake.

"What?" he asked, his eyes still shut.

"I told you that if you sleep in that damn chair, you'll get a permanent crick in your neck."

"Then you shouldn't have bought it for me, Mags," Daniel said as he pried his eyes open. *Mags? "Maggie?"*

Daniel sat forward in the chair, suddenly more awake than he'd ever been in his entire life. In front of him, kneeling on the floor by his feet with her chin on his knee, was Maggie, his wife who had been dead and buried for years.

"What?" he asked again, his heart pounding wildly in his chest. "What are you doing here?"

She gave him a wicked blue-eyed smile, her chestnut hair falling in waves around her oval face. She didn't look a day over thirty-five, younger than he'd ever seen her. In fact she looked breathtaking—so young, so beautiful, so untouched by the pain and suffering the cancer had inflicted on her, the cancer that had killed his beautiful wife.

"Merry Christmas, Daniel."

Daniel didn't bother asking any more questions. How Maggie got there...why she was there...he couldn't care less. He came out of the chair, dragged her to her feet, and held her more tightly in his arms than he'd ever held anyone in his life. He didn't know what to do—hold her for eternity or drag or to the ground and make love to her for the rest of his life. While he decided, he kept his arms around her, pulling her even harder against him.

"Good thing I'm dead," Maggie gasped in his ear, "or you might kill me."

Daniel laughed through tears as he buried his face into her hair and inhaled. Vanilla. Maggie's hair always smelled faintly of vanilla.

"Don't say that. Don't say you're dead. I know I'm dreaming so at least let it be a good dream," Daniel whispered, pulling her even closer, so close he could feel her heart beating against his chest. He loved that feeling—heart to heart. After sex he would stay inside her a few moments just to relish in that sensation as long as possible.

Maggie reached up and pinched him viciously hard on his arm. Flinching, Daniel laughed and pulled back to look at her face.

Maggie grinned at him. "You're not dreaming, Daniel."

"Then how are you here?"

She shrugged and her eyes gleamed with secrets. "Someone upstairs decided you needed something special for Christmas. Something that wouldn't fit into a box. Not even one this size." She held up the tiny box of Tiffany blue.

"Look, I can explain—" Daniel began but Maggie cut him off.

"I've been gone a long time." Maggie kissed him quick and

soft on the lips. "You're allowed to move on, fall in love, get remarried…"

Daniel shook his head. "I know I'm allowed. I even know that's what you wanted…"

In the months before Maggie died, she'd brought up Daniel's future without her several times. She did everything she could to persuade him that not only should he move on after she died, she wanted him to. Even in her last hours, she'd whispered to him, *I'm going to die but you're going to live for a long time. Promise me you won't live alone… You're the best man I've ever known. Don't let that go to waste… Don't give up on love, on life… Promise me…* And through his tears he'd nodded and replied with a hoarse, *I promise, Mags.*

"Then what's the problem?" Maggie arched an eyebrow at him. How many times had she asked him that question during their marriage? He'd never figured out a good answer to that question.

"Anya. She's…too young, too…" Pausing to search for words he could only sigh. "She's not you."

"Very true." Maggie nodded sagely. "And for that you should be eternally grateful."

Daniel's eyes widened in shock. "What is that supposed to mean?" He glared at her. "You were the best thing that ever happened to me."

"And you were the best thing that ever happened to me, too. Our marriage was strong most of the time. I didn't know I could love anyone as much as I loved you. Didn't even think I was capable of that kind of love and happiness. But."

"But?"

Maggie smiled at him again, a mysterious other-worldly smile. In life he'd never seen her smile like that.

"But…for such an intelligent man, you have a very bad

memory," Maggie teased as she raised a hand and ran it through his hair. She tapped him on the forehead.

"I remember nothing but amazing days with you. And even more amazing nights," he said, running his hands up her arms. She wore red silk pajamas, a pair he'd gotten her for Christmas one year. Boxy and boyish, they hid her incredible curves but she needed something to wear when family came around. And nothing turned him on more than stripping her out of them and slowly revealing the female figure hiding beneath the masculine cut.

"Really?" She pursed her lips at him. "Let me show you something. Close your eyes."

"I always loved this game," Daniel said, closing his eyes as she'd asked.

"Don't get your hopes—or anything else—up, you wicked man. Open your eyes."

Daniel opened them and inhaled in surprise. The dark and quiet living room had suddenly been transformed. Light came in from everywhere—the tree, the Christmas candelabras in the windows, the lamps, the red and green candles. Voices filled the room with laughter. Two dozen of his and Maggie's relatives were intermingling as Christmas music played in the background.

"Shit." Daniel grabbed Maggie's hand and pulled her against the wall as another Maggie passed them holding a bottle of wine and three empty glasses.

"No one can see us," she said, squeezing his hand. "This is just a memory we're in."

Daniel glanced around. He saw himself standing by the fire-place with Maggie's sister Carol, talking softly and smiling. He knew this memory. Christmas number three with Maggie—the Christmas they'd decided to invite everyone in both families to her house in the country. "God, it is. I do remember this. You gave me a watch that year."

"A Daniel Roth watch—seemed fitting."

"And I gave you..."

"This." Maggie held up her hand to show a three-stone diamond ring on her right ring finger.

"One diamond for each year of happiness you'd given me." Daniel took her hand and kissed the ring.

"I loved being married to a man who knew how to buy jewelry."

Daniel grinned as he surveyed the scene. "This was a good Christmas. I loved having my parents here, your parents, the sibs..."

"The kids," Maggie said, nodding toward Rachel and Jayson, Maggie's niece and nephew.

"Yes. The kids." Daniel swallowed as eight-year-old Rachel stuck a bow on top of four-year-old Jayson's head. Jayson ripped it off and slapped it onto Rachel's head and the screeching laughter of the children echoed off the walls.

Maggie led Daniel toward the fireplace, where he and Carol whispered back and forth while sipping at their wine.

"So will you finally talk my sister into having children?" Carol asked, smiling at Rachel and Jayson, who now had become enamored of the toy train that wound around the Christmas tree.

"She says she doesn't want kids," Daniel watched himself say. "I think she means it."

"Motherhood would be so good for her. She's just Type A, always has been. Having a baby would calm her down. All your priorities change when you have children. You want them, don't you?"

Daniel watched the younger version of himself inhale

deeply, saw his eyes soften as he watched Jayson staring with silent fascination at the toy train.

"I do. Very much." Daniel knew "very much" had been an understatement. Once the shock of being married to a goddess like Maggie had worn off, all he'd wanted was to have a child with her. A daughter with Maggie's mind and wit, a son with his love of books... He ached to add to their family of two.

"Talk to Maggie. Maybe she'll come around." Carol smiled at him. "Do it soon. She's running out of time."

"I'll talk to her tonight." The younger Daniel lifted his wine glass to his lips while the older Daniel could only wince.

"I remember that conversation," Daniel said as Maggie took his hand and led him away from the fireplace, away from the memory. "It didn't go as I'd hoped."

"I remember it, too. It went a lot like this." Maggie bent over and blew out one of the candles. Every light in the room went out but for the ones on the Christmas tree. In the darkness, Daniel heard harsh whispering.

"Keep your voice down," Younger Daniel ordered. "The kids are sleeping downstairs."

"Yes, let's worry about the kids," Maggie from the memory said. "They matter so much more than we do."

"I never said that."

"You don't have to say that. I told you before we got married I didn't want children. I have my work. I have my life with you. I have everything I need or want. Asking me to have kids is like asking me to take on a second job. Why would I do that when I love my first one so much?"

"But having kids...it's not supposed to be a job."

"What would you call something that involved non-stop manual labor, Daniel?"

"Are you actually angry at me for wanting to have children with you?"

"Yes. Yes, I am. It's not who I am. It's not what I want. You're asking me to be someone and something I don't want to be. How would you feel if all of a sudden I decided I wanted us to be vanilla? No more kink, no more submitting to you in bed... and elsewhere? No more you being in charge in the bedroom?"

Daniel watched his younger self blanch at the question. "I'd be furious," he admitted. "And I'd hate every second of it. But it's not—"

"It *is* the same thing," Maggie countered. "Exactly the same thing. Deciding we're going to be a vanilla couple from now on is just like you asking me to be a mother. It would be a total betrayal of my very self. So either you accept that kids are just not part of our future...or I'm not part of your future. What will it be, Daniel? Your decision."

Maggie in the memory had fallen silent. And Daniel watched his younger self fall silent, too. Neither of them spoke.

Not a single word.

"Close your eyes, Daniel," Maggie whispered to Older Daniel, who obeyed readily, wanting to get out of this memory as quickly as possible. When he opened them again, they'd returned to the present, to his living room, with his Anya still angry and secluded upstairs in her room.

Daniel could barely meet Maggie's eyes.

"I hated myself for weeks after that," Daniel said. "Not for talking to you about having children. But because I didn't answer when you asked me 'What will it be?' I should have answered immediately. I should have said, 'You, Maggie. No matter what.' I'm sorry. I'm so, so—"

Maggie stopped his apology with her fingertips on his lips. "It's all right. You were upset and hurt and sad. You had dreams, and I crushed them."

"You had your own dreams that I was asking you to give up."

"You were. But I stood my ground. That night and every single time we had the fight about kids."

"We didn't fight that—"

Maggie snapped her fingers and before Daniel's eyes a parade of memories flashed.

We've discussed this before. I'm done talking about it.

We can adopt. You don't even have to—

How many times do I have to tell you—

You would be an amazing mother. Once you had a baby, you would—

What? Be miserable?

And on and on it went. Seven years of marriage, heated conversations, subdued fights, resentments waxing and waning...

The ghosts of a hundred arguments past went silent and Daniel could only press his hand against his forehead to steady himself.

"You know, if I hadn't gotten my diagnosis," Maggie said, gently prying Daniel's hand off his forehead, "we would have gotten divorced in a couple of years."

Daniel shook his head. "No. That... No."

"I'm not conjecturing. I know." She smiled sadly at him. "I know."

"Divorced...you and me?" Daniel reeled from the very thought of it. They'd had such a good marriage. Divorce seemed utterly inconceivable. And yet so many fights he'd forgotten. Time had erased all those bad memories.

Maggie sighed. "Divorced. Yes. And the consequences wouldn't have been pretty."

"I can't..." Daniel said. "No. I don't—"

"But you need to, darling. You need to see..." Maggie touched his face, closed his eyes for him, and Daniel braced himself.

When he opened his eyes, he found himself standing in Maggie's office at her Manhattan law firm. She'd been a partner and had made millions in her practice. Her office gleamed with money and success and power.

And yet...

"Maggie...no..." Daniel whispered as his eyes came into focus.

She said nothing, only crossed her arms over her chest like she always did when embarrassed or nervous.

Another Maggie sat at her desk. No, not sat. Not really. Slumped over would have been the words Daniel would have used. This Maggie, the divorced-from-Daniel Maggie he'd never met, reeked of alcohol. A dusting of white powder marred the otherwise pristine surface of Maggie's black desk.

"Jesus, Mags..."

"I never told you that in my late twenties I had a little bit of a drug problem. Manhattan law firm. High-powered. High stress. Me trying to deal with all the pressure. I indulged more often than I should have. Behaved much better in my thirties. But after you and I divorced, I threw myself into my work and all those old bad habits came back."

Daniel said nothing. He walked around the desk to get a closer look at this Maggie he'd never met before. One tiny drop of blood had leaked from her nose and onto a contract on her desk before her.

"She's alive." Maggie nodded at herself. "Physically, at least. Emotionally, spiritually...gone. It's Christmas Eve and this Maggie is supposed to be auditing a contract. But this Maggie will work herself into an early grave by age fifty. She won't need cancer to kill her. She'll do it herself."

Daniel knelt by her chair. He started to touch her hair but pulled his hand back. "She's not real." He stood up and walked back to his Maggie. "I refuse to believe she's real."

"She's not. She's merely a shadow of what could have been. Let me show you another shadow."

"Whose?"

Maggie exhaled heavily. "Yours."

With a single blink Daniel disappeared from the penthouse office and discovered he now stood in a cramped and dingy apartment. Glancing out the window, he saw narrow brownstone houses, trash in bags piled high on the street, plastic faded Santa Clauses illuminating the dirty front porches. It appeared to be Queens or the Bronx.

"Where am I?" Daniel asked. He'd never set foot in this place before.

"Home sweet home. After we divorced you refused a cent of alimony from me. You took the first library job you could get. Small branch in the Bronx. You spent most of your days at work trying to keep homeless people from moving into the bathrooms."

Daniel shrugged. "At least I'm working in my field. Sort of."

"You took the first job you could find after our divorce...and married the first woman you dated after our divorce."

"I did?" Daniel stared at Maggie in shock. She nodded.

"You did. A page at the library named Mara. A couple years younger than you but already with two small children."

At that Daniel had to smile. "I'm a stepfather?"

"You *were* a stepfather. The marriage lasted about six months. You bonded with the kids far more than their mother. Mara was jealous that you seemed to love them more than her. And you did. Vanilla woman, wouldn't even consider any D/s in the bedroom much less anything kinkier. She left you and took the kids, and this is your Christmas that year."

Daniel heard a key in the door and saw a different version of himself come in. That Daniel looked tired, haggard, older than he had any right to. In his hands he carried a bag of Chinese take-out.

"Your family in Canada invited you back home for Christmas. You had too much pride to tell them you couldn't afford the airfare this year. You lied and said you had a new girlfriend and wanted to spend Christmas with her. But it's just you alone with Chinese food. It'll be the same Christmas after Christmas. You'll give up on love, on marriage, on your dreams of fatherhood. And this will be you until you die..."

Daniel watched himself sink into a battered armchair and turn on the television to an American football game. He didn't even like American football. But it was noise, light, movement... Dozens of women during his life had told him he was sexy, handsome. He'd even gotten gorgeous a time or two. But this Daniel had gone soft around the stomach, with a heavily lined face, and there was nothing behind those blue eyes of his that so many women had swooned over. Nothing at all.

"I'm a wreck."

"Yes, you are. At least you don't have a nose full of coke and a fridge full of vodka."

Daniel looked at Maggie. "You're telling me that it's for the best you died of cancer? I can't...I won't believe that."

Maggie gave him a look of deepest compassion. "I'm telling you that things happen for a reason. Even the bad things. That's all."

Daniel turned away from the vision of himself. "Can't you show me something good? Something that doesn't make me feel like throwing up? Please, Mags?"

Maggie took his hands again and kissed his now bare ring finger. "I can show you something absolutely beautiful if you really want to see it."

"I do. Please let me see something beautiful. A good

Christmas memory. We had as many of those as the bad ones. Didn't we?"

"We did, my love. We absolutely did. But I won't show you a good memory of us. Not yet anyway."

"What could be more beautiful than you and I having a good Christmas together?"

Maggie raised her hand, snapped her fingers, and Daniel now stood outside the bedroom where Anya had hidden herself away from him.

"What your Anya is doing right now," Maggie said.

Daniel looked to the door in embarrassment. "She locked me out," he said.

"Smart girl. You need to be locked out every now and then so you can get your head on straight. But she didn't lock *me* out."

"I hope you've got a key then."

"Oh, Daniel..." Maggie said, clicking her tongue. "Where I'm from we don't need keys."

And with that she took him by the hand and swept them both right through the door.

DANIEL'S HEART tightened in his chest at the sight that greeted him. Anya had taken the blanket off the bed and wrapped herself in it for warmth. In the corner of the bedroom she huddled on the floor next to the heating vent, a telephone pressed to her ear, with her gray furball of a cat, Leonard, curled up at her feet.

"Anya." Daniel spoke her name softly and stepped toward her. "Sweetheart, I'm so—"

"She can't hear you." Maggie took him gently by the wrist. "We're not really here."

"She's got to be cold. Of course she'd pick the coldest room in the house to hide in."

"Crying women with breaking hearts don't always make the best decisions, Daniel. Remember when we got into that fight on our fifth anniversary and I ended up backing the car into a duck pond?"

"That one duck is still in physical therapy because of you."

Maggie grinned at him. "Exactly. Now shush and listen. I'll translate if you need me to."

Back in the old days, Maggie would have gotten The Ouch for telling him to "shush." The Ouch had been her name for a particularly vicious stare Daniel would given her when he was annoyed with her or—even better—he was pretending to be annoyed with her for the purposes of inflicting erotic punishments. She always called it The Ouch because whenever she saw it, she knew she'd be in pain the next day.

But now Daniel couldn't take his eyes off Anya long enough to give Maggie The Ouch. His little girl looked miserable with the blanket pulled tight around her and her beautiful face lined with dried tears. It killed him that he couldn't gather her in his arms and hold her until she felt warm and safe and loved again.

"It's okay, my love," Maggie whispered to him as she squeezed his arm. "Where I am, there's no pain, no pettiness, no sorrow or jealousy. It doesn't hurt me to see you look at her."

Daniel smiled at Maggie and his heart swelled with his old love for her. It felt comfortable and warm like his favorite pair of jeans pulled straight from the dryer. His new love for Anya felt completely different. It scared him, exhilarated him, dug into him like fingernails in his back.

Kneeling down next to Anya, Daniel studied her face as he listened to her soft voice speaking into the phone. He'd had to learn French and learn it quickly once he and Anya had gotten together. His little spitfire *Québécoise* lover took a little too much pleasure in correcting his errors. She took so much pleasure in it that he started correcting any and all of her mistakes with English. The wooden ruler he kept in his office and her perfect round bottom had gotten very well acquainted.

"Did everything arrive in time?" Anya whispered. "We had a heavy snow, and I couldn't walk to the post office for a few days."

She paused and someone on the other end answered her.

"Who is she talking to?" Daniel asked Maggie.

"Here," Maggie said. "This might help."

Daniel watched as Maggie reached out and touched a large mirror hanging on the wall. The image in the glass wavered and turned into a new picture. A young man stood in the middle of a narrow hallway holding a cordless phone to his ear. He had shaggy auburn hair and pale skin, hazel eyes, and a face that would turn handsome in a year or two once he put on a little weight.

"That's Etienne, Anya's brother. Haven't met him yet. Just saw a picture."

"He's the guardian of the family, now with Anya in America.," Maggie explained. "Their father is useless."

"Anya told me the same thing." Daniel looked back at Anya on the floor. In the mirror, Etienne walked down the hallway to a living room. A small tree barely three feet high with only one sad strand of white lights decorating it stood guard over a mountain of presents wrapped in elegant silver and gold paper.

"I can't believe you were able to afford all this," Etienne said, staring at the presents. "How did you do it?"

"Daniel asked me to stay with him. With the money I saved on rent I could buy the presents."

Etienne winced. "I would rather you hadn't gotten the presents. I don't trust rich men."

"He's a good man," Anya protested. "Very good. The best.

And he's so kind to me. And so handsome, I can't... Never-mind." She smiled a little, no doubt realizing her brother was the last person on the planet who'd want to hear about her attraction to her boyfriend.

"If he's so kind to you then why do you keep so much from him? Hmm? Did he know you had a mountain of presents to mail when you walked them to the post office?"

Anya grimaced. "He would have driven me if I'd asked. But if he'd seen the presents, he would have wanted to know where the money came from. And if I told him it was all I had, then he would have made me let him pay for them."

"You should have let him, if he has that kind of money."

"I have some pride, Etienne."

"Too much pride, Anya."

"I have to agree with him," Daniel said, wanting badly to touch Anya. Why couldn't she see him? Why couldn't he hold her? "The girl is ninety percent pride and ten percent spite."

Maggie nodded and grinned. "And one hundred percent in love with you."

"I like that kind of math." Daniel turned his attention back to Anya. Of course the girl took every last cent she had and spent it on her six younger siblings. He should have known, should have helped. He'd been so caught up in finding the perfect engagement ring, creating the perfect Christmas for the two of them, that he'd forgotten she had her family back in Quebec that she worried constantly about. What else was she keeping from him?

"Are the little ones asleep?" Anya asked, tucking the blanket tighter around her.

"It's Christmas Eve," Etienne said with a roguish grin. "Of course they aren't sleeping."

Oh yeah, Daniel realized. That kid was going to be a heart-breaker. Better keep Kingsley away from him.

"Can I talk to them?" Anya asked.

"They'd never forgive you if you didn't. They're all in Camille's room trying to get her to sleep."

Etienne carried the phone back down the hallway. Daniel winced at the sight of the house. House? It looked more like a two, maybe three bedroom apartment. Small, cramped, dark and dismal. Old carpet, stained walls. The place looked clean but only the presents under the tree gave any hint that love lived in the home.

Inside the mirror, Etienne opened a door to a tiny room that held twin beds. Children somewhere between the ages of eight and fourteen piled on top of or around the bed. The smallest girl, Camille, clung to a pink elephant stuffed toy and whispered to one of her sisters.

"Beautiful family," Maggie said, and Daniel saw his late wife smiling at the children. "I do love kids. Other people's kids. Just never wanted any of my own."

"I did," Daniel said with a sigh. "So much. I loved the thought of taking care of these little people who couldn't take care of themselves."

"You always took such good care of me. You'll make a wonderful father someday. I'm sure of it."

"If that day ever comes..." Daniel watched the scene in the mirror. Etienne entered and told them Anya was on the phone. Smiles crossed all the children's faces, but Camille lunged for the phone and ripped it from Etienne's hand.

"Anya?"

"Hello, my little monkey," Anya said and Camille giggled. "Are you ready for Santa Claus?"

Camille's small, sweet face clouded over. "Papa said he wasn't coming this year."

"Don't listen to Papa," Anya said. "He's on the Naughty

List. You listen to me. Santa's coming for all of you. He told me so."

"He did?"

"Yes. Santa spends a lot of time Christmas shopping in New York City."

"That's where you live."

"I did live there. Now I'm in a big house out in the country. It's so pretty." Anya wiped a tear off her face. Daniel could hear the pain in her voice beneath the forced levity.

"Can I come visit you?"

Anya's eyes seemed to flinch at the question. "I'll come visit you first. I miss you. All of you."

Camille sighed heavily and sadly, far too sadly for a child so small. Daniel wanted to pick the little girl up and hold her in his arms and tell her silly stories until she smiled again.

"I miss you too. Nobody's here to sing to me."

Anya gasped loudly in feigned shock. "Not even Etienne? He won't sing to you?"

Camille shook her head. "He says he can't sing or it'll ruin Christmas for everybody."

"He's right about that, actually," Anya said and Daniel chuckled. "But I can sing to you if you'll get into bed and turn out the lights. Promise?"

"Promise, promise," Camille pledged, solemn as a judge. She told Etienne that Anya was going to sing to her. Etienne took the phone from her hand and pushed a button to turn the speakerphone on. All the kids gathered even closer to the bed. Camille laid her head down on the pillow and pulled her pink elephant in close, holding him by his fuzzy foot.

Anya cleared her throat and closed her eyes. Quietly, in a voice both melodic and tremulous, she began to sing an ancient carol in her native language.

"The first Noel, the angels did say, was to certain poor shepherds in fields where they lay..."

Daniel's throat tightened at the sweet sound of Anya's singing voice. Rarely had he heard her singing before and never like this, never to soothe a child on Christmas Eve.

All of Anya's brothers and sisters listened intently to the words. Until the chorus when the two older girls, Aimee and Nicole, began to sing along.

"Noel, noel... Noel, noel... Born is the king of Israel..."

"She has a beautiful voice," Maggie said, her voice nearly a whisper.

"And a beautiful heart..." Daniel stood up. It physically hurt not being able to touch Anya and comfort her. Her grumpy gray cat Leonard slept at her feet but couldn't do much for her other than help keep her toes warm.

"She does have a beautiful heart. And soul. And face and body," Maggie teased. "You're lucky. She's a catch. But then again, so are you."

"I don't feel like much of one right now." In fact, Daniel felt horrible. He'd made Anya question his love for her—and on Christmas Eve, of all days.

"Come here. I want to show you one more thing." Maggie tugged on his arm and Daniel reluctantly let her lead him away. He didn't want to leave Anya. Not now. Not ever. But since he couldn't help her, couldn't talk to her, it was best to just leave until he could again.

Maggie took him from the guest bedroom and down to the living room, back to the Christmas tree.

"Beautiful tree. She did a good job decorating it." Maggie nodded her approval.

"She's a designer. You should see the clothes she makes for herself."

"She made an all-new wardrobe for her sisters for Christmas."

Daniel stared at Maggie.

"What?" Maggie asked. "I peeked."

"That girl amazes me sometimes. Who am I kidding? She amazes me all the time."

Maggie only smiled into the tree. She reached up and lightly touched the little sock monkey ornament.

"A young woman named Eleanor gave that to me," Daniel said. "She's a—"

"Oh, I know exactly who Eleanor is." Maggie's eyes widened. "I know who she is even better than you do. Just thank your lucky stars you didn't end up with that one."

"Well, I know she doesn't want kids either."

"Least of your worries, I promise. Her future..." Maggie whistled through her teeth. "Let's just say it gets...interesting. But I won't say any more. I'd hate to ruin the surprise for you. I'm almost out of time anyway. And there's something else you need to see."

Daniel's heart clenched at the words *out of time*. He wasn't ready to let her go again. Not now. Not ever.

"What is it?"

"Nothing much," she said with a sly smile. "Only this."

Maggie waved her hand and the living room exploded with light and sound once more. Daniel heard laughter and music. Voices everywhere speaking French and English. Spinning around, he saw a room full of children and teenagers wrapping and unwrapping gifts. And in the middle of it all stood Anya looking beautiful and flushed and frazzled.

"Where are we?" Daniel asked before realizing the absurdity of the question. "I mean, When are we?"

"One possible future. You've invited Anya's siblings to come for Christmas. Anya's never been happier."

Daniel watched as another version of him came into the living room, Camille slung over his shoulder.

"Did anyone ask for a Camille for Christmas?" Daniel bellowed to the room. "Santa left her on the front porch. Anyone?"

"I did!" Anya came to him and took a squealing, giggling Camille from his arms. "I wanted a Camille to do my dishes for me. And cook. And clean. And brush Leonard and scoop his poop."

"No! No! No! Not poop!" Camille cried out in giggles. "Give me back to Santa!"

Daniel couldn't stop staring at the other version of himself, the future version. He looked like an idiot, grinning from ear to ear like that as he gazed at the room full of children and Anya, beaming like a new bride. New bride? Daniel glanced at future Anya's hand and saw his engagement ring shining on it. In this version of the future, he'd asked her to marry him and she'd said yes. He liked this version of the future. Whatever it took, he'd make it happen.

"I've never seen you look happier, either," Maggie said. "Not even on our wedding day."

"I was terrified on our wedding day."

"Thought you were making a mistake?" Maggie asked with a wink.

"Thought you were."

"Marrying you was the smartest thing I ever did." Maggie waved her hand and the lights dimmed, the laughter died, and the future faded away. They had returned to the quiet, Christmas tree-lit present.

"We were good together, you and I," Daniel said, taking her into his arms and holding her close. He felt her fading on him already and refused to let her go. Not just yet, anyway.

"Better than good." Maggie relaxed into his arms and slowly

swayed. "I can sing too, if you recall. *Have yourself a merry little Christmas,*" Maggie sang softly into his ear in a voice lower and huskier than Anya's, but no less beautiful.

"Not this one," Daniel begged, spinning Maggie as she sang the song, an old favorite of his. "This one's so depressing."

"No it isn't. It's just honest," she protested. "*Through the years we all will be together...if the fates allow...*"

"The fates didn't allow," Daniel said as he pulled her tight to him. "I wish they had, sometimes."

"I know, my love. I know you do. And I did too, once upon a time. But the fates had other plans for us. And in time you'll be standing where I am, and the whole course of your life will stretch out before you like an open scroll...and you'll see and understand. And then you will be grateful things happened as they did. I promise."

"I believe you. I do. Only it's hard...hard to believe." He closed his eyes and inhaled the scent of vanilla on Maggie's hair.

"I know it is. It's like trying to see in the dark. But someday you'll stand in the light."

"And we'll be back together?" he asked, hoping in some way he would be reunited with Maggie, with everyone he'd ever loved and lost.

Maggie smiled once more at him. One more smile. One more wink. One more soft kiss on his lips.

"If the fates allow," she whispered.

And then she was gone.

Daniel started, stunned by her sudden departure. "Maggie?" he called out, and heard no answer.

A mantle of sadness settled over him. Once more she had left him before he was ready. He sat back down in the chair. The box of Tiffany blue rested on the arm of it. In his hand he held the little box tight and knew what he would do. But not yet. Not quite yet. Not until morning.

Sleep came for him as he relaxed into the chair. Visions of Christmases future danced in his head. He and Anya...they would get married and they would be happy together. And all her brothers and sisters would come live with them, and he would finally have the house full of children he'd always wanted. And it wouldn't matter one bit that they weren't his own children. He would make them his children by loving and treating them like the father they deserved. They would sit at his feet and listen to the stories he would read them. Even now he could feel Camille's chin on his knee.

"*Monsieur*...you'll hurt you neck if you sleep like that."

Daniel slowly opened his eyes. Sunlight and snowlight filled the room. And Anya, his beautiful Anya, sat at his feet.

"You're right. I shouldn't sleep in this chair. I'll get a permanent crick in my neck if I do."

He reached down and pulled Anya off the floor and into his arms.

"What are you doing?" she demanded as she wiggled on his lap.

"Playing Santa. Tell me what you want for Christmas."

"It's Christmas morning," she reminded him. "Shouldn't we have had this talk weeks ago?"

"Just tell me. We'll see what Christmas miracles I have in my pocket."

Anya sighed as she rested against him. Nothing felt better than Anya's head on his shoulder.

She raised her hand and touched his face, his lips. "I have you. There's nothing more I want or need."

Daniel's chest tightened. He knew he should be on his knee for this but it felt so much more natural to have Anya on his.

"Not even this?" He held up the Tiffany box and laid it in the center of her palm.

Her eyes went wide as the sky when she opened the box.

"But..." she started to protest and Daniel stopped her mouth with a kiss.

"But nothing," he said. "Marry me, Anya. That's an order."

He took the ring from the box and slipped it on her finger. Tears flooded her face as she threw her arms around him.

"Yes, sir," she breathed in his ear.

"Good girl." Those two words were all he could push past his throat. He'd never been so relieved in his life.

For a few minutes they merely held each other and cried and laughed and kissed. But finally Daniel came to himself enough to start teasing her again. He couldn't go five minutes without teasing her.

"Now that ring cost a fortune. So I expect something equally valuable right now in return as my Christmas gift. Pay up."

Anya blushed from ear to ear. "I have a present for you. I do."

"Good. Go get it. I want it. If it's not at least twelve pairs of new socks, you will be roundly punished until next Christmas."

"I can't go get it," she said, nervously turning the new ring on her finger. "It'll be late."

"Shipping problems are unacceptable. No excuses. How late are we talking?"

Anya took his hand and kissed it before she slowly settled it flat onto her stomach.

"A little less than nine months."

FIN.

A MIDWINTER NIGHT'S DREAM

AUTHOR'S NOTE

This particular novella is a little different, and it's all your fault, dear readers.

I did an Instagram giveaway of two holiday books: A Christmas Promise by Mary Balogh (a Regency Christmas romance) and One Hot December by moi (a contemporary rom-com set in a ski chalet on Mt. Hood in Oregon). I asked readers where they would prefer to spend Christmas—an English country house or a sexy ski chalet on Mt. Hood. Again and again, readers replied they wanted to spend Christmas in an English country house...if Søren and Kingsley were there.

And thus was born A Midwinter Night's Dream—an Original Sinners novella set in Victorian England. It stars not Father Stearns but Baron Stearns, and not Eleanor but a reformed pick-pocket who is the baron's ward. Kingsley, of course, plays Baron Stearns's valet...a valet devoted to all his master's needs.

So in the spirit of "Once More, With Feeling" (the musical episode of Buffy the Vampire Slayer*) and "Atomic Shakespeare"* (*the legendary* Taming of the Shrew *episode of* Moonlighting*), I offer you this Original Sinners Victorian Christmas novella.*

To Anthony Trollope, my favorite trollop

ONE

23rd of December 1871
London

THE BARON WAS DEAD. *Long live the baron.*

Those had been Kingsley's exact words when his master received the news that his dearly despised father had finally kicked the bucket. The new baron was properly addressed as "Lord Stearns," "my lord," or, after acknowledging the title, as "sir." Yet, Kingsley and the new baron had known each other—intimately and biblically—since the ages of sixteen and seventeen respectively, and therefore when Kingsley addressed the newly minted Baron Stearns, he did so in his usual manner.

"Søren," Kingsley hissed, then gently kicked the new baron in the shin.

The new baron—"Søren" to his intimates, as it was the name his beloved mother, not his detested father, had given him—lowered his copy of the *Times* just enough to peer at Kingsley over the top of it.

"We're back in England," Kingsley said.

Søren glanced out the train window and said, "What do you

know? We *are* back in England. This is why I keep you in my employ. To remind me what country I'm in at all times lest I forget."

"Also to beat me and bugger me."

Søren held up his newspaper. "Yes, also that."

"Søren," Kingsley said, kicking the new baron in his other shin.

"As you reminded me," Søren said, "we are in England again. You'll have to at least *pretend* to respect my rank while we're here."

"Yes, my most honored and gracious lord and master."

"Better. Now what do you want?"

"Will we be paying a visit to Lady Claire while we're in town?" Kingsley asked. Town meaning London, of course. "Or returning to Paris immediately?"

"I hadn't thought about it."

"Lying sodding bastard."

Søren lowered his newspaper again and arched his eyebrow at Kingsley.

"I mean, lying sodding bastard, *my lord*."

Søren carefully folded his paper and set it on the empty seat at his side. They sat across from each other in a first-class train compartment, which would deliver them to London in now— Kingsley checked his pocketwatch—eight minutes.

"Valets who wish to keep their tongues firmly attached to their bodies will refrain from speaking when it is clear their master wishes them silent," Søren said. "In other words—shut it, Kingsley."

"You're more rude than usual now that you've got the title," Kingsley said. "And that's saying something. You were a high-handed knob to start with."

"You should be nicer to me," Søren said. "My father's just died after a long and difficult illness. I'm in mourning."

They met eyes. Kingsley looked at Søren. Søren looked at Kingsley.

They both burst into laughter. A train conductor walked past, and Søren kicked Kingsley in the shin.

Kingsley fell sideways onto the train seat, cradling his leg.

"You kick much harder than I do," Kingsley said. Søren merely stared out the window until their train pulled into the station.

They both stood, donned their overcoats and hats, and found the nearest empty cab.

"Mr. Fitzsimmons's office, Surrey Street," Kingsley instructed.

London somehow managed to be both frigid and clammy that December 23rd, and soon Kingsley was both shivering and sweating as the cab made slow progress to Mr. Fitzsimmons's office.

Søren, however, looked the picture of perfection, as always. Gray suit, gray waistcoat, tie white as new-fallen snow, shoes impeccably polished, and not a single strand of his golden hair was out of place.

"You're staring, Kingsley," Søren said. "Stop it."

"Trying to picture you with a beard. Look," he pointed out the window at the men of business on the sidewalks. "We'll have to grow enormous mustaches to fit in now."

"We'll just have to be unfashionable."

"Suits me," Kingsley said. "I've yet to meet a girl who ever got wet from a walrus. Unless one splashed her."

"Don't make me laugh," Søren said, glaring. "I'm attempting to look bereaved for our meeting. Is it working?"

"No," Kingsley said. "Try to think about how much your father suffered. Does that help?"

"It makes me want to break out into song. Are there any

songs about evil men dying of syphilis? If not," Søren said, "someone should write one."

"Won't be me," Kingsley said. "I can never remember how to spell 'syphilis.' Never know where to put the Y and if there are two Ls or one."

"I'll give you a dictionary for your Christmas gift," Søren said.

"I'd rather you just give me what you gave me last year."

"What was that again?"

"A beating and then you buggered me. That's also what you gave me for my birthday. And your birthday two nights ago. And the Catholic feast days, all two-hundred of them."

"Yes, well," Søren said. "I'm very devout, as you know."

The cab lurched to a stop in front of Mr. Fitzsimmons's impressive offices. Kingsley paid the driver enough to wait for them. This was sure to be a short meeting.

Mr. Fitzsimmons, a man as round as he was tall, greeted them heartily as they entered his private office, bowing and scraping to Søren and calling him "my lord" so many times, Kingsley thought for a moment they were in church.

"My deepest sympathies upon the death of your father, my lord," the rosy-cheeked solicitor said, hand over his heart.

"Shallow sympathies will more than suffice," Søren replied.

Mr. Fitzsimmons blinked. "Yes, of course. Shall we begin then?"

The solicitous solicitor indicated a large leather armchair. Kingsley stood behind Søren, waiting attendant as Mr. Fitzsimmons sat at his desk.

"I won't beat around the bush, Lord Stearns," Mr. Fitzsimmons began once he'd perched his spectacles on his nose, "you know as well as I do that your father was a very wealthy man. Investments he made paid off handsomely. The estate is free of all debts and the yearly income stands at..."

Mr. Fitzsimmons cleared his throat and mentioned a figure so large Kingsley's knees nearly buckled.

Søren only sighed, however. "He was as covetous as he was cruel. Did my father leave anything to my half-sister, Lady Claire."

"She'll inherit forty thousand on her twenty-first birthday."

"Better than nothing," Søren said. "Thank you, Mr. Fitzsimmons. I assume the rest of the estate goes to the Crown?"

"Not quite," Mr. Fitzsimmons said. "You, Lord Stearns, are also a beneficiary."

"Of what?" Søren asked, scoffing. "A one-pound note wrapped around a rock thrown at my face?"

"Your lordship inherits the title, of course, free and clear. As to the remainder of the estate," Mr. Fitzsimmons continued. "The townhouse at Regent's Park, the family seat, Edenfell, and the accounts...all yours, my lord."

"I don't believe that," Søren said. Neither did Kingsley. "My father would rather have left his fortune to a one-eyed tabby cat in Yorkshire than to me."

"He did insert a condition which you must fulfill in order to inherit. And...unfortunately, in order for your sister to inherit, as well." Mr. Fitzsimmons coughed.

"Go on," Søren said.

"You will have to marry to inherit," Mr. Fitzsimmons said. He coughed again. Then he said something that sounded like, "Today."

Kingsley blinked.

Mr. Fitzsimmons coughed a third time.

"Today?" Søren repeated. "I have to marry—*today*?"

"Or tomorrow morning, sir. You must marry within one day of the reading of the will. If you do, you and your sister will inherit. If not, then it's all to the Crown."

"That can't possibly be legally binding," Kingsley said. "Banns have to be read."

"Not if a license is procured—easily done if one has rank and wealth. And I understand Lord Stearns is a Catholic," Mr. Fitzsimmons said with some barely concealed distaste. "You'll simply need an official present at your ceremony to validate it."

"Can't Lord Stearns contest the condition?" Kingsley asked. "His father was mad as a hatter."

"I wouldn't risk it," Mr. Fitzsimmons said. "In the event Lord Stearns does not fulfill the condition, the Crown inherits. The courts routinely side with the testator's final wishes, no matter how eccentric, and they will have a vested interest in ruling against his lordship. Your father was..."

"Evil," Søren said.

Mr. Fitzsimmons replied, "I would have said 'cunning.'"

"Yes, that as well." Søren rubbed his temple and Kingsley couldn't stop himself from reaching down and squeezing his shoulder to comfort him.

"Forgive me, Lord Stearns," Mr. Fitzsimmons went on, "but it's now half noon. I don't mean to rush you along, but for your own sake..."

"Of course." Søren rose quickly from the chair to his full and impressive height. Mr. Fitzsimmons rose as well, at once. "Good day, Mr. Fitzsimmons. We'll be in touch, I'm sure. Come along, Kingsley."

Kingsley followed Søren out of Mr. Fitzsimmons's office and onto the street where their cab waited.

"Death by syphilis," Søren said, "was too good for the man."

TWO

KINGSLEY WAITED until Søren was in the cab before giving the driver their address. The cab lurched forward. Once they were moving, Kingsley drew the shades down. They were master and servant no more, but two lovers, alone and talking.

"Just when I thought," Søren said, eyes closed and head back, "that I had plumbed the depths of my father's evil...he does this to Claire."

"Marriage isn't evil," Kingsley said. "Boring, useless, and monotonous, but not evil."

"The last time I spoke to my father," Søren said, "I swore to him I would never capitulate to any of his schemes to make me marry. Now he's found the one way to do it—by using my love for Claire as a weapon against me. I almost want to applaud him for his ingenuity."

Søren's tone was light, but Kingsley sensed the brewing rage underneath his words.

"Your father's in Hell being spit-roasted on the fiery cocks of Satan and Beelzebub as we speak."

"You're trying to cheer me up. It's not working."

"Just get married," Kingsley said.

"Just get married? Wonderful idea. Tell the driver to stop by the Bride Shop. I need to buy a bride. We'll take two. One for me and one for you. Perhaps a third to keep as a spare. Grand idea. Brilliant."

"There's no need for sarcasm. You're a fucking baron with the face of Adonis, the body of Michelangelo's David, and the cock of...I don't know. Some mythological or biblical figure with a very large cock. There are dozens of poor lords in this town who'd sell their daughters to you for ten quid and a new horse."

"You get what you pay for," Søren said.

Kingsley sighed. The time for joking was over. "Søren, you know—"

"Don't." That one word was an order and a threat. Kingsley ignored both.

"Talk to her," Kingsley said. "That's all."

"She's my ward," Søren said. "She's barely out of the schoolroom."

"She's nineteen now, almost twenty. More than old enough to marry."

"She despises me."

"Who doesn't?"

"We haven't spoken in three years. My first words to her can't be 'Hello, Eleanor. Sorry I left you without saying good-bye, but I was wondering if you'd be kind enough to marry me?'"

"She was destined for prison or the workhouse before you came along and saved her. She owes you."

"I'll tell her that," Søren said. "But I'll make certain you're standing in front of me so that when the gun goes off, the bullet hits you, not me."

"I'll take that risk."

Søren fell silent a moment.

"He knew I wanted her," Søren said softly.

"Your father?"

He nodded. "I took Eleanor in, made her my ward, and somehow he found out. When I saw him last, he mocked me, saying for all my pride, all my self-righteousness, I was no better than he was, taking home a fifteen-year-old girl."

"Your father forced himself on your mother when she was barely seventeen, and he only married when he found out she was carrying you. And that was the least of his crimes. All you did was give a good home to a poor motherless girl whose wastrel father had forced her into a life of crime. You didn't lay a hand on her."

"I wanted to, though," Søren said. "God, I did want to. The thoughts I had..." He closed his eyes, took a long shuddering breath. "At midnight, the night before we left, I found myself standing outside her bedroom door, the doorknob in one hand, a leather strap in the other. She was sixteen by then, and I was twenty-nine. What decent God-fearing man dreams of strapping and sexually violating his sixteen-year-old ward?"

Most of them, Kingsley imagined, but he didn't say that aloud. He knew a rhetorical question when he heard it.

"You didn't do it. That's what matters. I want to slit your throat most mornings when I'm shaving you," Kingsley said. "I don't. The thought isn't what counts, only the deed. You did not do the deed. Not only did you not do the deed, you packed up and left for three years. You are nothing like your father. In fact, you are his opposite."

Kingsley knew what he had to say to convince Søren to talk to Eleanor. He hesitated to say it because it was as manipulative and cruel as it was true and certain. But needs must when one is being buggered from the grave by an evil, insane baron.

"If you don't marry your Eleanor, someday...some other man will."

Søren's eyes flinched, just his eyes, and Kingsley knew then exactly the expression Julius Caesar wore when he saw the knife in his belly put there by his dearest friend, Brutus.

"Tell the driver to take us to Regent's Park," Søren said.

Regent's Park. The townhouse where Søren's sister lived. And Eleanor, his ward.

Kingsley replied, "Where do you think the driver's been taking us the last ten minutes?"

THREE

LADY CLAIRE GREETED them with an enthusiasm most unladylike. Kingsley stood behind Søren in the elegant entryway of the townhouse. Claire, a pretty brunette with her brother's aristocratic eyes and nose, but not his cold beauty, appeared at the top of the stairs in a fetching gown of lavender. She squealed in delight and practically threw herself down the stairs in her rush to greet them.

"Frater!" She yodeled the word before launching herself off the penultimate step and into her brother's arms.

"Yes, quite lovely to see you as well, Soror," Søren said. *Frater* and *Soror*—tender pet names for each other, Latin for Brother and Sister. Kingsley found it stupid, but that was his jealousy talking. He'd had a sister, Marie-Laure. Not that he'd ever met her. She'd died of scarlet fever the year before he was born.

"Spin me," Claire said as she clung to her brother, her dainty lavender slippered feet a foot off the floor. "I've been dreaming of this moment for three years, and in my dreams you always spin me."

"Must I?" Søren asked.

"I'll kiss Kingsley if you don't."

Søren spun Claire in two complete rotations before he set her down on her feet again, her hands on his shoulders, his hands on her waist.

"Calm down," Søren said, then pushed down on the tip of Claire's nose.

"Very well." She turned her chin up to allow Søren to press a sedate chaste kiss onto her cheek. "I see you've brought your shadow with you."

"Follows me wherever I go," Søren said.

Claire held out her hand and Kingsley kissed the back of it.

"Have you been taking good care of my brother?" Claire asked him.

"He's not dead yet," Kingsley said.

"Well done." Claire patted his shoulder. "Morning room? I'll ring for tea."

In minutes they were ensconced into Lady Claire's cozy morning room seated on yellow velvet chairs drinking tea from dainty cups.

"How is your Aunt Adeline?" Søren asked, as if this were a simple social visit.

"She's well," Claire said. "Went to buy a gown in mourning black. Said if I won't wear mourning, someone in the house has to."

"You could wear green and white stripes for all I care," Søren said. "In fact, you should. Let's go to the shops and buy garish clothing for all of us."

"Frater," Claire said. "You're stalling."

"Possibly," Søren admitted.

"Do I want to know what Father..." Claire paused to feign spitting after saying his name, and continued, "...did to us?"

"You don't," Søren said, sitting back in his chair. "But I'll tell you anyway."

Claire listened as Søren recounted the terms of the will. Her mouth opened slightly, she gasped, and her eyes widened hugely. And then...at the end...she laughed.

"That is not an appropriate response," Søren chided.

"I can't help it. You always said you would never marry, even with a gun to your head. And there's no gun to your head. It's just me. Father—" She feigned spitting again, "held *me* to your head. He was a clever arsehole, wasn't he? Before the pox made mincemeat of his brain, I mean."

"Claire!" Søren sounded like an appropriately scandalized older brother.

"Oh, piffle." She waved her hand. "I've been living with Eleanor for the past four years. She's taught me all the good bad words. Shall I go and fetch Eleanor then? So you can propose to her?"

"When did I say anything about proposing to Eleanor?" Søren demanded.

"Who else would you marry?" Claire asked.

"Goliath," Kingsley said.

"What was that?" Søren asked.

"Yes, what was that?" Claire asked as well.

"Earlier I was trying to think of a mythological or biblical figure with an enormous—"

"Kingsley," Søren said.

"Head," Kingsley said. "Goliath. He was a giant. So he must have a giant head. We were discussing hat sizes of biblical figures."

"Did you really mean 'head' or were you talking about—" Claire lowered her voice, "cocks?"

"For God's sake, Claire." Søren shook his head. "I suppose Eleanor taught you that word as well."

"Twas..." She pointed at Kingsley.

"I am the sole adult," Søren said, "in a world populated entirely by tall and abominably behaved children."

"He means us," Kingsley said to Claire. "We're abominable."

"Cheers then," Claire said. Kingsley and Claire clinked their teacups together like sailors down the pub.

Søren stood at the front window, one hand on the sill and one on his hip, head down—the very picture of deep contemplation.

"Eleanor's missed you," Claire finally said.

Søren turned around. "Has she?"

"I caught her throwing darts at your portrait last week. She has marvelous aim. I won't tell you where the darts landed, but it was a poor choice to be painted full-length, Frater. Let's hope your portrait self wasn't planning on children."

"She's been a bad influence on you," Søren said.

"Yet, I've never been happier. Funny that." Claire stood and walked to him, took his hand in hers. "Frater, I would rather live on the streets selling matches than see you unhappy. The only reason I'm telling you to marry her is because I know you want to, even if you can't admit it."

"I am her guardian," Søren said. "If another man in my position who was like me in every important respect came to me and asked permission to marry her, I would tell him no, absolutely not."

"Of course you would." Claire poked him in the chest, "because you wish to marry her yourself. And if you tried to stop her from marrying the man she wanted to marry, she'd run away to Gretna Green with him after leaving a dead snake in your bed."

"Live snake," Kingsley said.

"True," Claire said. "I hate to break the news to you, but you are her guardian in the same way I am a lady—in name only."

Søren sighed. Kingsley couldn't imagine how difficult this was for him—his conscience at war with his heart. What a blessing, Kingsley thought, that he didn't have a conscience. Made life much easier.

"If you're happy with her," Claire said, "and I know you will be, then Father loses. The last thing he'd ever want is for you to be happy." She put her hands on her brother's chest and gazed up at him. "He drove my mother into her early grave just as he did yours. I have an equal right to hatred, but I would rather see him forgotten and you happy. And me, as well. She's been a sister to me for four years. If I could have one thing from you for Christmas, it would be to have her for a sister-in-law."

Søren said nothing and the nothing he said said everything. He kissed Claire on the forehead. She smiled, triumphant.

"I'll go and fetch her," Claire said.

"I'll do it," Kingsley said. "She might be armed."

Kingsley left and strode upstairs. When he walked past Søren's official portrait hanging in the hall, he saw the holes in it from the darts. Dozens of holes. A hundred, perhaps.

Eleanor's door was slightly ajar, and Kingsley peeked in before announcing himself. She sat at her writing desk in a pale green gown with an ivory lace collar scratching words onto a sheaf of parchment. She glanced at him. Once.

"Can't even face me himself," she said. "Had to send his lapdog."

Kingsley barked.

She looked at him and arched her eyebrow. He remembered the day she demanded Søren teach her how to do that. Clearly she'd been practicing.

"Writing another of your lurid scandal stories?" he asked, stepping into her elegant white and gold bedroom, a far cry from the cramped and filthy room she'd been sleeping in with six other girls, all pickpockets, when Søren rescued her from her life of crime.

"I'm writing about a wicked rogue with dashing dark hair and a devilish smile. A man designed by God to wear tight trousers."

Kingsley was, in fact, wearing tight trousers. Fitted riding breeches and polished Hessian boots with brass buttons. Might not be fashionable, but he'd yet to meet a lady who'd complained about how he dressed.

"Ah, my biography then."

"A murder mystery, actually. You make quite a handsome corpse, even disemboweled."

"Is my killer a beautiful black-haired girl of nineteen? With green eyes, delicious lips, and a bad temper?"

She sat up straight and tore her paper in half.

"Damn," she said, "you guessed the ending. Back to the drawing board."

Her voice was lower than Kingsley remembered, huskier, more womanly. A voice like running one's hand backwards across velvet.

"Lord Stearns would like to speak with you."

"He can speak to the devil for all I care."

Kingsley strode to her writing desk and stood looking over her.

"When the constable was seconds away from hauling your thieving hide off to gaol, the sainted son of a baron—the very man whose wallet and pocketwatch you stole—intervened. He paid off your debts. He bought your freedom. And if that wasn't enough, he took you into his home and treated you like his own sister. I don't care what you'd rather do, you will go—*now*—and speak to him, or I will carry you."

She rose from her chair and remained there, unmoving.

Kingsley smiled. "I was hoping you'd do that." He swept her

up and into his arms. If she was surprised, she didn't show it. He carried her to the bottom of the stairs.

"There." He pointed at the door. "Go."

She started to brush past him, but he caught her by the waist and held her in place.

"I didn't want to leave," he said. "I serve him, in every way, as you know, but you and I were close, in our own way. Being there with you and him and Claire, it was as if I had a family again."

"Then you should hate him, too."

"Kiss me," he said.

"Why should I?"

"To spite him. If you really hated him you would. But we both know you don't—"

She kissed him. Her lips brushed his and he pulled her body flush against him and deepened the kiss with a nip of teeth on her bottom lip. A potent kiss, the sort that went straight from the mouth to the groin.

She broke the kiss and ran her hand through his hair.

"You need a haircut, Kingsley," she said. "You look like a pirate."

FOUR

ELEANOR ENTERED the drawing room and shut the door behind her. Søren sat at the piano, playing Beethoven's "Für Elise." He'd removed his jacket and rolled up his cuffs a turn. She came closer, watching him play, watching his long and lovely fingers waltzing across the ivories, watching his noble head as it bowed over the keyboard.

One courageous strand of his perfect golden hair threatened to fall over his forehead. She longed to reach out and brush it back. But she didn't. She wouldn't. The piece ended and the notes rang out and died. He looked at her.

"Hello, Little One," he said and smiled.

"I tried to grow as tall as I could while you were gone," she said, "so you couldn't call me that ever again."

He slowly rose from the piano bench and looked down at her. He held his hand at the top of her head and moved it to rest at his collarbone. He sat again, point made.

"I said I tried. I didn't say I succeeded, Lord Stearns."

"We know each other too well to be formal."

"Once, yes. But now? You're a stranger to me, my lord."

He met her eyes once and then put his fingers at the keys again. "Am I?" he said and began to play.

She recognized the piece at once. "Lo, How a Rose E're Blooming," an old German Catholic Christmas hymn. Her mother's favorite hymn, which Søren knew. She'd told him that during their first Christmas together four years ago, after he'd just brought her into his home. He'd gone to six different churches and chapels until he'd found a hymnal that included the song so he could learn to play it for her.

The piece ended. His fingers stilled.

"Eleanor, I need you."

She almost laughed. "You need me? Where were you when I needed you?"

"You wanted me. You didn't need me."

"I told you I loved you," she said, gazing down at him, fire in her eyes. "Do you know how hard it was for me, sixteen, to say those words to you, almost thirty? You, the son of a baron and me, the common daughter of a common thief. Do you know how hard it was for me to tell you what was in my heart?"

"Very hard?"

"No," she said. "It was the easiest thing I'd ever done or said. Because I trusted you."

He had the decency to look away as if ashamed.

She remembered that moment like yesterday. A winter evening at Edenfell and the air was fragrant with the scent of sleeping trees and falling snow. A week before Christmas. Claire had gone to bed early with a novel. Kingsley was likely off debauching his favorite local widow. Søren sat in the low club chair by the fireplace going over the estate's accounts. With his father in the sanitarium, Søren had taken charge of the estate. It flourished under his tender care and so had she. It had been exactly a year since he'd made her his ward. A year of new dresses and Claire's easy friendship and lessons with tutors and dancing masters and horse-riding instructors. And her favorite part—Mass on Sundays with Søren at the small Catholic chapel two villages away. That night as Søren made little notes in his ledger, she sat at his feet in front of the fire and laid her head on his knee. Between one mark and the next in his ledger, Søren rested his hand lightly on the back of her head. With one gentle knuckle, he'd stroked her neck from her ear to throat and back up again. Had she been a cat, she would have purred. But she was a girl in love, so she turned her head and smiled up at him.

"I'm in love with you," she'd said. "And I know you're in love with me. If you came to my room tonight, I wouldn't turn you away."

He didn't reply, not in words. Instead he caressed her lips with his thumb, a sensual touch that thrilled her even to recall it three years later. And when he pressed the tip of his thumb into her mouth and touched her tongue, she knew for certain he would come to her bedroom that night.

But he hadn't. He'd left the house by morning, taking Kingsley with him. No note. No explanation except a letter to Claire a week later saying "business" had called him away. That night at his feet in front of the fire had been the last she'd seen of him for three years. Until now.

"You abandoned me," she said.

"You were left with Claire's Aunt Adeline who treated you like her own daughter."

"But you were my guardian."

"And I left so I could better guard you."

"That makes no sense."

"I can't explain further, but I do apologize for the hurt I caused you."

"All's forgiven," she said though it wasn't. "Happy now?"

"You're in the same room with me. Of course I'm happy."

She closed her eyes and took a deep breath.

"What would you do if I stood on your piano and screamed my head off?" she asked.

"Quite frankly, I'm surprised you haven't already," he said.

Quite frankly, so was she.

She took a deep breath and temporarily silenced her desire to scream.

"Now...what do you need of me?"

"I need you to marry me."

He looked at her and she at him. In her nineteen years, no one had ever shocked or surprised her more.

"What?"

"You heard what I said." He began to play again.

Eleanor shut the fallboard, nearly closing it on his fingers. He managed to pull them out just in time.

"Marry you?"

"Sit," he said. "Here."

He pointed at the piano bench. She sat. She was too addled to fight him.

Once seated, he began to speak. He told her quickly of the condition in his father's will, how they couldn't risk contesting it, how fulfilling it meant Claire would have a home always, and she would never have to marry for money or security, how if they failed to fulfill it...they would lose all. This house. Edenfell. The money. They only had until half-noon tomorrow.

"Father had sworn for years he was leaving everything to Claire to punish me. I shouldn't be surprised that he lied even about that. I can't support her and you on my own, or I wouldn't presume to ask this of you."

"This is madness," she said.

"This is revenge. I told him, more than once, I would never be the son he wanted. I wouldn't marry, wouldn't have children, wouldn't use my title...I would reject everything he was and stood for and wanted. I went so far as to nearly join the Jesuit order and take a vow of celibacy."

"You never told me that."

"There are many things I've never told you."

"How many?"

"How many things haven't I told you?"

"Yes. How many secrets are you keeping from me? I want to know the number."

He raised his hands in surrender, but then she saw him ticking off his fingers as if counting.

"Four," he finally said.

"Four. What are they?"

"If I told you they wouldn't be secrets, would they?"

Eleanor growled and stood up. Not to leave but to put some distance between her and Søren. She couldn't think when she sat so close to him. He was far too beautiful. Her fingers itched to touch that spun gold hair of his. His eyes were grayer and wilder than she remembered, like a stormy December sky, and when she breathed in, she could smell the scent of him—like frost on a pine tree in a snow-deep forest.

"I know you despise me now," he said. "I'm not asking for a true marriage. We'll have an arrangement. We'll marry, and you can live at Edenfell with Claire. Or here if you prefer. You'll have a generous allowance. Kingsley and I will return to the continent, and you'll be free of me."

"Not good enough," she said.

"Name your price."

She turned and faced him. "Everything."

"Everything?"

"You asked my price. My price is everything. I do want a true marriage with you and *everything* that comes with it, including your secrets."

"You can't imagine what you're asking."

"Why? Because I'm a virgin?"

"That's certainly part of it."

"There's this marvelous book called a 'thesaurus.' Have you seen it? It lists synonyms for words. If you look up the word 'virgin' it in, you'll find 'naïve' is *not* listed among its synonyms."

"Of course not," he said. "They're entirely different parts of speech. One's a noun, the other's an adjective. 'Virginal' is the adjective form of 'virgin.' "

"'Virgin' may also be used as an adjective," she said. "Example: *He trampled the virgin snow under his feet.* No one would call it 'virginal snow.' That would be snow that's never been sexually defiled."

"And what would you know about sexual defilement?" Søren demanded.

"It was discussed in a religious pamphlet Aunt Adeline made Claire and I read."

"And what did the pamphleteer have to say about sexual defilement?"

"He was against it."

"And you?"

"I thought it sounded quite nice, myself."

He laughed first, softly and she laughed next, just a little louder.

"Tell me, Søren. Please?"

It seemed he couldn't look at her. He turned his head away as if mesmerized by the low fire in the grate.

"Is it Kingsley?" she asked.

"No," Søren said. "If you didn't know about he and I...then yes. But as you do..."

She did know. Her first summer at Edenfell, she'd seen them share a clandestine kiss. She'd gasped and run off. When Søren caught up with her, she'd been certain he would send her away for good to keep his dangerous secret. Instead, he'd trusted her with the truth—that while he and Kingsley both desired women, they also desired each other. They were lovers and had been since they were very young men. She'd loved him more after that, not merely for trusting her but because she knew when he told her he desired women, he meant that he desired *her*.

"I would never ask you to cast him out of your life," she said. "Only to let me in as well."

He said nothing. His face was expressionless.

She touched his shoulder and at once he put his hand over hers, clutching it. "Was I mad to think you desired me? Or simply stupid? I must have been one or the other for you to spurn me and then to offer me a loveless marriage."

"You are neither mad nor stupid and God, yes, Eleanor, of course I desired you. You knew. Kingsley knew. Even Claire knew. But I made a vow—"

"Damn you and your vows to your father. He's dead."

"I meant my vow to you." He met her eyes.

"To me?"

"The night I took you from the police station, the night I said I would make you my ward, you were frightened. Don't deny it."

She had opened her mouth to deny it, but her denial would have been a lie. He was the son of a wealthy baron, powerful in his own right—anyone who looked at him wanted to bow or curtsy. If he'd wanted to violate her, enslave her, even kill her... he could with no consequences. She knew better to think a handsome face was proof of a good soul. Her father had taught her that.

"That night in the carriage, when I brought you home from the police station to this house...I vowed to you that you would always be safe under my roof. I would never give you any cause to fear me."

"I am not afraid of you," she said.

"And I wish to keep it that way," he said. "A wife should never fear her husband."

"A woman has every right to fear marriage. If I marry you, you will *own* me. Legally I will be your property *forever*. Forever," she repeated. "There is no divorcing for Catholics. I spent three years pining for my guardian. I won't spend the rest of my life pining for my own husband. Either we have a true marriage or none at all."

He said nothing. She had her answer. Eleanor nodded. She turned to leave.

"Yes," Søren said.

Eleanor turned.

Søren stood from the piano bench and walked over to her.

"Yes what?"

"Yes," he said. "We can have a true marriage if you insist. You do give up a great deal to marry me. It's not fair of me to give you so little in return."

"Oh," she said.

"You will marry me then?"

"Yes, of course," she said quickly before she could change her mind. She held out her hand to shake. "Forever."

He took her hand in his.

She expected him to shake her hand. He didn't. He lifted it to his lips and turned it, wrist up. Then he pressed a long hot slow kiss inside her palm.

He whispered, "Everything."

FIVE

THAT EVENING they were married at the Royal Bavarian Chapel. Søren knew the Rector, and was able to talk him into performing a wedding mass on very short notice. Eleanor borrowed Claire's best white gown and white fur-trimmed cloak. Søren wore a dark gray suit with a matching waistcoat. Claire acted as maid of honor. Kingsley was Søren's best man. Claire's guardian, her Aunt Adeline, was the sole guest, not including two nuns who watched from the wings.

Mr. Fitzsimmons and a civil official were also in attendance. Of course they were there. This wasn't a marriage for love but to secure an inheritance.

The night was dark and cold. The chapel was lit only by a few white candles on tall iron candle holders. The altar was decorated with country greenery for Christmas.

There was no music when she walked down the aisle toward Søren and her footsteps echoed. She imagined Søren could even hear her heart beating in the silence.

"*In nómine Patris, et Fílii, et Spiritus Sancti,*" the priest intoned.

Together, Eleanor and Søren replied, "Amen."

And so it began.

Did Lord Marcus Lennox Søren Stearns, Baron Stearns, promise to love her, comfort her, honor and keep her, in sickness and health?

He did.

Did Eleanor Louise Schreiber promise to obey him and serve him, love, honor and keep him, in sickness and health?

She did.

A gold band was slipped onto her finger. A brief kiss was pressed upon her lips.

Then it was done, and Eleanor—the daughter of impoverished German exiles from the failed revolutions of 1848—was now Lady Eleanor, Baroness Stearns.

They returned to the townhouse in Regent's Park. Eleanor ate a late supper with Claire while the men ensconced themselves in the drawing room, drinking port and discussing the transfer of the old baron's properties.

"Nice to know we won't be out on the streets," Claire said after the servants cleared away the dishes. "I doubt I'd survive long. I'm fragile and easily susceptible to cold."

"Like every member of the aristocracy, you're spoiled and pampered and mostly useless," Eleanor said.

"Are you happy?" Claire squeezed Eleanor's hand.

Eleanor forced a smile. "Never happier."

They left the dining room and Eleanor saw Søren and Kingsley in the hallway, saying their goodbyes to the solicitor, Mr. Fitzsimmons. The man bowed to her and said, "Goodnight, Lady Stearns. My heartiest congratulations."

"Thank you," she replied.

"Lady Stearns," Claire said to herself. "That used to be my mother. Now it's my sister."

"Eleanor, I need a word with you," Søren said.

Eleanor looked at Claire but there was no escape. She was married now.

"Goodnight," Claire said and kissed her on the cheek. Eleanor went into the drawing room with Søren.

"Where's Kingsley?" Eleanor asked. Søren stood by the fireplace, warming himself. She joined him.

"Sending a telegram to the staff at Edenfell. We'll go there tomorrow, if that's acceptable to you. The news of my sudden marriage will be all over town by morning. Claire will stay behind for a few days to put out the worst of the rumors. She'll join us on New Year's."

"That's acceptable, yes."

"I know you always liked it there," he said. Then, "Sleep well. We'll leave early."

She knew she was being dismissed and wouldn't stand for it.

"You promised to give me everything, Søren."

"Yes, but I didn't promise to give you everything *tonight*."

"I'll go to bed," she said. "But I'll say to you now what I said to you three years ago. I love you, and I know you love me. If you come to my room tonight, I won't turn you away."

With that, she went upstairs and into her bedroom.

THIS FUCKING marriage had better work or Kingsley was going to dig the old baron out of his grave just for the pleasure of kicking the corpse. He sat in Søren's bedroom by the fire, drinking brandy when he heard footsteps in the hall, heavy and male. A moment later, a door opened to Søren's bedchamber.

"There you are," Søren said, shutting the door behind him.

"Here I am. Brandy?"

"Immediately," Søren said.

Kingsley grinned and stood slowly, feigning a relaxed

languor he did not feel. He poured a steep brandy and passed the snifter to Søren.

Søren drank and deeply while Kingsley watched, merely sipping his brandy. He sensed an interesting conversation was about to take place, but he knew better than to try to get Søren talking before he was ready or willing.

When the brandy snifter was empty, Søren set it on Kingsley's fireplace mantel.

"I have a problem," Søren said.

"Oh?" Kingsley smiled behind his own brandy. "Do you?"

"I want her."

"I knew you were depraved, but you've gone too far this time. You want to bed your own wife? You disgust me."

"You can't be serious for one minute?" Søren demanded.

"Fine. I'll be serious. If you want her, have her."

Søren turned and rested his elbows on the mantel. Kingsley leaned back against it, next to Søren.

"I don't beat women."

"First time for everything," Kingsley said.

"I'm having a moral crisis, and you're making jokes again."

"I confess I am enjoying this a little." Kingsley took his brandy glass off the mantel. "Seeing you flagellating yourself like a medieval monk for the shameful sin of wanting to make love to your own wife. It's entertaining. Better than the opera."

"It's not the sex that is the issue at hand," Søren said. "How many times do I have to tell you—"

"Yes, I know. You don't beat women. Although you really should. It's great fun when they like it. Half the girls at Magda's were twice the perverts I am."

"She invited me to her bedroom again."

"Has she?"

"What should I do?"

"Fuck her," Kingsley said. "Obviously." Seemed obvious to Kingsley.

Søren turned, glared at him.

"She's a virgin."

"What of it? So was I. Once. I think. I assume so at least. Must have been at some point." Kingsley shook his head. "A dark time in my past. I must have blocked it from my memory."

"Why aren't you talking me out of this?" Søren asked. He stood up straight and crossed his arms across his chest, leaned back against the mantel.

"Do you think I'm that petty? That jealous?"

"Yes."

Kingsley threw up his arm in surrender, turned his back on Søren and filled his snifter again. He turned around.

"You're terrified."

"I am," Søren stared into the fire. "This was a mistake."

Kingsley set his brandy aside and went to stand in front of Søren.

"Tonight in the chapel, when Eleanor walked down the aisle toward you, I have never seen you look at any woman the way you looked at her. And the only time I've ever seen you look at *anything* like that..." Kingsley smiled.

"When?"

"One night when we were about eighteen or nineteen," he began, "we spent the night in the Cathédrale Notre-Dame de Paris. The night, the moon was full. You remember? And it shone through the famous Rose windows and turned the cathedral colors I never dreamed existed. You said to me that night, 'How can you not believe in a loving God when you see that?' You looked at her like you looked at the moonlight through those windows. You looked at her like you'd just found another reason to believe in God."

Søren smiled, but he didn't deny it. He met Kingsley's eyes.

"I look at you that way, too."

"Did you?"

"Yes, but only when you aren't looking."

Kingsley stepped even closer. Søren put his arm around Kingsley's waist. They kissed, quickly but tenderly, and when the kiss ended, Kingsley pressed his forehead to Søren's.

"You are not your father. He beat his wives though they begged him to stop. You wouldn't even take me to bed me until I'd begged you on my hands and knees to do it. I think you enjoyed making me wait and beg for it as you did actually doing the deed."

"Oh, but I made you regret begging for it, didn't I?" Søren asked.

"I regret nothing I've ever let you do to me. Nothing. *Rien*."

"And I've never once regretted my nature," Søren said. "Not since I found you. Not until I fell in love with her. How do I tell her? How does a man tell his beautiful young bride, a woman he wants like a man wandering in the desert wants water...how does he tell her he's impotent unless he beats her?"

"You could beat me, you know."

"I plan to. Often."

"No, I mean now," Kingsley said, the idea coming to him at once. "Beat me now and go to her when you're aroused."

"And what then?" Søren demanded.

"Shall I show you pictures? I have my collection."

"I'm fully versed in the mechanics, you ass. I can't simply throw open her door and toss her on the bed."

"You could, actually. She wants you to. Come on, what's stopping you other than stubbornness? She invited you to her bed. Beat me. Go to her."

Søren just shook his head.

"Fine," Kingsley said. "She kissed me today and it was

incredible. If you won't be a husband to her, I will." Kingsley started for the door.

Søren grabbed him by the collar and thrust him against the wall. Though no force was necessary, Søren forced Kingsley's mouth open and pushed his tongue inside it. Being with Søren required Kingsley to fight his instincts. He wanted to embrace Søren, tear at his clothes, kiss back twice as hard. But Søren wanted submission of the most abject kind. So Kingsley must stand there, back pressed against the mantel as Søren bit his lips and his neck. He had to stand there while Søren opened Kingsley's shirt and pushed it off his shoulders and onto the floor.

Without a warning, Søren turned Kingsley toward the fireplace.

"Stay," Søren said. Kingsley stood and waited, head down on the mantel while Søren retrieved whatever implement of torture he wanted that night. He didn't have to wait long.

Søren struck Kingsley. The pain was swift and furious, and Kingsley had to bite into his own arm to silence a scream. He knew at once the source of the pain. A Scottish school tawse. The pain it caused was unique. Nothing else felt quite like it. Kingsley loved it and hated it in equal measure. Søren brought it down again. And again. Faster. Harder. Quicker. Crueler. Kingsley's back burned like Søren had dowsed it in linseed oil and thrown a match on it.

And then it was over. Søren turned Kingsley to face him. Kingsley stood there, panting like a dog, ready to fall to his knees and serve. He looked up at Søren and found his master's eyes glowing like candlewicks. Kingsley dared to touch him and found Søren brutally hard. Even through his trousers, Kingsley felt Søren throbbing against his hand.

"There's Goliath," Kingsley said, grinning.

Søren kissed him again, as Kingsley stroked him. When the kiss broke, Kingsley forced himself to smile.

"Go and fuck your new bride," he said to Søren. "Do it well and tell me all about it tomorrow."

Søren held Kingsley's neck in his large, strong hands.

"I love you," Søren said.

Then he left and Kingsley was alone with his thoughts again. They were the same thoughts as before.

This better fucking work.

SIX

ANNETTE, Claire's lady's maid, came to Eleanor's room and helped her out of her dress and corset and into her nightgown. While Eleanor sat at her dressing table to take the pins from her hair, Annette pulled the covers down the bed and built up the fire. Soon the fire was blazing bright and roaring.

"Are you trying to warm the whole house?" Eleanor teased.

Annette laughed softly. "Your wedding night, Lady Stearns. No man likes it to be cold when he takes his clothes off. Anything else, Ma'am?"

Eleanor caught herself blushing. She didn't do that very often...or ever.

"No," she said. "Nothing else."

"Goodnight then, my lady." Annette gave her a curtsy and a saucy little smile before leaving the bedroom.

God, it was humiliating. And what was more humiliating—everyone knowing it was her wedding night and acting like her world was about to be turned upside-down by an act that men and women had been doing since the foundation of the world... or that she'd sleep alone, rejected by her new husband on their wedding night?

Eleanor ran the brush through her hair one last time. She rose and lit a candle in the fire and carried it to bed. As she was setting it in its brass holder onto the bedside table, Søren opened the door.

She stared, shocked, as he closed the door behind him. Then he locked it.

"Søren." It was all she said, all she had time to say.

He strode to her and took her by the waist, pulling her to him. He kissed her.

She was so stunned by the kiss she didn't do anything at first except allow it. She didn't flinch or gasp, didn't move away, didn't push him back. She stood and let it happen. But only for a moment.

Then she kissed him back. She lifted her hands to his chest and clung to the soft linen of his shirt as she pressed her lips to his. His tongue touched her lips, and she opened her mouth to him, giving herself up to him and the kiss.

She felt the kiss everywhere, all over her body. She burned and shivered, the kiss hot as a summer sun, the scent of him like morning frost on a windowpane. He tightened his hold on her, molding her to him. She felt the hardness of him pressing against her lower stomach and it excited her so much she couldn't help but push her hips against him and it. She wanted to touch it, touch him, all of him, for hours, all night until morning. Eleanor tried to break the kiss to tell him that, to ask him to undress, to lay in bed with her so she could explore his body and let him explore her. But when she tried to pull away, he dug his fingers into her hair, gripping her by the nape of the neck, and deepened the kiss.

He raised his other hand to her neck and yanked hard enough on her gown to tear a button as he pulled it down her shoulder, baring her right breast. Eleanor shivered as his large hand cupped her breast, his skin warm, almost hot. Her nipple hardened against his palm, and he pinched it so hard she gasped. At her gasp he shuddered and released a soft sound of pleasure from the back of his throat. He broke the kiss, finally, but only to lower his head and take her nipple into his mouth. His arms were around her, forcing her to arch her back. She dug her fingers into his golden hair and breathed his name. His mouth was hot on her and hungry, and he suckled her hard enough it hurt but it hurt in such a way that she wanted to hurt that way forever.

Eleanor thought she might faint if he didn't stop but he didn't stop and she didn't faint. But her breathing was fast and heavy. She felt she was drowning in sensation, it was all happening so quickly. She wanted to tell Søren to slow down, let her catch her breath, but she didn't have the breath to say it. And he did not slow down.

He rose up and captured her mouth, forcing his tongue inside for another brutal kiss. She'd lived under his roof—ate every meal with him, spent every evening with him, walked and talked every day with him—that perfect year before he'd left her. Never once had she seen him speak too sharply to a servant, lose his temper with his sister, drink too much or lose control of himself in any way. He'd always been temperate, restrained, and in total command of himself.

Until now.

Without a word—of tenderness or affection, of lust or warning—he lifted her off her feet and put her on her back onto the edge of it bed. He pushed her gown up to her waist and instinctively she tried to push it down again.

"Don't deny me," he said and it wasn't a request but an order. She obeyed it because she didn't want to deny him, not now or ever.

His hands were under her gown at her hips and he pulled her to the very edge of the bed. He pressed her legs open and roughly drew them around his waist. He cupped her between her legs, and his fingers rubbed along the seam of her body, pushing and opening her until he found what he was looking for. Eleanor cried out as he worked a finger inside her. Although at night, alone in bed, she had touched herself there a thousand times, it hadn't prepared her at all for what it felt like when it was his finger inside that tight and aching place.

He turned his hand and pushed his thumb in, and Eleanor whimpered in pain. The sound seemed to do something to Søren. His head fell back and his eyelashes fluttered. She'd never seen him like this before. Before she had thought she'd wanted him, and knew what it meant to want him, but not until then did she feel an almost animal need to take him into her body as deep as he could go.

Søren seemed to share the need. He took his hand from her and he opened his trousers. Though she'd wondered about it, dreamed about it, she'd never seen his cock until then. It was larger than she'd expected, long and thick and she ached at the sight of it. She'd heard of women fainting on their wedding nights at the first sight of their husband's organ...Eleanor thought she could, but faint from the wanting of it, not the terror of it.

She wanted to tell him what she thought of it but didn't have the chance. He took it in hand, guided it to the entrance of her body and pushed.

Eleanor flinched as the thick tip of it found resistance. She didn't want to resist it. She wanted all of it, all of him, inside her. But her body had other ideas. Søren held her by the hips, pushed again, and the barrier gave way, and he was inside her.

The agony was acute, overpowering all her other senses. Desire fled. Pleasure fled. Even her love for him was forgotten in that terrible moment when he wrenched her open. It was too much, too hard, too solid, too thick and too deep. It burned. It burned and it scared her.

"Søren, it hurts," she said. Her voice sounded small and young to her own ears. "It hurts."

She clutched at the sheets, and moved her hips, trying to find a way to accommodate so much of him inside of her. When she moved, though, his eyes fluttered again, and he thrust into her, then again. If he'd only stop moving, she could breathe, ease into it, take it, enjoy it, but he seemed like a man lost to the world.

She needed to touch him to bring him back to her, back to himself, but she couldn't reach him. His head had fallen back and his eyes were closed as he worked her on his cock.

Eleanor slipped her hand between her legs and touched herself where he impaled her. She felt her own tender flesh, wet with desire or blood or both. She touched the organ that split her, sliding her fingertips over it as it penetrated her. Søren must have felt her touch. His eyes opened at last, and he looked down at her.

"Søren," she said. Some awareness seemed to come back to him. He touched her face, stroked her cheek. She turned her head and pressed a kiss into the palm of his hand. "Søren," she said again. He lowered his hand to her left breast, caressing it through her gown. He grew impatient and yanked her gown down again, down to her waist, baring both her breasts to him. The cock inside her slid deeper, touching her womb. She flinched and the inner muscles of her body clenched around him.

"Do anything you want to me," she said, arching her back to show she was giving herself to him, all of her to all of him. "Anything."

"Don't say that, Eleanor," he said. His tone was sharp. She ignored it.

"Why shouldn't I? We're married."

He wrapped his arm around her lower back, lifted her and impaled her.

"Anything..." she said. He withdrew from her and impaled her again. "Anything...anything you want..."

He turned his head and she saw him looking at something. What was it? There was nothing on her night table but a book and the candle still burning.

"Anything." She said it because she meant it. Because she would do anything, allow anything, give him anything as long as he was inside her, spearing her.

Søren wrenched himself away from her, out of her body. He stood at the foot of the bed and straightened his clothes.

"Go to sleep, Eleanor," he said.

"You're going? Now?" She pulled her gown up to cover her breasts. "Why?" Her voice broke on the question.

"Goodnight," he said and then he was gone.

KINGSLEY WAS HALFWAY through a bottle of red when he heard Søren's footsteps in the hall.

"Coward," Kingsley muttered, thinking Søren had gone to Eleanor but changed his mind and come back to bed. But the footsteps passed the door and kept walking, fast. Curious, Kingsley went to the door and looked out in the hallway. Søren was at the steps and descending.

Kingsley ran to the banister at the top of the stairs. Sure enough, in the entryway, Søren threw on his coat and walked out the front door.

At night. In winter. Four hours after getting married and not fifteen minutes after going up to Eleanor's room.

Eleanor...

He crept up the stairs and stood at her door. She sat at the edge of her bed, eyes wide open as if in shock, her torn nightgown clutched in her hand at her throat.

Fuck.

Kingsley withdrew to the hallway, leaned back against the wall and put his hand to his forehead. What had he done? From inside the room, he heard Eleanor softly weeping.

Without knocking he went into her room. She looked up at him as he came to her and offered her his wine glass. With a visibly trembling hand she took it from him and drank deeply.

"He left," she said and her voice was hollow. "He came to me. We..."

"Did he hurt you?" Of course he had. There was blood on the bed.

"Some," she said, shaking her head. "But that was...it was...I didn't want him to stop. But he did. And then he left. He just... he left me."

"Shh..." Kingsley said, not wanting her to get overwrought. "Drink your wine."

She drank again, and he stroked her hair.

"Did I do something wrong?"

"It isn't you," Kingsley said gently as he took the empty wine glass from her. "I'll talk to him. I'll make it right. Try to sleep."

She looked up at him, her eyes wide and green and angry. "You know all his secrets. Why did he leave me?"

Kingsley shrugged. "He doesn't want to hurt you."

"Then why," she said, "does he keep doing it?"

SEVEN

Christmas Eve, 1871

AT FIVE THE NEXT MORNING, Kingsley was awoken by a light slap on the cheek followed by an order to get dressed. They were taking an early train. Eleanor and Annette would be coming on the later train apparently.

Though he despised early mornings, Kingsley got up, got dressed, and flagged down a cab to take them to the station. They had a first-class compartment to themselves, which Kingsley took advantage of by stretching out as best as he could on the rear-facing seat, arm thrown over his eyes.

"You're sleeping?" Søren asked, his tone scoffing.

"With your permission, my lord. And even if I don't have your permission."

"You don't."

"Fuck your mortal soul," Kingsley said.

"Have I ever told you that you are a bad valet?"

"I'd rather be a bad valet than a bad husband."

"And what, precisely, is that supposed to mean?" Søren demanded, his tone clipped and crisp.

Kingsley peeked out from under his arm and looked at Søren. "You know."

"Do I?"

"You left her? Again? How could you do that to her? And on her wedding night?"

"What did or did not happen on my wedding night is none of your concern," Søren said.

"In *coitus interruptus*," Kingsley said, "you pull your cock out of her cunt before you come. You don't pull it out of the entire fucking *house* before you come. Do I need to draw you a picture?"

"You spoke to Eleanor?"

"Someone had to go to her when she was sobbing her heart out after you ran away."

"I never, in my wildest dreams, imagined that my male lover would side with my wife against me."

"You need to have wilder dreams then, *mon ami*. And don't call me your 'lover.' I hate that word. Implies I love you. I don't. I barely tolerate you. I'm your 'bare tolerator,' if that. Good day."

At that, Kingsley rolled over onto his side, away from Søren.

"Kingsley."

Kingsley held up his hand, fingers clenched, indicating Søren should shut it.

"We will finish this fight," Kingsley replied, "in four hours when I wake up. Until then, I want you to sit there and think about what you've done."

"Have you forgotten who you are addressing?"

"Have you forgotten I'm French? In England you bow and scrape to your aristocracy, but in France we cut your fucking heads off. Pardon me—we cut your fucking heads off, *my lord*."

To that, Søren had no rebuttal. A sure sign he did feel some remorse. Good.

A little over four hours later, Kingsley woke up. He found coffee and the toilets and enjoyed them both and in that order. Revived, he returned to his compartment and found Søren behind the *Times* again. Kingsley pulled down the shades to give them privacy. If this fight dissolved into fisticuffs, he didn't want any witnesses.

"I am now willing and able to continue our fight," Kingsley announced. Søren did nothing. Kingsley attempted to kick Søren in the shin, but Søren had seen it coming and moved his leg at the last second.

"Bastard," Kingsley said.

Søren lowered his newspaper, folded it, tossed on the seat next to him.

"She said I could do anything to her," Søren said. "She said it more than once, as if she meant it. And for a few seconds, I came dangerously close to taking the candle off the table and pouring scalding wax on her breasts. And if you think me leaving mid-coitus hurt her, imagine the alternative scenario, if you will."

Kingsley's eyes widened. He blew hard through his lips. "Fair point," Kingsley said. "That would throw even me off my game if you hadn't warned me first."

"I'll accept your apology the moment you offer it."

"You'll accept my foot in your arse," Kingsley said. "Just because I agree it was better for you to leave than douse her in candle wax without warning doesn't mean you win this fight."

"What was I supposed to do?"

"Tell her. Just...tell her. Tell her what you are, what you do, what you want. Tell your wife who her husband is."

"And watch the girl who loves me come to hate me?"

"She'll hate you anyway if you keep leaving her like that. And who knows? She might not hate you. She might like it. If she told you to do anything to her...she might have meant it, you know?"

Søren shook his head. "What is your game?"

"What?"

"What are you playing at? Trying to talk me into telling Eleanor about my...proclivities? What do you get out of it?"

"A full fucking night's sleep," Kingsley said.

"If you didn't want us to marry, you should have told me."

Kingsley furrowed his brow at Søren in confusion. "I did want you to marry her. Nice enough way to get rich overnight, marry a beautiful girl. If I was against it, I would have stopped it."

"I kept waiting for you to stop it, to try to talk me out of it."

"I didn't," Kingsley said. "If you'll recall, I talked you *into* it."

"Yes, which is highly suspicious the more I think about it."

"What do you think this is about?" Kingsley asked. "Can't I just want you to be happy?"

"No," Søren said. "You know I know you too well for that."

Søren paused and Kingsley lived and died in that short agonizing silence.

"Are you planning on leaving me?" Søren asked. "Is that what this is about?"

Kingsley only stared at him, stunned speechless.

"You sit there and berate me, swear at me, and insult me for not being honest with Eleanor. But you're not being honest with me, are you? I ask you again: are you planning to leave me?"

"Why would you think that?" Kingsley asked, too stunned to muster a defense.

"You encouraged me to marry her, encouraged me to bed her, and you are now encouraging me to tell Eleanor everything about myself. You seemed determined Eleanor and I have the same sort of relationship you and I do. Are you hoping she can be to me what you are so you can leave me with a clear conscience? If so, tell me and tell me now. I don't know if I could bear it but I can hardly bear not knowing either."

"I..." Kingsley lifted his empty hands to show he was without words.

"You were seeing a woman in Paris," Søren reminded him. "Usually you boast about your other lovers, but you rarely spoke of her. Is it her? For God's sake, Kingsley, tell me."

Their compartment was silent but for the steady chugging of the train on the iron tracks.

"I'm almost flattered," Kingsley finally said. "No, I am *certainly* flattered that you think I could leave you. Even if I wanted to, I couldn't. My love for you is a beast so unholy strong not even Hercules could slay it. Now that I've said that, I imagine Hercules was a mythological figure who also must have had an enormous cock."

"Kingsley."

"No. No. No. Never. I would never leave you. No, a thousand times, no. A million times. A billion. You own me, you know that. You should no more worry about me leaving you than your own hat growing legs and running away."

Søren exhaled and visibly relaxed. "You are being honest with me?"

"Yes," Kingsley said. "I swear on my mother's grave. The woman in Paris...I do care for her. She's only twenty-eight and her husband's an old man, too old to give her children. She asked me if I would...and I was considering it when we received the news your father died."

"She asked you to give her a child."

Kingsley nodded, knot in his throat.

"But if you're married," Kingsley pushed his words past the

knot, "and you're happily married then someday you'll have children. And I could be like a second father to them. You would let me be close to your children, wouldn't you?"

Søren only stared at Kingsley a too-long moment. Kingsley waited and Søren finally spoke a command. "Come here."

Kingsley came and sat at Søren's side. Søren took Kingsley's face in his two hands, forcing Kingsley to look at him.

"Yes," Søren said, his tone emphatic. "Yes, I would let you be close to my children. I would let you be a second father to them. And while we're at it...yes to everything you ever want from me. Anything you wish for, hope for, dream of...yes to it all."

Kingsley rested his head against Søren's chest. Søren wrapped one arm around Kingsley's back, the other around his head. Kingsley felt Søren pulling his too-long hair off the back of his neck. Søren kissed him on a tender spot, just above his collar. "Yes," Søren whispered then kissed Kingsley's neck again. "Yes." A hundred kisses were punctuated with a hundred yeses.

Yes. Kiss. *Yes.* Kiss. *Yes.* Kiss. *Yes.*

It went on and on until Kingsley couldn't tell the yeses from the kisses. He raised his head, and Søren gave him a long slow deep yes on the lips.

Eventually, the kiss ended. With his thumbs, Søren wiped away the tears on Kingsley's cheeks.

"Why haven't you ever told me you wanted children?" Søren asked. His tone was gentle now, not commanding, only wondering.

"I never wanted you to think you weren't enough for me," Kingsley said. "It was hard enough convincing you to be with me. If you knew there was something more I wished for, something we could never have, you'd send me away, probably saying it was for my own good or something stupid and selfless like that. As stupid and selfless as running away from

Eleanor for three years just because you wanted to take her to bed."

"It was the right thing to do," Søren said.

"It was," Kingsley said. "Then. Leaving her last night with no explanation? No."

"No," Søren said with a sigh. "It wasn't."

"But it wasn't right of me, either, sending you to her like that. It was selfish. When I saw her last night weeping...I wanted to break your neck for hurting her. Then I realized you must feel the same. You want to hurt anyone who hurts her."

"I'm supposed to be her guardian. How do I guard her from myself?"

"I never imagined I could love a woman you loved," Kingsley confessed. "I know I'm jealous. I'm not proud of it but I am. And when you brought her home, I thought you'd lost your mind. If a man wants to buy himself a Christmas gift, it's usually a new horse or a silver-tipped walking stick. Not a young girl he wasn't even planning to bed. And that girl? She was scared witless she would do something wrong and you'd send her back where you found her. She came to me in private and begged me to teach her which spoon to use and how to curtsy and how to address an earl and how to speak French like any well-bred young lady must. She's common as dirt and so am I. Neither one of us knew what you were doing with us. I still don't most days."

"You never told me that."

"I'll never forget when the Earl and Countess of Godwick came for tea. They thought Eleanor had gone to finishing school in Switzerland as she spoke French so well and behaved so gracefully. I was as proud of her that day as any father had ever been of his child in the history of the world." Kingsley shook his head and met Søren's eyes. "Just between you and me...you may not even deserve her. You've never in your life had to work as hard as she did that year to fit into your world. You certainly won't deserve her if you don't tell her the truth. I'm begging you to tell her, not for my sake or whatever imaginary children you'll have someday, but for her sake, and because I love her, too."

Søren kissed him again and Kingsley didn't know this time if it was a kiss or a yes. For Eleanor's sake, he hoped it was a yes.

EIGHT

EIGHT HOURS on two trains and then one long carriage ride finally brought Eleanor home to Edenfell.

The winter sun had long set by the time the carriage turned into the drive, but the lane glowed like morning. Four years ago, after a carriage had run off the drive, Søren had ordered lamp-posts to be installed. A dozen on each side of the lane were lit and it seemed as if she were being carried to a magic castle in a fairy story.

Edenfell was a great gray box of a house, an old Georgian manor, square and sturdy and safe. Her happiest days had taken place in this home before Søren had left her. And her loneliest nights after he was gone.

The carriage pulled up and she saw Søren on the grand main steps waiting with Kingsley at his side. He came down the stairs and did the footman's job of putting down the step and opening the door for her, helping her out.

"Welcome home, my lady," Søren said, and pressed a cool kiss on her cheek. Kingsley escorted Annette into the house leaving her all alone with Søren.

On his arm she entered the house and found no one to greet

her, but the house itself. The hall glittered with candlelight reflected off the freshly polished brass chandelier. The warmth enveloped her.

"Where is everyone?" she asked.

"I've ordered the official welcome of the lady of the house to wait until tomorrow," Søren explained. "The staff wasn't pleased with me, they're so happy we're married. I imagined you'd be in no mood for a raucous welcome."

She wasn't and found the silence a relief. "You left early today," she said.

"I had preparations to make for your arrival," he said as he steered her into the drawing room. "You see?"

Eleanor's eyes widened. Søren had brought in a Christmas tree—a fine tall spruce with silver baubles and candles on it all aglow. And greenery decorated the hearth and hung from the ceiling.

"I wanted to give you back the Christmas I took from you when I left so abruptly," he said.

He was trying so hard to please her. Did he still not understand?

"May I show you something?" she asked. "Outside?"

"Of course," he said and though he looked puzzled, he followed her from the decorated drawing room, through the garden door out to the snow-filled veranda. Eleanor pulled the hood of her cloak up as Søren slid on his gloves. She led him down a pathway and to the old wood and stone gazebo.

"Here," she said as she stood at the railing and looked up at the bright and shining new winter moon. "This is where I would go to be with you after you left. Every night that winter."

"Be with me?"

"I couldn't cry in front of Claire, or she would start crying, too. I told her once how you smelled like winter and she laughed at me. She said you smelled like shaving soap and nothing else.

But you do. The snow collects in here and the night wind, too. I can't explain but in here is where I would find you. And I would close my eyes and breathe you in again and again until I had filled myself to the brim with you." She turned to him and found snow dusting his golden hair and his gray eyes glowing silver in the moonlight. "Did you know I wanted you that much that I would stand in the winter in the cold and the snow at night just to catch, for a moment or two, the scent of your skin?"

"No," he said.

"I did. Yet I think...I think you forgot me the moment I was out of your sight."

"You think that, do you?"

"Is it not true?"

"I will tell you what is true." He moved to stand closer to her so she could feel the warmth of his body radiating even through his coat and her cloak. "In Paris at mass, a girl with black hair like yours would attend every day. I would sit two pews behind her so I could stare at her hair and pretend she was you. I kept an orchid in my room because its scent reminded me of your soap and I wanted to smell you whenever I lay in bed. The hart tie pin you gave me? I wore it every day until the clasp broke and even after I kept it with me. Even now," he said and pulled from inside his breast pocket the small silver stag pin. He slipped it back into his pocket.

"You gave Claire and me 'pin money.' I never had pin money before. I thought you were supposed to use it to buy pins. So I bought that for you. My hart. My heart." She put her hand over her own heart.

"Your heart. I carry it against my own."

Before she could speak, he took her face in his gloved hands and kissed her roughly and deeply. This was no tender kiss, not loving either, but possessive and aching and desperate. She had no choice but to open her mouth to the kiss and receive it. His mouth pressed hers open, his tongue touched hers and she moaned. Without thinking, she found herself twining her arms around his neck and pushing her breasts against his chest. He gently but insistently pressed her back against the gazebo railing. Her fingers found the nape of his neck and clung to it.

"You make me ache inside," she whispered into his ear.

"You can't say something like that to me," he said, "and not prove it."

Before she could demand what he meant, he kissed her again and pulled her hard against him. He opened his heavy coat and wrapped her inside it and it was like stepping into a warm room.

And once she was warm against him, he began to lift her skirts.

"Søren," she gasped against his lips but he pressed his tongue into her mouth to silence her. He brought her skirt and petticoats all the way to her hips. In the shelter of his coat she barely felt the cold. What she did feel was his hand, still encased in his supple calfskin glove, sliding along her upper thigh and then between her legs. He wouldn't, would he? Here? And with his gloves on?

He would. He did. He pushed his finger through her folds once and then twice, a third time while she moaned against his mouth. When he found her entrance, the tender hole, he stroked it and Eleanor gasped and thought she might faint.

"You do not hold the patent on frustrated desire, Little One. Even if you did invent it, I perfected it in the three years we've been apart. The three longest years of my life," he said and slid his finger up and into her. Eleanor shuddered as he entered her, and she pushed her hips into the palm of his hand.

"Again," he ordered and she pushed into his hand again. Pleasure rippled through her stomach and hips. Then again. She couldn't stop herself even if she wanted to.

"I can feel your heat even through my glove," he said into her ear. She was too lost to speak. She had to grip the railing behind her to stay standing as he worked her on his hand. When he started to push a second finger inside her, she had to raise her leg and place her foot on the stone bench to open herself to him. "God," he breathed as he went deeper into her.

He gathered her wetness with his fingers and brought it to the knot at the apex of her thighs. He slicked it over her and kneaded it until it throbbed against his finger. Then without warning he entered her again. His gloved fingers felt thick inside her. She could feel the seams of the leather stitching grazing all her tender places. Inside her passage, he spread his fingers apart, opening her and her inner muscles contracted in protest and pleasure.

"I imagined this," he said and his breath turned to steam. "Touching you inside until you came apart in my arms. I had to leave a piano recital once because they played Beethoven's 'Moonlight Sonata,' and I couldn't stop picturing your thighs straddling me at the piano bench."

"You always played it for me," she said.

"Which is why I can't hear it without thinking of you." He thrust into her with his fingers, again, and then again. He thrust with his hand as he had last night when he took her. Though she knew this time he would not stop until she had reached her peak. She breathed hard as he stroked her so intimately, not at all gently but firmly, vigorously, obscenely. "Release for me, Eleanor."

Even if she wanted to disobey him, his searching stroking fingers would not let her. He moved in and out of her wetness, sliding across that throbbing knot again with his gloves as he entered her. Her hips pushed into his touch and soon the most intimate and delicious flutters began. There was no stopping it now and she came, crying out and shuddering. The pleasure went on and on as he stroked and caressed her.

"Tell me again," he said as he held her cupped in the palm of his large strong hand, "that I forgot you."

She reached between their bodies, took him by the wrist and pulled his fingers from her. She pushed her skirts down and smoothed them, stepped back and away, her hands pressed into her lower stomach where the muscles still fluttered.

"Tell me why you left me—three years ago and last night."

"Eleanor, please—"

"I thought once it would be enough if you desired me even half as much as I desired you," she said and all her pleasure turned to sadness. "But it isn't enough. Legally I am your property and cannot deny you your rights as a husband, but I ask you to never touch me again until we can have a true marriage. And it can be no true marriage without the truth."

She pulled her hood up and returned to the house. She was cold now and shivering, and not because it was winter.

NINE

ELEANOR FOUND ANNETTE waiting in her new room—the mistress of Edenfell's chamber. As Annette helped her out of her clothes and into her best blue nightgown and robe, Eleanor examined her new bedroom. Blue and ivory walls, ivory wainscoting, a large brick fireplace and over it, a portrait of Søren's great-grandmother, a handsome woman who had been the first Lady Stearns when her husband was given a barony as a reward for some vital service to the Crown.

The canopy bed was dark blue with oak posts and piled high with soft down pillows and a blue silk coverlet. A camelback love seat covered in striped blue and ivory fabric sat under the curtained windows. All this was hers now. All this beauty. All this wealth. The house. The land that stretched for a thousand acres or more. The trees. The gardens. The stables and the horses.

She would have traded it all for the truth from Søren.

Exhausted from the day's travels and last night's trials, she dismissed Annette and sank into the armchair by the fire with a book she had no intention of reading.

Just then she heard a soft knock on her door. Not the main

door but the connecting door between her room and the master's suite. Before she could answer, Søren entered.

He'd removed his gray jacket. He looked quite dashing in his waistcoat and shirtsleeves and his usually perfect hair rakishly disheveled. He stood at the fireplace, arms crossed over his chest, not three steps away from her. She pretended she didn't see him and stared through him into the fire.

"You wish to know the truth," he said. "I will tell it to you though you might not like what you hear."

"Anything is superior to not knowing."

"Very well. But do not say you were not warned." He paused and took a breath. "Are you familiar with a certain tale by a man named John Polidori called *The Vampyre*?"

"Of course," she said. If it was lurid and strange and sensual, she'd not only read it, she'd read it twice. "Why?"

"The reason I left you last night and three years ago is because...I am a vampire, Eleanor. And when I come too close to beautiful young maidens, I'm overwhelmed with an insatiable need to drink their blood. That is why I left you and keep leaving you—to save you from my bloodlust."

She stared at him. His face was utterly serious and solemn. His tone was truthful and his eyes earnest.

"Are you truly?" she breathed.

"No."

Eleanor threw Shakespeare's *Complete Works* at him. Luckily, as it was an expensive and rare volume, he caught it and set it neatly on the mantel.

"How could you?" she asked. "How could you leave and then mock me like that?"

"Because I am a cruel and wicked man. And also because if I prepare you for the absolute worst, then perhaps you'll take the truth a little better."

"I don't wish to hear it anymore."

"Nonetheless, you will. Come into my bedroom."

"I don't enter the bedrooms of vampires or men who pretend to be vampires."

"Generally, a good rule of thumb. But tonight, you will come into my bedroom."

"I shan't and that's the end of it."

"Eleanor, I am your husband, your lord and master, *pater familias* of this family and you are required by the Church and the Crown to obey my every will, whim, and command, no matter how immoral or arbitrary. You are my property, and you will no more tell me no when I give you an order than a chair will refuse to let me sit in it."

"What will you do to me if I go to your bedroom with you?" she demanded. "Throw me on the bed again, use me, and abandon me?"

"I will sit you on my lap and make you look at French pornography with me."

"Oh," she said, blinking. "You will?"

"Yes."

Eleanor rose to her feet and said primly, "You only had to ask."

The master's suite was far larger than the mistress's and as dark and masculine as her bedroom was light, airy, and feminine. While her room held only a dainty little writing desk, his bedroom contained a large desk in an alcove surrounded on three sides by windows that looked down on the lake. The room was brightly lit—every candle blazing, the fire hot and high, and not one but two oil lamps burning on the large desk.

He sat in the red velvet-covered desk chair and pulled her down onto his lap. She tried to ignore the bed behind them—the grand four-post bed with the silk covers the color of red wine and the fire burning in the brick fireplace.

"Kingsley was kind enough to lend me his collection," Søren

said as he opened a large leather folio. It felt delicious to sit on his lap, one arm around her waist holding her against him as he turned the pages of the folio.

"I have a question for you," he began. "The night you invited me to your bedroom, three years ago. What did you want to happen that night?"

The question took Eleanor aback. Of all the things to ask...

"The obvious, I think. That you would take me to bed with you."

"What precisely were you picturing would happen? Was it this?" He turned to a photograph in the folio—a naked woman with voluptuous breasts lay draped over a divan, a swarthy naked man braced over her, his large cock entering her body. Her face was a mask of pleasure—real or feigned for the photographer, Eleanor couldn't say. But her heart raced madly at the sight of it. She'd never seen photographs like this before. Drawings of naked women, or paintings, yes, but photographs? Of people engaged in the sex act?

"I...oh my Lord." She laughed, shocked and delighted.

"Or this?" Søren turned to another photograph. In this one, the woman was on her hands and knees, the man behind her, cock entering from behind. Eleanor could only stare and squirm on Søren's lap.

"Or perhaps this?" Søren turned another page and there was the woman seated on top of the man, his hands on her naked hips and his organ entering her from below. "Well?"

"I suppose," she said. Her toes curled up in her slippers. "Any of them would do. I...I knew how it works, of course."

Her face was burning hot and her stomach was terribly tight and fluttering.

"What did you dream would happen with us?" Søren asked again. "Don't be shy. We're married now, and these are things I need to know, just as there are things you need to know about my desires."

"I stayed up," she said, "reading. I wanted you to see the light on under my door so you would know I was awake. I..." This was so hard to speak about. She was so good at saying outrageous things when she wanted to shock people, but when she was alone with Søren and he was asking her to tell him her private thoughts, she found herself flustered and tongue-tied.

"Go on." He pressed a soft kiss on her neck under her ear.

"I thought you would come into my room and...and you would kiss me again and we would undress and get into bed. And we would touch each other. After that it's all a bit...hazy. As I said, I knew how it worked, in theory. But in practice...I hoped you would tell me what to do once we were in bed, that you would instruct me so I could please you."

He nodded, smiling as if her answer had pleased him.

"I need to show you some etchings now," he said. "You might not like them nearly as much. These are from an illustrated edition of one of the stories of the notorious Marquis de Sade. A violent and depraved man who engaged in sexual acts so brutal he nearly killed several of his lovers. He's French, of course. That should explain everything."

Eleanor tensed as Søren turned a few loose pages until he came to a drawing of a naked girl in some sort of bare stone room or dungeon. Her wrists were bound above her head to an iron ring and a man stood behind her, whipping her with something like a cat o'nine tails.

"This is a flogging," Søren said. He turned the page to an etching of another naked girl, bent over what looked like a church's prie-dieu though it was clear the girl was not praying. A man was using a belt of some kind to beat her buttocks. Her face was contorted in agony.

"God," Eleanor breathed. The room had grown uncomfortably warm.

"You asked me about my secrets," Søren said. "Here is one of them. The night you rested your head on my knee, told me you loved me and invited me to your bedroom...I did come to your room."

"You did?"

"I came as far as the door, as far as putting my hand on the doorknob." He pointed at the leather strap in the hand of the man in the etching, "In my other hand was that, a leather strap."

"A strap?"

"For beating you," Søren said. She turned her head, met his eyes. He returned her gaze.

"Beating me?"

Søren pulled out the photograph of the couple having intercourse on the divan.

"This," he said, "does not arouse me. Not alone. Not the photograph of it. Not even the act. This, however, does." He put the etching of the man strapping the girl's bottom next to it. "This is what arouses me—inflicting pain. Until I do so, inflict pain, that is, I'm unable to become aroused enough to do this." He pointed at the copulating couple. "I wanted to be with you like this..." He pointed again at the couple mid-coitus. "But to do so I would have had to hurt you in some way, which is why I brought the strap with me. And when I caught myself outside your door, strap in hand, I knew I had to leave, immediately, and put as much distance as possible between us."

"That's why you left? Not because you didn't want me but because you did?"

"A month after you came to live at Edenfell," he said, "you ran away. Do you remember?"

"Of course. I had a cough and I was frightened that I—"

"You thought you had consumption," he said. "It killed your

mother and for years after, even a little cough would make you afraid you had it and it would kill you, too," he said. "And that's why you ran away. You wanted to protect all of us—from you. When I caught you, you said you hated me and that's why you were leaving. You wanted to go home to London. All lies."

"I knew you wouldn't let me leave if you thought I was ill. I had to lie." Eleanor shook her head. "Why are we talking about this? It was years ago."

"I had seen my father terrorize his wives—first my mother, then Claire's. He enjoyed making them fear him. He wouldn't always beat them. Sometimes the threat alone and the terror in their eyes was enough to...delight him. Every little cough scared you into thinking you had what your mother had. Imagine how it is for me, seeing his cruelty and fearing, all my life, I am also infected with that same cruelty."

"But I didn't have consumption," she said. "Only a cold. And you are not cruel like your father. Whatever he had, you are not...infected."

"It's simple enough to believe that when I'm with Kingsley. He enjoys receiving pain as much as I enjoy giving it. But no woman in her right mind would enjoy the sort of pain I give him. And if I tried and I hurt you and you hated me for it...I'm not sure I could live with myself."

"I'm confused..." She shook her head. "Last night you were aroused. You did want me and you did...you were inside me."

"Kingsley volunteered to play whipping boy. I beat him with a tawse. When I grew aroused, I went to you. If I hadn't beaten Kingsley, I would not have been able to...perform. Without inflicting pain first...Eleanor, I simply can't."

He took a deep shuddering breath. "Last night, you were a virgin, your body unopened. When I opened you, there was pain and tearing and that aroused me even more. I came very close to losing control of myself. Which I have done in the past and Kingsley's body paid the price for it. You invited me to do anything to you. 'Anything' you said over and over. I saw the candle and nearly poured scalding wax onto your breasts. That's why I left you so abruptly and walked for an hour out in the cold until I was calm again. Because I wanted to hurt you, so much it terrified me."

"Søren—" she began. He held up his hand to silence her.

"There are more secrets I have to tell you. I loved it here at Edenfell mainly because my father hated country life and wanted nothing to do with the place. I spent most of my time at school or here. When things grew unbearable between my father and Claire's mother Annabelle, she would stay here without him." He took a breath. "I was fourteen and Claire was about two years old. I'd spent the day playing with Claire, carrying her around the house, talking to her, petting the horses with her. It charmed my stepmother apparently. That night she came to my bedroom. And...she kissed me."

"Oh, God," she said.

"I was shocked but...she was a beautiful woman, only twenty-four years old, and I let the kiss go on longer than I should have. She invited me to have her, and I did want to, if only to punish my father. Things progressed and I pushed her onto her back. Then I...I held her wrists so hard she cried out. She pushed me off her and slapped me. She said, 'Damn you. I thought you were different, but you're just like your father.'"

Eleanor had no words. Only tears.

"That was when I left home," he said and wiped a tear from her face. "I packed up my things and what money I had, and booked passage to Rome. There I entered a Catholic seminary and began my training to join the priesthood someday. I thought I should never be close to anyone again because of what I was. And I would have been a priest if I hadn't heard some of the other seminarians whispering about a notorious Roman brothel run by a woman named Magdalena. Not a normal brothel, but a place where men went to either beat pretty naked girls with birch rods or to be beaten by pretty naked girls with birch rods. Or boys."

"That's where you met Kingsley?"

He nodded. "After his parents died in a carriage accident, and his father's estate was sold off to pay the debts, he had nothing. He ran away to Rome where he thought he had distant family somewhere. Instead he was picked up by a police officer on Magdalena's payroll. She took him in, put him to work. Very quickly, he rose in the ranks. He was, as you see, quite special."

He turned a page to reveal a faded daguerreotype of a teenaged girl in a sumptuous gown draped over the arm of a fainting couch, her lips slightly parted, her figure a perfect hourglass, an otherworldly beauty surrounding her like an aura.

"You could say Kingsley was the first girl I ever fell in love with," Søren said. "Magda called him her *Principessa*. Princess."

"Oh, she's so beautiful," Eleanor breathed. "No wonder you wanted her." Impossible to think of the "her" in the photograph as a he, even knowing it was Kingsley in a dress. She was simply too female, too lovely...a true Princess.

"I desired women," Søren said, "but I refused to beat them, which meant I could never be with a woman. With Kingsley, I had a beautiful girl who I could beat as viciously as any man. A girl trained to take beatings. A girl who loved them. And after some time, it didn't matter to me if he were dressed as a boy or a girl. After Claire's mother killed herself, I came home to see to it that Claire was safe with relatives—not my father. Once she was safe with her aunt, I swore I'd never set foot in England again. It was only when my father had been deemed 'insane' by his physicians and needed putting away that I finally returned. And it so happened, during a trip to London to meet with Father's solicitors, a girl bumped into me on the street, and the next thing I knew, my wallet and pocketwatch were missing."

The pocketwatch had been a gift from Søren's maternal grandfather, also named Søren. All the pawnshops in London were on alert for it, generous reward promised. That was how she'd gotten caught. There in the police station, while awaiting her fate—hard time in a brutal workhouse, undoubtably—Søren himself came to pay her bail and see about her release.

"Four years ago this month," she said. "Do you remember what I said to you in the police station?"

"You asked me," Søren said, "'*Are you one of them wicked lords who takes poor girls off the streets and does all sorts of nasty things to them?*'"

"And you said 'no.' And I said—"

"You said, '*Pity.*'" Søren smiled. "The absolute cheek. The constable nearly slapped you in the face. Meanwhile...I think that was the moment I began to love you."

And it had been when she'd fallen in love with him, when he'd first come into the police station, sat across from her, and asked her if she was cold. He'd offered her his coat, and she'd been too ashamed of his kindness to accept it, though she had been freezing. He put it round her shoulders anyway.

"Are you angry?" Søren asked. "Hurt? Frightened? Disappointed?"

"I am..." She took a long breath. "Intrigued."

"Intrigued? Better than horrified."

"No, no, certainly not horrified. Relieved, I think, too. That I know what it is now that was coming between us all this time. I wish you'd told me before but now, I do understand."

"I want us to have a happy marriage," Søren said. "If you wish it, we can be as we were last night. I can hurt Kingsley and then come to you. I think with time and patience, we—"

"No," she said.

"No?"

She rose from his lap and went to the fireplace. She took the candle in its brass holder from the mantel, lit it in the fire and returned to Søren.

"Hurt me," she said. "Please?"

"Eleanor..." He rested his forehead on his hand, rubbing the bridge of his nose.

"Did I do something wrong?"

"No." He lifted his head. "Never. It's only..."

"What?"

He closed his eyes. "I have dreamt of this. I have dreamt of you asking me to hurt you. You speak so matter-of-factly as if you don't realize you're bringing every dream I've ever had to life."

"What don't you do what you dream then?" she asked.

"There is no sin in a dream. You kill a man and it isn't murder. You bed a woman and it isn't adultery. But done awake, it is a sin."

Eleanor set the candle on his desk. She went again into his lap.

"But we aren't awake," she said softly. "Didn't you know? All this...you and me, this house, our marriage...it's only a dream. Mine? Yours? Someone else's a thousand miles and a hundred years away. And you know what happens in dreams? Anything. Anything at all. You can swim under the ocean like a fish or fly in the sky like a bird. You can walk on the moon and dance among the stars and touch the sun and not get burned. Or be as wicked with your wife as you would ever want to be."

"Are you sure it's a dream? It feels quite real to me."

"I'll prove it. You say no woman in her right mind would desire the pain you describe, yes?"

"Yes."

"Am I in my right mind?"

"I saw enough of madness at my father's sanitarium to know you are of perfectly sound mind."

"And yet..." She lifted the candle from the holder and dripped the hot wax from it onto the inside of her own wrist. Søren's chest heaved as the wax fell. It hurt but it was worth that pain times a thousand for the burning look in his eyes.

"See?" she said. "I liked it. I want more. Must be a dream."

Eleanor gave him the candle and stood. She took off her robe and sat on his lap again, straddling his thighs, facing him. Then she unbuttoned her nightgown and pulled it open to bare her breasts.

"Only a dream," she said again. He let a drop of wax fall. It landed on the top of her right breast. It stung and burned and she flinched and hissed. Then laughed at her flinching.

"Too much?" he asked.

"Not enough."

His eyebrow arched. His mouth quirked into an almost smile. He let another drop fall. Then another and another. It hurt, yes, but it excited her as well. The anticipation, the sudden thrill of pain, the way Søren looked at her as if he was seeing her again for the first time, and the power in knowing his most intimate secret and playing with him this private game.

She could have taken a cathedral's share of candles on her body to please him but it seemed a dozen drops or more was enough to arouse him. He set the candle on the desk. He lifted the skirt of her gown, opened his trousers, and lifted her up and guided his cock into her. When he pushed her into her this time —unlike last night—there was no resistance. She was still wet and open from his fingers not an hour ago inside of her.

Eleanor moaned, clinging to his shoulders as he lifted and lowered her onto him again. Once fully inside her, he kissed her mouth, her neck, her breasts. She returned his kisses and caresses, finally allowed to touch him as she wanted since her first night under his roof. She unbuttoned his waistcoat, his shirt, touched his broad, strong naked chest, the ivory tower of his neck, and ran her hands through his golden hair.

She throbbed between her legs, throbbed inside the passage he filled, ached where they joined. She reached between their bodies, touching his organ as it split her, touched herself where she ached. Her wetness was all over him.

"Little One," he breathed into her ear. In reply, she tilted her hips and sealed herself to him. And then he stood, lifting her on him and with him, pressing her down onto the desk and there he took her, making her his wife and claiming her as his own. Her body tensed and froze and when she came it was with a cry loud enough the servants would all know that the baron and baroness had a very happy marriage indeed.

Søren buried his head against her neck and held her close as he released into her, filling her with his seed and at last consummating their marriage.

Drowsy and happy, she wrapped her arms around him as he held her again in his lap on the red velvet chair.

"What shall we dream next?" she asked between tender kisses.

Søren replied, "Let's dream about Kingsley."

TEN

KINGSLEY SAT ALONE in his bedroom, a book in his lap—unread—and a wine glass in his hand—half drunk. As Søren's valet, he was always close to his master, so when the new baroness came, he heard it quite clearly from his room across the hall.

"Well done, my lord," Kingsley said aloud. "And you, my lady."

Silence followed and he wondered if he pressed his ear Søren's door, could he hear what they were saying to each other. Or, even better, peek through the keyhole...

Someone knocked and Kingsley nearly spilled his wine in surprise.

Before he could say "Come in," Søren opened the door.

Kingsley's eyes widened. Søren was dressed though his shirt was open at the neck and wrinkled and his throat sported a red mark, likely courtesy of the young baroness's teeth.

"You presence is required in our chamber," Søren said.

"Is it? I take it your little talk was a success."

"You know perfectly well it was. Now go into my chamber at once and stop grinning, you degenerate French whore."

Kingsley obeyed the first order, disobeyed the second. He followed Søren into the master suite. The baroness looked beautiful, bright-eyed and well-fucked as she sat propped on her pillows, counterpane pulled to her waist, gown barely buttoned past the top of her ample breasts.

"My lady," Kingsley said.

"Sit," Søren said. "On the bed. We're all friends here."

Kingsley sat next to the young baroness and waited for his next orders. His heart was running wild. Had he once dreamed of being allowed into the intimacy of Søren's marriage bed? Yes. But he'd never expected it and certainly not this soon.

"Eleanor," Søren began, "if you'll recall, during our wedding, as I put the ring on your finger I spoke these vows—'With this ring I thee wed, with my body I thee worship, and with all my worldly goods I thee endow.'"

"I remember it quite well," she said, smiling tiredly.

"I've wedded you and worshiped you with my body," he said. "Now it's time I endow you with all my worldly goods. And so I give you Kingsley, the most valuable of all my worldly goods."

And Kingsley said, "As I am his, I am yours."

"Is that so?" Eleanor said. "I knew when I married I'd receive gifts of fine China and linens. I didn't know I would also receive a handsome Frenchman. Marriage is full of surprises."

To Kingsley, too. He'd never felt so owned by Søren as he did right now. For wasn't this the ultimate proof of ownership? That Kingsley could be shared, lent, and used by others?

"Eleanor is now aware of what I require in bed," Søren said. "Although I'm certain there will be times she wishes for pleasure without taking pain first. And when those moments come, Eleanor? You may have Kingsley serve you."

She lifted her hand and ran her fingers through Kingsley's hair. This time she didn't tell him to get it cut.

"Would you enjoy serving me?" she asked.

"I would," Kingsley said. "Very much."

"Perhaps you should serve the baroness right now," Søren said from where he stood at the end of the bed, watching them.

"Søren," Eleanor said, blushing. "But what if—"

"Don't argue," Kingsley said to her. "Pointless. Entirely pointless with him. Nothing makes him happier than ordering me about. And nothing makes me happier than obeying his orders." That being said..." Kingsley leaned close and put his mouth at her ear. "I'll only obey this order if you wish it."

"No whispering," Søren said. "Against the rules."

Eleanor cupped her hand around Kingsley's ear, ignoring Søren's edict entirely.

"I wish it," Eleanor said to him. "Though I don't know what to wish for."

"Demerit," Søren said and pointed at Eleanor and then at Kingsley. "One for each of you."

Kingsley spoke to Søren sharply in rapid Italian that he knew Eleanor couldn't understand.

"What did he say?" Eleanor asked Søren.

"He said I am an ass, and I should stop frightening you," Søren translated. "Is that true?"

"You aren't frightening me, no," she said. "But you are an ass."

Kingsley's head fell back in delighted laughter.

"You married well, my lord," he said to Søren. Then he looked at Eleanor. "Shall I show you how I could serve you? And then when the time comes and we're alone or you're in need...you'll know what to ask of me?"

"If you please," she said.

Kingsley raised a hand and stroked her face. It was burning bright and hot, like she had a fever. He leaned over her and brushed his lips across hers. Then he kissed her again, deeper.

She opened her mouth to his tongue and he was pleased to hear her moaning softly for him.

He smiled down at her. "Like that," he said, "But here." He slid his hand under the counterpane, over her stomach and then between her legs. He felt her warmth and her softness under his hand. It pleased him when she opened her legs a little wider for him.

"Kiss me? There?" she asked, seemingly astonished. "That wasn't in the pamphlet Aunt Adeline gave us."

"I have much better pamphlets," Kingsley said. "Or perhaps I should demonstrate."

Before her nerves got the better of her and she stopped him, Kingsley pulled the counterpane down to her thighs. When he started to push her gown up to her waist, she stiffened and covered Kingsley's hand with hers.

"Don't be shy, Eleanor. Remember...we're only dreaming," Søren said.

"This," she said, "is a very wicked dream."

"It's about to get wickeder," Kingsley said. "Wickeder? More wicked? Fuck, I hate English."

"Less talking, Kingsley," Søren said. "Put your tongue to better use."

"You see what I put up with?" Kingsley said, shaking his head, as he lifted her gown up again. This time she didn't try to stop him. "A brute. An absolute bastard."

In one easy practiced motion, Kingsley moved between her legs and opened her thighs. He looked down at her, at her open body. With his fingers, he explored her—the soft black curls, the red and tender flesh glistening wet, the inner lips so lovely and delicate. And when looking wasn't enough for him, he lowered his head and tasted her.

Eleanor gasped as he flicked his tongue over her open body. Gasped again when he did it once more. He tasted her wetness even more, he tasted Søren's seed inside of her. The cocktail was potent and he couldn't stop himself from wanting to drink every drop out of her.

Kingsley stretched out on the bed, buried his head between her beautiful thighs and served her with everything he had. He served her with his tongue, licking and lapping at her, stroking her with his tongue and lips. He used his fingers to carefully pull back the flesh that surrounded her clitoris and licked the little bud with the very tip of his tongue. Eleanor gasped his name softly and he did it again, and then again, and over and over until she was pumping her hips into his mouth.

He felt the bed shift and he glanced up to see Søren sitting at Eleanor's side. He opened her gown and ran his large hands over his wife's full breasts, stroking her pale red nipples, licking and sucking them. The sight of it excited Kingsley even more. Though he'd dreamed of it, they'd never shared a woman between them before and that it was Søren's young bride, which made it all the sweeter.

He wanted to please his master and mistress more than anything. And to please the master, all he had to do was please the mistress. He worked a finger into Eleanor and when she contracted around it, he pressed in another. He found the soft hollow on the front wall of her vagina—did she know these words or would he have to teach them to her?—and kneaded it. That was the magic touch for her, it seemed. She came then, her hips hovering two inches off the bed as Kingsley licked her roughly. She released a low hoarse whimper and all around his two fingers, she clenched and contracted with delicious womanly flutters.

Kingsley could have lived between her thighs all night but Søren tugged his hair. He rose up and before he could wipe the wetness from his mouth, Søren kissed him. He didn't merely kiss him, he licked Kingsley's lips in one of the more sensual, sexual wicked kisses Kingsley had ever experienced in his life. Søren was tasting Kingsley's mouth, his wife's cunt, and his own seed in one long deep kiss.

Bliss.

"I've died," she said, "and gone to Heaven."

"You've come three times in one night, Eleanor. You aren't dead. You're spent," Søren said.

"You're a liar, you know," she said to Søren. "You *are* one of them wicked lords who takes poor girls off the streets and does all sorts of nasty things to them."

Søren laughed low and soft. "You're welcome."

As the new couple kissed their goodnights, Kingsley slipped out, across the hall, and into his bedroom where he collapsed back against the door and breathed and breathed again.

That had been a rather unexpected turn of events.

Before he even had a chance to catch his breath, someone knocked on his door. He opened it and Søren entered.

"What..." Kingsley said, his voice trailing off before he could ask the question on the tip of his tongue. *What* was *his lord doing here?*

When Søren grasped him by the back of the neck and pulled him in for a kiss, he knew what Søren was doing there.

Søren pushed him against the closed door and began to strip him of his clothes—his waistcoat, his tie, his shirt, his trousers... Kingsley was hard, painfully so, and needed using, especially after tasting Søren inside his young bride.

Then Søren slapped him. Once. With the back of his hand. Right across the cheek. Hard enough to hurt. Not hard enough to leave much of a mark.

"That," Søren said, pointing at Kingsley's face, "is for your insolence." He slapped Kingsley again. "And *that* was for keeping secrets from me." Søren grabbed Kingsley by the throat and kissed the breath out of him. "And that was for making my wife very, *very* happy."

"Forgive me. Forgive me. And..." Kingsley said. "...my pleasure."

Søren pulled Kingsley in front of the fireplace where a low smoldering blaze still burned. And then there, on the floor, on the rough Persian rug, with Kingsley on his back and Søren over him and inside him, they coupled like two beasts in a forest. Kingsley was spread wide as Søren pushed himself in deeper and deeper with every thrust. The pain was potent and the pleasure obliterating as his lover's cock speared him.

Søren's weight bore down on him, and Kingsley lay pinned by the wrists and split beneath him. It had been some time since Søren had used him so roughly, and Kingsley's body sang with the bliss of it. Søren gripped Kingsley's cock and stroked it, bringing him to the edge of release and holding him there. The organ rammed into him mercilessly. And when Søren released into him, filling him with his thick hot seed, Kingsley couldn't hold back another moment. He came onto his own stomach and chest with a dozen or more powerful spurts. And when it was done, and Kingsley lay limp on his back, and Søren knelt above him and over him that his master said the loveliest words Kingsley had ever heard spoken.

"And that," Søren said, "was for me."

"The baron is dead," Kingsley said. "Long live the baron."

ELEVEN

ELEANOR WOKE from her sleep when she felt the bed shift. Søren slipped in next to her, naked, and took her into his arms.

"What time is it?" She asked, certain only minutes had passed since he'd kissed her goodnight.

"After one," he said. "Christmas."

She laughed sleepily. "Happy Christmas, my lord."

"Happy Christmas, my lady. Now go back to sleep."

She nestled her back against his chest, luxuriating in the heat of his long lean body.

"Four," she said.

"Hmm?" he said.

"You said there were four secrets you were keeping from me. One was that you did come to my room that night I invited you though you didn't come inside. Two, that you must inflict pain to become aroused. Three was your stepmother attempting to seduce you and that's why you left home. What's the fourth secret?"

"You don't want to know, I promise."

"Go on, tell me," she said, rolling over to face him. "If I can take all the others, I can take the last one." She touched his strong chest and felt the steady rhythm of his beautiful heart under her hand.

"If you insist," he said and kissed her lightly on the lips. "The last secret is this...I can't live without you, Eleanor."

"That's the last secret?" She smiled, half-asleep and fading fast. "That's the most beautiful secret of all."

"I can't and I won't," he said. "So please, wake up, Little One. Come back to me."

"What? What do you mean? I'm here, right here."

"No, you aren't," he said.

Eleanor opened her eyes.

TWELVE

Christmas Eve, 1998
Manhattan

ELEANOR OPENED her eyes into a room dark and cool and smelling vaguely of bleach. Søren sat in a chair by the head of her bed, his hand brushing her hair from her forehead, and his eyes searching her face. He looked strange to her. He was her husband, of course. Same golden hair. Same marble gray eyes. Same age or thereabouts. But instead of his gray suit and waistcoat he wore a black long-sleeved t-shirt with jeans.

Jeans?

"Søren? What time is it?"

"Oh, thank God," he breathed. He kissed her forehead. "Thank God. Thank God. Thank you, God. *Deo gratias*."

"Where am I?"

"You're in the hospital, Eleanor."

"Hospital?" Her mind was a fog.

"You had the flu," he said. "You've been unconscious almost all day. They gave you IV antibiotics. Do you remember any of this?"

"The flu? No...no, I was with you."

"Yes, the flu, and a very bad case of it. So bad they thought it might be meningitis."

Everything was coming back to her. She'd ignored the aches in her body, busy as she was with finals and term papers. Her mother was out of town, spending the holidays with some religious order she'd gotten obsessed with so Eleanor was staying at Kingsley's townhouse over Christmas break. She'd blamed her extreme exhaustion and upset stomach on end-of-semester stress. She'd gone to bed early on the night of the twenty-third in the blue guest room at Kingsley's. That was the last she remembered.

"What happened? Did I faint or something?"

"Kingsley found you burning up with fever this morning and barely conscious. He brought you into the ER. I came as soon as he reached me."

"Is it...Christmas?" She thought she remembered Søren telling her it was Christmas.

"Christmas Eve. Nearly midnight."

"You should be—wait—shouldn't you be saying Midnight Mass?"

"Father Ballard is taking my place. He'll tell the church I was called away to be with someone deathly ill. Not a lie, unfortunately. God, you scared me so much." He moved from his chair to her hospital bed, sat next to her and leaned down and kissed her forehead.

"Kingsley? In a hospital? You sure?"

Søren pointed. Eleanor raised her head and saw Kingsley, all six feet of him, curled up awkwardly in a hospital room armchair, white blanket draped over him, sound asleep.

"He carried you in his arms into the ER. He stayed with you and made sure you were put in a private room. He read to you while you were resting. Even when I arrived, he still wouldn't leave until you woke up."

"Read to me?"

"The book you had in your backpack." Søren picked up the book, still on the side table.

"*Christmas at Thompson Hall*," she said. A book by Anthony Trollope, the other great Victorian writer. "I read it for my Victorian lit seminar this semester. Oh my God."

"Eleanor? What's wrong?"

"I had the craziest dream," she breathed.

"While you were unconscious?"

She nodded. "We were in Victorian England, and you were a baron, and I'd stolen your pocketwatch and you'd made me your ward so I wouldn't go to jail. And we..."

All at once, she began to cry when it hit her that when she'd woken up, she'd lost her husband.

"Eleanor?" Søren pulled her to him and held her in his arms.

"We got married," she said between her wrenching sobs. "I was your wife, Søren. I was...and you were my husband."

"Please stop crying, Little One. You'll make yourself sicker."

But she couldn't stop. It had been so beautiful and so real and so true. And she'd been so happy there, married to Søren.

Her dream tumbled out in fits and starts. "I was so in love with you, and you were so scared to tell me you had to hurt me to make love to me. But you did and then it was wonderful. And Kingsley was there, being your wicked valet."

"Of course he was."

"Ah, it was so real. It was like being in a movie and reading a book all at the same time. I can still see everything—you and Kingsley on the train. He kicked you in the shins. Not very hard. But then you kicked back, really hard. And Claire's lavender dress and the morning room and you played 'Lo, How a Rose E're Blooming' on piano. And I remember it all."

She told him everything. How Kingsley had been a cross-dressing teenaged prostitute named Princess in Magdalena's Roman brothel. How Søren had left seminary because he'd fallen in love with Kingsley. How he'd had to marry because of his father's will. How Kingsley had wanted them to get married so he could have children in his life. Proof positive it was all a dream—who could imagine Kingsley as a father? Or even wanting to be?

The dream was so real, Eleanor had to remind herself this was New York, not England. She was twenty-one, a senior at NYU, not a nineteen-year-old former pickpocket-turned-baroness. This is what happened when a stressed-out college student took a Victorian lit class *and* a nineteenth-century British history survey in one semester.

"I was your baroness," she said to him. "Lady Eleanor Stearns. We lived at Edenfell. I'll never forget how the house looked as the carriage drove up the lane. All those lampposts, it was so magical. You'd put a Christmas tree in the drawing room for me. There were even real lit candles on it."

"This dream version of me was not wise in the ways of fire hazards." Søren took a tissue from the box on the side table and wiped her face.

"God...I feel like I'm still there." She put her hand on her forehead, closed her eyes. "We sat in this red velvet chair, tufted. We looked at old porn and then we fucked on the desk. And I knew nothing about sex, which should have told me it was a dream. That and all of us having English accents—except King. He was still French. And horny. You watched while he ate me out then after? You reamed that man. Like, fucked him to next Christmas and back. Third-degree rug burn on his back. If he was an apple, you would have cored him. I mean—"

"Yes, Eleanor, you've painted a sufficiently vivid picture."

"You also finger-fucked me in a freezing gazebo, *while wearing leather gloves*, you pervert."

"That wasn't a dream," he said. "That happened two years ago on New Year's Eve. And I wasn't wearing gloves because I was a pervert. I was wearing them because it was thirty degrees out."

"*And* you're a pervert."

He surrendered with a smile. "That may have been a contributing factor."

She laughed to herself. Her head was splitting and she was so thirsty and she had to pee or die, but she couldn't quite let Søren go yet.

"You're here," she said, "but I miss you. The other you." Her husband.

He gently rubbed her back while rocking her against his chest. "I love you and always will," he said. "Here and in your dreams."

When she stopped shaking, he slowly lowered her back onto her pillow.

"I'm sorry you didn't get to give your Christmas homily," she said.

"There's always next Christmas."

"What was it about?"

Søren took her hand in his and twined their fingers together, not easy to do as his hands were so much larger than hers.

"Saint Joseph," he said. "He's a mystery to me, always has been. Mary conceived Christ with the Holy Spirit. No Joseph necessary. Yet God still wanted Mary and Joseph to be married. God sent angels to Mary and Joseph when she became pregnant with Christ and angels announced his birth, but when it was time for her to give birth—arguably the most dangerous part— there were no angels anywhere to be seen. She had to go it alone in a stable, never having given birth before, with no one to help her but Joseph. I think that means something, that God could have sent angels to Mary then, but He didn't, because He didn't have to, because—"

"Because her husband was there." Tears sprang into her eyes again.

"Exactly," Søren said. "I suppose the theme was the sacredness of ordinary human love, that although God could have done it all Himself, He still brought Joseph and Mary together as if the love people show each other and the way we care for each other is its own sort of divinity. Better even than angels."

"In sickness and health," Eleanor whispered.

"Eleanor?"

"Just thinking of the wedding vows—in sickness and health. I'm sick as a dog, probably contagious, and you're here anyway. It is like we're married."

"What matters more?" Søren brought her hand to his lips and kissed it. "The ceremony and saying the vows? Or living them when it counts?"

"Marriage is a sacrament, though," she said, smiling weakly at him.

"Love is a sacrament." He squeezed her hand. "Oh, and don't worry. Most priests get flu shots. When you drink after as many people as we do..."

Funny. For Christmas that year, Eleanor had asked for a threesome with Søren and Kingsley. A silly request, as silly as asking for snow in winter in New York. Whether she asked for it or not, she was *definitely* getting it.

She'd wanted to spend the night with both of them in bed. And here she was, in bed, with both of them there—Søren at her side and Kingsley asleep in the hospital armchair. Maybe not as fun as a kinky threesome, but somehow she knew it was a bigger thing she'd received, a better, truer gift.

And there would be plenty of threesomes when she was well again.

"Kingsley," Søren said, whistling softly. "She's up."

Kingsley stirred and opened his eyes.

"Hi, King," Eleanor said from her bed. She waved tiredly at him. "Sorry I ruined your Christmas Eve."

He walked to her hospital bed and leaned over her.

"Not giving me a blow job by the tree is how you ruin my Christmas Eve, Elle," Kingsley said, pointing at her face. "You die, you ruin my *life*."

Eleanor winced. "Was I that sick?"

"You had a fever of 104. And you were talking out of your head when I brought you in."

"Shit, what did I say?"

"Out of nowhere you looked up at me and said, 'Get a hair cut. You look like a pirate.'"

"I was dreaming," she said.

"About me?"

"You were a former cross-dressing teenaged kinky prostitute named Princess."

"Ah, in my dreams," Kingsley said, hand over his heart.

"Søren also beat you and fucked you half to death."

Kingsley rolled his eyes. "In *his* dreams."

Søren slapped Kingsley in the stomach with the back of his hand.

"Go home, Princess," Søren said. "Get some sleep."

"You don't have to tell me twice," Kingsley said. He held up two fingers. "Second time in two years you've ended up in the ER. Two's the limit."

"Yes, your majesty," she said. Kingsley turned and started to leave. As he was pulling on his coat at the door to her room, Eleanor said, "Hey, King? Thanks for taking care of me."

He bowed his head, magnanimous as a true king. "My

pleasure."

"King?" Eleanor said. Kingsley turned back around. "Leave the tree up. There's always New Year's Eve." She winked at him.

"It's a date," he said, then left.

When he was gone, Eleanor used the bathroom and drank a glass of water before sinking gratefully back into the hospital bed. A nurse came, checked her vitals, gave her ibuprofen, and pronounced her on the road to recovery.

"Will you stay the night with me?" she asked after the nurse left.

"All night," he promised.

"You're a very good husband," she said.

"In your dream?"

"I meant now." She squeezed his hand. "Merry Christmas, my lord."

"Merry Christmas, my lady."

He kissed her again on the forehead and she closed her eyes. Then Søren spoke again.

"Eleanor? Did you say...you said in my bedroom at Edenfell in your dream, there was a red velvet tufted desk chair?"

"Right. You sat on it and I sat on you while you forced me—entirely against my will—to look at kinky porn and talk about sex with you."

"There was a red velvet tufted chair in my father's room in New Hampshire growing up. It had been at Edenfell for a hundred years in the master's bedchamber."

Eleanor's eyes opened, opened wide. She stared at him. No way. There was no way she could have known or guessed that...

"Are you serious?" she asked.

"No."

Fin.

A WINTER SYMPHONY

AUTHOR'S NOTE

This story takes place between the fourth and fifth Original Sinners books, The Mistress *and* The Saint.

It's the story of how and why the Unholy Trinity's move to New Orleans came about...and no, it was not because of the beignets.

Although that was a factor.

Dedicated to Bethany Hensel, Merci, Mon Ami

FIRST MOVEMENT

NOVEMBER ALLEGRO

ALLEGRO:

At a brisk, lively, or cheerful tempo.

ONE

KINGSLEY WAS HAPPY.

Very, very happy.

This came as a surprise to him. It would have come as a surprise to anyone who knew him, too.

On the list of adjectives frequently used to describe him, one might find the following:

- dangerous (of course)
- sexy (he had his fans)
- sleazy (he also had his detractors)
- ruthless (fact)
- insane (not quite, though he had his moments)
- brooding (fair point—he was French, after all, and contemplating the ultimate meaninglessness of his own existence was in his DNA)

But one would not include "happy" on any list describing Kingsley.

Apparently, he needed a new list, because now he was a

very happy man. True happiness, that is—*joie de vivre*, joy in living.

Had he ever felt this depth of joy before? Maybe once? Maybe on the last warm autumn night in Maine, when he was sixteen and Søren seventeen? Maybe that moment, after the beating and after the sex, when he lay across Søren's lap under the wild stars? Maybe that moment when Søren's fingers stroked Kingsley's naked back, tender from welts, and softly said three words...

You did well.

Yes, that was the last time he'd felt this much happiness. Once, he might have thought it would be the only time he'd ever feel it, until the night Juliette said three even more beautiful words to him.

Je suis enceinte.

The reality of this newly-discovered *joie* occurred to him on the night of his forty-seventh birthday. November 2nd in a year when winter came early, rudely shoving autumn out of the spotlight. Outside it was cold enough to chip teeth from chattering. Inside Kingsley's small private sitting room in his Riverside Drive townhouse, it was warm, however. The fire burned cheerfully behind the grate. He'd forgone his usual after-dinner wine for a milky cup of coffee—decaf—and he held Juliette lightly against his chest as they lay on the large antique fainting sofa. Out of nowhere, Juliette gasped as if in pain. A gasp followed by a laugh. She grabbed Kingsley's hand and put it on the swell of her pregnant belly.

"Someone is rehearsing for the Rockettes tonight," Juliette said, laughing again as she was kicked from within.

"Or there's a football practice going on in there," Kingsley said, feeling another tiny foot or hand press against his palm. The wave of joy rushed over him, leaving his head swimming and his throat almost too tight to speak.

"Back to sleep, Coco," Kingsley said softly to Juliette's stomach. "It's past your bedtime."

Coco wasn't the baby's name. They'd already decided on Céleste for a girl, Hugo for a boy (after author Victor Hugo). In French, *coco* was a child's slang term for an egg. At one of Juliette's early obstetrician appointments, her doctor had said their growing fetus was now about the size of an egg.

"I think Coco's trying to tell you 'happy birthday,'" Juliette said as she eased onto a pile of silk cushions. She wore a silk turquoise bathrobe, the tie of which kept sliding over her belly and under her breasts now that her narrow waist was long gone.

Kingsley put his mouth to her stomach. "Is a card in the mail too much to ask?"

Juliette smiled tiredly and adjusted the pillows underneath her as Kingsley drew her long and lovely dark legs across his lap.

"Did you ever think at this time last year, *this* is how we'd be spending your birthday?" she asked. "Alone together. No party. No wine, even. Just the two of us sitting here, being boring and reading?"

They were being very boring. Kingsley was almost finished reading *The Immoralist* by André Gide. Juliette was reading a book on her iPad, and he occasionally saw her smile at something in it.

Yes, this was certainly a very different scene from last year's birthday, which he'd celebrated in high and mad style. His townhouse had been bursting at the seams with guests dressed for the French Revolution, inspired by Kingsley's heritage and the upcoming release of the film *Les Misérables*, though the theme had not been *Liberté, égalité, fraternité* but *Liberté, égalité, sodomie*...

"This is better," Kingsley said.

"Are you certain?" she asked. Fear flashed across her dark eyes. They were lovers and they were in love, and this had been the case for several years. But they weren't married. Kingsley didn't practice monogamy, or even really believe in it. As for Juliette, she suffered from a marriage phobia, though he couldn't blame her. A rich, powerful man had once practically owned her, using her mother as leverage to keep her in his home and his bed. Men all over the city—especially Brad Wolfe, that asshole —showered her with gifts and attention and declarations of devotion. She played with them and took their presents, of course, and enjoyed every minute of it.

But now she and Kingsley were having a child together, and this easy open love affair of theirs was changing. A welcome change, she admitted, but Kingsley knew she worried that it wasn't so welcome for him.

After a long pause, he answered, "You know I've wanted children for as long as I can remember."

"I have wanted to dance on the moon since I was a little girl, but if NASA came to our front door and told me it was time to go, I would be terrified."

"I'm happy," he said. "This is what I want."

"I know it's what you want. But is it *all* you want?"

A good and fair question from the woman who was having their child. A question that had to be answered, if not that night then soon. Very soon. Little Coco wasn't going to wait forever for him to decide.

"Are you asking about Søren?" Kingsley said. He ran his hands up and down her smooth bare calves. She took long baths these days, enjoying the buoyancy of the warm water, and Kingsley would shave her legs for her now that she had trouble reaching her ankles. "Do you want me to give him up?"

"No," she said. "That's the last thing I want. Someone has to beat you, and it's not going to be me. All I want to know is...is it enough for you? *Finally*, do you have enough?"

Kingsley started to answer, to say yes, of course it was finally enough, that she had nothing to fear, that nothing and no one was going to come between them.

There was a knocking at the front door—loud, insistent. Juliette sat up and put her hands protectively over her stomach.

Kingsley jumped to his feet. More pounding on the door. Shouting now. It sounded like someone was trying to beat their way into the house. Kingsley looked at Juliette. "Stay here," he said.

He left the sitting room and strode down the hall to the grand front doors, wishing he still had his dogs. As he neared the doors, he heard his name and drunken laughter. The tension eased. He unlocked the door.

A half dozen men and women stood on his front porch wearing *outré* party clothes under their coats.

"Long live the King!" one woman shouted, hefting a bottle of champagne in the air. "About time! I'm freezing my tits off."

She and the other intruders started to press toward the door. Kingsley held up his hand. "What the hell are you all doing here?"

"It's your birthday, right?" the woman with the champagne bottle said. "We're here for the party."

He recognized her. Her name was...something that started with an R? Manhattan socialite—she'd tried on kink like a new outfit and decided she liked the way it looked on her. He recognized a few other faces, men and women who'd frequented his clubs in the past. Kat, the daughter of the ex-governor. Tate, her high-functioning alcoholic boyfriend. Another girl wearing only a red, white, and blue bikini under her coat. In the old days, he might have saluted her flag. Tonight he just wanted to tell her to wrap up before she contracted hypothermia.

"*Mon roi?*" Against orders, Juliette had come out of the sitting room and now stood by him. "Who is it?"

"Oh," Roxy said, eying Juliette's round belly. Kingsley

instinctively moved in front of Juliette. "No party this year, I guess?"

"No," Kingsley said to Roxy, to Kitty, to Tate, to the city itself. "The party's over."

TWO

AFTER THE REVELERS HAD LEFT, Juliette laughed at how scared they'd been of a few drunks at their door. She kissed him on the lips and went up to bed. Kingsley promised to be up soon. First, he had to check all the locks.

He wandered from room to room, not only checking that the front, back, and side doors were locked, but the windows, too. Never before had he locked the doors of the townhouse, believing it a sign of fear and weakness. His old arrogance shamed him. The woman he loved was pregnant with his first child.

He was almost tempted to hire bouncers to guard the door. After checking the locks, he returned to the sitting room to make certain the fire was out completely. How could he live with himself if he let the townhouse catch on fire with Juliette inside? Was this paranoia? He wished. But no, just weeks ago, secrets from his past had finally caught up with him. Søren and Nora had nearly paid with their lives. At night, as soon as he closed his eyes, he was back in that room, ears ringing from the loud claps of gunshots, and there was every chance in the world he would not survive to hold his newborn baby.

Everything changed in that room. And everyone came out of that room a different person from the one who'd walked into it. Especially him. The man who went in never locked his doors. The man who came out checked the seals on the windows to make sure not even an ant could crawl inside his home.

A mirror hung over the fireplace, gilt-framed, antique, and he caught a glimpse of the King that looked back at him—dark olive skin inherited from his Italian grandfather, dark eyes. Not a single gray hair, not a single wrinkle despite this being his forty-seventh birthday. Thanks to his good genes he didn't remotely look his age.

Ah, but he felt it. Here he was, creeping toward fifty and yet still kicking drunks off his stoop at midnight.

Roxy had looked at him like he'd grown a second head when he'd opened the door. It was his attire—no suit, no boots. Instead, he had on dark brown trousers, a black pullover, and the glasses he wore when reading. He looked, in a word, vanilla.

A year ago, he might have cared. Maybe even a few months ago. But the moment Juliette began to show, the moment when her pregnancy became real and not hypothetical, was the moment he stopped giving a single fuck about anyone and anything but her, the baby, and the few people in his life he considered family.

Nora. Søren. Griffin...

The list was short and getting shorter all the time. The dogs were gone. Sadie had been killed, and Dom died not long after. Old age. Brutus and Max were living with Calliope in the Hamptons. He'd lied to Juliette, saying since the dogs were so old, he wanted their last months to be spent somewhere they could run and play by the water, not cooped up in the townhouse. But the truth was, the first time he'd seen one of his enormous Rottweilers jump up on Juliette, nearly knocking her over, he couldn't get them out of the house fast enough.

God, he needed a drink. Except since Juliette wasn't drinking, he'd also cut back.

The dogs living with Calliope? Staying home on his birthday to snuggle up with Jules and read? No wine? He knew becoming a parent entailed making sacrifices. So far, they'd all been surprisingly easy. He couldn't help but wonder what harder, more painful sacrifices were to come?

He placed his glasses on top of his book on the side table. Juliette had left her iPad behind, and he picked it up to take to her upstairs. He tapped the power button, curious to see what she'd been reading. The screen came to life and displayed a photograph of one of the most beautiful houses he'd ever seen. A red-brick mansion with white columns and a grand portico. Elaborate, almost tropical landscaping. He read the caption: "One of many mansions on St. Charles Avenue, seen from a New Orleans streetcar."

It was a page from a travel guide to New Orleans. No surprise, as he was taking her there the day after Christmas for a two-week "babymoon," which was like a honeymoon. Supposedly. He had never heard of such a thing until Griffin had told him it was *de rigeur* now to take one's pregnant wife or girl-friend on a last big vacation before the first baby came along. Sounded painfully bourgeois to him, but when he mentioned it to Juliette, her eyes had widened. She'd said at once, "Could we go to New Orleans?"

As he flipped through the pages of the book on her iPad, he saw massive ancient trees dripping with Spanish moss, old mansions, brightly painted houses, Christmas lights hanging in palm trees, and French words everywhere—*Mardi Gras* (Fat Tuesday), *banquette* (sidewalk), *Vieux Carré* (Old Square, the French Quarter), and *bien sûr—laissez les bons temps rouler* (let the good times roll).

He wished they were leaving right now.

As he started up the stairs, his phone began buzzing in his back pocket. He pulled it out and saw he had a text message from Leo, one of the bouncers at The 8th Circle.

Guy ODed outside on the sidewalk. Ambulance on the way. Orders?

One of ours? Kingsley replied. If the man were a member of the club, he would head over there right away.

Never seen him before.

Kingsley told Leo to keep watch over the man, to keep him warm until the authorities arrived. And he should try to keep everyone inside the club until the police and EMTs were gone.

These calls were coming more and more often—poor souls overdosing in the bathrooms of his clubs, in the alleys behind them. Opioids were almost always the culprit. It seemed like a lifetime ago he'd found Griffin Fiske passed out drunk on the floor of one of his clubs. A more innocent time. Booze and coke were child's play compared to the *au courant* drugs people were on these days.

Kingsley knew these calls would keep coming. And people would keep showing up at his door, expecting an invitation into the non-stop orgy that had been his life for so many years.

When he said the party was over, he'd meant it.

But how did you un-invite an entire city to a party they'd thought would never end?

SECOND MOVEMENT

DECEMBER ADAGIO

Adagio:

At a slow tempo.

THREE

WHEN SØREN CALLED, Kingsley answered. Even when the call was nothing more than an invitation to dinner.

In the late afternoon of a bright mid-December day, Kingsley drove himself to Wakefield. He parked the black BMW he used for private trips in the church's parking lot. As he walked to the sanctuary, he gazed up at the church. Bathed in the watery light of a winter sun, it looked like a Currier & Ives calendar. Perfectly picturesque. Pure New England. Before going inside to find Søren, Kingsley glanced around, taking in the scene, committing it to memory.

Usually, Kingsley looked forward to his nights with Søren with a sense of anticipation bordering on feverishness. Not today. It wasn't going to be easy being with his lover and not telling him the momentous decision he'd made. Six weeks ago, he'd asked himself how he could un-invite the whole city from the party that had been his life. Now he knew the answer.

If the party won't leave, you leave the party.

He had no plans to tell anyone what he had decided—not Søren, not Juliette, not anyone—until after the holidays. He didn't want to ruin Christmas, not after all they'd been through this year. Kingsley walked on toward the church.

Two enormous wreaths of greenery tied with red bows hung on the great double doors of Sacred Heart Catholic Church. He went inside, where he heard voices coming from the sanctuary. Sounded like an argument. One male voice, unmistakably Søren's. A younger woman's voice—not Nora's.

Kingsley poked his head through the doors and saw Søren sitting at the bench of the church's grand piano with a young woman—Maxine, who used to play soccer with them on Sacred Heart's intramural church league team. She was college-aged now, with short dark hair and an athlete's compact build. For some reason, she was thrusting her left hand out at Søren and pointing at it.

"One hard whack," she was saying. "That's all I ask."

Catholics were getting stranger all the time.

"What's going on?" Kingsley asked as he came to stand by Maxine. She turned to face him, gasped at the sight of him, and threw herself into his arms.

"King!" she yelled in delight.

"Missed you, too," he said, returning the embrace with affection.

She pulled back, but left her hands on his shoulders and gently shook him. "You're having a baby!"

"Not exactly," Kingsley said. "I've outsourced that part to Juliette."

"I'm so happy for you." Maxine shook him again. She really was a very sturdy girl. Kingsley's brain bounced around his skull like a pinball until she let him go.

"I'm very happy for me, too," he said. "Or will be when the concussion subsides."

Søren was watching this whole show with an expression of

barely concealed amusement. He shook his handsome blond head, turned back to his piano, and played a few notes.

Maxine grinned, showing all her teeth. "Could you do me a favor, King?"

"Sexual?"

"Not today," she said. "Can you please tell Father S to hit me as hard as he can with a Bible?"

"No, no, no," Søren said, punctuating the no's with three descending notes on his piano.

"Why do you want him to hit you with a Bible?" Kingsley asked. "Other than the obvious."

"I have a tumor," she said, wincing.

"A what?"

"Maxine is exaggerating," Søren said. "She has a small ganglion cyst in her hand that requires minor medical attention, not being slapped with a Bible. Especially not by me."

"Look at it." Maxine held up her left hand and pointed to a tiny bump on the back near her wrist. "Isn't it disgusting?"

"Grotesque." Kingsley could barely see it.

"Right? It's called a Bible bump," she said. "It's called that because the way you're supposed to get rid of it is by hitting it hard as you can with a Bible to make it pop. Nobody around here can whack harder than Father S—"

"This is very true," Kingsley said.

"But he won't do it. Says it's 'assault on a parishioner' or some bullshit like that. Sorry, Father S."

"Assault or not, if you want your cyst gone, call a doctor," Søren said. "Hitting it with a Bible is an old wives' tale."

"Sexist," Maxine said.

"I'll do it," Kingsley said.

"Good Lord." Søren sighed and returned his attention to the piano, playing a slow, melancholy tune.

"Father S, do you mind?" Maxine said. "We're trying to do a medical procedure here."

Søren swiftly stood up, closed the fallboard on his piano, and walked out of the sanctuary.

"Thank God," Maxine said, shaking her head. "Now, will you really whack me with a Bible?"

"It would be an honor and a pleasure."

Kingsley never turned down an opportunity to take a whip, paddle, or a New Revised Standard Version Bible (red leather, how apropos) to an attractive young woman.

He had Maxine duck behind a pew and grip the rounded top, giving him a clean target. With her head down, she recited the Latin *Pater noster* in hushed tones. Kingsley narrowed his eyes, readied the heavy leather Bible, and just as he had hefted the holy book over his head, he felt it plucked from his hand.

"What?" Kingsley turned. Søren stood there, the Bible tucked under his arm.

"Here," he said and held out a small scrap of paper. "Maxine, you have an appointment this week with Dr. Liz Rayden, an orthopedist. She's booked until March, but she said she'd see you this week."

Maxine looked up at him and rolled her eyes. She stood up, took the paper, and tucked it in her pocket.

"Fine. Fine. See if I ever ask you for help again," she said. She threw her arms around Kingsley for another hug and said into his ear, "You're going to make a great dad, you know."

It was the sort of bland nicety people said to expectant parents, but Maxine had said it with such sweet and easy faith in him, he felt a lump in his throat. "*Merci.*"

"And when your kid's big enough, they can join the Sacred Heart Attacks!"

"I still despise that team name," Søren said.

"You were outvoted," Maxine said. "Get over it." She

released Kingsley from her hug and pointed at Søren. "Merry Christmas, and thanks for nothing. Me and my tumor are out of here."

She started for the door, and Søren began to say, "It's not—"

"Don't," Kingsley said. "Just don't."

"I can't believe you were actually going to hit Maxine's cyst with a Bible. What if you'd broken her hand?"

"There were two positive outcomes either way," Kingsley said. "Either it would work, and goodbye cyst. Or...she'd learn once and for all to listen to you."

"Fair play," Søren said.

A few minutes later, Søren locked up the church, and they started off down the path that led them through the small snow-shrouded woods and to the rectory.

In the last rays of daylight, the trees shimmered like diamonds.

"Stop," Kingsley said. "I need a picture of this. For Juliette." He took out his phone and snapped a few pictures of the scene —the light on the white trees, the little rectory hidden behind snowy branches.

Søren was staring at him as he took his pictures, studying him.

"What?" Kingsley said in French. "It's pretty."

"Yes, it is. It's pretty every year. First time you've ever bothered to notice."

Kingsley heard a question in that statement, but he refused to answer it. "Everything's different this year."

"That it is." Søren seemed to accept that as a good enough answer. They carried on, ducking under a canopy of tree branches and deeper into the little dark forest, made silver with snow. The moment they were out of the sunlight, the temperature dropped, but Kingsley didn't hurry toward the house, though it looked as cozy and inviting as a cottage out of a children's storybook. He inhaled the icy air, so clean and pure and cold, listened to the sound of the crisp snow breaking and crunching under his boots, a sound like no other. He even slipped his bare hand out of the pocket of his wool coat to gather snow off a low-hanging limb and feel it turn to water in his palm. If Søren hadn't commented about Kingsley's sudden interest in photography, he would have tried taking a few more pictures—the dark trees, the snowy path, the cottage with the gray stone chimney patiently waiting for a fire.

And Søren... He wanted a hundred, a thousand, a million pictures of Søren. Especially the picture of him he was tattooing onto his memory, Søren just as he was right then and there—tall and blond (with a touch of silver, just like the trees), and starkly handsome in his black coat with his Roman collar peeking out of the open top button.

He wanted to record everything, every sight and sound, every taste and smell. Not for Juliette, as he'd said. For himself. A king and a priest walking through a snowy wood... It sounded like the beginning of a story. The beginning, not the end.

They entered the rectory through the kitchen door, and Søren shucked off his coat with one casual move, slipped his finger under his dog collar and popped it out of his shirt. Kingsley hung his own coat on the hook.

"Where did you want to go to dinner or—" he started to say but then was cut off by Søren pushing his back against the door and kissing him.

The kiss was hot as summer but tasted like winter—that pure electric taste of ice-cold air that made the blood wake and the skin shiver. The kiss was possessive, and Kingsley let it possess him. He surrendered his weight against the door and lifted his chin to give Søren more of his mouth. There they were, those hands on his neck, holding him in place. Those hands he'd spent years wanting, dreaming of, remembering like a man in prison remembers the best meal he ever had in his life...

Kingsley returned the kiss—with his mouth, with his tongue, with his hands seeking Søren's skin at his throat, his beautiful bare throat. Kingsley found that perfect hollow with his fingertips.

The kiss broke, leaving them standing at the door close together, breathing each other's breaths.

"No dinner," Søren said. "You. Upstairs."

"Here?"

Søren smiled. "Why not?"

"We've never...here."

"Yes, we have."

"With Nora. Not alone."

"Really? Never?"

"Never," Kingsley said.

"I thought for sure..."

"You must have imagined it."

"I did imagine it," Søren said. "More times than I'll admit to."

"Admit to it," Kingsley said. "Please."

Søren laughed softly, though Kingsley wasn't joking. They had gone to bed together at the rectory many, many times over the years, always with Nora there between them. Never alone, never just the two of them, not here. There were two things Kingsley wanted in his life, wanted so badly he would have sold everything he owned down to his very soul: to have Søren, and to have children with Juliette.

And now, as if by magic, the universe had handed him both at the same time. But it was a trick, he realized. He was given both. He could keep only one.

"How many times?" Kingsley asked again. "I want to know. I spent too many years thinking you didn't want me at all. No more secrets, no more lies. I'm asking—how many times did you want to call me and ask me over, but you told yourself no?"

"I didn't count," Søren said, still smiling as if Kingsley were joking. But then, as if he finally saw how serious Kingsley was, he said, "Not even I can count that high. Is that what you want to hear?"

"Yes."

"Good. Now are we going to stand here in the kitchen while you ask me questions all night, or are you going to come upstairs with me so I can beat and fuck you?"

And while Kingsley did want answers...

Reader, he went upstairs with him.

FOUR

TONIGHT WOULD BE the first time they played alone together in Søren's bedroom. And eventually, one night would be their last time. So when Kingsley followed Søren up the stairs of the rectory to his bedroom, he counted the steps—eleven. And he memorized the particular shade of sunlit gold that gilded the dark hardwood floors. And the smell... The rectory was tended by the world's most Italian Catholic grandmother, and it always smelled clean, like pine and fresh linens. And winter, of course. It always smelled like winter, even in summer, because the man who made this little cottage his home smelled like winter. His skin like snow. His hair like ice. And, once upon a time, Kingsley would have said his heart was frosted over like a windowpane on a January morning, but what man with a heart of ice could say something like, "Not even I can count that high," when asked how many times he'd imagined them making love in his bedroom?

Once inside that bedroom, Søren went to the window and drew the white curtains open. There was nothing like the last light on a winter's day, the way it filled a room with a strange and sacred silence.

Kingsley felt almost lightheaded. He leaned against the bedpost to steady himself.

"I still can't get used to it," Kingsley said breathlessly when Søren turned to face him.

"What can't you get used to?"

"That we're doing this again," Kingsley said. "You want something for your whole life, and you get so used to wanting it, you don't know how to get used to having it."

Kingsley stood at the bedpost nearest the door, as if he couldn't bring himself to accept he was here, really here, an invited guest, a wanted guest.

Søren came to him. "I sent you away too many times. I shut you out too long. I wouldn't blame you if you hated me, if you walked out the door right now to punish me."

"Would it punish you?"

"I can't think of anything I want less right now than for you to leave."

Kingsley met his eyes, his steel-gray eyes and saw the truth shining in them, turning them silver. Søren was afraid that Kingsley might walk out—that this was too little, too late.

Kingsley went to the door, and paused at the threshold—he was a sadist himself, after all—before shutting the bedroom door.

The clicking of the brass bolt into place was one of the more erotic sounds he'd ever heard.

"I knew you weren't going to leave," Søren said, grinning slightly. "Come here."

Søren pointed to the old oval country rug at the foot of the bed. Kingsley committed the rug's colors and placement to memory, as he did with the entire room—the four-poster bed, the tops of the posts so tall they nearly brushed the ceiling. The quilt, downy white. The leather armchair and small side table, where a brass reading lamp sat.

Kingsley took his place on the rug. No one, unless they had submitted to someone they loved and respected, could ever understand the beautiful freedom of taking orders given by someone you trusted with your heart and your body. Nora had the best explanation for it. He remembered a lazy night at The 8th Circle, sitting around a table with Griffin and a few others, when one of the club's dominatrixes demanded Nora explain why she still sometimes submitted to Søren, why she'd take the servant's role to a man when she was born to be a master.

And Nora had said, "Imagine you know a guy—an investment banker, maybe—and you know that even if you handed over every penny of your fortune and watched him walk away with it...that when he came back a day later, or a week later, it would be with double your money, triple even. Imagine giving up all you have to someone, knowing you're going to get it back and then some. If you knew that guy, you'd love him, wouldn't you? Even if you didn't love him, you'd love him. You'd kiss his fucking hands, wouldn't you? You'd kiss his fucking feet."

The dominatrix who'd challenged Nora conceded defeat and kissed Nora's boot in penance. She was right. No denying. And if Kingsley hadn't been ordered to stand there on the rug by the bed, he might have dropped to his knees and kissed Søren's fucking hands, his fucking feet.

Søren lifted his hand and cupped the back of Kingsley's neck. "What do you want from me tonight? I'm in a giving mood."

Kingsley knew there was no right or wrong answer to that question. It wasn't a sincere query, just a way to make Kingsley squirm a little, embarrass him by making him talk about his fantasies. It took a lot to embarrass Kingsley, but Søren's steady gaze on him—his waiting, watching, judging regard—always turned him back into a nervous teenager, terrified of saying the wrong thing.

"The usual, I guess. Sex and kink, and it's all very hot and intense, et cetera, et cetera."

"Et cetera, et cetera?"

"I'll leave the 'et cetera' to you."

"Sex and kink, et cetera." Søren's tone was stern but amused. Professorial, like a teacher trying to find a kernel of sense somewhere in a very stupid pupil's reply. "Could you possibly be more specific?"

He could, actually. Kingsley remembered who he was then—not a skinny, scared teenager anymore but a grown man, a man other men were rightly afraid of.

And he knew exactly what he wanted.

Søren's bed was beautiful, two hundred or more years old. Oak with handcarved spindles. No surprise that after two hundred years, the wood was scuffed and scratched. It wasn't time that had left its mark on the bed, but rather Søren and Nora. Kingsley had watched with his own eyes, lying on those pillows, as Søren had flogged her while she was cuffed to the bedpost. Flogged her then fucked her. All those scratches, those gouges, those grooves, they were all souvenirs of her nights here.

"You have gouges and scratches all over your bed," he said. "Did you ever notice that?"

"I've noticed," Søren said, touching a deep dent in the footboard. "If I ever leave, I'll have to have the bed refinished."

"All these are hers," Kingsley said. "You tie her up here and flog her and whip her and beat her. None of them are mine. I've never left so much as a scratch."

"Would you like to leave a scratch or two on my bed?"

"I'd like you to fuck me so hard the bedposts break off, but I'll settle for one or two of these of my own." He stroked the marks left by handcuffs, by snap hooks, by desperate fingernails.

Kingsley wanted to leave his mark there, too. Something

permanent. Something left behind that declared to the world, KINGSLEY WAS HERE.

"Let's leave some marks then." Søren brushed his lips lightly over Kingsley's and whispered two words that left Kingsley breathless.

"Deep ones."

FIVE

SØREN ORDERED HIM TO UNDRESS. Kingsley obeyed, but slowly. He wanted everything to be slow tonight. No rush. No hurry. Make the evening last as long as possible.

He took off his suit jacket, tossed it over the back of the chair. Then the button-down, deftly freeing one button at a time. Meanwhile, Søren had unlocked the big steamer trunk. Hidden under the neatly folded sheets and quilts were all of Søren's toys. Floggers. Whips. Handcuffs. Misery sticks. Leather cuffs. Snap hooks. Spreader bars. Ankle cuffs.

Kingsley grew more and more aroused as the seconds passed and the silence grew heavy with possibility. Shoes off. Socks off. Trousers off. Then there was nothing left to take off.

Søren emerged from the chest with a ring. A large metal ring. Definitely not a cock ring, unless the cock in question belonged to a bull elephant.

"What's that?" Kingsley asked.

"You wanted to leave marks on my bed," Søren said, placing the metal hoop over the top of the wooden spindle, where it stayed like a ring tossed onto a peg during a carnival game. "Your own marks. She can't reach that high. I think you can."

Søren picked up two leather wrist cuffs. Kingsley was six feet tall, but even so, he would have to stretch if he were cuffed to that ring. The higher his hands were tied, the less secure footing he would have, and the more vulnerable he would be—no doubt precisely why Søren had thought of it.

Søren casually tossed the cuffs onto the bed, then unbuttoned his shirt. He threw it at Kingsley, who knew what to do. He neatly folded the shirt and laid it over the back of the chair, and just like that, he was sixteen again. This was how it had been. This is how it would be. Only this time, he hoped, without the terrible ending.

From the toy box, Søren removed a flogger with oiled leather tails. Kingsley closed his eyes, breathed a silent "*Merde.*" Oiled leather was bad. Oiled leather meant sharp, stinging sensations. Oiled leather was not for beginners, because oiled leather could cause serious pain.

"You don't use that on Nora, do you?" Kingsley asked.

"Never. Though she's been threatened with it. Keeps her in line, more or less."

He gave Kingsley a wicked, almost demonic grin. Then Søren moved closer, pressed his bare chest to Kingsley's. The skin to skin contact was delicious, electric. Kingsley's cock stiffened. It ached for touching and sucking, but the night had only just begun. Relief was hours away.

The flogger hung on Søren's wrist by the strap, and when he cupped Kingsley's neck lightly—and then not so lightly—Kingsley felt the tails gently brushing his naked back.

"I would never use this on Eleanor," Søren said, meeting Kingsley's eyes. "I've been saving it for you."

"What did I do to deserve the honor?"

"You showed up."

Søren's mouth found his again, kissed him deeply but too briefly. He raised Kingsley's wrist to his lips and bit him hard, over the pulse point, hard enough to break the skin. Just a nip of teeth, but it sent a jolt of sharp pain through his entire body. The blood welled up, not much more than a pinprick, but Søren's pupils dilated at the sight of it until there was more black in his eyes than gray.

Slowly, Søren lowered Kingsley's hand and placed it flat against the center of his chest. Kingsley could feel Søren's steady, strong heartbeat against his palm. Then Søren picked up one leather cuff and wrapped it around Kingsley's wrist, buckling it with his quick, agile fingers...fingers that had done this so many times, on so many nights, that surely he could have done it in his sleep. The leather cuff abraded the small bite wound on Kingsley's wrist. With every flinch, every twist, he would feel it again.

Which was, of course, precisely why Søren did it.

When both wrists were cuffed, Søren took out a snap hook and ordered Kingsley to face the bedpost and raise his arms. He could just barely reach the ring, standing on his toes. Søren, four inches taller, had no difficulty strapping him in and stretching him further in the process. Kingsley clenched his teeth as the muscles of his arms and back went taut and lengthened as if pulled on a rack.

In a proper flogging, the top warms the submissive up with a light start. The pain goes slowly and gently from a one to a two, a two to a four. Gradually, carefully, and with respect.

But this was Kingsley, a whore for pain.

And this was Søren, a man who made pain sluts cry for their mothers.

The first strike was brutal. Brutal and beautiful, just like the man who delivered it. Kingsley was caught so off guard by the pain that he cried out. When no second strike immediately followed, he knew he was in trouble.

"We're in the rectory of a Catholic church, Kingsley," Søren reminded him in his most insufferable tone. "Let's keep it down, shall we? Or do I need to gag you?"

Kingsley gave that question serious thought. Oiled leather flogger? No way to move into or away from the pain?

"Better gag me," he said.

Søren silently retrieved a gag from his toy box and tied it around Kingsley's head.

"Shall I continue?" Søren asked in his ear. "Oh, you're gagged. You can't answer. I'll take your silence for consent."

Kingsley's silence *was* his consent. His presence was his consent. When it came to Søren, Kingsley's existence was his consent.

"I promise I'll stop if you pass out from blood loss," Søren added.

This was a joke. At least Kingsley hoped it was. With Søren, one could never be sure...

The second strike was as hard and as harsh as the first. A line of fire burned across Kingsley's back. Then the third strike, and the fire went wild.

Kingsley braced himself as well as he could against the bedpost, shoulder to oak, and let the fire rain down on him. On his shoulders, on his sides, on his ass, thighs; even the tender skin on the back of his knees wasn't spared. The sensation went beyond stinging and burning to a place of absolute obliterating conflagration. If someone had doused him in gasoline and thrown a match on him, he might not notice. His body was a sacrificial bonfire and Søren the god for whom he burned. Everything turned to ash in the fire: His fears for the future. His dark memories of the past. His ego. His needs. His wants. His hopes. He was nothing but a body.

Then it was over, the cool air kissing his raw skin. He hung limp from the bedpost, covered in sweat and shivering, panting against the gag.

Søren pushed his bare chest against Kingsley's back. Kingsley almost passed out from the sudden wave of pain as Søren's sweat stung his wounded flesh.

But it was worth it. God, was it worth it when Søren wrapped his arms around his stomach, put his lips to his ear, and said, "Thank you."

Søren kissed him on the back of the neck where the strap of the gag had rubbed his skin red. He kissed Kingsley's shoulders, still burning, and the back of his head. Søren's lips dug hard into Kingsley's skin like he was close to coming, and it was true—he could feel his lover's powerful erection against his back.

This was one of those rare and perfect moments when Kingsley felt Søren's need, so much greater than his own. No matter how much Kingsley wanted it—and he did want it, beyond love or money—Søren *needed* it, like food, water. Like air. And if you needed air and didn't have it, wouldn't you put your lips to the ear of the man who'd given it to you to whisper your thanks?

Søren finally unbuckled the gag and pulled it gently out of Kingsley's mouth before dropping it onto the rug. Then he reached up and unhooked the snap hooks. Kingsley's arms fell down to his sides like deadweight. His knees nearly buckled. But he didn't have to worry that he'd fall. Søren had him. Kingsley leaned back against him, resting there. Søren's arms were around him, his chin on Kingsley's shoulder.

"Happy now?" Søren asked softly, laughter in his voice. "Now that you left your mark on the bed?"

Kingsley opened his tired eyes and saw the steel ring had cut gouges into the top of the bedpost, gouges so deep they'd exposed the pale wood underneath the dark stain and varnish.

Blissfully, he smiled.

"Very, very happy."

SIX

KINGSLEY STOOD ON HIS FEET, steady again, and turned around, kissing Søren with hunger and need. But kisses weren't enough to satisfy the craving. He went onto his knees and kissed and licked Søren's bare and beautiful stomach, tasting the sweat.

As much as Kingsley wanted his cock and wanted it right then, he made himself slow down. Made it last and last. If he'd learned anything this year, it was that everything could change in an instant. Everything could, with a knock on the door or a call on the phone, just...disappear.

Slowly, he opened Søren's black trousers and lowered them down past his jutting hipbones. Kingsley had to bite them, or he would die right there on the floor of the rectory's bedroom, which would undoubtedly put Søren in an awkward position. So he did them both a favor and bit them, nipping the pale flesh with the tips of his teeth. Søren flinched and caught his breath. Søren had a sadist's respect for pain. A connoisseur of it, really, and happy to be on the receiving end if and when the pain was inflicted on him by an overly enthusiastic submissive.

Søren was hard, his cock stiff and thick. Kingsley slid his palm up the shaft and wrapped his fingers around it, holding it as he bit Søren's left hip a little harder. Not too hard. Just hard enough to leave teeth marks and a bruise that Nora might see in a day or two. Kingsley was in a mood to leave his mark on Søren tonight—his bed, his body. He'd tattoo his name on the man's soul if he could find his way to it.

Kingsley brought the tip of Søren's penis to his lips, licked it, and circled it with his tongue. Then he slowly....slowly....slowly....drew it into his mouth. He held it by the base and took as much of it as he could. He tasted salt again, but not sweat. He forced his jaw to relax so he could take as much as possible into his throat, and once it was there he pumped his mouth around it.

Søren's hands found Kingsley's hair and stroked it, then gripped it to hold him in place.

He tilted Kingsley's head back slightly, and Kingsley let it happen without protest or struggle. He let Søren use his mouth as he knelt there and took it. This was what he'd craved for years, this giving up of self and will and autonomy. It wasn't always good to be a king. There was much to be said for being a servant, especially with this man as his master.

Kingsley opened his eyes and looked up. Søren was astride him practically, his legs parted and his hands holding Kingsley's head right where he wanted it. His bare chest glistened in the lamplight, his tight stomach muscles moving with each of his breaths. His eyes were closed as if in prayer.

Kingsley slid his hands up Søren's thighs and to his back, his long and muscled back. He dug his fingers into the tender skin, wanting to draw Søren deeper into his mouth.

Søren gasped—a sound as wild and welcome as sudden thunder on a stifling summer night—and released into Kingsley's mouth. Søren's come filled his throat, and he had to swallow fast or choke. He swallowed every drop and licked his lips when it was done. Søren stood over him, hands still in Kingsley's hair.

Kingsley leaned his head against Søren's hip and rested there. When Søren laughed softly, Kingsley looked up.

"I didn't plan on doing that," Søren said.

"Good," Kingsley said, resting his head again on the center of Søren's stomach. "I liked making you lose control."

"Doesn't happen very often." Søren ran his fingers through Kingsley's hair. "Did you do that on purpose?"

Kingsley sat back on his knees and watched as Søren zipped up his trousers. "Suck your cock like my life depended on it? Yes."

"Make me come."

Kingsley shrugged. "If I didn't make you come now, I knew you'd fuck me. And I didn't want you to fuck me now. I wanted you to fuck me later."

"Usually you want me to fuck you immediately."

"I suppose I'm in the mood to take things slower tonight. I don't want it to be over too soon."

"No matter what, you can stay as long as you like."

Hearing those words made him feel almost as good as swallowing every drop of Søren's come had.

"I told you...I'm still getting used to us being together again. I may never get used to it," Kingsley said.

Søren reached down and stroked Kingsley's now-swollen bottom lip. His face was solemn, his eyes stern.

"Get used to it."

SEVEN

SØREN SENT KINGSLEY downstairs to find a bottle of red wine and two glasses. While in the kitchen, Kingsley checked his phone and found Juliette had sent him a photo of her and Nora at the theater in their box seats, both women looking elegant in their evening gowns. They'd be out late, so Kingsley didn't have to hurry home. Juliette was always happy to have a night off from his hovering attentions. Yesterday he'd tried to convince her to move their bedroom to the ground floor so she wouldn't have to climb the stairs. To that she said, "I'm pregnant, not dying." And that was the end of that.

He started up the stairs with the wine. From down the hall, he heard Søren on the phone. Kingsley walked quietly to the office and peeked inside. Søren was standing behind his desk, phone to his ear. While Kingsley had been downstairs, Søren had changed into a soft gray t-shirt and black and gray plaid flannel pants. How did he still look like a priest even in his pajamas?

Søren waved him inside the office.

"Did she ever wake up?" Søren was saying to whoever was

on the other end of the line. Then a pause. "I'm so sorry, John. Your mother was an incredible woman." Another pause. "Go home. Get some sleep. Your mother's not there anymore. The nurses will take good care of her." Pause. "No, I wouldn't tell the girls tonight. Let them sleep. Tell them after breakfast tomorrow morning." Another long pause. "I'll be over at ten. You don't have to do anything tonight but rest up for tomorrow. Everything else can wait."

With quiet compassion and the subtle note of command in his voice, Søren counseled the man. It was always so strange to witness this side of Kingsley's enigmatic lover. How did he reconcile such compassion and kindness with his sadism? Kingsley wondered if Søren had invisible grooves on the bottom of his feet from walking that tightrope his entire adult life.

"John, you know as well as I do that if your mother were still here, she would tell you to go home and take care of her grand-daughters. Put them first, and you'll get through this." Pause. "Yes, Diane and I will see you in the morning. We'll take care of everything."

Another pause. Søren said goodnight and hung up the phone, setting it down lightly on the desk.

Søren met Kingsley's eyes. "Parishioner lost his mother. He'd taken her into the ER on Tuesday, when she was having a stroke. He said he couldn't bring himself to just leave her there in the hospital with strangers."

"She's dead."

"He knows, but it hasn't quite sunk in yet. He just needed someone with a little authority to give him permission to do what he already wanted to do."

"You're his dominant."

Søren softly laughed, winced. "I admit that thought has occurred to me on more than one occasion when it comes to my parishioners." Søren accepted a glass from Kingsley and took a deep drink of wine. "I needed that, thank you."

"You're a good priest."

"Not as good as they deserve," he said with a shrug, settling down behind his desk. "But I do my best. I need to call Diane about John's mother. Give me two minutes, and you'll have my full attention again."

"No rush. I'll let you—"

"You can stay," Søren said, picking up his phone again.

Kingsley decided he would do that. He'd rarely had a reason to go into Søren's office. In fact, he'd probably been in this room only half a dozen times in the seventeen years Søren had been at Sacred Heart. Although he vaguely recalled a time they'd crawled out of the large picture window with the bench seat behind his desk, the easiest route to the roof of the rectory. Window to ivy-covered iron trellis to roof. Was that how they'd gotten back in again? No, they'd broken the trellis, he remembered. The rest of the memory escaped him.

As Søren spoke with his secretary, Kingsley studied the office. Seemingly nothing had changed since the last time he'd been in here—and it had been years. Years and years. The walls were painted a creamy white and the hardwood floor was covered by a large faded Persian rug that had once been blue and gold, he would guess, but was now a dull gray and an even duller yellow. Floor-to-ceiling built-in bookcases held Bibles and dense theological tomes, some in Latin and Greek, languages that Søren read as comfortably as he read English and French. The desk was large, but not grand. Honey-colored oak, like an old-fashioned schoolteacher's desk with an antique brass lamp on top. None of the decor seemed particularly "Søren," and Kingsley assumed everything in the office had been here when he'd moved in and would stay here if he ever moved out. Except Kingsley couldn't imagine Søren anywhere but in Wakefield, celebrating mass six days a week, presiding over funerals and weddings, and coaching a ragtag team of co-ed intramural soccer players—the Sacred Heart Attacks, their mascot a cartoon heart brandishing a broadsword.

The Heart Attacks' second-place trophy from the 2010 church league tournament was perched on a small metal box on the shelf. Fucking First Presbyterian had taken the championship. Again.

The trophy wasn't the only addition to the office, though. Hanging on the wall was a small round sampler Kingsley hadn't seen before.

TRUTH MAKES LOVE POSSIBLE; BUT LOVE MAKES TRUTH BEARABLE.

— ACHBISHOP ROWAN WILLIAMS.

A gift from a parishioner to Søren, Kingsley guessed, reading the tiny sewn-on letters at the bottom: TO FR. MS FROM KJ.

Søren got off the phone with Diane and sat in his office chair, swiveling it to face Kingsley who stood at the bookcase by the window.

"Sorry," he said, sitting back in the chair. "Priests don't work nine to five."

"It's fine," Kingsley said. "Really." He turned and sat down on the window bench, though the glass was cold and there was nothing to see outside but the dark, icy branches of an elm tree. "Who is KJ?" Kingsley asked, nodding toward the sampler on the wall.

"KJ? Oh, Katherine Jensen. She's in the choir, does embroidery in her free time."

"Does she have a crush on you?"

"She's ninety-one. But yes, I think she does."

Kingsley smiled. "You put our trophy in here."

"I was hiding it in shame," Søren said, feigning disgust. "I will never forgive First Presbyterian for beating us again. You know they cheated."

"How?"

"By having better players on their team than we did."

Kingsley sipped his wine and set his glass down. "What's in the box?"

"Which box?"

"The locked one. Under the trophy."

Søren glanced over his shoulder at the box, and his eyes were different when he looked back. "Just letters."

"In a lockbox."

"They're from Elizabeth," Søren said. "Old letters from when I was in school."

Elizabeth, Søren's sister with whom he shared a troubled past. She'd been abused by their father as a little girl. When she was twelve and Søren eleven, she'd instigated an incestuous abusive relationship with him. Her own brother. Søren had said before how difficult it was to even be in the same room with her, that it brought back disturbing memories.

"I shouldn't have asked," Kingsley said.

"You can ask me anything," Søren said gently, as if he were talking to a scared child about to make a difficult confession. "You know that, don't you? If it's something I can answer, I will."

"Really?" Kingsley shook his head. "Forgive me for being skeptical. I feel like you've been keeping yourself a secret from me for years."

"I know," Søren said with a solemn nod. "I was. In my mind, I'd convinced myself I was protecting you. I think the truth is, I was protecting myself just as much, if not more. But I'm trying to be more honest with all of us. If you want to know something, ask it."

"You'll regret saying that."

Søren grinned. "Try me."

EIGHT

TRY HIM? That blond monster was as arrogant as he was
beautiful. Kingsley would show him.

"All right. First question. Where did you get your pajamas?
Is there a pajama catalog just for priests?"

"You like them? Eleanor got them for me. And red ones
covered in candy canes, too."

"They make those in your size?"

Søren picked up his wine glass. "Apparently so."

"They're very cute."

"Thank you. I always wanted to be cute." He took a drink.
"That's your question?"

"I have more."

Søren held out his hand, palm open. "Ask away."

"Why do you keep your sister's letters?"

Søren sat back again, exhaled hard. "The pajama question
was much easier to answer. I've wanted to burn them many
times. However, since Elizabeth writes about my father's abuse
in them, destroying them would feel like destroying evidence.
Stuart Ballard—"

"Who?"

"The priest who's my confessor—he suggested I put them in a locked box, throw away the key, and set them on a shelf where I might see them every day until I'm used to them, and they no longer hold any power over me. It's called exposure therapy. Seems to have worked. Now they're just letters in a box. They have some sentimental value, too, I suppose. Apart from the occasional threatening letter from my father, no one ever wrote to me at school. I felt completely abandoned there. Finally, after two years, Elizabeth somehow found out where I'd been sent, and she started writing to me in secret. The first letter I received from her was a godsend. I can't tell you how crushing my loneliness was there." He smiled. "Until a certain French whore and masochist came along and changed my life."

Happiness again, pure happiness, potent as cocaine, hit Kingsley's brainstem and shot through his whole body.

"Does Nora know that you have those letters?"

"I don't think so. She's never asked. I've asked her not to ask. Shockingly, she's obeyed."

"There's a small horrible part of me that's happy I know, and she doesn't."

"I don't think that's particularly horrible, just understandable, considering. Any other questions?"

"Tell me something else she doesn't know." Kingsley grinned, feeling deliciously evil.

"Something Eleanor doesn't know? Let's see... Well, this is hardly a deep, dark secret, but I didn't tell her that I was recently offered a theology professorship at the Gregorian in Rome."

Kingsley's eyes widened. "When was that?"

"About a month ago. They wanted me to start next summer."

"Rome?"

"Rome."

"And you told them no?" If Søren wouldn't leave Sacred Heart for a cushy teaching position in Rome, he'd never... Kingsley pushed the rest of that thought aside.

"After everything we've just been through, I could hardly ask Eleanor and you and Juliette to uproot yourselves and come with me, could I? And I wasn't going to leave without you."

Kingsley ignored a pang of guilt. "Did you want to take the job?"

"I miss teaching. Being the only priest at a parish this size is exhausting. In a perfect world, I'd be teaching, but we don't live in a perfect world."

"If you weren't planning on taking it, why keep it from Nora?"

Søren met his eyes briefly, then looked away. "She's fragile right now," he said. "Doing better than most people would after what she went through, but she's not quite there yet. I've lost count of the times I've called her over the years and said I needed her to come over and be with me. Never once has she called to say she needed me."

"And now?"

"Three times in as many months. Which isn't many on paper but it's a lot for her. Most of the time, she swears she's fine, and I believe her. But sometimes when she's alone...sometimes she just can't be alone."

"You like that, don't you? That she needs you now."

"It's gratifying, yes. I wish the cause were different, but since we're being honest, it means..." He paused and smiled. "It means *everything* to me. Just mentioning to her the possibility I might go away—even if I'm not planning to, which I'm not—it would worry her. And worry is the last thing she needs, especially since she's starting to get back to her old self." He smiled. "Any other brutally personal questions?"

"One million. Give or take."

"How about one more, and then we go to bed? Surely we could save the other 999,999 for tomorrow?"

"What's something you never told me? Something about us."

Søren raised his arms and clasped his hands behind his head, the picture of deep contemplation. Kingsley would have killed to be inside that blond head, seeing all those memories flashing across his mind's eye like a montage from a black-and-white film.

"I got you a Christmas present," Søren said.

"That's not a secret. We get each other Christmas presents every year."

"Not this year. Back then."

"When we were in school?"

Søren nodded. "By the time it finally arrived, you were already gone and not coming back."

Kingsley sat up straighter, looked at him. "What was it?"

"You used to brag that you were scouted by Paris Saint-Germain FC."

"I had been, I swear."

"I believed you. That's why I wrote Elizabeth and asked her to buy a PSG football shirt when she was in Paris for Christmas that year and ship it to me. She did, but the post was slow, and it didn't arrive until a week after you were gone. It sat wrapped in brown paper with twine—the only wrapping paper we had at school—until the end of the term. Sat on my dresser taunting me every day, reminding me you'd left and weren't coming back. When I went to France to look for you after the term ended, I took it with me, but I never found you. When you join the Jesuits, you have to give up all your worldly possessions. That shirt was the very last thing I gave away. A homeless man was begging for change across the street from the building. He looked about your size."

Kingsley stared at Søren and didn't speak at first. In the silence, a branch from the frozen elm tree outside scratched the frosted window. The wind blew softly, but he felt it creeping through the cracks in the old and drafty cottage. The moment was already becoming a memory, one of his most important, one that would keep him warm in any season, safe in any storm.

There was nothing you could say to a confession like that, that the man you loved more than your own life had clung to a scrap of fabric for months and months and had only let go at the very last second, like a bride turning back one last time before walking down the aisle to make sure the man she truly loved wasn't coming to claim her. Or like Lot's wife looking back at Sodom before being turned into a pillar of salt.

Since there was nothing to say, Kingsley said nothing. He went over to Søren, sitting in his office chair, and he went down onto his knees on the rug in front of him and rested his head in Søren's lap.

Søren put his hand in Kingsley's hair and just held his head against his thigh. Kingsley inhaled deeply and smelled the scent of winter, the scent of trees encased in ice, but earthy and bursting with life within.

"I have a problem," Kingsley said. "I've gotten used to it."

Søren laughed softly. "It shouldn't be a problem. I told you, it's not going away."

No, maybe not, Kingsley thought. Maybe Søren's love wasn't going away.

But Kingsley was.

NINE

"COME TO BED," Søren said, and Kingsley obeyed.

Kingsley went first, and Søren walked behind him. Once inside the bedroom, Søren shut the door. Kingsley heard the click of the door latch, his new favorite sound.

Talking was over. All the secrets that would be told that night had been told. As soon as the door shut and the world was outside it, Søren took Kingsley's face in his hands, possessively, forced his head back, and kissed him like he owned him. He did own him, had every right to him.

Quickly, roughly, Kingsley's clothes were stripped from his body. Buttons unbuttoned. Shirt tossed aside. He was hard already from the kiss, but his penis stiffened even more when Søren pushed him onto his back on the bed and crawled on top of him.

Even six months pregnant, Juliette was light as a feather compared to the sheer breathtaking mass of the six-foot-four man on top of him. Was there anything like being kissed while fighting for air that made one feel more used? More owned?

The quilt was soft against Kingsley's skin and cradled his body as he sank into the bed.

White handmade quilt, antique bed, light from an old brass lamp. It was like making love in another time, another world, a world so removed from the real one that Kingsley was able to forget that their nights like this were numbered.

Søren rose up on his knees, straddling Kingsley's waist. "Do you want to leave marks on the bed?" he asked.

Kingsley answered, "I would carve my name across your headboard if you let me. I'd leave teeth marks in your footboard. I'd let you bleed me into the mattress so deep the stain would never come out. I'd..."

Kingsley paused as Søren's eyebrow reached his hairline.

"So that's a yes," Søren said.

Søren left the bed to go to his steamer trunk, his box of tricks. While he was gone, Kingsley moved fully onto the bed, lying in the middle, head on a pillow. Søren returned with two sets of steel handcuffs. Two? Søren straddled him again, putting one set on each wrist. The snapping of the lock into place and the cool touch of the metal on his already tender wrists made Kingsley desperately hard. His cock throbbed, wanting to be touched. Once the cuffs were on, Søren turned him onto his stomach. Kingsley lay there, prone and defenseless as Søren cuffed each wrist to a bedpost, his arms locked in a wide V.

Kingsley relaxed at once, surrendering himself entirely to the grip of the cuffs. He closed his eyes and rested his face against the quilt, soft from a thousand washings and smelling clean as a spring dawn.

His back was covered in bruises from the earlier beating, and even the slightest touch hurt. So that was all Søren administered at first, light touches on his tender back. His large and heavy hand stroked the wounds, lighting them up like signal fires with every touch.

"It wouldn't be right," Søren said, his tone quiet and gentle, "to put bruises on top of your bruises. It wouldn't be right at all, really. But it will be very, very enjoyable."

Not would be. *Will* be.

Kingsley registered the switch in verb tense at the exact moment Søren brought the short crop down onto his back. Not only onto his back, but directly onto a fresh bruise. Kingsley buried his face into the quilt to muffle his cries. The pain was staggering. Tears filled his eyes, and he pulled hard enough on the cuffs that bound him that he could feel the metal digging into the wood.

Then it was over, and Kingsley panted against the pillow, his back as hot and throbbing as his cock. Cool air soothed his raw skin, but the respite was brief. Something touched his bruises again, and Kingsley cried out softly. He felt it again and knew what it was this time. Not a hand. Not the crop. Søren was kissing his back, kissing his bruises. Kissing them softly, but even Søren's softest kisses caused him pain. Those were his favorite kisses, the ones that hurt.

Søren kissed a wandering path up Kingsley's body from the small of his back to his sides, his ribs, between his shoulders, and then his neck. Søren was naked. Kingsley felt Søren's cock pushing against the back of his thigh. A dizzying sensation, to be desired by this man.

He felt Søren's hands slide up his arms. Then the handcuffs were off and tossed onto the floor with a metallic clatter. Kingsley's body was loose and listless after the rush of pain. He let Søren turn him onto his back. He returned to full awareness at the moment when Søren laid down a black towel onto the bed, then picked up a small scalpel off the bedside table. No words were spoken, but Kingsley's heart pounded loud enough he could hear it beating in his ears.

"Hold very still," Søren said, his voice tender and soothing. "I don't want to hurt you."

Søren was going to cut him with a scalpel, but he didn't want to hurt him. Only to a sadist and the masochist who loved him did such a breach of logic make any sense. He meant that he didn't want to hurt Kingsley unintentionally. He did, of course, want to hurt him—entirely on purpose and in exactly the manner he desired. That was Søren.

Kingsley, as ordered, did not move.

The chosen spot was on Kingsley's hip, in that hollow of sensitive skin near the bone.

"You left your marks," Søren said, head down and leaning over Kingsley's hip. "Now I'll leave mine."

Kingsley watched Søren with hooded eyes, devouring the sight of his lover's tender concentration. The beauty of a sadist at work. The intensity in his steel-colored eyes. The steadiness of his hand. A lock of silver-blond hair falling over his forehead. The lips parting in pleasure as the skin slit under the sharpest edge of the knife...

A small cut, but precise and in the shape of an S. Blood welled to the surface. Søren's pupils dilated and took over his eyes.

"Are you all right?" Søren asked.

"I have never been better."

Truly, only Søren could wield kisses like a knife and a knife like a kiss.

Everything happened fast after that. Søren moved Kingsley onto his side, opened him with wet fingers slick with lubricant. And then he was inside him, moving deep with long strokes. Side by side, Søren's chest to Kingsley's back and his hand clutching the bleeding hip, four legs entwined, breaths ragged and rushed.

Slow thrusts. Deep thrusts. Kingsley felt them all the way into the aching core of him. Søren's hand on Kingsley's cock. A wet hand wrapped around a thick cock. Stroking in time with the thrusts so that Kingsley felt overwhelmed by pleasure, pleasure in and pleasure out. He wanted to come more than he wanted to breathe, but even more he wanted to hold back and come with Søren.

He shut his eyes tight and breathed shallow breaths, even as his climax built. With his own hand on himself, he could have held back easier, controlled his arousal. But with Søren's hand, so firm and grasping, it took herculean effort to hold back. The muscles of his stomach tightened painfully even as his hips worked into the hand that held him, and the cock inside him speared him completely.

"Come," Søren ordered into his ear, and Kingsley couldn't disobey. His back bowed and he let go, coming in spurts onto the white sheets even as Søren pounded into him with rough thrusts Kingsley barely registered through the wild haze of orgasm. As soon as he was empty, he was filled again. Søren came inside him as Kingsley lay limp and spent on the bed.

Then it was over, and they lay together, breathing together, bound together.

Søren slowly held out his hand and showed it to Kingsley. He saw the blood from the cut on his hip, staining the fingers and palm.

"It looks like my blood is your blood," Kingsley said.

And Søren replied, "Your blood is my blood."

Kingsley closed his eyes and asked himself how he could possibly leave this behind.

He didn't know how, only that he would.

TEN

SLOWLY THEY DISENTANGLED from each other. Søren pulled on his black flannel pajama pants and left Kingsley naked and spent on the bed. Shortly, Søren returned, his hands freshly washed—no more blood—carrying a first-aid kit.

Søren gently swabbed the cut on his hip, then applied ointment and gauze.

"You know," Kingsley said, never able to resist a chance to taunt Søren, "the famous Mistress Nora uses Snoopy brand Band-Aids when she cuts you up in her dungeon."

"Yes, well, the famous Mistress Nora is slightly demented, I hear."

"That's what we boys pay her for."

"Yes, I've heard that, too."

Kingsley smiled as Søren snapped the first-aid kit shut. "You're handling it better," he said. "Her work. When did that happen?"

"I'm still not thrilled about it, but how could I deny her what I won't deny myself?"

"Easily. You'd done it for years. So what changed?"

Søren looked at him. "You were in that room. We all were. You know what changed."

Everything. Everything changed and there was no going back.

"How could I deny her anything now?" Søren said. "All that matters is that she's alive and safe. And you."

Søren slipped out of his clothes again, turned off the lamp, and slid into bed with him. Without thinking, Kingsley curled up against him and laid his head on Søren's stomach.

"Don't let me fall asleep," Kingsley said. "I want to be home by midnight."

"What happens at midnight?"

"Juliette will want crêpes."

"You make her crêpes at midnight? Midnight crêpes?"

"She's six months pregnant with my baby. If she wants crêpes at midnight and blood oranges at dawn and a rack of lamb for lunch, she gets it."

"Maybe I want midnight crêpes."

"Are you pregnant with my child?"

"Not at the moment."

"Then make your own fucking crêpes."

Søren's stomach moved under Kingsley's head, rolling like a wave as he quietly laughed.

In the silence, Kingsley asked a question he'd been afraid to ask before. "Are you all right?"

Søren took a deep breath before answering. "Strangely, I think I'm better now than I was before. And Eleanor will be, too, eventually. Sometimes she has nightmares, and so do I, but there's a new honesty between us, a new certainty. Neither of us are content to wait for happiness anymore. She and I wanted to be together. We are together. You and I wanted to be together. So here we are—together."

"It does change your priorities, realizing you could die, doesn't it?"

"How did it change yours?"

Dangerous question. One Kingsley wasn't prepared to answer yet.

"I'm leaving your bed to go and make crêpes for Jules," he said. "Does that answer your question?"

"You're doing that because she's pregnant, not because of what happened to us. What's going on?"

Kingsley raised his head, saw Søren looking at him. "What are you asking?"

"For weeks now, you've been acting differently. And tonight...when did you start taking pictures of my church? Of the trees? You hugged Maxine earlier like you might never see her again. And all evening you've been asking me to be honest with you, which makes me wonder if you're not being completely honest with me. Is there something going on you aren't telling me about?"

As much as Kingsley wanted to stay there, resting his head on Søren's stomach for another hour or century, he slowly sat up and gathered the sheets around him.

Søren switched the lamp back on and sat up, too, back against the headboard, white quilt at his waist. "Kingsley?"

"Something happened on my birthday," he began. "You know how I said I didn't want a party."

"I remember."

"All I wanted was to be alone with Juliette all evening. She had a meal delivered from my favorite French restaurant, and then all we did was curl up in my sitting room and talk and read. Then I heard something. People were pounding on the door, yelling my name. Juliette was scared. But you know who it was?"

"Who?"

"People I've known for years. They were dressed up, drunk, ready for a party. And I couldn't get rid of them fast enough."

Søren smiled, looked relieved. "Is that it? You've realized you're over your playboy ways?"

"It's more than that. I was scared. Me. And the reason they were pounding on the door was because I had locked it. I never used to lock the doors. I didn't want anyone thinking I was scared. But now I am. All the time. Day and night. Juliette carries pepper spray wherever she goes. I'd carry a gun with me, if she'd let me. But I have them in the house, which I'm under orders to get rid of the second the baby is born."

"You're about to be a father. Things have to change."

"I read something a long time ago that's stayed with me. Tacitus, the Roman historian, said, 'Great empires are not maintained by timidity.' I have never been as happy in my life as I am now. And I've never been so afraid."

"Are you afraid your empire is going to fall?"

"Fuck my empire. Burn it to the ground. I don't want it anymore."

"What do you want, then?"

"I want to take Juliette and the baby and move to the other side of the world. That's what I want." He paused, met Søren's eyes, and said the hardest words he'd ever said. "And that's what we're going to do."

ELEVEN

SØREN STARED. The silence was so profound that Kingsley heard a tree limb scratching the roof.

"You're leaving New York," Søren finally said. "You and Juliette."

Kingsley nodded.

"For how long?"

"Forever." Before Søren could ask another question, Kingsley started to explain himself. "We're not safe here. I made too many enemies. I've crossed the mafia. I've pissed off the police, politicians... I know the secrets of too many powerful people. Next time someone knocks on my door in the middle of the night, they might have a gun in their hand instead of a bottle of champagne. I have to think of Jules. I have to think of the baby. You told that man tonight on the phone he had to put his children first. That's all I'm trying to do."

Another silence, loud enough that Kingsley heard the quiet ping of the carriage clock on Søren's fireplace mantel downstairs. It was getting late. He climbed out of bed, started to dress.

"There's no reason to worry," Kingsley said, though he himself was sick with worry. "Closing up a small empire takes time. And Jules loves her doctor here, so I know she won't want to give birth somewhere else. We won't move until the baby's at least six months old." He pulled on his trousers as he talked. Talked, and tried to explain it so clearly that it made so much sense, no one could even think of questioning the decision. "We'll probably even have one last Christmas here before we leave."

"One last Christmas."

"Which is over a year away," Kingsley reminded Søren. And himself. He wasn't leaving tomorrow or the next day. A year, more or less. An entire year. Longer than they had together the first time. It would be enough. It would have to be enough.

"And you're going...where?"

He slid his feet into his boots, a good way to avoid eye contact. "Not certain yet, though I'm thinking a villa in St. Bart's."

"St. Bart's? You mean Saint Barthélemy...the island in the Caribbean." Søren's voice sounded strangely flat.

Kingsley shrugged. "It's French. It's safe. It's close to Haiti. It's beautiful."

"It's 2,000 miles away."

"Only 1,700 miles. I looked it up."

"And that's where Juliette wants to move? St. Bart's?"

"She doesn't know we're moving yet. I'm going to surprise her when we're on holiday in New Orleans."

Søren's eyes widened slightly. "This was *your* idea?"

"What? Do you think Juliette put me up to this? This was my decision. And she'll understand it. I hope you can, too."

The pause before answering was no longer than the space between breaths, but Kingsley felt it like a breath he'd been holding for an hour.

"Of course," Søren said. "If you think for one second that you can't raise your family here safely, then you should go."

"Thank you," Kingsley said. "You know, I didn't make this decision lightly."

"No. Of course you didn't. It's just—"

"What?"

Søren shook his head. "Nothing. St. Bart's is beautiful, I hear. We'll try to visit, if I can."

If.

That word was a bucket of ice water over his head.

If.

Not when.

If.

St. Bart's wasn't a long drive away. St. Bart's wasn't the sort of place one went for a weekend getaway. You could only get there from New York by flying. Not an easy trip for a smalltown priest under a vow of poverty. And if he did come to visit—*if*—where would they go to be alone together? A hotel? It felt tawdry and sad already.

"I'll visit you," Kingsley said.

"Of course."

Another *Of course* and Kingsley would scream. Was that all Søren could say?

"Will you tell Nora or should I?" Kingsley asked.

"No, you can tell her when you're ready to make the announcement. I'd only ask you to wait for a few months. This summer, when it won't hit so hard. Not the holidays."

Was this a punishment, telling Kingsley he had to break the news to Nora himself? *You want to go, you get to tell her the bad news, not me.* Unfair, he knew. It was Kingsley's secret to tell, not Søren's. That's all he meant by that, wasn't it? How terrifyingly fast the doubts were creeping and crawling their way into his brain...

Was Søren already pulling away from him? Shutting him out? De-vesting in their relationship and silently reminding himself, *Now I remember exactly why I chose Nora over you, and why I'll do it again.*

"She'll understand, too," Søren said. "But she will be disappointed. She wanted to be part of the baby's life. She's an only child. No nieces or nephews."

"She can visit anytime. You can, too. I know it's not so easy for you to—"

"We'll be fine."

We'll be fine.

Who was *we*? Was "we" Søren and Kingsley? Søren and Nora? Søren and Kingsley and Nora? All of them? Would they be fine?

An hour ago, he'd felt secure enough to ask Søren the sort of personal questions he wouldn't have dared even think of asking six months ago. Now he couldn't even bring himself to ask who he meant by "we," and who would be "fine" when they were gone.

"I should be going," Kingsley said. "See you soon."

"Of course."

The door waited for him. He'd have to open it and walk through it to go downstairs to leave the house to get into his car to go home. Easy enough, and yet he stood there.

He wanted to kiss Søren goodbye, but he didn't want to risk trying to kiss Søren goodbye and being rejected. Or worse, receiving a tepid kiss. How had a decision that had seemed so simple in theory become so painfully, impossibly difficult?

"If I don't see you before Christmas, I hope you have a nice one," Kingsley said.

A nice one? Was he talking to his lover or a salesgirl at Tiffany's?

"I'm sure it will be fine. You, too. Have a nice time in New Orleans with Juliette."

"We will."

He opened the door. Might as well just do it, like ripping off a bandage. And then he remembered the gauze and tape on his hip and how he had a perfect bloody letter S there that Søren had carved into him, claiming him. He would not let this get between them. He wouldn't. He'd let so many secrets and lies, and his stubborn pride, get between them before. He wasn't a kid anymore, but a grown man with a child on the way. He would not be a coward.

"What were you about to say?" Kingsley asked.

"I didn't say anything," Søren said. He still sat up in the bed, sheets to his hip and his beautiful body suddenly out of reach.

"You started to, a minute ago, and then you stopped yourself. What were you going to say?"

Søren gave a little smile, a cold little smile. "The wrong thing. Trust me."

"I want to hear the wrong thing."

"You don't, I promise—"

"I do. Didn't we just say no more bullshit between us? Didn't we? Or did I imagine that?"

"Kingsley, I know you're—"

"What were you going to say?"

Søren met his eyes. His stare was icy and cold. "I was going to say, 'Don't do this to me again.'"

Kingsley lifted his chin, stood up straighter. "You were right," he said. "That was the wrong thing to say."

"I tried to warn you," Søren said.

"You knew I was in love with you for *years* and you—"

"I know. I know, Kingsley. Of course you have to go. Of course you do."

Kingsley nodded. "Of course."

And with that, he left.

There was no kiss goodnight. Of course there wasn't.

THIRD MOVEMENT

JANUARY MINUET

MINUET:

A slow, stately ballroom dance for two.

TWELVE

JANUARY 5TH and it was seventy degrees at ten in the morning. And, as if it couldn't get any better than that, Kingsley was having some of the better sex of his life, even if it was vanilla.

The window to their rented *pied-à-terre* on Conti Street was open, and a clean morning breeze blew into the bedroom, caressing Kingsley's naked back so lightly that chills rose all over his body. He was on his hands and knees, braced over Juliette, who lay on her back under him, thighs wide and eyes closed, a little smile on her beautifully full, soft lips.

"What are you smiling about?" he demanded, punctuating the question with a gentle thrust. She was so warm inside, warm and slick and so incredibly tight—thank you, pregnancy—that he could have stayed inside her all day.

"Just happy," she said, and slowly opened her eyes. "Very, very happy." *Très, très content.*

Kingsley was also *très, très content.* How could any man in bed with this woman not be *content*? He felt like he was young and in Paris again, in bed with this glorious woman in their elegantly simple—and simply elegant—apartment on the second floor of an old French Quarter double gallery home. Every morning they were making lazy love on the old creaking brass bed, the pale green shutters thrown open to let in the scent and sounds of city life—coffee, laughing voices, and the thick wet heat of Louisiana.

Juliette was wearing a short cotton nightgown that covered her growing stomach but left her long dark arms and chest bare. He covered her with a thousand soft kisses. Her shoulders, her collarbone, the valley from the hollow of her long throat to between her full breasts. Had they ever had so much vanilla sex in their lives, the two of them? She, who adored being on the receiving end of rough and possessive sex as much as he enjoyed being on the giving end? But there was no risking the baby. Now it was slow. Now it was soft. Now it was lazy and tender, not wicked and rough. Her hands were resting lightly on his shoulders, not tied to the bed. Her legs, hooked over his calves instead of strapped to the footboard, thighs forced open wide.

Eventually, they'd return to their wild nights and wicked ways. For now, Kingsley was more than content to enjoy these sunny, sensual mornings with her. He pulled out and she rolled onto her side, propping her knee up on a pillow. He slid back into her from behind this time, spooning her. While kneading her intensely swollen clitoris, he fucked her. Her breathing quickened, and her head fell back against his shoulder. It was a uniquely satisfying experience to make Juliette—pregnant and dressed in her innocent white cotton maternity nightgown—come so hard he felt her vagina clench around him like the grip of a strong hand, and so loudly, half the French Quarter heard her orgasm. As she was riding the wave of her climax, he pushed into her with ragged breaths and short, shallow thrusts and came hard himself—spending himself until there was nothing left to give her.

Panting and empty, he pulled out and rested his chin against her shoulder. Another soft warm breeze blew through the apartment and rustled the sheer white curtains across the room, making them sway like shy ghosts at a party.

"It's January," she said, laughing like it was a joke. "It's January, and we have the windows open."

"You missed that?" Kingsley asked.

"Warm winters? Oh, yes. This is heaven. You may have to go back to New York without us. We'll see you again in June."

"Coco isn't even here yet, and you two are already ganging up against me."

"Nothing against you," she said. "Only against winter. Ice is not a pregnant woman's best friend. But it's fine. I'll buy some of those spikes climbers put on their boots. What are they called in English? Tampons?"

"Crampons," Kingsley said.

She giggled like a girl. "That's it. Tampons wouldn't do much good on my shoes unless I walked through a puddle." She reached for her phone. It had buzzed while they were making love. "Lord," she said and groaned.

Kingsley took the phone from her. She had a text message from Brad Wolfe—that asshole—asking her out to dinner. "May I?"

"Please," she said.

Kingsley texted a reply.

This is King. Stop asking Juliette out on dates. She is pregnant with my baby.

He thought that would do it. Brad Wolfe—that asshole—wrote back immediately.

The more, the merrier.

Asshole, Kingsley replied, then blocked Wolfe's number before returning Juliette's phone to her.

"Not to blame the victim," he said, "but it's your fault you're so beautiful."

"It's a curse, I know." She laughed again, and he pulled her closer and gently cradled her belly.

"You think we woke Coco up?"

"I felt a little wiggling in there." Juliette placed her hand over his and moved it. "There. Feel it?"

He did feel it, the little hand or foot pushing against the walls of the womb. Sometimes Juliette would balance a small cup of water on her belly and wait for the water to dance in the glass. She would say, *Oh, no, the T-Rex is coming...*

"Does it hurt?" he asked.

"Not really. Coco is a good roommate. Lots more dancing since we came here, though. I think Coco likes the French Quarter."

"Coco likes all the beignets you've been eating."

Juliette gasped dramatically. "Beignets? What a wonderful idea..." She rolled over to face him, a maneuver she liked to call a walrus pirouette. "That's exactly what we should have after breakfast."

"After breakfast? What are we having *for* breakfast?"

"Blueberry waffles, coush-coush, and omelets."

"That's it?"

She poked him in the center of his chest. "Extra powdered sugar on the beignets, remember."

"Yes, ma'am."

He dressed quickly. Before leaving, he paused in the kitchen doorway and watched Juliette cook. She was singing *"Parlez-Moi d'Amour"* to herself as she sliced onions and mushrooms, massaged olive oil into the flesh of bright red bell peppers. She'd bought a New Orleans-themed cookbook on their second day here, and every morning she tried a new recipe.

In the two weeks they'd been here, Juliette had bloomed like a rose. He hadn't realized how much the cold of Manhattan's bitter winters bothered her until he watched her come alive under the January sun of New Orleans.

"I have a present for you," he said.

She glanced at him, gave him that sly smile he always loved to see. "Another one?"

"I saved the best for last. I'll give it to you after breakfast."

"We're taking the streetcar tour after breakfast."

"I'll give it to you on the streetcar."

"Ah, then it's not what I thought it was."

"Maybe it is," he said, "and I just want us to get kicked off the streetcar." He kissed her soft cheek. "I'll be back with beignets. Extra powdered sugar. Decaf coffee for you."

"Kink and caffeine—the only two things I miss from BC." *Before Coco.*

"I promise, after the baby's here and you're ready, we'll drink espresso and have kinky sex all night."

"That's all I ask," she said.

Kingsley turned to leave, and she gave him a playful pinch on his French derriere on his way out of the kitchen. Really, she was a changed woman here. Relaxed, giggly, walls down, as if the city had gotten her drunk. He was falling in love with her all over again. The first time he fell for her, it was for her sorrow. Now he found himself falling even harder for her joy.

If this is what life would be like when they moved to St. Bart's, then he was ready to pack up today and leave the empire dismantling to the lawyers. Only, he knew it didn't work that way. And even if it did, he'd promised Søren one last Christmas. How could he take that back? Especially since he hadn't made that promise for Søren's sake, but for his own.

He strolled along the breezy sunlit streets of the Old

Square, sunglasses on, which made it easier to note the appreciative glances he received from the female tourists that morning. Every sundress that walked past him did a double-take or, even bolder, shot him a smile. He was wearing his favorite jeans with a loose white button-down shirt half-tucked in, collar open, sleeves rolled up. He knew he looked like he'd just rolled out of the bed of a beautiful woman—which was accurate. When he passed the hostess at a French café, she smiled broadly at him. "*Bonjour*," he said, forgetting to switch to English. He and Juliette always spoke French when alone together.

The waitress replied, *"Bonjour, Monsieur. Voulez-vous vous joindre à nous pour le petit déjeuner?"*

"Not today," he replied—*Pas aujourd-hui*—hoping his look of surprise was hidden behind his sunglasses. "Maybe tomorrow."

She smiled broadly. A sure sign she was American, not French.

"Your French is very good," he said to her. She looked about twenty, a young Black college girl wearing the classic hostess uniform of a black skirt with a white blouse. "You've been to France?"

"Not yet. I graduated from the *Ecole Bilingue* last year," she said.

"It's a French school? Here?" He hadn't realized they had French immersion schools in New Orleans. He assumed it was as French as Boston was Irish—in symbol and spirit, but not really.

She nodded. "There are a few in town. They're trying to bring the language back."

"You had good teachers. And I'm from Paris, so only my opinion counts."

She smiled again and made him promise to come for breakfast tomorrow with his girlfriend. A pinky swear was demanded and given. As Kingsley walked off toward Café du Monde, he caught himself feeling that same happiness he'd felt the night of his birthday. Only here, now, the fear was gone. Had he left it in Manhattan or lost it in New Orleans? Either way, *laissez le bon temps rouler...*

THIRTEEN

AT NOON THEY BOARDED A STREETCAR—NOT named *Desire*, sadly—for a tour of the Garden District. Kingsley had been to New Orleans before. Mardi Gras, years ago. His memory of the city was only of its nightlife. He had stayed out until dawn, returned to his hotel, and slept all day before going out again in the evening. Other than the parties and the parade, he hadn't seen much of the city. He certainly hadn't done any daylight tourist activities. Not his style. But Juliette loved looking at old houses—she had a Gothic streak in her bones a mile wide—and what made her happy made him happy.

Shamelessly, Juliette took photo after photo with her phone, like every other tourist on the streetcar. When the tour guide, speaking in an almost-impenetrable Cajun accent, pointed out Anne Rice's old house, Juliette took a dozen photos of it and immediately texted them to Nora.

"She would love it here," Juliette said. Kingsley had to agree. Mistress Nora would do well in a city known as The Big Easy. Art. Literature. Sin. Booze. What more could a porno-writing Catholic dominatrix want? Maybe they would come back next autumn, all of them together for one last hurrah before he and Juliette decamped to St. Bart's.

"Are you sure we have to leave Sunday?" Juliette asked as they turned a corner, and the streetcar eased slowly down a street so dense with ancient oaks that they blocked the sun.

"We could try to get a hotel and stay another week, if you like."

"You probably have too much to do back home."

"If you want to stay, we'll stay," he said.

She smiled, almost wistfully, and put her hand over her belly. "We have a doctor's appointment on Tuesday. I shouldn't miss it."

"We can come back after." He put his arm around her shoulders. She nestled in closer to him...for about two seconds, before she decided she needed to hang out the side of the streetcar to take more photos. "I know you're not looking forward to another winter in New York."

"Who would be?" she said without turning.

"What would you say if I told you we only had to stay there one more winter?"

Slowly, she lowered her phone and ducked back into the streetcar, a dozen beautiful old houses sliding by unseen, forgotten.

"What do you mean?" she asked.

"I mean...I want us to move away, start over somewhere safer. Warmer."

They had taken their seats near the back so they could speak without interrupting the other tourists. He was glad now that they had a little privacy. Juliette covered her mouth with her hand and glanced away.

"It'll be for the best," he said. "I was thinking St. Bart's. Safe, beautiful. Our children will grow up speaking French. We'll get a villa there. No more winters."

She turned around and looked at him. "You can't mean it." She lowered her voice and added, "What about Søren?"

"He knows."

Her lovely dark eyes widened. "You already told him?"

"I already told him," he said. "A few weeks ago. It's done. Call it a *fait accompli*."

Because it was a *fait accompli* if he'd already told Søren. Because that was the hardest part, the biggest barrier, the only thing standing in their way. Nothing could stop them now.

"But the clubs—"

"We'll sell them. Or I'll find someone to take over The 8th Circle."

"Who would run it?"

"The King is retired. Long live the Queen?"

Juliette nodded. "Nora would do an excellent job. But the townhouse—"

"We'll sell it. We could buy ten of these," he said, pointing at a row of ivy-draped Louisiana mansions, "for the price of one Manhattan townhouse on Riverside Drive."

Juliette shook her head—not to say no, but because she was clearly in shock and couldn't quite take it all in yet. They rode the next few blocks in silence, not even hearing what their tour guide had to say about the cemetery, about the beads on the trees and fences...

"I never let myself dream," she said, and looked at him again. "But you already told him."

He nodded slowly.

Again, she shook her head. "I thought you'd never give up the city and the clubs and the power...then I thought you might, after all that happened. But then you and he—and you were so happy, and I was happy for you, but I told myself now it would never happen. And that was fine. New York is fine. It's only..."

"It's not where you want to be. And if you don't want to be there, I don't want to be there."

She rested against his chest again, her hand on his heart, and his chin on the top of her head.

"You were right," she said. "This is the best gift."

He kissed her hair. "You're missing a good house," he whispered.

She sat back up and turned with her phone to take a picture of an enormous white mansion with a black iron fence surrounding it, a large yard filled with tropical plants and an imposing portico with four white columns. It was the sort of house children dream of living one day. A true dream house. Even now, Kingsley was daydreaming of their children playing hide-and-seek in a garden like that, playing fetch with a dog in a yard like that, growing up safe and coddled and spoiled and loved in a house like that.

"If anyone has a spare eight million on them," the tour guide said, "that one's for sale. It's a fixer-upper."

Juliette laughed and looked at him. "How much do you have in your wallet?"

AFTER THE STREETCAR TOUR, they went out in search of lunch. Juliette joked she was on the hobbit diet now that she was pregnant: first breakfast, second breakfast, elevenses, lunch, dinner, tea, supper. Kingsley was happy to indulge her. New Orleans had surprised him with the incredible variety and quality of their restaurants. The whole city was putting Manhattan to shame.

As they strolled toward the cafe, hand in hand, Juliette said, "You know, St. Bart's is tiny. I mean...*teeny* tiny. I checked my phone. The whole population is less than ten thousand people. Could you survive living in a small town on an island?"

"For you I could."

"Have you ever lived on an island for longer than a month or two? It's harder than people think. Especially if you're not used to it. I was used to it, and even I got island fever."

"It doesn't have to be St. Bart's. I only thought of it because it was French and safe and one flight to see your mother. We could move to L.A. if you wanted, San Diego, Miami—"

Suddenly she stopped and gave a little laugh. "Look," she said, pointing.

Across the street came a row of children, girls, all of them about nine or ten years old. They were wearing matching dresses, gray plaid with crisp white shirts and black cardigans. A young nun in a gray habit led them, a goose and her goslings.

"Aww..." Juliette sighed and leaned against him. "They look just like Madeline."

"Who?"

"The little French girl in the children's books?" Juliette said as if he should know that. She recited a few lines for him:

> In an old house in Paris
> That was covered with vines
> Lived twelve little girls
> In two straight lines [...]
> The smallest one was Madeline.

"Boys didn't read Madeline books," he said.

"I wanted to be her so badly," Juliette said, shaking her head. "I had all the books and read them over and over. I remember getting in trouble for trying to color Madeline in with a brown crayon so she'd look more like me. But those girls, they look just like the girls in the books, except they *do* look like me."

The girls in the Catholic school uniforms were Black like Juliette. Even the nun was Black. Juliette raised her hand and waved at the girls as they passed. They waved back, smiling broadly.

"Are you having a baby?" one girl shouted across the street.

"Yes, we are," Juliette called back. "Soon!"

Some of the girls applauded and a couple *oooh*-ed, which prompted the nun to turn and shush them. Kingsley laughed. This was not something that happened in Manhattan. If you waved at strangers across the street and talked with them, people would think you were mentally unstable. It seemed so natural here. So easy.

Ah, The Big Easy. So that's how it got its name.

Juliette laughed, too, but her eyes were filled with tears, ready to spill.

"Jules?"

The girls turned the corner and disappeared. Juliette stared at where they had been and where they went as if she saw something he couldn't see.

"I never told you," she said, "but I've been here before."

More secrets.

"I thought this was your first trip," Kingsley said. Was everyone in his life keeping secrets from him?

"He brought me here, once. Only once."

He. The man who'd practically kept her a prisoner, blackmailing her into obedience. Juliette hardly ever spoke of him but when she did, she never said his name, only "he" or "him."

"I ran away from him here," she said. "I was on my own for two days. When I remembered he was paying for my mother's treatment, I went back. The two best days of my life were in this city." She smiled. "Until you."

He held out his hand to her and she took it, squeezed it, met his eyes. "Let's move here," she said.

"New Orleans."

"Why not? It's French. It's a big city, a real city. Far, far from New York. And Coco would grow up with children that looked like her, or him. And the music and the food..."

He held up his hand. "If this is what you want—"

"It's what I want."

"It's settled then," he said. "We'll start looking for houses."

"Good. But lunch first, please."

They sat at a table outside on the café's patio. Eating outside in January? Maybe August would be hell, but it would be worth going through it for this—Juliette in a bright yellow sundress and sandals in the middle of winter, happier than he'd seen her since the day she first felt the baby kick, when the theoretical had become so wonderfully real.

While Juliette was in the bathroom, Kingsley sent Søren a message.

We're still moving, but it's New Orleans, not St. Bart's.

Without waiting for a reply, he added, *I miss you,* and immediately he wished he hadn't.

Juliette returned, and he helped her into her chair. As she perused the specials, she suddenly looked up. She smiled, then hid her face behind the menu.

"What? What is it?" Kingsley asked.

"Don't look behind you," she whispered.

He immediately looked behind him. Two priests in black clerical garb and Roman collars—a white priest, white-haired, about sixty, and a young Korean priest, not more than thirty—took a table at the opposite end of the patio. Before they could say anything, their waitress came to the table with their coffee.

"Morning, Katie," the younger priest said with a wave to their waitress.

"Morning, Father Lee." She smiled at Kingsley and Juliette. "Cream and sugar?"

"Please," Juliette said. "And do you know those priests?"

"They're in all the time. Jesuits from the college. They get free coffee here."

The waitress walked over to the priests and joined them in friendly conversation.

"You think it's a sign?" Juliette said.

"Definitely," Kingsley said. "I'll just trade in my Jesuit for a new one."

Juliette reached across the table and took his hand in hers. "Thank you, my love," she said softly. *Merci, mon amour.* "We'll find a way to make this work. For all of us."

"Are you happy?"

"Very."

"Then it's already working," he said, squeezing her hand. "Merry Christmas, my jewel."

"Merry Christmas, *mon roi.*"

As Kingsley went to put his phone away—he considered texting during a meal to be a mortal sin—it buzzed in his hand. A cryptic reply from Søren.

Much better.

FOURTH MOVEMENT

FEBRUARY SONATA

SONATA:

An instrumental musical composition typically of three or four movements in contrasting forms and keys.

FOURTEEN

KINGSLEY GAZED into the pit below him. Quiet this Monday evening, far quieter than the madness of a Friday or Saturday. Not empty, however. A dominant man wearing only leather trousers and full sleeve tattoos worked his submissive girlfriend over with a flogger on a St. Andrew's Cross. One of the "littles" who belonged to a man called Papa Bear was swinging upside-down from a harness, her frilly panties on full display as her dress hung over her head. Otherwise, fairly subdued down there.

At least the dungeons were full. All four of his staff dominatrixes were hard at work, putting the fear of Goddess into their wealthy male clients. It was good, he reminded himself, that these people—his people—had a safe place to play. The equipment was of high quality. The pro dommes and subs were world-class. And when the party got going, it was like Hieronymus Bosch's wettest dream.

There had been a time when wild horses couldn't drag him out of the club. Now it was hardly ten at night, and already he was checking his watch, longing to be home with Juliette. They could read each other books about New Orleans, discuss renovations, paint colors, nannies... He tried to tell himself The Big Easy wasn't all jazz and booze, beignets and Mardi Gras. There was something called "termite season," apparently. And God, the lizards—they were *everywhere*. Devastating poverty in many of the wards, not to mention the rampant post-Katrina gentrification. And, of course, the summer humidity you could cut with a chainsaw. He reminded himself of all these downsides, but it didn't work. He still wanted to be there more than he wanted to be in this city.

The future tantalized him. The past dogged him. When he wasn't imagining life in New Orleans with Juliette and their baby, he was back in the past again, sixteen years old, following Søren one warm September night out to a clearing in the Maine woods, waiting to hear those three words again—

"There's my King," came a voice from behind him.

Wrong three words.

Mistress Nora put her hands on his hips from behind and rose up to kiss his cheek. He leaned into the kiss. She sidled up next to him at the railing. She was wearing a red leather bustier and red boots. A short flogger with scarlet tails hung from a cord around her wrist. "Watching the show?"

"Not much of one tonight. It's Monday," he said with a shrug.

She swept her thick black hair off her shoulders and pulled it up into a loose bun, then fanned herself. Must have just finished up with a client. Her hair was damp with sweat, and her heavy black eye make-up was becomingly smudged. Her dark eyes glowed bright by the light of the tall tallow candles that illuminated the VIP lounge. For a moment, he could imagine she was a Valkyrie, fierce, deadly, and wild.

"How was your session?" he asked. He wanted desperately to tell her what he and Juliette were planning, but Søren had asked him to wait for a few months so she could get her bearings. They'd been through a lot, especially her.

"It was all right. I think I broke his finger. Oops."

Oops? Not merely sadistic, but callous, too. Kingsley's blood stirred just standing next to her, and he wondered if he needed a beating tonight more than he needed his dignity. No, he told himself, not tonight. Tonight he would go home as soon as he could, get out of his clothes—obscenely snug black trousers, black shirt with the collar open, and black coat with tails—and into bed with Juliette.

"Is that bad?" he asked.

"Nah. He tips an extra grand if I break something."

"You don't sound excited."

She glanced at him out the corner of her eye. "Can I tell you a secret without you firing me?"

"You don't work for me anymore, remember?"

Painfully, this was true. Nora chose her own clients now. She kept all her money. She paid rent on her dungeon, but she didn't answer to him anymore. This arrangement had hurt his wallet but improved their relationship.

"Okay, fine," she said. "Can I tell you a secret without you kicking me out of my dungeon?"

"Of course."

"I broke his finger because I was bored, and I was trying to do something to get my head back in the game."

"I take it this didn't work."

"Worked for him." She rolled her eyes. "He came so hard I have to get the ceilings mopped tomorrow. Still, the whole time I was thinking about how I wanted to be anywhere in the world but in that room."

"You never think that when I'm in your dungeon, do you?"

She put her arm around his waist, patted his ass, and kissed his cheek. His tight trousers were getting even tighter. This woman was so vicious that breaking a man's finger bored her.

"Never," she said with a wicked gleam in her vicious eyes. "When I'm with you—dungeon or no dungeon—all I can think about is how much fun I have beating the shit out of you."

"*Merci.*"

He kissed her lips lightly, and they turned their gazes back to the pit. A few more people had trickled in. Play was picking up. Someone was getting their boots blacked. Someone else was getting pilloried and sodomized in tandem.

"I was torturing a billionaire, and I was bored," she said.

"And I'm watching a former child star get sodomized by a drag queen named Scarlet O'Whora, and I'm bored, too. What's wrong with us?"

"It's that room," she said, sober again, somber. He knew she wasn't talking about her dungeon this time. She wrapped her arms around herself as if suddenly cold. "Something happened in that room to us, and we're all different now. You feel it, don't you?"

"I feel it."

"Looking back, it feels like I spent my entire adult life playing with people."

"You did. That was your job."

"True." She sighed. "For years it was like the three of us were playing one big game with each other. Me and him versus you. You and him versus me. Me and you versus him. I don't know. It's like...after everything that happened, the game's over."

"Because we both won?" Kingsley asked.

She met his eyes. "Because maybe it was never a game to start with." She closed her eyes. "So many people got hurt. We hurt so many people. Real pain is a lot scarier than what they pay me for."

"Yes," he said. "Yes, it is."

"It's hard to be here sometimes," she said. "I keep trying to go back to the way things were, but I don't know... I'm starting to think I'm not supposed to go back. I'm supposed to go forward."

Had she told Søren that? Is that why he didn't want Kingsley to tell her they were moving, because she was feeling just as restless? If Kingsley and Juliette left, if they broke the bond that held them all together, what would stop Nora from leaving, too? Her black eyes glowed with an inner fire. No wonder Søren feared getting burned again.

Intrigued but unwilling to show his hand, Kingsley said simply, "Where do you think you are supposed to go?"

"I want to travel. Get out of here and not look back for a while. In fact, I was thinking..." She glanced at him out the corner of her eye. "You told me a long time ago about this place you went to in France after you got shot the first time. Somewhere in wine country or something. Your parents took you there when you were a kid?"

Kingsley furrowed his brow. "I told you about that? I don't remember."

She smiled. "You were drunk at the time. I think I was, too. You said you went somewhere to recuperate? Maybe that's what I need. A little time in wine country."

What she needed was a male submissive. A real one. Not her old houseboy Wesley or whatever his stupid name was, but a real submissive who would worship her for her power, not try to take it away from her. Someone to serve her, guard her, someone she could train and spoil and be spoiled by. Not that he would tell her that and risk being bludgeoned to death by Søren. Bludgeoning was one of his few hard limits.

He waved his hand to dismiss the idea. "You'll be bored," he said. "Just a little village called Mozet and a bit of beach. My father had friends there, I think. It's been so long since I've been."

"Didn't you have a girlfriend there?"

"No, I had a *wife* there. Only she was someone else's wife."

Nora laughed her low throaty laugh, and he had to remind himself—again—that he was going to go home as soon as possible. Any minute now.

"Mozet," she said as if committing the name to memory. "I'll look it up. Maybe it's just what the doctor ordered."

"Juliette had a good time in New Orleans, you know. You could take a few weeks there. We didn't want to come back."

"So I heard. Søren asked me if I'd seen you since you got back from your trip. You aren't hiding from him, are you?"

Kingsley exhaled heavily. "Maybe. I think I've gotten on his bad side again."

"What did you do?" Her tone was teasing.

"I told him something he didn't want to hear."

"That'll do it. But I don't think he's mad at you at all."

"Are you sure?"

"He's been playing Vivaldi's 'Winter' over and over again like some kind of Phantom of the Rectory. It's very adorable, not that I told him that. I think he's pining for you. I know he's not pining for me. He can't get rid of me."

Kingsley tried not to smile, though it was hard. Kingsley thought he was the one who did all the pining in their relationship.

"Perhaps he's just in the mood to play Vivaldi," he said.

Kingsley had written a report on Vivaldi back at their old school. Vivaldi, the "Red Priest" who taught music to orphan girls, turning many of them into violin virtuosos.

"He also just bought you another Christmas present," Nora said. "It's sitting on his piano with your name on it."

"He did? What is it?"

"No clue. He's being secretive about it. Then again, I'm being secretive, too." She brought the tips of her fingers together and wiggled them rapidly, like a mad scientist fiendishly delighted by the potion she was brewing.

He leaned close to her. "What secret are you keeping?" he whispered.

"If I tell you," she said, "it won't be a secret."

A soft buzzing interrupted them, a phone vibrating. Nora took her phone out of her bustier where she'd nestled it between her ample breasts. Lucky phone.

"I better go," she said. "I'm spanking the mayor's nephew in ten. This one I'm actually looking forward to. He's cute as a button when you put him in stockings, garters, and a Laura Ashley dress."

She kissed Kingsley on the cheek, but before she could pull away, he took her by the wrist. "Before you go, I was thinking..."

She waited, eyes wide, and he saw the real woman underneath the outrageous make-up—the blood-red lips and Cleopatra eyes. Nora. His friend. One of the very few people he trusted with his life.

"When the baby comes, I was going to take some time off to help Juliette," he said. "But someone has to watch over the clubs, you know. I was wondering—"

"Not me."

That surprised him. He thought she'd jump at the chance to rule his empire. "Not you?"

"I... This is going to sound embarrassing and entirely out of character, so please just forget I've said it after I've said it. Okay?"

"Okay..."

"Most nights, all I want is to be with Søren," she said. "Not even for sex or kink. Just with him. It's a good thing I've scared him off asking me to marry him. If he asked me to elope to San Pedro tomorrow, I might do it."

She was serious.

"And if you tell him that," she added, "I will kill you."

She was serious about that, too.

"Is it that bad?" he asked.

"Or good? I don't know. I just know I've turned down twenty clients this past month. I'm down to ten sessions a week. My therapist says that's normal, that it takes six months at least to get your bearings back after a life-altering incident. Unfortunately, the bills don't wait for you to get your shit together."

Søren had said Nora was struggling, that she was "fragile." And perhaps she was. But she wasn't fragile like a wine glass, Kingsley saw, but fragile like an egg. There was something inside her about to break out. No wonder Søren was scared. Was he scared *for* her or *of* her?

"You know I will help you if you need it," Kingsley said.

"If it comes to begging you for money, I'll start stealing cars again." Her phone buzzed. "I better run. Places to go. People to beat."

Her old joke, except this time she didn't smile when she said it. She kissed him one more time and turned to walk away.

Then she stopped and spun on her heel, turning like a music box ballerina. It was good to see that even if she'd lost her bloodlust, she hadn't lost her grace.

"I know who could run the place while you're on paternity leave."

FIFTEEN

IT TOOK a second for Kingsley to recognize the young man who answered the door. Shaggy dark hair, wide silver-blue eyes that somehow managed to look both innocent and intelligent at the same time. He wore baggy khakis on his thin frame and a navy-blue t-shirt with YORKE written across the front. Yorke College.

"Michael," Kingsley said. "You cut your hair."

"Ah, yeah," he said and ran a hand over his head as if still getting used to his shorter hair. "For Christmas. I was trying to look older since we were visiting Griff's family. Did it work?"

"You do look older. But why aren't you at school?" It was a Tuesday evening, and not a holiday as far as Kingsley knew.

"The furnace in my dorm died. The temperature dropped to forty indoors, so they sent us all home. Or, not home, you know, but—"

"Here."

Michael blushed becomingly. He really was a pretty boy. No wonder Griffin had fallen so hard for him so fast.

"If that's our Mexican," Griffin's voice carried all the way from down the hall, "the money's on the side table."

"I'm French, not Mexican," Kingsley called back before Michael could reply.

Griffin suddenly stuck his head into the short hallway of their apartment. "King, holy fuck."

Griffin ran to the door and slid the last few yards on his socks, coming to a stop only by grabbing the door frame. Kingsley took a self-preserving step back just in case.

"King."

"Griffin."

"I swear to God, we're getting Mexican food for dinner. We weren't planning a racist threesome."

"I assumed."

"God, I haven't seen you in forever, man. Get in here. Hug me 'til it hurts."

Kingsley sighed. Griffin was...Griffin. As usual. The hug was brief but painful, just the way Griffin liked it.

Before Kingsley knew it, he was sitting in a black club chair with a cup of a very good coffee in his hand. Griffin took a seat on the sofa, with Michael at his feet, shoulders between his knees. Outside, fresh snow was falling, and the sky had turned a strange smoky gray. The apartment was warm but not quite Kingsley's style. Exposed brick walls. Sleek, symmetrical black leather furniture. Funky cow-print rugs. A playful home, but definitely on the young side. Or maybe Kingsley was just getting to be on the old side.

Griffin grilled him about his "babymoon" while Michael listened quietly and politely, only occasionally offering his own questions or comments. Every time Michael did speak up, Griffin would gently squeeze his shoulder or tug his hair as if to reward him for talking. He was a shy kid, Kingsley knew, and Griffin seemed to be helping him out of his shell. He did have a way of making people comfortable, making them feel safe to be themselves. This would stand him in good stead if he took the job Kingsley came to offer.

"Since your dinner is on the way, I'll get to the point," Kingsley said as he set his empty mug on the rustic wood coffee table. Wood. Splinters. Sharp square corners. Not child-safe at all.

"Or just stay for dinner," Griffin offered. "We always order extra. Trying to fatten Mick up so we can share clothes."

"It's not working," Michael said. "So much for the freshman fifteen."

"I'll give you fifteen lashes later tonight," Griffin said. "That can be your freshman fifteen."

"You know we have a guest, right?" Michael pointed to Kingsley. "Like...right there. And he can hear you."

"King," Griffin said, "I'm going to give Mick fifteen lashes later tonight."

"As you should. He clearly hasn't learned his place yet." Kingsley winked at Michael.

"I'm just kidding. Mick knows he's perfect." Griffin leaned over and gave Michael a quick rough hug and a kiss. They were so easy together, so comfortable. Would Kingsley ever be that comfortable, that playful with Søren? He'd known and loved the man since he was sixteen years old, and he still couldn't imagine coming up behind Søren and giving him a hug. He'd probably end up in the hospital after taking an elbow to the liver.

"All right, so I'm curious now," Griffin said. "What's up?"

"First, I have to ask you to keep this a secret. For now. Just for now."

"From who? Everyone? Like, even Nora?"

"Yes."

"Should I go?" Michael looked up at Griffin. "I can go."

"Whatever he tells me, I'll tell you anyway," Griffin said. "King knows that."

"Yes, I know that." Ah, to be that young and naïve again.

Griffin and Michael listened intently as Kingsley explained the situation to them—Juliette's pregnancy, feeling unsafe in the city after what they'd all gone through, the enemies he'd made, and the decision he'd come to...and, of course, the need for someone to watch over The 8th Circle and its denizens.

"Mistress Nora herself suggested you," Kingsley said. "And I'm inclined to agree with her opinion."

Griffin looked incredulous. "Me? Seriously? Run The 8th Circle?"

"You. Seriously."

"That's a...that's huge, King. Are you really leaving? I can't imagine New York without you, or I guess...you without New York."

"I can imagine it very easily. And maybe when you're my age, you can imagine it, too."

"And this is like...a done deal?"

"We found a house," Kingsley said. "It's old, however, and in a city that's hard on houses. We're looking at a massive renovation that would take about a year. As I told Søren, we'll have one last Christmas here and then move next January, February at the latest. That's not much time to train a replacement to run an empire."

"So...you need an answer pretty fast."

Kingsley nodded. "I won't be angry if you say no. It's not easy."

Griffin shrugged. "Fuck, what else do I have to do besides keep him in line two days a week?" He tugged Michael's hair.

"Is that a yes?"

"Let me talk to Mick about it. I'll tell you in a week or two?"

Kingsley smiled. "*Parfait.*"

Griffin met his eyes and looked suddenly very serious. It

wasn't often one witnessed Griffin Fiske being serious. "What happens if I say no? You have a runner-up?"

"You don't need to worry about that."

"Why? Because it'll influence my decision?"

"You'll sell it," Michael said.

Kingsley glanced down at Michael's uncanny silver eyes, but didn't say anything. That told them everything.

"Shit," Griffin said, falling back onto the couch. "So it's me or the club folds."

"There are other clubs in town."

"There's no other 8th Circle."

"And there are very few people I trust," Kingsley said. "Nora said she's in no shape yet to take on the responsibility. She would trust you to do it, and so would I. But no one else."

Griffin blew out a hard breath. "All right. Let me think about it."

"It does make good money. Not that you need it, but it's been lucrative."

"Wouldn't kill me to have a real job for once in my life."

Kingsley agreed, but he didn't say so out loud. He knew far too many depressed and anxious trust-fund babies whose lives drifted along listlessly, without purpose or meaning.

The door buzzer sounded.

"I should go," Kingsley said. "I believe your Mexican has arrived."

He was on his way to the elevator when Griffin caught up with him. "Hey, King, wait up."

Kingsley turned and saw Griffin wearing that same uncharacteristically serious expression on his handsome face. His dark eyes were shadowed. His lips were tight.

"How's Nora doing?" Griffin asked. "Seriously."

Kingsley mulled that question over before answering. "I don't know. Søren says she's struggling. I saw her just last night, and she admitted to feeling not quite herself. None of us do, I think."

"Is that why you're not telling her you're moving?"

"Søren's asked me to wait while she gets her bearings."

"You know she'll be pissed when she finds out we're keeping something from her."

"There are two possible outcomes," Kingsley said. "One, she'll understand and appreciate that we were only trying to help her. Or two...she'll beat the shit out of me and Søren."

"Hey, win-win."

"And you."

"Not a win. Definitely not a win."

The ancient elevator door opened.

"Goodnight, Griffin."

"Hey, speaking of the sinister minister..." He lifted his chin. "What's going on with you and Søren?"

Kingsley only smiled and hit the Close Door button. "I said, *Goodnight, Griffin.*"

NO ROLLS ROYCE was awaiting Kingsley at the curb. He'd been traveling incognito since coming home from New Orleans, and caught a cab. He was planning to head straight home until he saw the glow of Central Park and asked to be let out there.

He buttoned his wool coat and walked with his hands in his pockets, enjoying the pleasant crunch of fresh snow under his shoes as he strolled on the snow-packed lanes. The park was straight out of an old postcard tonight. It was only one of the many things he loved about New York.

What was it Nora told him once about leaving Søren? That there are two reasons you leave someone you're still in love with: either it's the right thing to do, or it's the only thing to do. With her and Søren, leaving him had been the only way for her to live the life she needed to live. With Kingsley and Manhattan...ah, it wasn't the only thing to do, no, but leaving was the right thing to do. For Juliette. For Coco. For himself. He only hoped that someday Søren would understand Kingsley wasn't leaving him again, just the city that could no longer keep them safe.

Don't do this to me again.

Those words echoed in his mind. Søren had warned him it was the wrong thing to say. And it had been. That night.

But tonight? Tonight, Kingsley found himself smiling at the memory of those words, the heartfelt pain behind them. Kingsley had left Søren. That was a fact. He'd left, disappeared, not come back. And all the while, he later learned, Søren had been waiting for him, wanting him, even searching for him with a Paris Saint-Germain football shirt in his old schoolbag wrapped in brown paper and tied with twine.

That wasn't something a man without a heart would do.

That was something a man with a broken heart would do.

And what if Kingsley was breaking his heart again by keeping his distance? Only one way to find out.

It was embarrassing how much mental effort it took for Kingsley to call Søren.

As soon as Søren answered, Kingsley said, "What did you get me for Christmas?"

A soft mocking laugh. "Who told you I got you anything?"

"Nora."

"She'll be flogged for that. I was saving your present for our last Christmas together."

"You mean in ten months?" Kingsley said.

"Yes."

"You were going to keep a present out in plain sight for ten months? That's torture."

"Of course it is. The torture is half the gift."

Kingsley grinned and leaned back against a lamppost. "Can't we consider it a late Christmas gift from last year?"

"We can. But only if you come over tonight to open it."

A yellow cab moved slowly down the street toward him. Kingsley raised his arm.

"I'm on my way. I need to stop by the house first and pick up your souvenir from New Orleans."

"Why am I suddenly terrified?"

"Because you should be," Kingsley said. "See you soon."

"I miss you, too."

The cab pulled to the curb. Kingsley was frozen to the spot, though, phone to his ear. He couldn't believe what he'd heard. "What was that?"

"You texted me from New Orleans and said you miss me," Søren said. "And I said, *I miss you, too.*"

Kingsley nearly laughed. "You really do love me, then."

"I do. Are you finally getting used to that?"

Kingsley breathed out a thick exhale that hung in the air. "Almost."

SIXTEEN

WHEN KINGSLEY ARRIVED at the rectory, he heard music wafting through the door. He stopped before entering, listened. Was that Vivaldi's "Winter" from *Four Seasons*? He quietly opened the door.

He passed through the cozy old kitchen with its hardwood floors worn slick by time and stood in the arched entryway to the living room. The fire was bright in the fireplace and Søren sat with his back to Kingsley at the piano, still playing as if he hadn't heard Kingsley come into the house.

Kingsley told himself he shouldn't do it...but he also told himself he wanted to do it. He'd envied Griffin and Michael their easy way with each other. Yet he knew that would never be him and Søren. His lover didn't like being touched when he wasn't ready for it. And knowing that, respecting that, was a deeper, more meaningful type of intimacy than just walking up behind your lover and embracing them. So Kingsley waited until the piece came to an end.

Søren's fingers lifted off the keys, and he rested his hands on his lap.

Kingsley approached, with loud footfalls. Søren didn't face him until Kingsley was setting his gift on the piano.

Søren picked up the black bag. The cuffs of his black, long-sleeved pullover were pushed up to reveal his forearms. For some reason, Søren also liked to play piano in bare feet. Something about feeling the vibrations of the music through the floor.

"What's in the bag?" Søren asked.

"Just a souvenir from New Orleans."

"If it's not beignets, I'm going to be a little disappointed," Søren said.

"It's not beignets. I can't have those in the house without eating a dozen of them."

Søren pulled the tissue from the bag, revealing a mask in the old Venetian style. It was painted red on one side, solid white on the other, with elaborate gilding around the mouth and eyes. The work of a famous local artist, popular at Mardi Gras.

Søren examined the mask closely. "This is disturbing. I assume that's the point?"

"It might be."

Søren put on the mask and was transformed into a strange and mysterious blank-faced figure, a nightmare come to life.

"Take it off," Kingsley said. "It's too bizarre. This was a mistake. Huge mistake."

Søren didn't take it off. He just laughed a low sinister laugh. Nora was right. He was the fucking Phantom of the Rectory.

"Just toss it in the trash," Kingsley said.

"Oh no. I'll find a use for it." He set the mask on the top of the piano, where it looked like a face was trying to escape a pool of liquid ebony. "Thank you. It's good to see you again."

"Nora said you were pining for me."

"I do not pine. But," Søren said, his tone conciliatory, "you have been on my mind."

"She said you were playing 'Winter' in my honor. Why that piece?" Kingsley asked. "Vivaldi wasn't French."

"When I was twenty, living in Rome at school, I went to Magdalena's house for Christmas. I'd said something to her months earlier about you, how I was worried you might be dead. After losing your parents and your sister, it wasn't out of the realm of possibility that you'd commit suicide or drink yourself to death. That night, Magda had me play that song for her on her new piano. As she was turning the pages of the sheet music, suddenly....there you were."

"There I was?"

"A picture of you. She'd hired an investigator to find you."

Kingsley stared, wide-eyed. "You knew where I was?"

Søren shook his head. "Magda was too much of a sadist to tell me. She showed me you were alive, as I'd wished, and nothing else. Besides, I was already in the Jesuits by then, and I knew if you wanted me, you could have found me. All you had to do was—"

"Call our school. I did."

Now it was Søren's turn to be struck silent.

"I called a couple of times but never could bring myself to leave a message for you," Kingsley said. "Too much of a coward to face you. I didn't know you were worried about me."

"Every second of every hour of every day and every night. If you knew how white-hot my anger at you was for disappearing on me without a trace... It took until that room, I think, to finally forgive you for your disappearing act."

"You forgave Nora a lot faster."

"I knew where she was. I knew she was safe. And she was gone one year, while I didn't see you for a decade. When I did see you again, you were dying in a hospital bed."

Silence again. A deep and honest silence.

"So," Søren said as he stretched out his long legs and crossed them at the ankles, crossed his arms over his chest and shrugged, "That's why I tend to gravitate toward Vivaldi's 'Winter' when I'm thinking of you. It worked once before, playing 'Winter,' and then there you were. Maybe it would work again. And so it has, finally."

Kingsley took a tenuous step forward.

"I have a secret for you. It's not my secret but I'll tell you anyway."

"I'm intrigued," Søren said and leaned back on the piano bench, arms crossed, ankles crossed.

"It's about your piano. Do you know how *la maîtresse* was able to afford to buy you a fifty-thousand dollar Bösendorfer piano?"

"I've always been afraid to ask."

"A wealthy man came to me with some *special* requests. Nothing she hadn't done before...except he was the son of a mafia don. You know how she despises the mafia. She turned the job down flat. Then she saw your piano for sale and called me back, said she'd do it. That was when you two were apart because you were being such a bastard about her working for me. And still, she still did that for you."

Søren glanced away, at the fire.

"No piano is worth that," Søren finally said.

"You are, though. To her. Now for my secret, one I even kept from myself. All these years, I resented you and hated her because I told myself that you loved her more than you loved me...but really, I think the truth is, she loved you more than I did, and I knew it, and that's what I resented."

Søren said nothing.

"If not *more*," Kingsley went on, "then *better*. She loved you better than I ever did. A brooding sexual obsession with someone you dated in high school doesn't really count as a relationship, does it?"

Søren smiled. "Not quite."

"I made passes at you. She made sacrifices for you. If this *was* a competition between me and her and you were the prize, she should win, hands down."

Søren said softly, "It's not a competition."

As if to prove that, he picked up the package tied in brown paper and gave it to Kingsley.

"This really was going to be your gift for this coming Christmas. If you open it, you won't be getting anything else this year. You've been warned."

"Empty threat," Kingsley said, though knowing Søren, he probably meant it. Still...he couldn't help himself. Søren slid slightly to the side and made room for Kingsley on the piano bench. Kingsley sat next to him and untied the twine.

He flipped the package over. When he pulled the paper apart, he knew what he was going to see: red and blue. A Paris Saint-Germain football shirt. Not the one Søren had originally gotten him all those years ago, but a replacement. And every time Kingsley wore it in New Orleans, he would think of Søren and miss him.

But he didn't see blue and red. He saw gray.

Gray and burgundy.

He unfolded the t-shirt and stared at the scarlet words screen-printed across the heather gray fabric.

LOYOLA UNIVERSITY
NEW ORLEANS

The cartoon head of a red wolf peered over top of the college's name, baring its teeth.

"What..." Kingsley's voice trailed off. He had to catch his breath.

"I am, as of one week ago, on the shortlist to replace Father

Juan Domenico as a professor of pastoral studies at Loyola University. He's retiring at the end of the next school year."

Once again, Søren had stunned Kingsley into silence.

"Apparently I'm a 'shoe-in' for the position—a Jesuit priest with two PhDs and nearly twenty years of pastoral experience at my own church. I'll move to New Orleans next January or February. Just like you said...one last winter here."

Finally, Kingsley found his voice, and as usual, it was the voice of doubt. "And it's going to happen? You can just...make a phone call and leave?"

"They've been attempting to transfer me for years. I've done everything I could to stay here, but only because it was close to Eleanor. Close to you. I don't need this house or this church. I need you. I need her. I need my family. If my family is in New Orleans, that's where I need to be."

"What if you don't get the job?"

"I'll come anyway."

Kingsley felt like panicking. It didn't seem possible that this was real, and if it wasn't he would never survive the joke being played on him. His heart was pounding like a million horses racing across a thousand fields. He couldn't sit still. He rose from the piano bench and stalked back and forth in front of the fireplace.

"If I need to leave the Jesuits and join the Diocese of New Orleans as a parish priest, I will," Søren explained. "There are priest shortages everywhere. It won't be a problem."

"What about Nora?" He was almost dizzy with shock.

"She'll come, too."

"She will?"

"If she knows what's good for her."

How did Søren do that? How could he make a threat sound so sexy? Or sexy talk sound so threatening?

He was right, though. Nora would go. She'd said as much, that she would run off with Søren anywhere if he asked her.

"And don't worry about Juliette," Søren continued. "She called me weeks ago and asked if there was any chance we could join you all in New Orleans. She really does love you, you know. One of these days you're going to have to accept that I love you, too."

Kingsley had to sit down. He didn't even bother looking for a chair. He sat down on the rug in front of the fireplace, back to the fire, eyes on Søren.

He lowered his head and closed his eyes, breathed through his hands. The floor creaked and he felt Søren sit down by him on the rug. Then two strong hands drew him down across Søren's lap and fingers slid under his shirt to stroke his back.

They sat there by the crackling fire, suddenly boys again who would break every rule to be together, even if it were only at night and far away from the prying eyes of the rest of the world.

"That summer we were apart," Kingsley said, "all I wanted was to see you again. Then school started and one night...it happened. You took me out to the woods and it was the best night of my life. It feels like that night again."

Lips touched his temple. Then Søren spoke three words.

"You did well."

It was that night again.

Slowly, Kingsley lifted his head. He was still clutching the shirt. He smoothed out on the floor in front of him and folded it carefully and rolled it into the classic "ranger roll," which he'd learned to do back in his days in the Legion.

"I should get home to Jules," Kingsley said. No overnight visits for a long time. Juliette wasn't due quite yet but it was still possible she could go into labor at any moment.

"Of course," his lover said. "It isn't as if we're running out of time to be together."

Kingsley stood up and held the gray t-shirt against his chest, as if afraid to let it go. Søren stood, too, stood close.

"Another secret," Kingsley said. "I want you to kiss me."

"That's not a secret."

"It's—"

Before Kingsley could get another word out, Søren had fallen onto his mouth. Their lips met, their mouths opened, their tongues touched. Kingsley breathed deep. The logs on the fireplace crackled and delicious smoke wafted through the room. The taste of Søren—like snow melting on his tongue—and the scent of the fire, and the rough grip of strong, cool fingers on the back of Kingsley's neck, and the wind outside rushing over the windows...all of it came together and turned the kiss into a winter symphony, and all that was missing was the mistletoe above them, but it could wait. If not this Christmas, then the Christmas after, or after that.

Søren pulled back from the kiss. "I shouldn't have said, 'Don't do this to me again.' What I should have said was—"

He gripped Kingsley by the back of the neck, hard enough to leave bruises and bring tears to Kingsley's eyes. He tilted Kingsley's head back, forcing his chin up.

"What I should have said," Søren repeated, "was 'You will *not* leave me again.' Will you?"

"No," Kingsley breathed, growing hard.

Søren smiled. "Good."

Then Kingsley was free. He caught his breath, met Søren's eyes, gave a small laugh. "That's all you had to say."

Søren returned to the piano bench and sat, long legs out and crossed at the ankle. Kingsley lightly kicked the bottom of his bare foot.

"You know, Nora will kill you when she finds out you're keeping this a secret from her," Kingsley said.

"Turnabout is fair play. She's keeping something from us, too, if you hadn't noticed."

Yes, he'd noticed.

"So you aren't trying to protect her?" Kingsley said. "You're just getting your revenge?"

Søren furrowed his brow. "You seem surprised by this."

"I love you."

"That," Søren said, "is also not a secret."

With a last smile, he turned back to his piano.

Kingsley asked, "Just out of curiosity, what other secrets are you keeping from me?"

Søren said nothing, only began to play the piano again.

Kingsley rolled his eyes and walked out into the winter night. Eventually he might learn a few more of Søren's secrets, but not all of them. A little mystery was always good for a romance.

On the way to his car, Kingsley caught himself smiling.

He was happy.

Very, very happy.

FIFTH MOVEMENT

MARCH CODA

Coda:

The concluding section of a dance.

SEVENTEEN

"WHAT'S THIS?" Nora asked as she was putting away their toys after a long, delicious session of pain play and sex. "Who gave you a Carnival mask?"

Søren had just come back into the bedroom after taking a shower. He was naked but for a white towel wrapped around his trim waist. No man lost in the Sahara had ever longed to lap up water as much as she wanted to lick the water droplets off Søren's strong, flat stomach.

"Souvenir from New Orleans. Kingsley bought it for me but decided it was too bizarre, even for him."

She looked at the mask a long time, then held it out to him. "Try it on."

He raised his eyebrow, but took the mask from her and put it on, tying it with black ribbons around the back of his head. "What do you think?"

Nora stared at the eerily faceless man standing before her and was suddenly very cognizant that she was on her knees.

"I've had dreams like this."

❄

LATER THAT NIGHT, Kingsley's phone buzzed in his pocket. He took it out and saw he had a message from Søren.

Two words.

Thank you.

He replied, *For what?*

He wasn't surprised by Søren's response.

It's a secret.

F<small>IN</small>.

WRAPPED IN BLACK

WRAPPED IN BLACK

AUTHOR'S NOTE

This novella takes place during and shortly after the events of the Original Sinners short story "Christmas in Suite 37A" (available in the collection Michael's Wings). This is the Unholy Trinity's first Christmas in New Orleans.

CHRISTMAS EVE

THE GIFTS under the Christmas tree were wrapped in black. Black paper, gold ribbons and bows. This was Juliette's doing, an homage to the New Orleans Saints football team, though really, more of a tribute to their new life here. Kingsley was attempting to learn to love American football, but whenever he and Juliette had a game on, he spent the entire time trying to guess which of the linebackers (wasn't that what they were called?) was one of Nora's clients. That was new to him, not knowing the identities of her clients anymore. Then again, since moving to New Orleans, everything seemed new. New city. New house. New life. And, of course, new fears. It must be the French in him that saw the black boxes under the tree as slightly sinister, like a gift from an enemy, a gift that was also a threat. Although, now that he thought of it...Søren in his clerical attire...sometimes the best gifts come wrapped in black.

He sipped his red wine, a *Rosanella* Syrah from his son Nico's winery, as he carefully placed the rest of Céleste's gifts under the tree. At least Juliette hadn't wrapped their daughter's gifts in all black. Hers were covered in playful paper—pink and white and red, printed with candy canes, snowmen, and dinosaurs. Dinosaurs? When did dinosaurs become a Christmas symbol? Were there dinosaurs in the manger and the Bible left that part out? Childhood was very different today these days. When he was a boy, his gifts were wrapped in brown paper with twine or last week's *Le Monde*.

With the presents tucked safely under the tree, he stood up, went through the library to the French doors (all of his doors were French doors, he told Juliette who only rolled her eyes) and looked out over the back lawn. It was December 24th, six in the evening, and Céleste was wearing a sundress on her swingset though the sun had set nearly an hour ago. Juliette was gently pushing the swing, not too high, never too high, but high enough to make their little girl laugh and squeal.

As he watched them, he caught himself smiling. Just smiling. Simple stupid happy grinning. He couldn't help it. When Céleste laughed, he smiled. When she squealed, he laughed. He had been wrong about many things in his life, but this he got right—he knew he wouldn't be truly happy until he was a father. Now he had two children—Céleste and Nico, one very much wanted, and one quite a surprise. For more reasons than one.

Ah, well, that was just how life happened, wasn't it? You got nothing for free in this world. Nora had found his son for him—the son he didn't know he had but had loved from the second he'd learned his name and seen his face—but Kingsley wasn't the only one who'd fallen in love at first sight. If Nico was to be believed, he'd fallen in love with Nora the day he'd met her. "Not," as Nico had said to his face, "that it is any of your business." Looking back, it wasn't terribly surprising. Young men tended to fall hard upon meeting *la Maîtresse*. The only surprise in the whole insane scenario was that Nora had actually tried to tell the boy no, and for months. Not that she'd succeeded, but Kingsley appreciated the attempt. Apparently her loyalty to him ran a little deeper than either of them would have believed.

He could be philosophical about it now, even amused. He hadn't been quite so philosophical about it at the time.

So he got a son but at the price of what he had with Nora. *C'est la vie.* He could live with that trade.

But what, then, was the price for his Céleste? Fear. Even now, as he watched her swing a little higher than he would have liked, he imagined her tumbling onto the ground, hitting her head, blood everywhere, a mad rush to the emergency room.

Luckily, gravity was on their side today, and she came safely down to Earth and into her mother's arms.

He opened the doors and let Juliette inside, Céleste thrown over her shoulder like a sack of flour.

"Hello, Papa," she said, waving as they passed. "I have to take a bath."

"You do," he said. "You're covered in grass. How did that happen?"

"Someone," Juliette said with an elegant arch of her eyebrows, "decided to make grass angels since there's no snow."

"Did it work?" Kingsley asked.

"No," Juliette said. "But she had fun trying. Anyone here yet?"

He took Céleste off Juliette's shoulder and lifted her over his head and back down into his arms. Any excuse to make her laugh. "Not yet. They're on their way."

"I'll be ready soon." Juliette kissed him on the cheek. He set Céleste onto her feet and watched Juliette lead her out of the sunroom and upstairs to her bathroom.

How had it happened so fast? Only yesterday, she was a baby in his arms, barely seven pounds. Now she was walking and talking and demanding Griffin Fiske read to her and play ballet with her and kiss her goodbye, which he'd done last night since he was flying back to New York today. It had been nice having Griffin around again, even if he was moping over the not-terribly-surprising breakup between him and his Michael. Odds were always good that the boys would break up at some point. The age difference. The class difference. Griffin's tendency to smother. Michael's hidden but steel-strong backbone that would bend only so far. No, he hadn't been surprised at all to hear that Griffin had finally found Michael's hard limits. And he certainly wouldn't be surprised if and when he heard they were back together. The course of true—especially—young love never did run smooth. He and Søren were proof of that.

Kingsley glanced at his watch. He really ought to change clothes. Yet he stayed by the French doors looking out at the empty swing-set. Empty now because Juliette had dragged their daughter up to her bath. But how long before it was empty because Céleste had outgrown it? Until she'd outgrown her sundress? Outgrown her little pink bed? Outgrown her Papa reading her bedtime stories every night? How long before she noticed her parents were not married? How long before she noticed the locks on the rooms in the house she wasn't allowed inside? How long before he had to explain the gun cabinet and what Papa used to do for a living? How long before she started to notice that Papa and Uncle Søren were—

"With that look on your face, I'm afraid to ask what you're thinking right now."

Kingsley turned. Søren stood in the open doorway to the library. He looked even more distinguished than usual in his tailored three-piece suit. As his pale blond hair faded to silver with every passing year, with the waistcoat, the stern, and intelligent eyes, he looked like the world's sexiest college professor. Made sense. Although still a Jesuit, he no longer had his own church but instead taught pastoral studies at Loyola.

"I'm thinking you look very handsome," Kingsley said. How

many of Søren's students were as madly in lust with the good Father Stearns as he was?

"Thank you," Søren said. "You're lying."

"I was thinking you look very handsome. You make me wish I'd gone to college. I would have loved fucking my professors."

"I'm sure they would have loved that as well. Now tell me what you were really thinking about."

It was an order, and Kingsley knew Søren expected him to obey it. He remembered a line from that stupid Grinch cartoon he'd watched with Céleste last night—He thought up a lie, and he thought it up quick.

"I was thinking about Nico," Kingsley said. "That I won't get to see him this Christmas. Maybe not any Christmas."

Søren gave him a look of sympathy. "Believe it or not, I know how you feel."

"I know you do. Your son doesn't know you exist and probably never will. My son wishes I never existed."

"That is not true."

"Ah, he doesn't completely despise me anymore. We'll call that progress."

"Do you blame me for not getting to see him more often?" Søren asked as he stepped into the room. "I promise, I haven't banned him from New Orleans because of his relationship with Eleanor. Though I've been tempted." He smiled to show he was joking even though Kingsley knew...he probably had been tempted.

"*Non*. I can go to him as easily as he can come to us. But I don't think he's ready to share the holidays with us yet. Us. Me."

Once he'd said it, Kingsley realized it was only a half-lie he'd told. He hadn't been thinking about Nico and Christmas right then, but it was something that privately weighed on his mind and had ever since he called Nico a month ago asking him to spend Christmas with them here. His son had been very polite when he'd said, *Non, merci.* No excuse. No explanation. Just *non.*

"I know your relationship with him is...complicated. To say the least," Søren said.

"Almost as complicated as yours."

Søren laughed ruefully. "I have no relationship with him at all. Which is a necessary evil, I suppose. To keep us both sane. It is a shame, though. When I divorce my feelings about him and Eleanor from who he is as a person...he's an impressive young man. What he's done with his life, his work ethic, his devotion to the family vineyard. Any father would be proud of have him for a son."

"Until he starts sleeping with your ex-domme."

"Until then, of course." Søren raised his eyebrows.

Kingsley walked over to him, stood facing him. All the better to see his eyes and what secrets they were keeping. "How are you doing with that?"

"Eleanor and Nico? Fair is fair. I'm in no position to judge."

"That's a non-answer."

"Yes, it was," Søren said. "Either I can give you the real answer, or you can kiss me."

"I can't kiss you. You're better dressed than I am." Kingsley had a suit upstairs waiting for him, but he was still in his jeans and white button-down. Very appropriate for a day at home with his daughter. Not nearly as appropriate for Christmas Eve dinner.

"Doesn't happen very often," Søren said.

"I'll change, then I'll kiss you. Ten minutes."

He started out of the library. Søren put his hand on the doorframe blocking Kingsley as he tried to pass by him.

Søren said, "Kiss first."

There was no arguing with his tone.

Kingsley heard the water running upstairs in the bath. Odds were low that Céleste would see them...

With a grin—a very different one than he wore when watching his daughter on the swing set—he lifted his chin and waited. Søren brought his hands to Kingsley's neck, the thumbs stroking his jawline... The slight but firm pressure of those hands on his neck instantly raised Kingsley's heart rate, sent his blood pumping.

Breathless, he waited until Søren had made him wait long enough. Their lips met in a kiss, soft, growing harder, heavier as Søren slipped his tongue into his mouth and Kingsley returned the compliment. Søren even pushed him gently against the door frame, back to the wood. This wasn't a hello kiss between old lovers but a wet, hot kiss that belonged to the night with no clothes between them and no chance of interruption. The kiss went on, going deeper, getting hotter. Søren pushed his hips into Kingsley's, pressing him even harder against the doorframe.

And then it was over, just like that. Søren broke the kiss and stood back and waved his arm as if to say, You are now dismissed.

Kingsley stared at him, then sighed. "Sadist."

"It's why you love me."

"True, true," Kingsley said as he walked—painfully, due to the erection—away. "It's also why I hate you."

He heard Søren laughing softly as he started up the stairs.

NORA WOULD NEVER GET USED to Decembers in New Orleans. Christmas Eve and the high was sixty-seven. With Griffin gone back to New York, she had her house to herself again. Not that Griffin would have complained to see her walking around the house in her bra and panties, trying to remember where she put all of her cocktail gowns.

Finally, she found them in the back of the closet in the guest room—a row of black and red dresses she hadn't worn in months. Oh, and a pair of Griffin's boxer briefs somehow laying draped over the closet bar. She tossed them over her shoulder and onto the guest bed. She flipped through her dresses over and over again, trying to decide which one would be just the right amount of slutty for Christmas Eve. Briefly she entertained the fantasy of sticking Griff's underwear in an envelope and mailing them back to him. Instead, she'd just keep them for the next time he came to visit, hopefully with Michael if they worked things out and got back together. Which they would, she hoped. Well, Griffin had promised to call her and let her know what happened with their big dinner date tonight. Funny, it was like Griffin sensed something about her and Nico's secret relationship. He was twelve years older than Michael, and a few nights before he'd left for New York, he'd asked her if she thought there was any hope for something long-term when you were in love with a younger man.

Or, Griffin had wondered, had it all been doomed from the start?

She'd been very tempted then to tell him everything about Nico. She couldn't bring herself to do it while Griffin was staying with her, though. The number of questions he would have asked about the whole thing...she would have had to gag the man just to keep her sanity. And Nico's privacy. Privacy was not a concept Griffin Fiske had much use for. He would have put up billboards of him and Michael after they fell in love if Michael had allowed it, which he wouldn't have.

And someone really needed to tell Griffin about Kingsley and Søren, too. Both of them had mentioned that Griffin needed to be told before he found out some other way and was

wounded for life. It would have hurt her, too, in his position.
Griffin had taken over Kingsley's place in New York, running
the 8th Circle. Basically, he was the new—and much less scary
—King of the Underground. He'd be crushed to discover they
didn't trust him with something as important as King and
Søren's relationship, hers and Nico's. Well, she'd tell him later if
she needed to distract him from the heartbreak of things not
going as well with Michael as he'd hoped.

After looking at every dress twelve times, Nora finally
decided on a sequined black cocktail dress with a plunging
neckline. Slutty, yes, but also the sequins made it sort of Christ-
mas-y. She'd just stand by the Christmas tree lights and let them
reflect off of her.

This was a lot of effort for a simple Christmas Eve dinner
among friends. But this was the one thing Juliette had asked
from them for Christmas. She wanted to celebrate with a traditional, formal *Réveillon de Noël* with all of them. And Nora had
to admit, she didn't hate the thought of seeing Søren in his
three-piece suit.

Nora got dressed in her bathroom. She wore her hair down
but with a silver barrette and matching chandelier earrings,
subtle make-up but for her red, red lips, and her favorite shiny
black pumps with the ankle straps. Søren had a strange predilection for those shoes. He liked to strip her naked except for the
shoes and flog her senseless. Then in bed, he'd undo the ankle
straps with his teeth. Whenever she wore the shoes, it was an
open invitation for him to come back to her house and do just
that.

Except...with all those oysters she planned on eating...sex
might not be medically advisable. Oysters might be an aphrodisiac, but not when you ate your weight in them.

She decided to wear a different pair of heels. No ankles
straps. Just in case.

Kingsley's house was one street over, and she could walk there via the alley that separated their backyards. But not in these shoes. She'd have to drive. As she was leaving through the back door in the kitchen, her phone started vibrating inside her clutch handbag.

She didn't get many phone calls. Her clients sent texts since they knew better than to call her. And on Christmas Eve? Probably spam. She dug her phone out anyway, then smiled.

Nico.

"Hi, Moosh," she said when she answered.

He replied with a laugh. "It's good to hear your voice."

"You could hear it more if you called me more often."

"I like our letters."

Letters. He was the most old-fashioned young man she'd ever met. He wanted letters, handwritten. Calls were only for exceptional occasions.

"I do like our letters, yes, but it's good to hear your voice, too. Merry Christmas."

"*Joyeux Noël.*"

"You're up late." It must have been one in the morning in France.

"Christmas party. And I am a little drunk, and I miss you."

"I miss you, too. I love when you drunk dial me, but I'm on my way to your father's house for our Christmas party."

"Is he going? Or will he be at church?"

He. Søren. Nico preferred to refer to him obliquely. She knew how he felt.

"He's going. He doesn't celebrate mass as often now that he's teaching." There was a priest shortage in America, Nora knew, but not in New Orleans.

"Is he spending the night with you?"

Nora sighed. "Do you really want me to answer that?"

"No. Yes. No." He was quiet for a moment, then, "Yes."

"You are drunk, aren't you?"

"It's Christmas."

"He's spending the night."

"Bad Christmas."

"If it makes you feel any better, I plan to eat so much food tonight that sex would be a danger to both him and me."

"*Merci.*" He sighed. "I just wish it was me spending Christmas in bed with you. Not him."

Nora laughed. "Nico, you know how this works. He's the very forbearing husband I'm not actually married to, and you are my delicious concubine."

"Am I delicious?"

"Nico, if you remember, I once drank your semen out of a wine glass."

"Oh, I remember. I remember that about ten times a day," he said.

"You know I love talking to you, but I really have to go or I'll be late for dinner. Did you need me or just want me?"

"I need you. I was looking at pictures of you on my phone."

"I approve of that pastime," Nora said. "And...?"

"And I had an idea."

The way he said "idea" made her feel like she felt when Søren's teeth grazed her ankle.

Nora was intrigued. "I like ideas. Tell me."

"I know this will sound crazy, but, ah, you know how I'm going to New York next week? The meeting with our new investors?"

"You told me."

"I have a free night. I can fly down," he said.

"What? To New Orleans?"

"I have time. There's a direct flight. I would have to leave at ten the next morning, but I could do it. We'd have the whole night."

Nora smiled. She saw her smile reflected in the glass of the kitchen window. It looked like the smile the Grinch made when he had a wonderful, awful idea.

"I can do a lot with one night," she said. "But I have to ask You-Know-Who."

"Will he say yes?"

"He'll immediately remind me that I was just in France last month, and that I'm seeing you again in a few weeks." She already had plans to see Nico in January in France, which was the deal she and Søren had struck. Four months a year with Nico, one month a season. The rest of the year she belonged to him and only him.

"But your next visit is far away. Very far. Very very very very very very far. Weeks." Oh yes, he was definitely more than a little drunk.

"He'll also remind me that the deal was that you two don't encroach on each other's time with me. That was the custody arrangement."

"So it's a no?"

"It's a maybe."

"Only if you want to."

One in the morning. Nico would be in his bedroom. Probably naked under the covers. All young and firm and beautiful and warm and hard...

She wanted to. Very much. Very very very very very very much.

"Answer this question—what were you doing while you were looking at pictures of me?"

He laughed softly. "You know."

"On our Lord's birthday?"

"He gets to celebrate. So do I."

She wished he could see her smile. "I love you, Moosh."

"I love you, too."

"Merry Christmas," she said. "I'll let you know what his Lordship says."

Nora hung up, went into the bathroom, and checked herself in the mirror. She only hoped that the red in her cheeks would be attributed to the cool evening air when she got to Kingsley's house.

She needed that cool evening air to keep her from sweating as she walked as fast as she could in her pumps to Kingsley's house. If she was late, Søren, Juliette, or King would ask her why.

Oh, because Nico was drunk and masturbating in bed and decided to call me to see if I'd fuck him next week if he flew in from New York for a night.

That would go over like a house on fire.

SHE MADE it to the gate at seven on the dot, made it to the door at 7:01, and let herself in. After hanging her coat up in, she peeked into Kingsley's grand living room. It looked beautiful. The giant Christmas tree covered in white lights made a beautiful bright contrast to the dark, antique French furniture. They'd removed the Persian rug that usually covered the dark hardwood floors and replaced it with an enormous white fur rug that made the room appear as if had snowed inside the house. Juliette, dressed in a short shimmery off-the-shoulder gold cocktail dress, was taking Christmas pictures of Céleste, who was sitting prettily in the middle of the rug while *"Petit Papa Noël"* played in the background on the antique record player.

Nora stayed in the entryway, watching, not wanting to distract Céleste while she was actually holding still for a minute or two. She could hear voices coming from the kitchen—the caterers Juliette had hired. A step squeaked behind her, and she looked up to see Søren descending the staircase.

She put her finger to her lips to indicate that the photo session was still in progress.

He came to her and kissed her on the cheek. "Your cheeks are flushed. Why is that?" he said softly into her ear.

"It's cold out. Your lips are a little red. Why is that?"

"I had a sip of red wine."

"Are you lying, sir?"

"Are you?"

"Probably, knowing me."

"Then we're even."

He kissed her to stop her laughing. When the kiss ended, Céleste was running toward them. Nora picked her up and spun her.

"Merry Christmas, baby girl."

"You're pretty, *Tante* Elle," Céleste said in her little girl voice with her sweet little French accent.

"So are you." She put Céleste on her feet and watched her spin in circles, making her tulle skirt float around her. It must have made her dizzy because she started to fall over. Søren caught her before she hit the ground and picked her up. She wrapped her arms around his neck and squeezed like an octopus.

"Good catch," Nora said.

Søren quickly and efficiently peeled Céleste off of him and set her on her feet.

Juliette came into the grand entryway with a sigh. "It's time to go upstairs, my love."

This announcement did not go over well. Juliette reached for Céleste's hand, but the little girl wasn't having it. She dug in her heels, and her mother was forced to pick her up and carry her.

Céleste bellowed—there was no other word for it—all the way upstairs. No amount of soothing by Juliette could calm her. Céleste's night nanny met them at the top of the stairs and carried the still-screaming toddler to her bedroom.

Nora shook her head, blinked. Her ears were ringing.

"God, I'm so glad I don't have kids," she said without thinking. Søren's expression didn't change, but something flickered across his eyes. "Søren—"

"It's fine," he said quickly, too quickly. Nora kicked herself quietly. Søren's son Fionn was a tender subject. Sometimes she wondered if being around Céleste made it better or worse.

"I'm sorry. I shouldn't have said that."

"You're allowed to say anything you want," he said. "Unless you're gagged." He bent and kissed her cheek again. "Let's find the wine."

They knew exactly where to find the wine—in the living room at the wet bar. That's also where they found King.

"Red? White?" King asked as he poured himself a red. He was looking handsome as usual in a dark blue Armani suit, one of his favorites.

"White," Nora said. "White before dinner. Red during. Bourbon after. Speaking of...when do we get to eat?"

"Soon. Hungry?"

"I've been starving myself all day to make room for oysters. And turkey. And dessert. What's for dessert?"

"Whatever you can think of," King said, "Jules probably ordered it."

"I love that woman," Nora said.

As King poured the wine, Nora went to fetch the gifts she'd left in the entryway. She took them to the tree and tossed them unceremoniously onto the tree skirt.

"Socks, again?" King asked. He sat on the burgundy sofa, an

arm thrown casually over the back, legs crossed and his wine glass in his hand.

"Always," she said, standing up. "You two are impossible to buy anything but socks for. You—" She pointed at King, "can buy yourself anything you want. And you—" She pointed at Søren, "don't want anything."

"I can always use more black socks," Søren said. He stood by the fireplace mantel where a low fire burned, more for show than warmth. This was probably the first night King and Juliette had actually used their fireplace.

"It's getting a little boring, just buying you two socks every year. And what did you get me?" Nora asked King.

"I'm letting you date my son. That is your Christmas gift from now through eternity." King stood up, walked over to the record player, and swapped out Nat King Cole's "O Little Town of Bethlehem" for Dean Martin's "Let it Snow!"

"Ah, fine. What about you?" she demanded of Søren.

"Same." He smiled behind his wine glass.

"Assholes," she said, dropping into the armchair and crossing her ankles on top of the ottoman. She wanted to make sure Søren saw the shoes. No ankle straps. No sex tonight unless he thought of something better than socks for Christmas. "We should do something more fun for gift exchange than socks and first-born sons."

"What did you have in mind?" King turned around to face her. He was always up for a challenge. "I hope you're not going to say White Elephant. Does it look like we're a women's book club?"

"Just so you know, I've gone on some pretty stellar benders with women's book clubs. Show some respect."

He raised his hands in surrender.

"The white elephant gift has an interesting history," Søren said. "Shame it's become so... what's the word?"

"*Bourgeois?*" King offered and drank his wine.

Nora said, "Lame."

"The story is that the King of Thailand," Søren said, "would give gifts of elephants painted white to the people he wished to honor. Of course, everyone wanted the king to honor them, but...what do you do with a white elephant? Since the elephant was a gift from the king, you couldn't put it to work in your fields. It was an expensive pet. A blessing and a curse."

"So it was something you wanted but also didn't want at the same time," Nora said.

Søren nodded. "Exactly. I have no idea how it's become a game where people pawn off their worst trinkets and knick-knacks on each other. I thought that was what the St. Vincent de Paul charities were for."

A thought occurred to Nora, one that might send her careening straight to Hell if she happened to choke to death on an oyster tonight. But it was such a good—well, terrible—idea she couldn't resist. Especially if it meant getting Søren to allow her to see Nico next week.

"Let's do that then," Nora said as an idea came to her.

"A White Elephant Exchange?" Søren asked.

"Better," she said. "Cursed gifts."

"What?" King said. "Are you serious?"

Søren glared at her. "Eleanor, you haven't started practicing Voodoo, have you? We talked about that before we moved here."

She looked at them both. Cowards. "Come on, it'll be fun. Not actual cursed gifts. Just gifts that hurt. Hurt to give and hurt to receive, but you still want it."

"Ah, sadomasochistic gifts," King said, nodding. "Intriguing."

"Right? We'll give each other gifts that A—the other person wants, but B—also doesn't want, and C—hurts the giver to give."

"You mean like Nico?" King said, grinning rather menacingly at her.

She ignored the look. "Exactly. You let me date your son, which I want, but I didn't want it. For the record, I did not go looking for him for that reason at all, I swear on a stack of Bibles and ask Zach Easton if you do not believe me. He was there."

"I know, I know," King said and raised his hand in surrender. "Still."

"And you let me have him," Nora said, "although it hurt. Yes?"

King laughed softly. "Yes," he said and took a very long drink of his wine. "I'm all for it. I'd like to see what you come up with to give me. And you, especially—" He looked at Søren.

"I already have ideas galore," Søren said and gave King a look that would scare most men. King was not most men, however. And the brief look they shared was so intimate and personal, Nora knew she shouldn't have seen it.

King wrenched his eyes from Søren, turned to her again. "Are we planning this for next year?"

"Why not this year?" Nora said with a shrug. "We're Catholic."

"Speak for yourself," King said. "I'm a heathen."

"In the Catholic calendar," Søren said to Kingsley in the tone of a teacher lecturing a particularly stupid child, "Christmastide began today and ends on the Feast of the Baptism of Our Lord. Which is January eleventh—"

"See? There you go," Nora said. "Want to?"

King swirled the wine in the bottom of his glass. "If we're doing this, I'll need more wine."

"I admit I'd be curious to see what you two come up with for me," Søren said. "By curious, I mean slightly terrified."

"You are not," she said. He only smiled. "So... Are we in?"

"You know what you're getting me?" King asked.

"No idea. Do you know what you're getting him?" She pointed at Søren.

"Not a clue. Though it will be fun to think of something."

Nora held up her hands. "Shall we?"

"I'll play," Søren said. "If only to see what you have up your sleeve, Little One."

"Come on, Bad King Wenceslas," Nora said. "Want to play?"

He stood by the tree, wine glass in hand, a thoughtful expression on his face.

"More fun than socks," he said. He picked up a gift from under the tree and held it. A small black box. "Cursed gifts. Wrapped in black." He put the box back under the tree and turned to look at Søren.

"I'm in," King said.

"What are you in?" Juliette demanded as she swept into the living room. "Or do I not want to know?"

Nora quickly explained the game. Juliette listened in wide-eyed silence that might have been wide-eyed horror.

"Only you three," Juliette said, shaking her head. "Instead of a white elephant, it's black and blue. Of course you three would find a way to turn Christmas gift-giving into a mind game."

Nora grinned fiendishly, "Want to play with us?"

"*Non, non, non, non, non,*" she said, shaking her head and waving her hand. "I'm no sadist. And what I want for Christmas is what I want for every Christmas."

"Jewelry," King said.

"Exactly," she said. King pulled her into his arms and kissed her. "You know me well."

"All right, just the three of us then," Nora looked at Søren and then King.

"I only have one question," Søren said. "Will I still get my black socks?"

CHRISTMAS

THE DINNER PARTY ended shortly before midnight. Søren walked to St. Mary's, a Catholic Church only a few blocks away for midnight mass. Nora might have gone with him but didn't want anyone seeing them together. Søren knew too many of the other priests in town to take the risk. They'd all had too much to drink, so King walked her back to her house. The Garden District was safe, more or less. Still, no city was perfectly safe for a woman to walk alone after midnight, even on Christmas. Nico had actually threatened to buy her a guard dog since she insisted on walking alone in the evenings.

King escorted her all the way to the front door, which was very gallant of him. They stood beneath the oak tree in her front yard, festooned with Mardi Gras beads. She hadn't put the beads in there, but they always seemed to multiply. Søren thought she had a secret admirer in the neighborhood, but she guessed local drunks saw her tree and made a game of throwing their beads into the branches.

She expected him to kiss her cheek and head home right away, but he lingered. Clearly, he had something he wanted to say to her. She waited, tense.

"Was that my son you were texting with after dinner? You were smiling at your phone," he said.

No surprise King would have noticed that. He found phones at the dinner table the height of rudeness. Not that it ever stopped her.

"No, actually. It was Griffin. He was telling me that he and Michael worked things out." She opened her bag to get her keys, but she was ready to show him her phone if he doubted her.

"Ah, good for him." He looked a little suspicious. "That was a long text exchange for just that."

"I may have caught him up to speed on a few other things."

"You told him about Nico? Finally?"

He didn't seem angry about that, so Nora admitted to it. "Griff would have been really hurt if he'd found out from anyone but me. And since it seems like it might last a while…"

He nodded. "True."

She braced herself for another confession. "And…I might have let him in on you and Søren. He kind of needs to know that, too."

There were secrets you could keep from your friends, but something like this—being in a serious long-term relationship with someone—wasn't one of them.

Kingsley glanced away, his dark brown eyes reflecting the Christmas lights hanging on her porch.

"He knew a little already. It's hard to talk about, you know. What I am."

"What you are is Griffin's hero. And Griffin has never looked down on a switch in his life." She poked him in the upper arm. "Except if they're on the floor, and he's flogging them."

"Fair, fair."

She waited. He didn't leave. The night was cold now, but

she didn't mind it after all the food and the wine and the fireplace burning at King's house.

"I'm not angry about Nico, you know," he said.

"You aren't?" She leaned back against the door.

"Not anymore. I don't know if Nico told you this, but he said he wouldn't have agreed to have any sort of relationship with me unless you were part of the arrangement. He also paints you as the victim of his uncontrollable passions."

"He's a manipulative little motherfucker sometimes. Have you noticed?" she asked.

"I've noticed. Gets it from me. One of his finer qualities."

"Definitely. Does that mean you'll be getting me a different cursed gift this year?"

King shook his head from side to side as if he were shaking a Magic 8 Ball and the answer was...

"No."

"Fine, fine. After all, Nico is the gift that keeps on giving. And giving—"

"Stop. *Arrêt!*"

Sometimes Nora just couldn't help herself. "I will get you something, though. If I can think of anything mischievous enough." She grinned.

"I shiver at the very thought. See you at breakfast. Late breakfast. Ten."

"We'll be there."

He kissed her goodnight, one little air kiss on each cheek. A very different kiss from how he used to say goodnight. Not even the notorious Nora Sutherlin, she told herself, was deviant enough to sleep with a father and his son in the same week. Except for that one time when she was twenty-nine. And she didn't count that. He was technically a stepson.

Søren slipped through the back door of her house shortly

before one a.m. Nora was awake and waiting for him. She left her bed and went downstairs to greet him in the kitchen.

"How was church?" she asked after kissing him.

"Fine. Too much hugging. And I would have given a better homily."

"Of course you would. Let's go to bed. I'm exhausted from eating literally everything in the entire world." She started to leave the kitchen and return to bed when Søren gently gripped her by the arm and pulled her back to him.

"What do you want for Christmas?"

"World peace."

He glared at her. "You forget I know you. You came up with that game because you already have a gift in mind, don't you?"

"Maybe."

He took her chin in her hand and forced her to nod her head.

"All right. I do."

"What is it? I know I don't want to know, but that's the game."

She told him about Nico's meeting in New York next week, with the new investors in his winery, how he had a free night and could fly down to New Orleans. One night only.

"You're seeing him next month," Søren said.

"I told him you would say that."

"We have an arrangement."

"I also told him you'd say that." She ran her fingers through his hair, cupped the back of his neck, rose on tiptoes, and put her mouth to his ear. "You forget, I also know you."

She stood back on her feet and looked at him, arms crossed over her chest. This was deliberate. Her black nightgown was low cut, and by crossing her arms under her breasts, she created what she hoped was some distracting cleavage. Søren was a sadist with a singular predilection for pain, but, and this was a fact, even sadists liked tits.

"I'm not sure this gift would qualify under the terms of the game," he said. "It hurts me to give it to you, and it's something you want, but how is it also something you don't want?"

She met his eyes in the dark of the kitchen. "Because I don't want to hurt you. And it does. I wasn't going to tell you until after Christmas. But..." She took his hand in hers, squeezed his fingers, "you asked."

"I asked." He smiled rather ruefully at himself. Clearly, he regretted asking.

"While I'm with Nico, you can beat the shit out of King."

"I'm sure I will. And you, too."

She put her hands on his shoulders, looked up at him. "If it helps, he's much more jealous of you than you are of him."

"Is that so?"

"He never asks about us because he can't stand hearing the details. But he was relieved when I told him I was going to eat way too much tonight for us to fuck."

"You did eat an impressive, almost a concerning amount of oysters."

"Juliette went to all that trouble. So...is it a yes? I can tell him to book his flight?"

He took a moment before answering. She knew he already had his answer, but he was making her wait for it because he was a sadist, and because he could.

"Yes."

She smiled with relief. "Thank you, sir."

"But—"

"Oh, fuck."

"You will pay for my generosity."

She laughed softly. "Of course I will."

"Right now."

"What? It's after one in the morning. And I ate too much. I'm bloated and borderline nauseous. You can't stuff anything else into my body. There's no room."

Søren looked up as if trying to remember something. Then he simply said, "I don't care."

Nora winced. She wanted to get tied up and flogged right now about as much as she wanted to go running. Exhausted, stuffed, and she'd already told Nico she and Søren weren't going to have sex tonight. Which she'd made the mistake of telling him.

"Don't worry," Søren said. "I'll be gentle and quick."

"I don't believe that at all."

He took her by the wrist—gently, she had to admit—and pulled her into the living room. The urge to dig in her heels like Céleste was strong, but she gave in. Such was the plight of the submissive.

"But...it's Christmas."

"AS A CATHOLIC PRIEST, I am very familiar with the date," he said.

"You're really going to make me do kink on Christmas?"

"Christmas used to be such a hedonistic festival of sex and drinking that the Puritans banned its celebration. Let's say we're having an old-fashioned Christmas." He stood by the Christmas tree, the lights still on, and took off his suit jacket. The sight of him standing there in his elegant black vest, white shirt sleeves, tie still perfectly knotted, and a look in his eyes that said he would tolerate no argument...that helped.

He stood her one foot in front of him and held up a finger to indicate she should wait while he did whatever evil, awful thing he was going to do. What he did was bend down to take a present out from under the tree.

"You said too much hugging at church tonight, and now you want to fuck?"

"You know I don't like being touched except by you and Kingsley. And I don't, as you say, want to fuck. I want to make you suffer. And then fuck."

"You can't say 'fuck' at Christmas."

"You started it." He handed her a small box with her name on it. "Open it."

"If I have to."

"Little One."

"If I have to, sir." She had to. With a long sigh, she tore the red ribbon off and then the white paper. She had no idea what was in the box. It was about the size of a necklace box but a little too heavy.

Taking off the lid, she thought it might be a necklace after all. She saw chain links. Then she realized what she was looking at.

"Oh, joy. Nipple clamps."

She hadn't worn nipple clamps in a long time. They were more of King's thing than Søren's. Well, tonight they were clearly Søren's thing. He lifted the long silver chain out of the box. At each end were two clamps, wicked-looking and heavy. Softly he wrapped the long chain around her neck so she could feel the cold metal against her throat.

But the box wasn't empty.

Inside it was a silver ball—a silver bell?—small with a clip on the end.

Søren hung the little ball onto a pine needle on her tree. He only smiled.

Slowly he gathered the folds of her nightgown in his large hands and drew it up, up, up her body until she had to raise her arms. He pulled it over her head and tossed it lightly onto her sofa.

Now she stood naked in front of the Christmas tree. She hoped no Puritans were outside her house watching.

Søren went down on his knees in front of her.

"Never should have gotten my clit hood pierced," Nora said with a sigh. Now she knew what the little ball was. A weight.

"Are you whining? The great Mistress Nora, the dominatrix of dominatrixes, is whining?" Søren's voice was full of amused disdain.

"Guess what? Dominatrixes whine. Dominatrixes do whatever they want to do. That's why we're dominatrixes."

"I'm a sadist," he said. "We do whatever you don't want us to do. That's why we're sadists."

Nora groaned as he lightly fingered the little loop that pierced the folds of her clitoral hood. Blood rushed to her labia. Her breathing quickened. He was making her wet already.

There was just something wrong with being wet on Christmas.

Søren spoke his orders softly. *Spread your legs a little. Tilt your hips forward. Stop complaining, or I really will gag you.*

"I have recurring dreams where I'm telling the pope about the wicked shit you've been doing to me for the past twenty years. One of these days, I'm going to do it."

"Give my regards to His Holiness." Carefully he pulled on her piercing, holding it between his index finger and thumb. She moaned as her clitoris slowly woke and began to throb. He took the tiny silver ball off the branch, and by the light of the Christmas tree—oh, they were going to Hell for this—he clipped it onto her ring. It was about the size of a marble but heavier, and as he slowly let the ring go, she felt the weight of it pulling her clit hood. It hurt. Not agony. More like sensation, tugging.

If that wasn't enough, Søren leaned in and flicked the ball with his tongue. For a split second it was weightless, and then it came down again, feeling even heavier. Nora groaned softly.

Søren came up to his feet and walked in a circle around her as if inspecting her body. He seemed to like what he saw. He came to a stop behind her. She shivered as he ran his hands down both her arms until he reached her wrists. He took them in his hands and brought her arms up and behind her head. With her hands clasped behind her neck, she could only stand and wait while he stroked her body. Her sides, her hips, her stomach, and then, of course, her breasts. He cupped them, and she knew what was coming. He didn't disappoint. He took her nipples between his fingers and pinched them. Not too hard but hard enough, the pleasure grazed against pain. As if he had all the time in the world, he toyed with her nipples, pinching and rubbing them until her breasts felt heavy and her nipples were hard as diamonds.

Nora panted quietly as Søren brought his hands to the chain around her neck. She thought he planned to take it off, but instead, he pulled it tighter until she felt the cool links of the silver chain biting into her throat. Just for a moment, just for a breath or two or three, she felt the fear of suffocation, of choking. He let her feel it. She knew he wanted her to feel it. If that's what he wanted, she would give it to him, gasping his name once and quietly, a warning they were at the edge of what she could take.

And then it was over.

Søren tenderly kissed the top of her head, whispered, "Good girl."

God damn him, Nora thought. He could choke her and then make it feel like a point of pride she'd endured it all. And the insane thing was...it did make her proud of herself. Proud and aroused.

He was aroused, too. Hard. His cock pressed against her hip. He slowly, teasingly drew the silver chain off her, letting it slither over her naked skin.

One at a time, he cupped her breasts and placed the little clamps onto her stiff and throbbing nipples. Cold metal. Hot skin. Pressure like tiny teeth biting into her flesh. Before, she hadn't wanted this at all. Now she wanted nothing else but this.

Søren gripped her by the back of the neck and forced her to bend over. Thank God he hadn't ordered her to keep her hands behind her head. Nora placed her hands on the arm of the couch to steady herself for what was about to come.

"Wider," Søren said, and she knew he meant her legs. She spread her legs wider. His fingers found her labia, the little ball, and he toyed with it. Then he released it again, and she cried out as the weight made itself keenly felt on her clitoris.

"How on earth does a priest buy nipple clamps?"

"Griffin is useful sometimes," Søren said. "Not often, but sometimes. Wider. Arch your back."

She spread her thighs even wider and arched her back until she gave Søren a view of her cunt rarely seen except by her OB/GYN. Søren took his cock out and let it brush against her ass.

And all by the light of the Christmas tree.

The tip of Søren's penis pushed up against her labia. He guided it through her wet and swollen folds until it kissed the entrance of her body. He'd either slam it in with a single forceful thrust or enter her so slowly it would be equally torturous. As wet as she was now, she almost wanted the first. But of course, he would go slow. She felt the tip sink inside her, thick and pushing. He went in slowly. Slowly enough that she felt every inch as it slid in and up until it grazed her cervix. He still gripped the back of her neck. The bruise she'd have there would last a week. His other arm held her around the waist, keeping her in place. Her breasts ached from the bite of the clamps and the weight of the chain. Her clitoris was swollen and throbbing.

"God," she breathed. "I guess oysters really are an aphrodisiac."

Søren kissed the back of her neck. "You are an aphrodisiac."

HIS ENTRANCE into her might have been slow, but the next thrust was fast, rough, and deep. No more talking now. No more teasing. Just fucking. Quiet but for her soft cries and his hoarse breaths. He drove his cock into her again and again with no consideration for her comfort or pleasure. She wasn't comfortable at all, not bent over, spread out, and weighted down as she was. But there was pleasure. The pain gave her pleasure. The flood of sensations gave her pleasure. Her feet bare on the soft rug, her hair falling into her face, brushing her cheeks, his scent like the delicious distant smell of fireplace smoke in winter—it all gave her pleasure. And most of all, the thick cock that moved so deeply and easily into her slick hole. He worked her onto his cock with the grip on her neck. It had been a long time since he'd fucked her this roughly. The price she paid for seeing Nico. Worth it. It would have been worth it even if Søren had told her no.

The muscles inside her tightened, began to pulse around him. Every thrust stretched her back open again, pushed back against the tensing, clenching walls of her vagina. His hand moved from her stomach to between her legs. His fingers found the weight. He cupped her vulva with his palm, and the heat of his hand on her clitoris made her moan like a whore.

With a cry of release she couldn't stifle, she came all around him. A stream of hot fluids filled her and filled her.

After her orgasm, she went limp. Her head was dizzy. Her eyes couldn't focus. Søren slowly pulled his penis from her body. All the sadism had been spent along with his come. He was kind to her now, careful, gently pulling her up and around to face him. His warm mouth sought hers and found it. His tongue went deep, and she opened her mouth to take it all.

The kiss was drugging. She was almost ready to be fucked again when he broke it off. He cupped her again between her legs, pushed two fingers up and into her semen-slicked vagina.

"Mine," he said simply. "Mine to keep. Mine to give away."

There was only one thing to say to that.

"Yours."

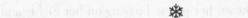

HE MADE her wear the nipples clamps until they were in her bed together. His naked body pressed against hers. She lay on her back, hands behind her head again as he removed the clamps. He massaged her sore nipples with his fingers and then, of course, with his mouth and his tongue. He was going to make her sleep with the weight on her clit ring. As long as she was laying down, she could barely feel it. But every time his hand strayed between her legs and he touched it, she inhaled sharply and was aroused all over again.

Using only his hand, he gave her another orgasm. Three fingers inside her body still full and dripping with his sperm. He opened her and stroked the quivering hollow above her pubic bone, working her until she lifted her hips into the air, froze in a final moment of climax before crying out and collapsing back onto the bed.

She might have fallen asleep right then if she hadn't heard Søren laughing quietly in her ear.

"It's not funny," she said. "I really had no interest in doing that tonight."

"Yes, I noticed you hated every moment of it."

"You know, no means no."

"For vanilla people," he reminded her. "With us, no means yes and your safe word means no. If you really didn't want to, you should have safed out."

"Yeah, but then you would have stopped."

He laughed again, louder, and then drew her across his chest. "I love you, Little One."

"Even when I'm a big whore with no self-respect where your cock is concerned?"

"Especially then."

"You're a bit of—" She was about to call Søren a whore himself when she heard her phone buzzing on her nightstand. "God, it's Christmas. Someone better have died and willed me a billion dollars."

She slapped her hand on her phone, brought it to her face. Blinking, she saw it was Griffin again.

"Griffin says he and Mick are still laughing about you and Kingsley getting together finally."

Søren made a sort of groaning sound, which she translated as, Everything I've ever done in my life I regret if it means I have to put up with Griffin's good-natured ribbing.

"I'm so pleased we can provide amusement for the two of them."

"I'm telling him to go to sleep. Apparently, he just fucked Michael half to death."

"Surely an exaggeration."

"I'll tell him you said that," Nora said, quickly typing out the message.

It was Michael who replied from his phone. "He's not exaggerating."

"Why is every man I know horny out of his mind tonight?" Nora asked. A rhetorical question. "This is not what the Lord intended for his birthday. Poor Juliette. Who knows what King is doing to her right this second."

"I doubt she's complaining. Bedtime, Eleanor."

"I'm telling him goodnight, I promise," she said, finishing the message. Another one quickly came back to her.

Goodnight, Griffin texted. *Merry Christmas. Give the Big Guy another hug for me.*

She showed the message to Søren. He groaned again. "Please no more hugs. Strangers hugged at Mass tonight."

"Need a Silkwood shower?" Nora asked as she obediently turned her phone off and tossed it across the room into the dirty laundry basket.

"Please." He was joking but she knew he wasn't really joking.

"I noticed you did pry Céleste off of you pretty quickly tonight," Nora said. She knew she was treading in dangerous waters here but felt like it was something that needed to be addressed. Especially after her stupid offhand remark about being glad she didn't have kids.

"Does Céleste make you think of Fionn?" Nora asked.

"Every child I see makes me think of Fionn."

"Is that why you don't like her hugging you?"

He didn't answer at first. She tensed, waited. She knew she shouldn't push him to answer.

"Part of it," he began, "is simply because I'm a priest. With all the scandals, I have a knee-jerk reaction to children touching me. I try to keep my distance as much as possible."

"What's the other part? I know you don't like being touched."

Again, he fell quiet. Outside the house she heard wind

blowing through her oak tree. A strand of Mardi Gras beads rattled against the window.

"If I'm honest with myself," Søren said finally, "I don't think that's the case really. I say it is, but it's more that I don't know *how* to be touched in a way that isn't sexual. I suppose that's a natural byproduct of only letting two people ever touch me, the two people I regularly have sex with." He paused, took a breath. "It's hard to explain. I promise I don't feel anything sexual when Griffin tries to hug me. Or Céleste. Or anyone but you and Kingsley. It's only that...I only understand being touched sexually, and when someone touches me for any other reason, it feels wrong. I don't know what to feel when someone wants to hug me just because they're pleased I'm there. I'll do it. I'll try. It's part of the social contract, like returning a handshake. But I'm tense the entire time, waiting for it to end. It never feels like I think it should feel. Like I imagine it feels when Céleste runs up to you and hugs you. My brain immediately tells me to step away when I'd much rather be able to enjoy it as a simple expression of affection." He sighed. "There's more to it, of course. Nothing I want to go into on Christmas morning."

Nora said nothing, only waited.

"I worry—"

"What?" she asked.

The silence after her question was long enough to scare her.

"What happens if I see my son someday, and I can't enjoy holding him?"

Tears sprang to Nora's eyes. She didn't have an answer for that. She could only rise up over him and kiss his face—his cheek, his temple, his forehead, his lips.

"I love you," she said. "I will love you all my life."

He met her eyes and smiled tiredly in the dark. "Then that's all I need for Christmas. Nothing else."

"Nice try," she said. "But you're getting your cursed gift whether you like it or not."

"Which is the point, yes?"

"Right."

"Any hints?"

She laid her head onto his chest, listened to the slow steady beating of his good strong heart.

"I think I have an idea."

JANUARY 5TH

THE EVENING of the fifth of January was almost cold, down in the low fifties. Nothing like New York in December, of course, but Kingsley really didn't miss the city or that weather. Although gray days like this made him wish for snow a little, if only to break up the monotony of the gray sky, gray streets, gray haze in the gray air. But that was fine. He was going to spend the night with Søren which meant he'd get all the winter he wanted in bed.

He took his least impressive car, a black Escalade that Juliette had wanted. It was big enough for Céleste's car seat and all the thousands of bags they had to take whenever they traveled with their daughter. Nora called it a "dad-mobile," and he would have been offended if it wasn't the truth. He didn't need the Dad-mobile tonight. He'd only taken it because it looked innocuous, and he was trying to seem like a normal person tonight. This was the first night Søren had ever invited him to the Jesuit House where he lived now.

The Jesuit House was a large, shabby-looking white Victorian with not much to recommend itself except a prime location at the edge of Audubon Park. He and Søren had kicked a soccer ball around the park a few times, and Kingsley had walked him back to the Jesuit House, but tonight was the first time he would cross the threshold. Made him miss Søren's old rectory at Sacred Heart. Back then, Søren had lived in the rectory alone, had privacy. Not here. He lived with a dozen other Jesuit priests in this old house. As he strode up the front steps, he was sweating a little, nervous, like the proverbial whore in church.

He rang the bell and an older man who wasn't dressed like a priest but most certainly was a priest opened the door.

"Can I help you?"

Kingsley almost said, "I'm meeting Søren," but then remembered this priest probably didn't know his name was Søren.

"Is Marcus here? I'm his brother-in-law."

"Yes, yes, of course. He said you'd be coming by. He's in the library."

The living room of the Jesuit House was cozy but looked almost as shabby as the outside of the house. The furniture might have been here since the Spanish were in charge of New Orleans. A few priests in lay clothing sat on armchairs and sofas, talking or watching the news on television. They looked up with curious eyes as Kingsley passed through the house. Kingsley had read the statistics that about half of all American priests were gay. The urge to wink at the one who stared at him the longest was almost overwhelming. But he had promised Søren to behave himself tonight.

"In here," the older priest said as he opened a door to the library. Kingsley stepped inside. Søren sat by a large picture window, reading by the fading light of the gray evening sky.

"There you are," he said, looking up from his book. "About time. We'll be late for dinner."

"We'll make it," Kingsley said. "I changed our reservation to 7:30."

They were not having dinner. They did not have reservations.

"Ah, then we have plenty of time. I'll change." Søren was wearing his clerical collar and black jacket.

"Can I see your room?" Kingsley asked.

"That's against the rules, I'm afraid," the older priest said.

Søren stood up and said, "Yes."

"Marcus."

"Will you tell on me?" Søren asked the man. His tone was light as if Søren knew he was a favorite and the rules didn't necessarily apply to him.

"Go on," he said, waving his hand at a door marked PRIVATE. "But quickly, please?"

"I'm sorry," Kingsley said as Søren led him toward the door. "I didn't know he was such an entitled prick."

The older priest laughed. "We knew."

Søren led him through the door and into a hallway. Kingsley couldn't say what he'd been expecting—he'd never been to the priests' quarters at their old school in Maine—but he hadn't imagined he'd be so disappointed.

"It's just a house," Kingsley said.

"Just a house," Søren replied. "What did you think it was?"

"Something, I don't know...spooky?"

Søren gave him a look. "We're Jesuits, not ghosts."

"You could have at least hung an antique chandelier."

"From these ceilings?"

They were normal ceilings, normal height. The normality of the place was almost stranger than if the place were actually strange-looking. The Jesuits had been around for centuries. He'd expected something more medieval, he supposed. But no, just a normal hallway, well-worn wood floors, scuffed green paint on the walls, and closed doors with numbers on them.

"Which one is yours?" Kingsley asked.

"Number eight, upstairs," he said. They turned a corner to take a staircase up. Kingsley guessed the younger, more ambulatory priests were sent upstairs so the older Jesuits wouldn't have to make the climb. As fit as Søren was, he was lucky they didn't put him on the roof.

They reached the second floor landing just as a young Black man came down the hall toward them. Young? Well, twenty-eight or nine. That was young to Kingsley these days.

"New recruit?" the young man said, smiling. He was wearing jeans and a long-sleeved t-shirt with LOYOLA across the chest. Kingsley had the same shirt, just short-sleeved.

"This is my brother-in-law, Kingsley Boissonneault."

"Right, the French one." He held out his hand and Kingsley shook it, said it was nice to meet him.

"Kingsley," Søren said, "this is Brother Eric, former captain, U.S. Army. Eric, this is Kingsley, former Captain, F.F.L."

"Really?" Eric sounded impressed. "The Foreign Legion?"

"Long time ago," Kingsley said.

"Much harder to get in than the Army, I hear."

"You said it, not me." Kingsley wouldn't have said it. He would have thought it, but he wouldn't have said it.

"Wish I could stay and swap war stories, but I have chapel in ten minutes. Nice to meet you. Come by anytime."

Eric jogged down the stairs. When he was out of earshot, Kingsley said, "Cute."

"Stop."

"Sorry."

Søren led Kingsley to the room with the 8 on the door.

"I'm tempted to draw a circle around it," Kingsley said, making an imaginary circle with his finger. He said this in French in case anyone was listening. Who knew how thin the walls were here?

"The thought occurred to me as well," Søren replied, also in French.

No lock on the door. No key. Must be the honor system around here. Søren opened the door and flipped on the light switch. No overhead light came on, only a simple floor lamp with a white shade.

"Not bad," Kingsley said, nodding. He'd braced himself for the worst, for hideous wall-to-wall shag carpeting and floral-print curtains. But no, it was a calm, clean, soothing sort of bedroom. Cool white walls and winter light coming in the large window that overlooked the park gave the room a contemplative ambiance. Oddly it felt more sacred in this plain, simple bedroom than in so many of the churches he'd visited. Kingsley took stock of the place, committing it to memory. An oak desk with a brass study lamp. A wooden cross over the bed. And the bed itself was an antique from the looks of it. Iron, sturdy, a twin but extra-long twin obviously. A simple white crocheted quilt covered the bed, one pillow, and neatly made. The only splashes of color in the room were a few red leatherbound books sitting on their sides on a floating wall shelf, and a painting hanging opposite the window.

"No mirrors," Kingsley noticed.

"There's one in the bathroom."

"Shared bathroom?"

"Of course."

"The horror." Kingsley shuddered in mock disgust. "What's this?" He pointed at the painting.

"One of my former parishioners is an amateur painter. She made this for me. Going-away gift."

Kingsley recognized it as a slightly impressionistic water-color rendering of Sacred Heart, Søren's old parish. The gray stone church surrounded by green grass and tulips brought

Kingsley back to the many times he'd snuck over to Wakefield to visit Søren.

"Do you miss it?"

"No. I miss a few of the people but it was time to move on. Past time. I belong here with you and Eleanor."

Kingsley had never told Søren how much it meant that he'd given up his church to move here. No matter what he said, that he kept a painting of Sacred Heart across from his bed was proof that it was a harder choice than he ever let on.

He turned from the painting in time to see Søren popping out his dog collar—he loved that Roman collars were called "dog collars" by priests—and unbuttoning his shirt.

"Need help with that?"

Søren gave him that look. Kingsley only laughed.

"I'm really not supposed to be up here?"

Søren took his shirt off and tossed it onto the bed. He opened the closet door. Kingsley sat in the one chair in the room, content to stare at Søren's back and shoulders for the rest of his life. Out of curiosity, he picked up Søren's discarded shirt from the bed and brought it to his nose, inhaled. Even his shirt smelled like winter. Kingsley—reluctantly—put it back onto the bed.

"It's not a hard and fast rule," Søren said, flipping through the clothes in his closet, about one-twentieth of what Kingsley had in his. "Father Lawrence, who you met downstairs, is very cautious. I can't blame him, but there have to be exceptions for family." He turned around.

"Right, right. Because I'm your brother-in-law."

"Of course you are." Søren's wicked smile disappeared as he pulled a black sweater over his head. A very nice black sweater. Too nice for a Jesuit. Obviously one Nora had bought for him.

Since they were speaking French, Kingsley didn't worry about asking, "I suppose Nora's never been up here."

"You are much easier to explain away than Eleanor. But Claire visited when I first moved in here. Sisters are allowed. Girlfriends are frowned upon."

Kingsley enjoyed the view of two very long, very muscular legs as Søren took off his black trousers and put on a pair of jeans. "Did she give you her gift yet?"

"Not yet, but I've given mine to her. And don't ask because you do not want to know."

"Something with Nico."

"No comment."

Kingsley sighed. "I wish I could say I was surprised. Make it up to me," he said. "Fuck me in your twin bed."

"Also frowned upon," Søren said. "But don't think I haven't imagined it."

"We had some very good nights in that cot back at school, didn't we?"

"Some of the best nights of my life."

He took a black jacket from his closet and slipped his feet into his shoes.

"Are you going to tell me where we're going tonight," Søren said. "I'll be disappointed if we really do have dinner reservations."

"In the mood?"

"Already ate."

He must have looked disappointed because when Søren passed him on the way to the door, he said, "And in the mood. Now tell me where we're going."

Kingsley leaned back against the door, smiled.

"You showed me your room. Now I'll show you mine."

❄

THE WINE in Nora's glass was red. The time was nearly nine o'clock—Nico should be there any moment. And the song on the radio was "The House of the Rising Sun." She'd thought this radio station would still be playing Christmas music, but no, it had gone back to its usual format. She didn't mind. She loved this song.

In her office at her desk, Nora sipped her wine and counted the minutes until her lover arrived. She still couldn't quite believe he'd gotten on a plane from New York to New Orleans in the middle of complex business negotiations for the sole purpose of seeing her. If he was coming this far and for just one night, she knew she had to make it good.

> There is a house in New Orleans
> They call the Rising Sun
> And it's been the ruin of many a young
>   poor boy...

Søren had made that joke when he'd entered her private dungeon upstairs for the first time, which she'd decked out in red and black and leather and steel. Ropes and whips and chains, oh my.

"Ah," he'd said, nodding with amused appreciation. "I've always wondered what the House of the Rising Sun looked like. Now I know."

She was looking forward to ruining Nico, her young poor boy, tonight.

What would he want? Sex, of course. All night, of course. He wasn't going to get it. Not until he'd earned it. In her left hand she held her wine glass. In her right hand she held a black silk blindfold.

> Oh, Mother, tell your children

Not to do what I have done...

Her mother had tried to talk her out of her life and the older Nora got, the more she understood those warnings. The more she'd known her mother had a point. But it was like trying to talk a leopard out of his spots. And really, once you've fucked your Catholic priest, everything else seems tame in comparison.

It's funny that she'd asked to play this game, this Black & Blue Elephant game. Give her a gift she wanted but didn't want? She'd been playing that game since the night Nico seduced her.

> *I got one foot on the platform*
> *The other foot on the train*
> *I'm goin' back to New Orleans*
> *To wear that ball and chain.*

One foot on the platform, the other on the train. That was her life now. One foot in Nico's world. One foot in Søren's. How long could it go on? She didn't know except that she was determined to ride the train to the end of the line.

Or until it derailed.

A car door slammed. Nico's taxi.

Nora finished her wine with a swallow and stood up. She walked slowly up the stairs to her dungeon, to her own private House of the Rising Sun. Behind her she heard the doorknob rattle. Then the door opened. Then footsteps. She'd already told him to meet her upstairs in the room at the end of the hallway.

She went into her dungeon and waited with her back to the wall. Outside the room, she heard Nico climbing the stairs. He paused at the top. He proceeded down the hall. The ancient wood floors of her two-hundred-year-old house creaked. He stepped into her dungeon.

Before he could turn his head and see her, Nora stepped forward and brought the black silk scarf over his eyes, blind-folding him.

"If you say a word," she said into his ear, "you'll spend all night in a hotel alone."

Nico—bless him—stiffened, breathed in, didn't say a word. Nora rarely made threats, but when she did, they were never idle ones. He knew that.

"Good boy," Nora said. "You'll get to speak when I tell you that you can speak and only then."

Nothing. Nothing but his shallow breaths.

She was in her highest high heels, which made it easier to pull the blindfold firmly around his eyes. She tied it behind his head.

"I'm going to hurt you tonight," she said. "This is hurting Søren so it's only fair I hurt you, too."

Slowly and almost imperceptibly, Nico nodded his head in agreement. He'd been drunk when he'd asked if he could come for a night. Now he was sober and realized just what he'd been asking.

"Hold still. I'm going to undress you. If you try to touch me, it'll be the last time you touch me tonight."

She knew it took all his willpower to obey, but he did it. He stood there unmoving, not reaching for her as she came to stand in front of him.

"I don't think I've ever seen you in a suit before."

She knew he'd gone straight from a lunch meeting in Manhattan with a potential angel investor to the airport. No time to change clothes.

Dark suit, crisp white shirt, collar open at the neck. But even in a suit he was still Nico. His hair was dark and curly and could use a cut but she'd cut the man who dared to cut it. His hands were calloused from hard work among his vines. He looked like a man who worked his ass off wearing the suit of a man who didn't break a sweat except at the gym.

"The suit is nice but it's not really your style," she said. "Let's fix that."

He stood still and quiet as she pushed the jacket off his shoulders and hung it on the hook behind her door. One by one she unbuttoned all his shirt buttons. Between each button she caressed his bare chest as it came slowly into view. His beautiful, young strong bare chest.

She looped her finger under the collar of his shirt and tugged it off as she walked a circle around him. A very nice, high-quality shirt—it slid off him like butter on hot bread. The next part was her favorite. She unbuttoned his suit trousers and brought them down and off of him. Underwear—black boxer briefs—went last. His shoes and socks were already off because he was a good boy who'd taken them off at her door.

She pushed him gently forward, moving him to stand in the center of her dungeon. She had a red vintage Chinese rug on the floor, a gift from a client from Hong Kong who worked in imports. In the dead center of the rug was a medallion and in the medallion was woven a lotus flower. She brought Nico to stand on top of the lotus. Then she stepped back and studied him.

There was nothing not to love about the naked body of a twenty-five year old man who worked his ass off in the fields of his family's vineyard. Dark olive skin, smooth and supple. Biceps she longed to sink her teeth into. Shoulders strong enough to survive her fingernails digging into them during an orgasm. Hips that knew how to move just right to bring about that orgasm. And the cock, of course, the beautiful young hard cock. She wrapped her fingers around it and stroked it just to hear Nico inhale.

She held it in her hand, the firm warm shaft, not stroking now, just holding. Owning it.

"I have to wonder what you're feeling right now," she said. "If I were you, I'd be furious. You probably thought we'd be in bed already, and this inside me. You thought we'd make love all night and it would be hot and sweet and delicious. And then I'd fall asleep in your arms and we'd make love again in the morning before you had to leave. And now here you are—blindfolded, under orders, don't even get to touch me. And you know I'm about to hurt you, very very very very very much. If you can answer in one word, you can tell me what you're feeling. Go on. Tell me. One word."

"Forgetful."

Nora narrowed her eyes at him. "Forgetful? Interesting answer. Now I have to know—what did you forget?"

"I forgot that the woman I'm in love with is a vicious bitch."

Then he grinned like he knew he'd given his teacher an A+ answer.

He had.

"I'd forgotten something, too," she said. "I risked my perfect life with Søren, the owner of my cunt and the master of my body... Søren, who is the most wicked, wonderful, brutal sadist God ever dared to put on this innocent Earth...to spread my legs for you, you little French brat. Now I remember why."

He opened his mouth to say something and then didn't. He'd almost earned a night in a hotel if he'd said a single word out of turn.

"Don't go anywhere." She flicked him on the end of his perfect nose. Quickly she found leather cuffs and a snap hook. The cuffs went on his wrists and his wrists went over his head and attached onto the sturdy hook screwed into the stud in her ceiling.

His smooth young skin was hot to the touch and the tip of

his cock was already shimmering with wetness. She dipped her head and lapped it off.

Nico's head rolled back and he gasped. But still, he didn't speak.

"I taught you so well. Let's see how I did on those pain control lessons. I have neighbors, you know. So when I make you scream, scream quietly, *s'il te plait*."

She went to the wall where her floggers hung in a pretty row. She didn't take one down. She didn't want to flog him. Flogging was too easy.

Instead, she picked up her whip.

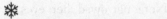

THE MARQUIS CLUB was Kingsley's New Orleans branch of The 8th Circle. At least that's what Nora called it. Downstairs it was a respectable jazz club managed by a former bartender and thirty-year veteran of a famous French Quarter bar. People might come and go and never know what went on upstairs.

Upstairs was where things got interesting.

He hadn't told Søren much about The Marquis Club other than the name, which Søren had rolled his eyes at before asking if Nora had put him up to it.

It was, after all, named for Donation Alphonse François, the most infamous erotica writer in history, otherwise known as the Marquis de Sade. The Marquis Club had found a home in a grand old double gallery house, white with black iron balconies. A former brothel, it had a large open salon on the main floor and a total of ten bedrooms on the second and third floors. Bedrooms that were now converted into dungeons. And one bedroom in particular—the biggest—had been converted into Kingsley's personal dungeon.

That's where he was taking Søren.

"I hope you like the new place," Kingsley told Søren as he pulled into the parking lot behind the courtyard.

"Does it have a dungeon and a bed?"

"Several of both."

"I like it already."

It wasn't by chance that The Marquis Club had a courtyard in the back. That was the main reason Kingsley bought it—privacy. He could park his car behind the club, open the courtyard gate, and slip in the back. No one from the street would see him go in. More importantly, no one on the street would see a well-known and much-liked Jesuit priest named Father Marcus Stearns slipping in the back as well. Luckily the club wasn't open tonight so they would have the place to themselves.

They arrived at seven and Kingsley parked behind the private courtyard, which was still decorated for Christmas. Kingsley unlocked the club door, but Søren paused before entering, gazing around the yard.

"I'll never get used to Christmas lights on palm trees," Søren said. "New Orleans is an interesting place."

"Tennessee Williams once said, 'There are only three great cities in the United States—New York, San Francisco, and New Orleans. All the rest are Cleveland.' Aren't you glad you don't live in Cleveland anymore?"

"As a matter of fact, I liked living in Wakefield," Søren said.

"Then move back there."

"I didn't like it that much."

Laughing, Kingsley let Søren into the club and locked the door behind them.

The atmosphere of the club was very different from the Jesuit House. This place was anything but cozy and contemplative. The wood floors were painted black. Crystal chandeliers hung from a tin tile ceiling. Even closed and locked up, the air in the club smelled of sweat and sex, red wine and candles. They took the back staircase to the third floor. Søren paused on the landing and looked down the stairs to the main floor below.

"Quite a change from the old place," Søren said.

"It's smaller," Kingsley admitted, "but I like that. Better food. More jazz. More intimate."

"Fewer bodily fluids on the stairs as well." Søren lifted his foot to look at the sole of his shoes. "Spotless. Not a drop of blood or come to be seen. First time for everything."

Kingsley glared at him. "The 8th Circle wasn't that bad."

"I thought about wearing a Hazmat suit on a few occasions, but I worried about overstimulating the vinyl fetishists."

"So it was a little gritty," he countered with a shrug. "Part of the charm."

There was no 8 on Kingsley's door. But there was a sign that said KINGSLEY EDGE. And a lock. Only Kingsley had the key. But not for long.

"For you," Kingsley said as he worked a key off the ring. "You get a copy of the key."

"I'm honored." Søren slipped it into his pocket.

"Hope you like the place." He opened the door but didn't turn on the light. This room wasn't made for overhead lighting. Kingsley knew it well enough by now to walk into the darkness and find the fireplace mantel and the matches he left on top of it. He struck a match and lit a row of eight white candles. Then he took one of the candles around the room and lit the others. Candles on the windowsills. Candles on the bedside table. Candles on an iron stand that stood next to the black leather St. Andrew's Cross.

All the while, Søren stood in the doorway watching him as he brought the dungeon out of the darkness. Soon the whole room glowed like a birthday cake. And Kingsley had a present to give.

Once all the candles were lit, he stepped into the room, closed the door behind him and locked it. Kingsley stood by the foot of the bed—not a twin but a bed big enough for two grown men. Which he hoped it would hold tonight. All night.

Kingsley was nervous all of a sudden. That didn't happen very often to him.

"I was thinking of you when I put everything together. Juliette and I can play at home but you and I need our own place. Like it?"

"Very much." He smiled. "Much more tasteful than Eleanor's private dungeon."

"You should see the dungeon she set up for her clients. It's like Sodom and Gomorrah in there."

"Yes, and this is just Sodom." Søren stared at him. "You're nervous."

Kingsley ran a hand through his hair. "I have your gift," he said. Søren raised his eyebrow.

There was a palpable tension in the room between them. Someone watching might think they'd never done this together before.

"It's up there, the black box." Kingsley nodded toward the fireplace mantel. The night was cool but not cool enough to justify a fire. But he liked it like this, the mantel covered in burning candles and the heart of the fireplace cold and dark.

Søren picked up the box and eyed it with obvious suspicion. "Very light," he said. He shook it gently. "No rattling. A pen?"

"I wouldn't be nervous about giving you a pen."

"A very small gun."

He snorted a laugh. "Just open it, you sadist."

With infuriating slowness bordering on psychological torture, Søren untaped the ends, pulled back the paper, revealed the box under the wrapping.

"Let's see," Søren said. "What were the rules? It has to be a gift you don't want to give me and yet you do want to give me and also a gift I don't want and yet I do want."

Then he opened the box. Søren's right eyebrow lifted. "Is this what I think it is?" he asked.

"What do you think it is?"

"Obsidian scalpel."

"With a fine bamboo handle," Kingsley said.

Søren set the box back onto the mantel. "You want to do blood-play with me?" he asked.

"Yes and no. You want to do it with me?"

"No and yes. But also yes, definitely. But also—"

"Scared?"

"Always. I've fantasized so often about slitting your throat, I'm worried one of these days, I'll do it."

"This is why I was on the fence about giving it to you. I've had it for months."

"Months?"

"I told myself we could 'christen' my new dungeon when it was finished."

"Christen it with blood?"

Kingsley pulled back the white duvet on top of the bed, revealing the black sheets beneath.

❄

THERE, Nora thought. *There's the reason I was born like this.*

Whip in hand, she stood a few feet away from Nico. His arms were hooked over his head. His eyes were hidden behind a black silk blindfold tied at the back of his neck. His long beautiful body was taut, his cock was hard, he was silent with respect for her and fear of what was coming next.

"And to think," she said as she walked a circle around him. "You never did kink before me. What a waste of such a delicious canvas." She slid the leather coil of her whip over his naked back.

She caught a glimpse of herself in the mirror on the wall as she made another circle around her favorite target. She'd dressed like she'd dress for a special client. Short tight black skirt, red corset, high heels. The only difference was she would have worn panties with a client. Not needed with Nico.

"Another question," she said. "Do you like it when I beat you? Or do you just like making me happy? You can answer. Be honest. Even if you say you only like it because I like it...I'll still do it."

Nico said something very softly, so softly she had to move a little closer. So close she could smell the scent of that morning's shower still on his heated skin.

"I like it," he said.

She was glad he couldn't see her smile at that. "Why?" Her voice was cold, demanding.

"I know I deserve it," he said.

"You deserve beatings?"

He nodded.

"Why?" she asked.

"What you said—I made you risk your 'perfect life' with your master for me. I should be sorry for doing that to you, but I'm not. And I should be sorry for hurting my father by sleeping with his former lover, but I'm not. I should be sorry for hurting your master, because he never did anything to hurt me."

"But you're not."

"I'm not," he said with total sincerity and disdain for anyone who would expect him to apologize for his desire for her. "How can I make it right if I can't be sorry? Like this." Even in his bonds he managed to shrug. "So beat me, Mistress Nora. I know I have it coming to me."

He didn't sound sarcastic when he said that. He sounded like he meant it.

"Only you," she said, shaking her head, "can twist me wanting to beat you into a point of male pride."

Wisely, he said nothing to that.

"Well, if you want to give up a pound of your flesh, I'm more than happy to take it."

She stood behind him, at the perfect distance measured many times so as not to strike too hard or too softly. She unfurled her whip, tested it a few times across the floor and into the air.

"I've never whipped you before, have I?" she said, pretending she didn't already know the answer. Nico said nothing. "You won't like it. Don't forget—the neighbors."

She let the whip go.

Nico didn't scream. But his body tensed and he flinched. And Nora was very happy.

It took a long time to learn how to use a whip the right way, the good way so that the tip danced across the skin, striking it like rain on a windowpane in a storm, not breaking the skin—or sometimes, just barely breaking it. Not like a cut with a knife but a thousand bee stings. A whip shouldn't slice but bite. Nora learned from the best how to make the whip an extension of her. Søren had taught her, begrudgingly, so she wouldn't accidentally put someone in the hospital.

Now she was as good, or better, than he was. Not that she ever mentioned that to him.

She loved her whip, loved the power she felt wielding it. To know she could, if she wanted, truly hurt someone. Instead, she was magnanimous, a merciful dark goddess. She didn't want the life of the person she was whipping. Just a little of their blood. Just a taste, a *soupçon*.

Nico took his punishment beautifully. He didn't scream but

he wasn't silent either. No one could be. But his cries were soft and stoic. A few gasps. A few full-body flinches when the whip kissed the very tip of a nerve and his entire body rang like a bell with the pain. Oh, she knew how it felt. She knew better than anyone how it felt. That's why she showed no mercy. If she could survive it, he could.

When he'd had enough, Nora stopped.

She stopped and she stared. Nico hung limp from the hook. His back and shoulders and hips were dotted with a thousand red and angry wounds. A few were bleeding. But only a little.

She walked up to Nico and touched his back, palm flat on his abraded skin. He winced, hissing through his teeth.

She put her mouth to his ear and whispered, "You just made me very happy." Then she kissed his earlobe.

Nico had been in her house one full hour and he hadn't seen her yet. She stood before him, letting the clock tick along with each of his panting breaths.

"You have no idea how tempted I am to keep you blindfolded from now until you leave my house. Should I? You can answer."

"What sin did I commit?" Nico wore a slight smile as if he were trying to play along but it was clear he was worried she might actually mean it.

"Not your sin. Mine. Only mine. Always mine."

"I don't agree."

Nora raised her eyebrow. "My toy thinks he has an opinion. I'm hurting Søren with you. I hurt you with Søren. How is that not a sin?"

"Storms can hurt us, too. There's no sin in a storm." For good measure he added, "Mistress."

Nora's heart clenched. She sighed. God, did she have good taste in lovers or what?

"I really should be ashamed of myself for sleeping with you," she said. "I should be. But I'm not."

With that, she untied his blindfold. He blinked his beautiful pale green eyes. For a moment she didn't say anything nor did he. She let him look at her and she let herself look at him looking at her. His eyes were bright with hunger and worship. No one looked upon his mistress the way a submissive man did. Like he was afraid to look and more afraid to look away...

"Do you think you've earned my cunt?"

"If you say I have, I have," he said.

She smiled. "You have."

She raised her hands and uncuffed him. His arms fell to his sides, then reached for her.

He was shockingly strong. She'd forgotten how strong he was. Or maybe she'd never known because he'd never used his strength on her. But when he did, she was powerless. In an instant she was on her back, on the lotus, and Nico was over her, straddling her. His knees forced her thighs apart. His hand went between her legs and stroked her pubic lips, then he pushed his fingers inside her. Her head fell back in a burst of pleasure. Her vagina was wet and open but still he opened her wider, spreading his fingers. Nora moaned at the back of her throat as he moved on top of her. His arm went around her lower back, lifting her. His hand pushed her skirt up to her hips. With a rough thrust he speared her, and she cried out. She grasped his shoulders, not caring that she was hurting him, and writhed under him as he fucked her. She lay back on the rug, her legs as wide as they'd ever been in her life, her vagina slick and open, her cunt throbbing as he worked his cock deep into her. She was overpowered, undone. Her orgasm shook her to the core.

Spent, she laid back on the floor, eyes open, vagina making little gasps around his cock. Above them on the ceiling were the mirrored tiles and she watched herself being fucked, watched

Nico's broken back arch and bow with every thrust, saw his body shimmer with his sweat, his head come up as he worked himself deeper. His eyes were closed. His lips parted. And then she remembered who was in charge here.

He was out of his mind fucking her. Easy enough to wrap her legs around his back, shift her weight quickly, push him down...his freshly-whipped and wounded back on the rough, rough rug.

Nico cried out in pain and pleasure as she clenched her cunt around him. The shock of the sudden pain made him come. His head and shoulders came all the way off the ground as he released his semen into her in a final series of quick rough thrusts.

After he came, he lay back in surrender, arms over his head. She could stay there all night straddling him, his cock soft inside her vagina, his sperm on her thighs, his mouth at her ear, his breaths tickling her neck.

"I'm still not sorry," he said.

"And that's why I love you."

After a few minutes, he stirred and pulled her down to him, kissed her face, her mouth, her forehead, her neck. He freed her breasts from her corset and sucked her nipples until they were sore. He grew hard and pushed her gently onto her back, started to fuck her again. Nora watched it all on the ceiling...her beautiful French brat who would rather take another whipping than stay another minute out of her cunt.

Best show in town.

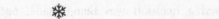

SØREN WALKED over to the bed, stood in front of him. Kingsley looked up at him. This was his favorite view of Søren.

"Are you sure?" Søren asked.

"I wouldn't have given that to you if I wasn't." He was speaking French again although they were alone, and there was no chance of being overheard. It was easier to lie in French.

Søren touched Kingsley's face lightly. Fingertips across his cheek, then to his ear, and then his fingers—those beautiful pianist's fingers—threaded into his hair. The grip was firm, possessive. Søren forced Kingsley's head back. Once it was back, Søren caressed his bared throat, held it lightly with his hand until Kingsley began to relax into the large palm pressed against his Adam's apple.

Then Søren ran a single fingernail slowly across Kingsley's throat as if slitting it. Every muscle in Kingsley's body knotted up. He couldn't help himself. It was pure instinct, like a cat's back raising at the sight of a snake.

He took a breath, laughed at himself.

"Flirt," Kingsley said.

"I have never felt you tense so hard as you did just now. I thought you were going to jump out of your skin."

"I might have pissed myself."

"It is a fantasy of mine to terrify you enough to make you do that."

"You got close that time."

Søren released his hair, moved his hand to Kingsley's mouth, ran his thumb across the bottom lip. "I like it when I scare you. I shouldn't, but I do."

"I like that you like it."

Søren said nothing after that, only stroked Kingsley's hair, his cheek, his mouth. The air was electric with waiting. He sensed a decision was being made, options considered and weighed, discarded, then reconsidered.

"No," Søren said.

"What?" Kingsley wasn't sure he'd heard right.

"Not tonight. Maybe someday but not yet."

"Why not?" He couldn't decide if he was disappointed or relieved.

Søren held up his hand for Kingsley to see. It was shaking slightly.

"It's usually me doing the shaking around you," Kingsley said.

"When I want something too much, I can't trust myself to have it. I think I might hurt you more than I should tonight."

He wasn't joking. Kingsley knew when Søren was playing the role of the wicked sadist and when he was being himself, a very concerned and careful sadist.

"You can, though."

Søren laughs softly. "Of course I can. I can do anything I want to you. But you were right about the gift—I want it, but I don't want it." He went to the mantel, picked up the box, and put the lid back on it. "But we'll save it for another time. And know that one of these days..."

He let the threat hang in the air. Kingsley knew what he wasn't saying—one of these days, he would slice Kingsley up like a Christmas turkey.

"What do we do then?" Kingsley asked.

"I can think of something," Søren said.

"You already have, haven't you?"

Søren's only reply was, "Stand up."

Slowly Kingsley stood up.

"You said I made you wish you had gone to college," Søren said. "Tonight, you can be my student."

"Student? I didn't go to college for a reason."

Søren lifted his chin, looked down at him, and said, "Recite."

God. Kingsley almost groaned aloud. He was really going to do this to him? Make him play the role of the bad student?

He'd object, but his cock was already hard, and it wasn't

easy to put up much of a fight with a painful erection.

"Recite what?"

"The work you memorized. It's ten lashes with the strap if you haven't memorized your work."

Kingsley's brain raced. What did he have memorized? Bible verses? No. Except for "Jesus wept," which he didn't think would satisfy Søren. Any great speeches? Four score and what? No. Everything had fled his brain. Everything except for one line of one poem bubbled up along with a memory of a girl reading it to him in bed after a lonely Christmas in Paris. He was twenty and angry and heartbroken. Everything he saw and touched and tasted made him remember Søren.

"You've forgotten your assignment?" Søren said. "I'll get the strap."

"*I crave your mouth, your voice, your hair—*"

Søren didn't have the decency to hide his look of surprise that Kingsley might actually have memorized a work of poetry.

"Go on," Søren said.

What was the next line? He remembered reciting the poem in his head as he walked through the cold and winding winter streets of the Latin Quarter, feeling hungry, feeling starved, no matter how much he ate. He continued:

> "*Silent and starving, I prowl through the streets*
> *Bread does not nourish me,*
> *dawn disrupts me, all day*
> *I hunt for the liquid measure of your steps.*"

"Pablo Neruda," Søren said. "Excellent choice. Go on."

Kingsley took a long breath, summoned the rest of the poem from the deep lizard part of his brain where his darkest hungers mingled with his most potent memories...twenty-one years old, the night he'd gone to bed with a tall blond man he'd met in a bar just to pretend Søren was fucking him again...how the man had put a knife to Kingsley's throat...the look of shock on his face when Kingsley had only laughed. As if that was the first time a lover had ever put a knife to him. The man had smiled, punched him across the face, and Kingsley let him finish inside of him.

> *"I hunger for your sleek laugh, your hands the*
> *color of a savage harvest,*
> *hunger for the pale stones of your fingernails.*
> *I want to eat your skin like a whole almond."*

Age twenty-two, a week's leave from the F.F.L., spent in Barcelona. In a crowd, he saw a blond head catch the morning sunlight. Kingsley followed the boy for blocks until he turned and saw the face didn't belong to Søren, but a Spanish university student, only eighteen. He seduced him anyway. Kingsley had beaten him with his belt at the boy's grandfather's villa, pretending to punish Søren for not being there to punish him. The boy had loved it, loved him. Kingsley left four days later, full of promises they would meet again. They never did.

> *"I want to eat the sunbeam flaring in your lovely*
> *body,*
> *the sovereign nose of your arrogant face, I want*
> *to eat the fleeting shade of your lashes."*

His twenty-sixth birthday was spent tied to the bed of a man twice his age because he was tall and Danish and had eyelashes like Søren's.

> *"And I pace around hungry, sniffing the twilight,*
> *hunting for you, for your hot heart,*

like a puma in the barrens of Quitratue."

As Kingsley recited, Søren had listened, eyes on his, his face again unreadable.

Anything could happen now that he'd finished the poem.

"Very nice," Søren said. "Now again, in Spanish."

"I never learned it in Spanish."

Søren sounded almost apologetic, though Kingsley knew he wasn't when he said, "Lazy students get the strap."

"I'm sorry, sir."

"Don't apologize to me. Apologize to Pablo Neruda. Now take off your clothes."

Ah, this was the part Kingsley had been waiting for. The pain. The humiliation. The baring of bodies. The baring of souls. His soul. Only his soul as Søren would keep his own modestly covered, as always. But that was fine. Kingsley wanted it that way, to be the one broken, and for Søren to do the breaking.

Kingsley unbuttoned his shirt quickly. He wanted it too much to go slow, to tease. Shirt off. Shoes kicked off. Jeans down and off along with the socks—the ones Nora had given him for Christmas. Worn on purpose. He stood naked, hard, hot heart racing.

"Here," Søren said and nodded toward a leather-padded bench, tall and wide and sturdy enough to hold the weight of a grown man.

"You want me bent over that, don't you?"

"You're a quicker study than you look."

The bench sat near the corner of the room by the fireplace. Kingsley went to it, the floor cold on the soles of his naked feet. And as he bent over it and let his hips and stomach press against the cool, slick leather, he tensed just as hard as he had when Søren had pretended to cut his throat. There was no more vulnerable position than this. And of course, Søren would find a way to make it even worse.

Søren knelt in front of the bench. There were leather straps that could be cuffed around the wrists at the base, and Søren used them to secure Kingsley in that defenseless position. He was trapped. He couldn't escape. He was there until someone freed him. It really was like being back in school.

However, he could turn his head, and he did, watching as Søren opened the closet door and pulled a red cord to turn on the light. A large walk-in closet, it was where Kingsley kept all his instruments of torture. Floggers and whips, cuffs and chains, all hanging on hooks in neat lines and rows.

"This is," Søren said, "the most magnificent closet I've ever been inside. I could sleep in here."

"Sometimes, when we're eating dinner with my family, I forget you're a madman. Thank you for reminding me."

"You're the one who said he wanted to eat my eyelashes." Søren seemed to be examining every strap and belt and flogger in the closet.

"I didn't say that. Neruda said that."

"Whoever said it, I'm sure I'll be in your mouth before this night is over."

"Do you make your Little One suck your cock as much as you make me do it?" Kingsley asked.

"No, actually, I don't."

"Because I'm better at it?"

"Because I don't feel nearly as guilty when I make you gag."

Kingsley moaned and put his head down. He should learn to never ask questions. He heard the distinct sounds of a man inspecting the hardware from inside the closet. "Are you ever going to come out?"

"I'm looking for your branding iron."

Kingsley laughed. "That I'm not 100% certain you're joking

is half the reason I love you."

"That you're not 100% certain you want me to be joking is half the reason I love you."

It never got old, hearing Søren say, "I love you." How many years had he wondered if Søren ever actually loved him? Or even remembered him? He would have sold his soul to hear those words when he was eighteen, nineteen, twenty-four, twenty-five. Sold his literal soul to the literal devil for them. And now here they were, given not just freely but free, as if they cost nothing, as if Kingsley could have them anytime he wanted.

Who knew? Maybe he had sold his soul to the devil to hear those words.

Maybe Søren was the devil.

Finally, Søren chose something from the closet and brought it back to the bench where Kingsley waited breathlessly, sweating fear and want.

Around his wrist was looped a long nasty-looking black strap. Leather, thin—the demonic love child of a paddle and a crop. Only a cane would hurt worse.

"Are you the devil?" Kingsley asked.

"No," Søren said, "but I do admire his methods." He touched Kingsley's back lightly. It felt like a threat. Kingsley tensed again, swallowed.

"Every muscle in your back just clenched," Søren said. He stroked Kingsley's spine from neck to hip and back again. "Do it again."

"Are you going to fuck me like this?"

"Do you want me to fuck you like this?" Søren laid the strap on his back, along his spine as if Kingsley were a mere shelf. He took his shirt off. Kingsley saw the black fabric land on the floor by his head.

"I haven't decided. Mostly I just wanted to hear you say 'fuck' again."

"Kingsley?"

"Yes, sir."

"Shut the fuck up."

He picked up the strap and brought it down, hard, onto the back of Kingsley's thigh. The sound of the slap echoed through the entire room, bouncing off the walls, loud as a gunshot in a library.

"I like that sound," Søren said.

"What?" Kingsley asked. "The report, or me screaming?"

"Both."

Kingsley didn't scream. He was too good at this to scream. But he couldn't stop himself from releasing soft cries and hard breaths. And swearing, obviously. Every hit on his back, his ass, his thighs brought forth a torrent of profanity. He even called Søren an evil bitch once. The man did not disagree.

It went on and on, not endlessly, but it almost felt like it. Kingsley would be hearing the sound of that strap against his bare skin in his dreams. If people on the sidewalk going past the house heard it, he wouldn't be surprised.

A rush of pain wiped Kingsley out. He went limp, relaxing in his bonds like a dead man floating in a pool.

Søren said quietly, "Are you all right?"

Kingsley's eyes were closed, his head hung down, his wrists were turning red in the leather cuffs. They would probably be bruised tomorrow. He wanted them to be bruised. He didn't want them to be bruised.

"I used to follow blond men through crowded streets in foreign cities," Kingsley said between breaths. "In case they were you. Or even looked like you. Even a little like you. One almost killed me, and it was still worth it. I would have cut off my right hand to be able to touch you with my left in those days."

"Kingsley," Søren said. He sounded almost wounded.

"And now I have you," he said. "And it's perfect with us. Except sometimes when you're beating me, I think...God, how will I explain this to my daughter someday? What will I tell her when she sees the bruises?" Then Kingsley said the thing he hadn't wanted to say. "And when I think about that, I almost wish you'd never come back to me."

"YOU'RE VICIOUS TONIGHT," Nico said. Nora smiled as she lay back against his chest. Hot water lapped around their naked bodies as they soaked themselves in her clawfoot bathtub. Christmas jazz wafted from the tiny speaker on the bathroom counter—Vince Guaraldi, Geri Allen, and Louis Armstrong. Nora had never been much of a jazz aficionado but moving to New Orleans had given her a new appreciation for it.

She laughed softly. "I'm vicious every night."

"Not with me."

Nora lifted her head, met his eyes. "I've been too easy on you."

"What do you mean?"

She'd said it like she was joking, just making dirty threats while they lazed together in her bathtub. But the tone of his question was serious, curious...Somehow he knew she wasn't really joking.

"I don't want to forget what I am with you," she said.

"Vicious?"

"In charge. You really, really shouldn't be here."

"You could have told me no."

"I could have, but I didn't. That's what worries me. We have to be more careful. I can't give you everything you want when you want it. It's for the best you don't get the idea that I can or I will. Okay?" She elbowed him gently in the side.

He was quiet again. She was used to him being quiet. Quiet was Nico's default state. She let him sit in the quiet and absorb what she'd told him without telling him that in the future, they would be sticking to their scheduled visits only, that her first loyalty was to Søren. It was okay if he didn't like that, but he did have to accept it. The song rolled through her head again... One foot on the platform, the other on the train... Had there ever been a better image ever written, ever sung of a person being torn in two directions?

"Vicious," Nico finally said and kissed her neck. That was all. He'd gotten the message, accepted it, and wasn't going to start a fight about it. Not tonight anyway.

Nora smiled. "Very vicious. You won't be taking your shirt off in front of anyone for a few weeks. I hope you're not in too much pain for your little business meeting tomorrow."

"I'd rather be whipped again than sit through that."

She sat up in the water and turned around awkwardly. It was never easy to spin around in a bathtub, especially if you had a guest. Facing him, she said, "It's a little old business lunch, Moosh, not hostage negotiations."

"It's..." He waved his hand in frustration. "You know, financial reports. It's projections. It's making promises I can't keep about what the harvest will be like, what the market will be like..." He rubbed his temples. "I'm a farmer. This isn't what I do. I was reading the investor's proposal on the plane, and I almost jumped out over those mountains in West Virginia I can't pronounce."

"Appalachian?"

"Yes, those," he said and made a hilariously bad French attempt at pronouncing them—*Ahh-pahl-aah-sheen*. But she didn't mock his efforts. After all, she was still trying to figure out Tchoupitoulas Street. That first goddamn T really threw her off.

They spent the next few minutes attempting to teach each other how to pronounce their shibboleths.

Ap-ah-lay-shun... Chop-ah-too-lus... Or, if Nico wanted to sound like a mountain man, he'd have to say *Ap-ah-latch-un*, which hurt his ears so much he put his head under the water.

Nora pulled him back out. "You know," she said, "about your meeting and those financials...there is someone who could help you."

"Please, don't say it." He tried to sink down into the water again. Once again, Nora fished him out.

"I have to say it," she said. "Kingsley is many things—most bad, some good—and one of the good things? He's a very successful businessman. He would help you in a heartbeat with those projections if you asked him."

Nico started to stand up and leave the bathtub. "I'm moving to the Appalachians. *Adieu, mon amour.*"

"Oh, stop moaning, you big French baby, and get back in here."

He sat back down in the bathtub as ordered.

"Now turn around," she said. "Let me see the damage."

Nico turned and let her see his back. The lights were low in the bathroom, but the lamp on the vanity was switched on, and she could see the red welts coming up all over him. Most of the welts weren't that much bigger than freckles.

"Beautiful," she said. "I do good work." She wet a washcloth with cold water from the tap and pressed it into the largest of the welts. "You could ask him. It wouldn't kill you. And it would make his year if you asked him for some help, especially since you do need it."

"Can't we just let your master whip me instead?"

Nora laughed. "I think he'd much rather whip me than you."

"Is he really angry at us?"

Nora thought about that before answering. "He wasn't thrilled, but he's not angry. You're on his time, you know. But we worked it out. You are actually a Christmas gift to me. We're playing the sickest, most twisted game of White Elephant ever. Of course, I thought of it."

She explained how the game worked and how the presents had to be blessings and curses simultaneously. Truly sado-masochistic gifts. They had to hurt to give and hurt to get. And yet...you still wanted it.

"I'm scared to ask what you're giving Kingsley."

Nora exhaled, leaned back in the bath. She and Nico were face to face now, his head resting on his arm casually draped over the side of the bath. His hair was wet with water and steam. His celadon eyes glowed in the low light. She was planning on spending half the night biting his lips, the other half sleeping in his arms. And when they woke up, they would make rough love up until the very last moment before he had to go to the airport. He'd be zipping his fly as the cab pulled up to the curb.

"I haven't thought of anything yet. What do you get for the man who has everything?"

"What do you want to do with me tomorrow morning?" he asked.

She told him the plan—rough sex and lots of it until the very last moment he had to leave to go to the airport.

"It's a good plan," he said. "But there's something else we can do."

Nora gave him a smile. She also gave him her foot. Reverently he took her right ankle into his palm and kissed the top of her foot, the arch, the dripping wet tips of her toes.

Like father, like son.

"I think you're starting to like him," Nora said as he traced a circle around her ankle bone with his tongue.

"Never," Nico said between kisses. "But I don't hate him anymore."

SØREN UNCUFFED KINGSLEY from the bench and helped him stand. He was dizzy at first, as the blood rushed from his head, but when he stumbled a little, Søren caught him, held Kingsley's head to his shoulder.

"It's what I was thinking," Kingsley said. "When you asked me what I was thinking on Christmas Eve. That I never want to have to have that conversation with my daughter. I'll have to, though, someday. Won't I?"

Søren's mouth was on his cheek, his ear. Kissing, biting, grasping. Now his mouth was on Kingsley's throat. Teeth on his shoulder, in his skin, grazing his collarbone. Hands on his back, digging in, holding him in place as their mouths met. Then Kingsley was on his back on the bed, and Søren was fucking his mouth with his tongue.

At once, the kiss was broken, but only so Søren could turn him onto his stomach.

What was happening? What had Kingsley said? What had he done to bring this sudden change in Søren from a dispassionate sadist to a passionate lover? He needed to know so he could say it again, do it again and again and again.

Søren's clothes came off, the rest of them, and the sound of them landing with a soft rush on the wooden floors was sweeter than any music this club ever played. There were no words. No orders. Nothing was required of him but to lay there while his strange and beautiful man prepared his body for deep penetration. Next, his knees were pushed apart. After, his hips lifted. After that, the tip positioned at the entrance of him. And after that, the slow, slow, slow opening, entering, filling of him.

Kingsley closed his eyes tight, breathed as he was taken. It was no easier now than it was when he'd been sixteen, in this same position for the same purpose but on a much narrower, smaller bed. Never easy but always sweet, always wanted, except when it wasn't. Tonight it was.

Søren stretched out on top of him, his chest on Kingsley's back. Gradually, so as not to overwhelm him, Søren let his whole weight settle onto—and into—Kingsley's prone body.

He never got used to this either—the sheer weight of the man. He was lean, all muscle, but tall, and though Kingsley wasn't small or weak in the least, even his lungs struggled against two hundred pounds of man stretched out along his back. But it was bliss to gasp for each breath with each thrust into him. And when his body opened, and the penetration became an obscene and decadent pleasure, it was easier to breathe. The cock went deep, and all the nerves in his body sang, his head lifted. He took a breath like a dolphin surfacing only to sink under the water, to dive back into the warm ocean of the bed before surfacing yet again.

Sometimes when they were making love, Kingsley would talk. He would have to. The words came out, and nothing could stem the tide but Søren's fingers in his mouth or a gag. Usually, he cursed Søren when it hurt or sang his praises when it felt like this, felt like God Himself sent one of his own angels to fuck him into the next life. Sometimes he debased himself, saying over and over—I love you I love you I love you I love you I love you. God, I hate how much I love you.

On those nights, Søren never gagged him but heard it all.

Tonight Kingsley said nothing, only listened to Søren's ragged breaths, his near-silent moans. There were two different sounds—the sound he made when he thrust his cock deep into Kingsley and the sound he made when he slowly pulled it out to the tip.

And then, quietly, into Kingsley's ear, Søren asked, "Does it hurt?"

And Kingsley's quieter reply, "It only hurts when it's over."

It went on. It went on for a long time. Sometimes it was fast. Sometimes it was slow. Sometimes it was endless until the moment it ended. That was tonight. Søren was going to spend all night inside of him. He felt teeth nip at the back of his neck. Kingsley turned his head to give up more of himself. He opened his eyes for a moment and was shocked to see himself. The dungeon was new. He'd never used it before. He'd forgotten about the antique cheval mirror he'd placed near the bed, and for this reason, so he could watch Søren fucking him.

It was dark in the room, dark but for the candles still burning. Kingsley saw his own eyes glinting, the outline of his face, his body in shadow, and the candlelight shimmering on Søren's long pale body, turning it gold.

This was his favorite part, when he was so open and relaxed he almost couldn't feel the cock impaling him. It was as much a part of him now as his own. He settled into the bed, let it hold him, the black sheets caress him, as Søren gently used him like the shameless greedy whore he always had been and always would be. And Kingsley watched. He couldn't stop watching. He couldn't look away from the slow undulations of Søren's hips, the dip at the small of his back, the taut muscles of his thighs as he worked himself in deeper. What was that joke Elle had made to him once, that Søren fucked like a freight train? Was it a joke or the perfect metaphor? He thought of the times he'd gotten trapped at a railroad crossing watching as the train rumbled heavily, steadily across the tracks. All that endless, unstoppable, tightly controlled power...

"Did you laugh?" Søren said into his ear.

Had he? He must have been thinking of the train. "Are you going to fuck me forever?"

"Yes," Søren said and grasped his hair hard, pushing his head into the pillow. "So settle in."

He settled in.

But still, he watched.

That face, Søren's face. Michelangelo's David come to life, the stone turned to flesh. His lips were parted as he breathed, his eyes were closed, and with each thrust in, the wince, the slightest wince of pleasure and need. And what was that? That look on his face as he pressed his lips to Kingsley's hair and breathed as if trying to breathe him in? Love. It was love. Kingsley had seen it, and even in the dark, he knew it for love.

"I love you," Kingsley said.

"I know you do. I know."

He knew he did. Despite what he'd said before, that he sometimes wished Søren had never come back to him. Not that it wasn't true, but that two things could be true—that he wanted Søren like a man lost in the Sahara Desert wants water—and that he didn't want Søren, like a man saved from the Sahara Desert didn't want sand.

It had to end sometime. It felt like he'd been lying on his stomach all night when Søren finally increased the pace of his thrusts. Kingsley's hips ached, felt full. His cock throbbed into the sheets, dripping. Søren slid an arm under his hips, lifted him to his elbows and knees.

Kingsley could move now, and he did, pushing back against Søren as he pushed in. His head was down. He breathed shallow breaths as he arched his back, let himself open even more. Had he ever been penetrated this deeply? He could feel Søren in his stomach.

Every nerve in his lower body sang and every muscle tensed. In the mirror, Søren pounded him. He watched until it was too much even for him. He arched his back again, closed his eyes, gasped as Søren's strong wet hand wrapped around his penis and stroked. That's all it took, and Kingsley was gone. His head came up. He released with a shudder, semen spurting wildly onto the sheets, white on black.

Silently Søren released inside him, filling him with his hot fluid.

They broke apart like waves break apart on the beach, crashing into pieces only to recede back into the ocean and come back together. Kingsley knew this was only the beginning of a long night.

And the scalpel was still there on the mantel.

They lay naked side by side on the bed, breathing. Søren's arm was flung over his eyes and forehead, the picture of a man utterly spent.

"You don't even have to try to humiliate me anymore," Kingsley said. "I do it for you."

"Tell me the rest," Søren said. "Tell me what you didn't want to tell me."

"I think Céleste will believe I'm cheating on her mother with you, and it kills me."

"Juliette will tell her that's not how it is."

"Will she believe her? Will she think her mother's making excuses to keep the peace the way my mother did? How do I explain to my daughter that the best sex I have with her mother is the night after the best sex I have with you because Juliette has a fetish for playing nurse when I'm injured? What do I say? 'Don't worry, *ma petite*. Your *maman* is as much a freak as I am.'"

Søren reached out, squeezed Kingsley's thigh. "I don't know what you should say, only that it'll be a long time before she knows to ask."

"I knew. When my father and mother fought, I always knew. It's so easy to hurt a child without even trying." Kingsley turned his head to face Søren. "I'm sorry. I didn't want to tell you. And you didn't want to hear all this."

"You did want to tell me, though. And I did want to hear it."

Kingsley smiled. "So there's your gift then. Not the scalpel, but the truth from me. Something you want but don't want. What about you? What aren't you telling me that you want to tell me that I don't want to hear?"

Søren was quiet for a long time. Kingsley knew there was something that needed to be said. He could probably guess what it was.

"I wish you'd tried harder to put a stop to it," Søren finally said.

Nico and Nora, he meant. He didn't have to say any more.

"I tried. My son has, as we say, *une tête de mule*." Literally, the head of a mule. Stubborn as hell, *en anglais*.

"You didn't tell him everything, though, did you? That she wasn't just someone you had sex with sometimes."

"No. I didn't tell my son that his new lover used to burn me, whip me, and fuck me up the ass with a strap-on. Do you think I should have told him that instead of her being a girl I fucked every now and then, that she was important to me? That she was special to me? That would have made him want her even more because it would hurt me more. And when he had her— and by that point, he'd already had her—it would have been a sweeter triumph."

"Probably," Søren said, his tone conciliatory.

He hadn't told Søren about how Nico had stood his ground when Kingsley had tried to confront Nora, how he wouldn't even let him speak to her. How they'd almost come to blows over it.

You don't talk to her, you talk to me. You don't look at her, you don't go near her...

If he hadn't wanted to strangle his son, he might have been proud of Nico for standing up to him. Not many people stood up to Kingsley. And even more, he was proud of Nico for not letting him or anyone else blame Nora. When there was an affair, the woman was always assigned the blame. Always. And Kingsley was guilty of that himself, thinking Nora had seduced Nico. But Nico had taken all the responsibility, 100% of it. *I went to her because she was feeling weak, and I knew it. I went to her to have her, and I wasn't going to take no for an answer. And I didn't.*

What was that saying about the apple not falling far from the tree?

"You know you have no right to tell her she can't have him. None. If she had a whole army of lovers, she'd still barely break even with you."

"Because of Fionn."

"Because of Fionn."

"She loves Fionn."

"She does. But having sex four months out of the year with a handsome younger man will never compare to you having a child with another woman. Even if she didn't want children."

"I know," Søren said. Then again, "I know."

"You took it well when it happened," Kingsley said. "Better than I did."

"Marie Antoinette took it well when they led her to the guillotine."

Ah, the guillotine. He remembered something Nico had said that day of their fight, that Kingsley wasn't angry because he thought Nora had seduced his son. He was jealous. *She's known you for years and me for months, and she still wants me more. You know it, and it hurts your stupid pride.*

No surprise a Frenchman had invented the guillotine. Only the French could kill a man with a single cut.

Kingsley smiled. "It's not that bad, is it?"

"I never thought it would be this serious between them. When she hinted at what was happening, I thought—unfairly, I suppose—that it was payback."

"For Grace."

Søren nodded. "Believe it or not, I was relieved. I'd behaved horribly in a moment of temporary insanity. She'd behaved horribly in a moment of temporary insanity. I'd almost lost Eleanor. She'd just lost her mother. It made sense in a way. We could call it even. But no, it wasn't that at all."

While they were telling each other the truth, Kingsley had one more confession.

"You have no idea how hostile he was to the thought of me being his father. We joke now about Nico hating me, but in the beginning, he did. If not me, personally, the idea of me. If I had put a stop to it, to them, that would have been the end of my relationship with him. I couldn't do it. I wasn't strong enough to do it. I wanted my son too much."

"I know. I do, I promise."

"Do you? Do you know how it feels that he beat me at my own game? He made me grateful that they're together. *Grateful*. My ex-domme and my son and I'm grateful. Because if it wasn't for her, he would have nothing to do with me. Why can't he be greedy for my money like normal children? People used to be terrified of me. Now I'm terrified that a twenty-five-year-old farmer who speaks French like a, well, a *farmer* will decide one day he doesn't want to talk to me anymore. And it will kill me and he knows it and—and this is what hurts—he enjoys it. I will say this to you and only you, but I have, more than once, imagined punching my own son in the face. Nothing makes you weaker than love for your children. I hate being weak. I should have gotten a vasectomy at age fifteen."

He tried to sigh, to laugh, but it came out a groan of real anguish.

"Could be worse," Søren said. "Could be Wesley."

Kingsley laughed so hard he almost fell out of the bed. "Bastard," he said and elbowed Søren in the side. "Don't make me laugh when I'm trying to be maudlin."

"Admit it, her taste in boy toys has definitely improved."

"My son is not a boy toy," Kingsley said. Søren turned his head toward him, arched his eyebrow. "He's a man toy. Speaking of Wesley, is he still dating your—"

"Safe word."

"Fine, I won't bring it up." He rolled onto his side facing Søren. "Are you angry? I know it's been hard, but she's content for once in her life, and you and I, we have fun together when she's out of town, no?"

"We do," Søren said with a grin. "If I ever was angry, I'm not anymore. I only wanted to tell you the truth. Except I didn't want to. And you wanted to hear it."

"Except I didn't." Kingsley laughed again. "Merry fucking Christmas."

"My sentiments exactly."

Søren turned toward him and drew him against his chest. "Can you stay all night?"

"All night. Can you?"

"All night. I have to leave early, though." Søren didn't sound happy about that.

"Church or something?" Kingsley asked.

"I have to pick up Eleanor's gift for me. I think. No telling with her. She gave me an address and told me to be there by eight. Really, I don't want to know. But that's the game, isn't it?"

"That's the game," Kingsley said with a sigh. "Stupid game. Let's never play it again. Until next year."

They lay together until they were moved on to other games. And after there were no more games to play, they spent the rest of the night tangled up in each other, wrapped in black sheets.

JANUARY 6TH

AT 7:30 in the morning, Lucky arrived at work. Since her first appointment was at eight, she needed to prep the space. She turned up the heat a little, put down a new bed warmer on her table, fresh sheets and blankets, and lit a pine-scented candle on the side table. After she changed into her work uniform of black slacks and a white polo shirt—square as hell but it made the clients comfortable seeing her in the same boring uniform every time they came in. Consistency and routine were reassuring for people who didn't have a lot of stability in their lives.

When everything was ready, she went to the front desk and opened her book to see who was coming in that day.

Oh yeah, now she remembered. One of her favorite clients, Nora, had bought a session as a gift. New client. She checked her notes. Lucky got out her iPad and scrolled to the name Nora had given her. One name. No last name. Søren.

All right, what was up with Mister Søren?

Lucky shook her head as she read the notes over. Usually, clients told her standard boring stuff like, *Don't touch my feet, sciatica, old right shoulder injury, can't use anything scented...*

But not these notes. They were probably the weirdest notes

she'd ever taken on a client's massage needs. More warnings than notes.

He doesn't know about this, and he's not going to be thrilled when he turns up. Seriously. Be prepared for a big sexy bitch on wheels.

No, he's never had a professional massage before, and he'll probably hate it. If you can even get him on the table, I'll tip you fifty bucks for every fifteen minutes.

Lucky remembered asking Nora why she'd booked a two-hour massage when she only expected it to last fifteen minutes.

It'll take him a while to agree to it. No hard feelings if he backs out.

When Lucky asked why she'd be massaging a man who didn't want a massage, Nora had given her a sad sort of smile.

He doesn't like being touched. But he doesn't like that he doesn't like being touched. I thought you could work your magic.

And one last warning:

Don't take any shit from him.

That wouldn't be a problem. Lucky didn't take shit from anyone.

Her office was in a quiet street in the Irish Quarter, a small blue and white shotgun house converted into a massage and "healing touch" practice. She didn't get a lot of motorcycles roaring in this neighborhood before eight in the morning, but suddenly there was one. Through the front window, she spotted a big black motorcycle. She didn't know anything about motorcycles, except this one was pretty and sort of European-looking. A male-shaped person on the back of it. It rolled up to a stop near the front door. He turned off the engine and dismounted. (Is that what motorcycle dudes called it? Dismounting?)

"Fuck," Lucky said out loud. This was Nora's friend? She'd expected your average good-looking white dude. This was not your average good-looking white dude. This was not your average anything. This was a human tree. Tall dude. Big dude. Not big like beefy but big like, well, just a big dude. Like someone crossed a soccer player with an Olympic swimmer, added twenty pounds of muscle, and put him on the back of a motorcycle. Good thing she'd bought the longer massage table.

She watched, curious and a little nervous, as the man paused outside her door. He took off his black motorcycle helmet, and she caught her first look at his face.

Oh, so not just a big, tall dude but a big, tall hot dude. He wasn't Lucky's type. Men, in general, weren't her type, but she knew a pretty boy when she saw one. Silver-blond hair, straight nose, serious eyes, seriously handsome. It looked like he wasn't going to come through the door when he saw the sign on the front of the building. But after a pause, he opened the door and walked inside.

"Good morning," Lucky said. She usually tried to sound professional with new clients—before she let her true self come out. "Are you Søren?"

"Unfortunately, yes," he said. The man's glare could melt the glue on the wallpaper.

Big sexy bitch, for real.

"Did I pronounce that right?"

"Not even remotely, but rest assured, I'm used to it."

She believed that but didn't care. "How do you pronounce it?"

"It doesn't matter." Good voice. Unhappy voice but a good voice.

"It does to me." She tilted her head to the side, waiting for his response.

He looked at her, and she got a weird feeling his estimation of her went up a notch. A very, very small notch, but still, it was progress.

"I'll answer to Surr-n, Serr'n, or Sore'n, so say whichever you'll be less likely to mangle."

"All three of those sounded like literally the same word to me."

Was that a smile she almost saw on his lips? Maybe?

"In certain circles, I'm called Mr. S, if that makes it easier on you."

"I like Mr. S. That's cute. Nice to meet you, Mr. S and/or Sore-en."

"I assume I'm expected."

"You're expected. I'm Lucky, the therapist here." She held out her hand to shake. He paused before shaking it. Big hands. Very big hands. But nice. Sculpted. No calluses. He didn't do construction for a living, that was for sure.

"You're an infant," he said, releasing her hand.

"I'm twenty-two. How old are you, Mr. S?" Rude question. She was curious if he'd even answer it.

"Fifty," he said without hesitation though if he'd said "forty," she would have believed him immediately. "I could be your grandfather."

"Maybe, I guess." She gave it some thought, did the math out loud. "Fifty minus twenty-two divided by two... Factor in some early puberty and bad parenting... It could work. Nice to meet you, Granddad. Want to come on back?"

"No."

"Are you going to come back anyway?"

"What happens in the back?"

"We talk for a few minutes."

"About what?"

"About what we're going to do? I know you've never had a massage before, but have you ever, like...*heard* of them?" She couldn't keep all the sarcasm out of her voice. Just most of it. He didn't seem to mind.

He narrowed his eyes at her. "I've heard rumors."

She laughed. "Nora warned me about you."

"What did she tell you?"

"Come on back, and I'll answer that question."

He took a long breath, almost exaggerated. Well, nice to see he had a little bit of a sense of humor about the whole thing.

"Don't be afraid," Lucky said. "I know I'm super scary-looking, but I'm not dangerous, I promise."

"You look like a Smurf."

Was this rude? Well, she did have blue hair, and she wasn't very tall. The man had a point.

"You think that's an insult, but I love the Smurfs." She waved her hand, beckoning him to follow her to the back. Fifty-fifty odds on whether he'd come back or not.

He stood stock-still in front of the desk. Her heart clenched in sympathy. This really wasn't easy for him.

"Hey," she said, "Nora told me she loves you. She wouldn't send you to me if she didn't think I could help you. And I promise you, Søren, nothing's going to happen that you don't want to happen. Nothing."

He sighed another exaggerated sigh.

She grinned.

"Lead the way," he said.

✳

USUALLY, she'd take a client straight into the therapy room for a quick convo before the massage started. But with him, she decided to take it easy. She led him into the recovery room, which was just a nice spa-like sitting room. Two brown leather chairs, low light, soft music, a waterfall fountain, pale green walls, cushy rugs, and filled with the soothing scent of sandalwood incense. She took one chair and beckoned for him to sit in the other.

"So," she began, slapping her hands on her knees. "Søren—"

"How does someone only twenty-two have their own massage practice?"

"Deflection. Nice," she said. "But Nora booked me for two hours, so if you want to hear my entire life story—"

"I wouldn't mind."

"Fine. Short version. Maybe it'll make you more comfortable with me."

He didn't look comfortable. He looked stern, closed-off, ready to bolt.

"I grew up in the middle-of-nowhere backwater hellhole Louisiana, with a roughneck dad and a half-Indian mom, which made me very popular in the swamp, as you can guess. That's sarcasm, by the way. Oh, and then it turned out I was queer. So, guess who got bullied all the time?" She smiled broadly and pointed at her face with both thumbs. "But I'm smart, believe it or not. At sixteen, I dropped out of high school, took the G.E.D., passed with flying colors, moved here, and got a job working the front desk at a massage clinic. Fell in love with the whole thing. I'd found my calling. So I saved my money, went to massage school, got a bank loan, and here I am. This is a massage and healing touch practice."

"Healing touch?"

"I use touch to help heal the body and the spirit. Also, you should know this is a queer-only practice and safe space. My clients are all gay, lesbian, bi-, non-binary, trans, kinky. If Nora sent you here, I assume you fall into one of those groups."

"Yes, I'm a lesbian."

She held out her hand for a high-five. "Right on, Granddad. Samesies."

He looked at her hand. She waited, waved it. Finally, he slapped it gently. "I can see why Eleanor likes you. She's obnoxious, too."

"Thanks," she said. "Nora's cool. She came to me for flogging elbow. It's like tennis elbow, but you know, because of flogging. I don't think she plays tennis."

"She does not." He didn't say anything for a moment. Then he said, "Kinky."

"You're part of Queen Nora's crew. No shock there."

"And, ah...bisexual."

She nodded, smiled. "That was hard for you to say."

He looked away, his eyes resting on the little waterfall fountain trickling quietly in the corner. "I don't really think of myself in those terms."

"Big gorgeous white dude, manly as fuck on your big fuck-off motor-bicycle out there. Probably hard to see yourself as queer, yeah?"

"Queer people are vulnerable."

"And you're not."

He met her eyes. "No."

"You're scared of getting a massage. I think there's some vulnerability there."

"I'm not scared. I'm uncomfortable with the idea. Very different."

"You want to talk about that discomfort? Unpack it a little?" She leaned back in her chair to give him breathing room.

"What's to unpack? I had a difficult childhood like so many others. It leaves scars."

"Abuse?"

"Yes."

She waited, gave him time.

"Sexual," he said. "And physical. And psychological."

"So the works, huh?" She'd learned through long practice to put people at ease by not overreacting to painful and traumatic revelations. They needed to be able to tell her anything without worrying they were upsetting her. Sometimes her clients' stories made her sick, made her want to cry, and she did, but only after they were gone. She owed them that much. She owed them the chance to speak freely, without concern for anyone's comfort but their own.

He nodded.

"And you don't like being touched as a result?" she asked.

"I associate touch with either sex or suffering. Even a hug from a friend feels like something I have to quietly tolerate."

"I could refer you to an excellent Reiki practitioner if you really don't want to be touched. They do energy work more than touching. It would be a good place to start."

"As tempting as that is, I do want to overcome my aversion. And if Eleanor trusts you...I suppose I can try." He fell silent a moment, then said, "I don't want to be like this. I don't want to let my past win this battle."

Lucky wished he liked being touched. She would have hugged him for his trust and his courage.

"For what it's worth, I'm sorry that happened to you, Søren. I can't change the past, but I can help with some of the after-effects if you're interested. But I need a little more information. When does your aversion to touch usually flare up? No offense, you give up strong 'fuck off' vibes. I can't imagine many randos are coming up to you on Bourbon Street and pinching your ass."

"Only Eleanor," he said.

"I can believe that. Where does it get bad for you?"

"At church mostly," he said. "Are you Catholic?"

"Come on. Look at me. Smurfs aren't Catholic."

He laughed, almost. Not a real laugh, but she could tell he was warming up to her.

"During Mass, there's a moment called Passing the Peace. That's when we're supposed to shake hands and kiss and hug each other."

"Sweet."

"It's intolerable."

"That bad?" she asked, trying not to smile at his disgust at the very mention of hugging and kissing strangers.

"Handshakes are fine. Anything else seems..." He exhaled. "Excessive. To say the least. Unfortunately, it's unavoidable."

"A whole lot of people don't like being touched by strangers, or even by friends. And a lot of them weren't even abused. They just have strong boundaries around their bodies. There's nothing wrong with that, and I don't believe in trying to fix what isn't broken." She'd never touch anyone who didn't really want to be touched. It went against everything she believed in as a therapist.

"I know. However," he surprised her then by smiling, "I have a son."

"You do? What's his name?"

"Fionn." Then he said it again, slowly and sarcastically so she could hear how to pronounce it. "*Fionn*." F'yawn.

She smirked at him. "Thanks, Mr. S. Tell me about your Fionn."

"He lives in another country with his mother and her husband, but there's a chance I may see him someday soon. I told Eleanor that it worries me that I may not feel comfortable holding him. If it weren't for that, I'd happily go on tolerating the hugs. But—"

"You don't want to just tolerate being hugged by your son?"

He was quiet, then said, "Yes. That's it exactly."

She took a deep breath, slapped her knees. "All right. We can work on that. We'll start small. On a scale of one to ten, how much would you hate it if I held your hand right now?"

"We're going to hold hands?" He looked like he was on the verge of laughing at her. Good. Better than tears.

"Why not? I hold hands with a lot of my friends. It's not romantic, not sexual. Just keeps us from getting separated in crowds."

"We're not in a crowd."

"Yeah, but I don't want you getting separated from me anyway."

His eyes met hers. "It wouldn't be terrible," he said. "Maybe a four out of ten."

"Four's not bad. Most people would feel pretty uncomfortable holding hands with a Smurf."

"That was rude of me. I apologize."

She shrugged. "You didn't hurt my feelings. I don't have any feelings."

His gray eyes brightened a little. "You are an unusual young woman."

"True, but I'm very good at holding hands."

She held out her hand, palm up and open, a peace offering. But also a test. If he couldn't even let their hands touch for longer than the span of a handshake, he wasn't going to be on her table today. Maybe not ever.

"It'll be all right, Granddad," she said. "It's just a little old hand." She wiggled her fingers.

"Since you are my granddaughter, I suppose it wouldn't be that out of the ordinary to hold your hand."

He reached out and took her hand like he was going to shake it, but he didn't shake it. He held her fingers. Lucky leaned forward in the chair and held onto his hand. His hand was so much bigger than hers, but it was still a good fit, like a child's hand in a grownup's. She closed her fingers around his, and he let her. A few seconds passed. She waited for him to pull away. He didn't.

Lucky knew she was pushing her luck, but that's how she got her name. Luck only came to those who pushed for it. She brought her other hand over his. Now she held his right hand with both her hands. She almost joked, A hand sandwich, but she managed to keep it on the inside.

"I know you probably can't feel it," she said, "but right now, I'm sending everything good that's in me into you. I'm sending my hopes and dreams and my kindness and my caring and my humor and my prayers for your healing into you."

He smiled. "You can do that?"

He was sitting back in the chair, right arm out, right hand in hers. She could tell he was tolerating it well enough, but he didn't seem to be getting anything out of it yet.

"I can do that. And if you let yourself feel it, you'll like it. It feels like a warm light shining into you."

She sent more into him through that sacred place where their hands met, where the healer met the one who sought healing. She sent the memory of Nora's love and concern for him, the image of him holding a baby boy in his arms and smiling. She sent him the love she had for her work, her passion for her calling. And she sent her own little love she felt for him, for this man who teased her about her blue hair and let her call him "Granddad" without being the least insulted. Rare in any man.

He leaned forward in his chair and brought his left hand to wrap over hers. They both leaned forward as if they were saying a prayer together, both their hands in each other's hands. And the room glowed with the light of compassion, which she knew he probably couldn't see, but she could.

"You want to come back and get on my table?" she asked. "I have more light to give you."

He exhaled. "I'm willing to try."

She squeezed his hands. He squeezed hers back. Without breaking the contact, she stood up and led him by the hand back to her table.

❄

"THREE THINGS you need to know for your own comfort and safety," Lucky said as she brought him into the therapy room. Only when she gestured for him to take a seat did she release his hand. "First of all—I'm going to lock the front door. The back door's also locked. I'll set the alarm. Nobody can get in here without us knowing. I pay for private security, and they're good. No cops are going to raid this place and arrest you for unpaid parking tickets."

"You must work with victims of violent crime."

"A lot," she said. "Too many. Second, I don't care if you're naked or if you're fully dressed. Seriously. I can work with any variation of clothed or unclothed, and you'll have a good experience."

"My mother was Danish so—"

"Inherited that Scandinavian naked gene, huh?"

He laughed softly. "Yes."

"I'll kick up the heat a little more then. Third—you're in charge. If I'm touching your leg, and you don't want me to touch your leg, tell me, 'Lucky, back off my leg,' and I'll back off."

"I appreciate that."

"Any injuries or pain you want to tell me about?"

"I run, which leaves my feet and ankles are always slightly

tender. And a little soreness in the right shoulder from last night."

"Flogging? Whipping?"

"Strap and flogger."

"Giving or receiving?"

"Giving."

"Cool, cool." She picked up her iPad, made her notes.

"Are you writing 'flogging injury' in my file?" Søren asked her.

"I'm a professional, Mister. I called it 'repetitive-stress myalgia in the right shoulder.'"

"The gentleman on the receiving end would find that amusing. He just called it a 'good night.'"

She smiled. This was good. He was getting more and more comfortable with her. Maybe they'd make some progress today.

"How do you feel about George Winston?" she asked.

"I'm not averse," he said.

She queued up George Winston's album "December" on her iPhone and adjusted the volume. She asked Søren a few more housekeeping questions, gave him the usual spiel about stopping for bathroom breaks, water breaks, and then it was time. Only one question remained.

"You want to start face up or face down?"

He stared up at the ceiling as if it could give him the answer.

"Both sound equally appalling."

"I work with a lot of dudes. If you get a boner from a foot rub, I don't care. It happens. The body has a mind of its own. Just don't point it in my direction, please."

He exhaled. "I suppose face up."

"All right. I'm going to step out for five minutes, let you undress, get on the table under the sheets and blankets, and I'll be back to get started."

At that, she dimmed the lights to low and stepped out of the room. First, she locked the front doors. Second, she set the alarm. She turned up the heat another notch, and then it was time. She knocked softly on the door and then went inside.

Søren lay on his back on her table under the blankets.

"Comfortable?" she asked in a soft and careful voice. She was always gentle with her new clients.

"I'm not completely miserable."

Probably as good as it was going to get from him. Lucky made sure to tell him everything she was doing as she did it. *I'm going to put a bolster under your knees now. I'm going to straighten the blankets. I'm going to adjust the table height. Surprises were never good for nervous clients.*

One thing she noticed, without meaning to notice, was that he had a good body. A very good and very naked body. And definitely Scandinavian—the carpet matched the drapes.

"You should know, Nora said she'd pay me fifty bucks extra for every fifteen minutes I keep you on the table. Don't let that influence you. Just wanted you to know my ulterior motives."

Søren seemed to think about that for a moment. Then said, "Bleed her dry."

Lucky laughed and put her hand on his hand. They'd established that much of a comfort level with each other. He squeezed her fingers and then let his hand go lax in hers.

"So you said hugging made you uncomfortable, but handshakes don't, and handholding isn't that bad either. So it sounds like your area of issue is your chest and stomach. What I'll do is start on the outside—hands, feet, head, neck—and spiral my way in before I go near your chest, hips, and core."

His only response was a slight nod. She went to work thinking, *Magic hands, don't fail me now.*

Lucky got out her best massage lotion, scented like the sea, and squeezed it into her palm. As promised, she started on his hands. A lot of people told her the hand massage was their favorite part anyway. So much typing, so much wear and tear on the fingers in everyday life that everyone should get their hands massaged every now and then. And his were nice to massage, not only because he had beautiful hands, but they emanated a gently vibrating aura, vibrating almost audibly, like music.

"You a musician?" she asked.

"Pianist. Did Eleanor tell you?"

"No. But sometimes I can feel music in people."

"You can feel music in my hands?"

"I can sometimes sense stuff about people through touch. Don't let that freak you out."

"I'm skeptical, but I am not 'freaked out.'"

She worked on both hands, felt the vibration grow louder and lovelier the more his hands relaxed into hers. She was almost sad to let them go when it was time to move on. The next stop was his feet. He'd warned her he was a runner. His feet showed it.

"You beat the hell out of your feet," she said as she worked her fingers up and down the top of his right foot, to the ankle, and back to the toes. "How much do you run a day? A thousand miles?"

"Seven miles three to five days a week."

"Damn. Please tell me you eat an entire sleeve of Oreos sometimes."

"Never."

"Shit."

He was silent for a moment and then said, "However—"

"Yeah?"

"Thin Mints," he said. Lucky laughed. "Don't tell Eleanor."

"What happens on the table stays on the table." Sometimes she talked the whole time during a session. Sometimes she said nothing at all. The talking seemed to distract him from what was happening, but that might not be a good thing if they were trying for comfort. Comfortable and distracted weren't the same thing. She shut her mouth and went to work on the soles of his feet. She concentrated on imparting white healing light through her fingers and into his well-used feet. Feet were important. They carried the body on its journeys. She sensed that he was at the beginning of a journey. A journey to a crossroads and that choice of paths would be the most difficult choice of his life. She didn't say anything to him about that. There was no stopping it, no warning him off of whatever the universe was bringing to him. But she could help him be stronger for his quest, steadier on his feet. She pictured a white ball of pure healing light in her hand, and she pushed it through the tender arch of his right foot.

Søren flinched. It was so sudden she almost gasped. Only years of training kept her from reacting. She never ever let herself react. Only a client was allowed to react.

"Did I hit a sore spot?" she asked, keeping her voice calm.

"No, it...it felt good."

"Good," she said brightly as if she had been expecting that reaction all along. She kept working at the sole of his right foot and then moved to the ankle. She gave the tendon extra attention. He released a little breath.

"Bad or good?"

"Good," he said.

She smiled to herself.

"I saw that," Søren said.

"I'm allowed to be happy that you're enjoying this."

"I'm enjoying...parts of this. Not all of it."

"Would you like a warm compress for your eyes?"

"Are you trying to get me to stop watching what you're doing and commenting?"

"Maybe."

"I wouldn't say no."

Not quite "enthusiastic consent," but that was probably as enthusiastic as he was going to get today. She took a compress out of the towel warmer and laid it over his forehead and eyes.

"Isn't that nice?"

"It's...tolerable."

"Such a flatterer. I'm imagining the Yelp review right now—'Not the worst thing I've ever experienced. I would rather have been shot in the eye, but since that wasn't an option, this was an acceptable substitute. Five stars.'"

"Four stars," Søren said. "You called me Granddad."

"Relax, Granddad. You might actually like this part." She grabbed one ankle at a time and pulled gently, shaking the leg, which was her go-to technique for stubborn clients. It felt impossibly good, at least to her. She had no idea what sort of magic that worked, but on runners especially, it was almost—

"God," Søren said.

"Better than sex, right?"

"Close."

"All my drag queens love that one. Those insane high heels they wear fuck their lumbar spine up."

"Always delighted to be in the company of drag queens."

Feeling ludicrously triumphant after that victory with Søren, Lucky went all-in on him, giving him everything she had to offer. All her best techniques, all her concentration, all her strength, and all her compassion. She worked on his shoulder, giving more attention to the right than the left as that was the one experiencing pain. It was her favorite part of the job, feeling a knot of tension dissipating under her fingers.

Slowly she worked her way in from the outskirts of his body to the center of his being. To his chest where he kept his lungs and his heart. To his pelvic area where he kept his power, his sexuality, and the suffering he carried from whatever happened to him as a kid. His thighs were like steel—from the tension, not the running. She was in dangerous territory here, and she tread lightly, carefully. Every time she moved closer to his hips, she let him know.

"Since you're a runner, I want to work on your hip flexors. You okay with that?"

"I'm fine with it."

He sounded tense, and she felt the tightness in his body, but he'd agreed to it, probably because he knew he needed it, even if he didn't want it. She went in carefully, uncovering first his right hip and massaging the tendons before going to his left. It had a bruise on it.

"Don't ask," he said.

"I've seen bite marks in stranger places."

She worked around the bruise, massaging until the tightness in his hip turned supple and soft.

And that was it.

"Ready to turn over?" Lucky asked softly. This was a big moment.

"No."

"We can stop now if you want. I know prone isn't really the most comfortable position for a lot of people."

He took a long breath. "We can try."

She held the blankets as he turned over and laid his arms down the length of his body. She pulled the sheets back to his hips. He had the most beautiful sculpted, muscular, sinewy, strong back of any man, woman, or non-binary person she'd ever seen on her table. Angels blew their trumpets when he took his shirt off. She'd heard of marble statues that looked like human flesh, but his human flesh looked like a marble statue. She was almost surprised it was so warm and supple under her hands. But she didn't let his physical beauty intimidate her. Everyone was equal on her table, young and old, ugly and beautiful, sinners and saints.

Slowly she worked her way from his shoulders to his mid-back to his lower back where she felt so much tension she was shocked he wasn't in active pain. It was like his midsection was wrapped in a band of black iron. This was where he carried the weight of his secrets and his suffering, right here in the very core of him. She gathered all her empathy, all her strength again, so much she knew she would be drained for the rest of the day... gathered it into a golden ball and worked it into the small of his back with the heels of her hands. The pain was darkness. She shone the light onto it. The darkness feared the light and fled from it.

A soft sound came out of Søren's throat, and she knew the pain was gone.

At least for now. The pain never stayed away for long. But that's what she was here for. She'd fight it as long as it needed fighting because everyone who knew what chronic pain was like knew that even one day without it was a gift.

When the massage was over, she lifted her hands off his body like a pianist lifting their hands off the keys after a final note.

"We're done," she said quietly.

He turned over onto his back, stared up at the ceiling, exhaled. "Thank God."

"I'm almost hurt." Not almost. That did hurt. But she smiled anyway, for his sake.

"No," he said. "That's not what I meant. I meant, thank God it was...not unpleasant."

Her heart danced. "You liked that?"

"Parts of it. Parts were difficult, but some of it was pleasant. And a few moments were...sublime."

"The leg-pull thing?"

"That should not feel as good as it does. Thank you for that new experience."

She smiled, put her hand on his. He immediately squeezed her fingers. She felt the joy of a parent feeding their child waking from a coma, clutching the hand like a signal, a message that said, I'm alive, I'm alive, I'm still alive...

She squeezed his hand back, said, "I'll let you get dressed. Sit up slowly. You might feel dizzy. When you're ready, you can meet me in the recovery room. Would you like water, hot tea, or coffee? I make a mean masala chai."

"Masala chai would be very nice."

As she started to leave the room, he sat up and ran his hand through his hair. Knees up, head down, and breathing...he looked drained, like he'd just run a marathon or endured a powerful test.

"I'm proud of you, Søren," Lucky said. "I know that was hard for you."

He turned his head, smiled at her. She could tell he was trying not to laugh. He probably didn't have Smurfs telling him, "I'm proud of you," very often.

And he was very handsome when he smiled. In fact, he looked nothing like a granddad, especially not hers.

"Thank you, Lucky."

Ten minutes later, she had his masala chai ready. One for him and one for her. He came into the room, took the cup from her hand, and took a long sip.

"Very good." He took another sip, then another, then set the cup down. "I should be going."

"Let me get the door for you." The after-party was always a little awkward with a new client. She smiled and led him to the front door, unlocked it for him.

"It was nice to meet you. I hope I see you on my table again someday."

"My life doesn't allow me these sorts of luxuries. Please

don't be offended if you don't see me again. It's nothing personal."

She was touched by his concern for her feelings.

"What do you do for a living? Or should I not ask?"

"I wouldn't ask. But suffice it to say, it doesn't pay well. Don't let my 'motor-bicycle,' as you called it, fool you. It was a gift." He pulled on his black leather motorcycle jacket and zipped it.

"I'll tell Nora to pony up for your birthday next time she's here."

"Then I'll see you in December."

"I'd give you a hug goodbye until then, but I know—"

He stepped forward and took her in his arms. She was so surprised by the hug she almost forgot what to do. Then she remembered, and she wrapped her arms around his back and patted it like she was the grandfather and he the grandchild.

It was a short hug but sweet. He turned, walked out, and got on his motorcycle.

She stood in the doorway. "You're a good hugger, Granddad."

"And you're an excellent therapist. Five stars."

With that, he put on his helmet, turned the key to the engine, kicked up the kickstand, and rode away.

She had a feeling she'd never see him again.

Too bad. Mr. S really did give good hugs.

IN THE OLD DAYS, Kingsley couldn't have told anyone what 8:30 in the morning looked like. He thought of that time as B.C. —Before Céleste. Now he'd been up for an hour, and Juliette even longer. Breakfast was over, and he and Céleste were in the back yard. Although it was a cool sixty degrees that morning, she'd wanted to swing. So he'd bundled her into her shoes and her coat, and here he was, pushing his daughter on her swing set, laughing as she squealed every time she went a little higher, a little higher.

Even in these happiest moments, melancholy threatened. He'd never gotten to do this with Nico. Did Nico even have a swing set growing up? They probably had a tire swing or a thick rope tied to a sturdy tree branch. His son had a good childhood, Kingsley reminded himself. Even if he wasn't a part of it. And though it hurt to admit it, even if only to himself, that if he'd been a part of it, it probably wouldn't have been so good.

"Higher?" he asked Céleste when he caught her in the swing and held her suspended in his arms. She loved when he did that—grabbing her on the upswing and letting her feel the gravity before he let her go again.

"Can we do water balloons?"

The non-sequiturs that came out of his child's mouth never ceased to surprise, amuse, and confuse him.

"Water balloons are for summer, not for January."

She was about to argue when Kingsley heard a voice behind him.

"Can I push?"

Kingsley pulled Céleste off the seat of the swing immediately and turned around, twisting her away from danger, if there was danger. His old instincts always lurked under the surface, no matter how relaxed he might seem.

He stared across the yard to the gate in the back fence, the one Nora always used when she came and went from the house.

Nico was standing there. Only fifteen feet away. Nico. Standing there. Nico was in jeans, a dark jacket, a black weekender bag over his shoulder. He looked healthy but tired. He looked like a man who'd had a long but very good night.

Nico. And Nora, too. She stepped in after him, looking

sheepish in her tan wool coat and black boots. So this was Søren's "gift" to Nora—a visit from Nico.

He was too shocked to say anything but, "What are you doing here?"

"I was in town. I have to go to the airport soon, but I had time to stop in for a few minutes. *Bonjour,* Céleste," he said, smiling. "You remember me?"

Shyly she shook her head. She didn't have much long-term memory for faces at her age.

He swallowed. "That's Nico," Kingsley said. His heart was lodged like a rock in his throat. "That's your brother. Can you say hello?"

She gave the tiniest little wave.

Nico started forward. Juliette came out onto the back patio. She gasped, smiled.

"It's good to see you," Juliette said. "What a surprise."

"Nice to see you, always," Nico said, unfailingly polite to Juliette. Not nearly as polite to Kingsley.

"I have a client who needs me this morning," Nora said. "Can you take Nico to the airport?"

"Can I go?" Céleste said.

"We'll all go," Juliette said. She came to Kingsley and took Céleste out of his arms. "Come in and have some breakfast if you have time, Nico. I'll pour some coffee." She left them alone. Alone but for Nora. This was a good gift for their game. He knew giving up even an hour with Nico had to have hurt her. And it certainly hurt Kingsley to know Nico had been one street away all night, and his son hadn't told him. But no regrets. He would take what he could get, including the pain.

Kingsley looked at Nora. "Thank you."

She smiled. "Merry Christmas, King." She took Nico's arm and kissed him on the cheek. "See you soon." She said something in his ear, some private whisper. Nico smiled and nodded.

Then she turned and was gone.

"You didn't have to give up your time with her for me," Kingsley said to his son.

Nico walked slowly toward him, shrugged. "I wanted to see Céleste."

"She'll remember you when she gets older. You can spend a little time with her before we go."

Nico looked past him at the house. He seemed to be working up the courage to say something. Probably, *This is the last time we are going to meet. I've decided I don't need or want you in my life at all. Stop trying to replace my real father...*

"I have a meeting in New York with some investors today. Would you go over their prospectus with me, so I know what I'm getting into?"

Kingsley couldn't believe what he was hearing. He would have given Nico an arm, a leg, and a kidney if he'd asked for it.

"Of course. Come inside."

Nico walked up to him, and together they went to the French doors that led to Kingsley's office. Kingsley opened them for Nico. Nico paused, studied the floor before finally meeting his eyes.

"I'm sorry I forgot to call on Christmas."

"It's fine. You're busy at home. We know that."

"*Joyeux Noël,* a little late," Nico said.

"Better late than never."

He followed Nico inside.

Next year, they were definitely playing the game again.

NORA HEARD the tell-tale purr of a classic Ducati engine outside her kitchen in the alley behind her house. She had just finished cleaning up the mess she and Nico had made. Good timing.

She went out and met Søren in her back garden.

"So, how did it go?" she asked with a nervous smile. "Did you absolutely hate it?"

"You owe Lucky two-hundred dollars."

Nora's eyes widened. "You made it a whole hour?" She was so happy she threw her arms around him and kissed him on the mouth.

"One of the longest hours of my life," he said after she stepped back, but he did seem relaxed. Or as relaxed as Søren ever got with his clothes on. "But not universally awful."

"Did she do the leg pull and shake?"

"Why does that feel so good?" he asked, his voice hushed with awe and wonder.

"I have no idea. Probably Voodoo. Are you mad at me?"

"For forcing me into an uncomfortable situation that I did not ask for? I should be."

She crossed her arms, met his eyes. "Seriously, are you pissed at me?"

He touched her cheek. "No. It was...nice. Enough."

He pointed at her nose. "Never do it again."

"Yes, sir." She rose up on her toes and kissed him again. "Come in. I'll make you breakfast. A good massage always makes me hungry." Nora wasn't the world's greatest cook, but she'd learned how to make kick-ass French toast from Nico. She'd joked that they probably just called it "toast" in France. No, he told her, it was called *pain perdu*—lost bread. Only the French, she'd said, could make French toast sound bleak.

He glanced at the back door. Nora knew what that look meant.

"He's gone. He's at King's house."

"Really? That's...surprising. Isn't it? Your orders?"

She raised her hands. "Nico's idea, believe it or not."

"Even more surprising. Kingsley will be thrilled."

"As they say—Christmas comes but once a year. Luckily, I'm not Christmas."

No, she came at least three times last night alone.

"Breakfast sounds very nice."

They went into her kitchen. Both of them had slept with someone else the night before, and yet as soon as she and Søren were together again, back in her kitchen again—he made the coffee, she started breakfast—it was like they were an old married couple once more. Contented. Happy. Comfortable.

"You think we should play the game again next year?" Nora asked as she took the plates from the cabinet. Søren poured two cups of coffee.

"I prefer our traditional Christmas celebration, actually," he said, leaning back against the counter, cup of coffee in his hand.

"Right, right," she said. "Sodomy under the Christmas tree. Noted."

He lifted his cup in a salute. "Yes, and a priest can never have too many pairs of black socks."

FIN.

ABOUT THE AUTHOR

Tiffany Reisz is the *USA Today* bestselling author of the Romance Writers of America RITA®-winning Original Sinners series.

Her erotic fantasy *The Red*—the first entry in the Godwicks series, self-published under the banner 8th Circle Press—was named an NPR Best Book of the Year and a Goodreads Best Romance of the Month.

Tiffany lives in Kentucky with her husband, author Andrew Shaffer, and their two cats. The cats are not writers.

Subscribe to the Tiffany Reisz email newsletter:

www.tiffanyreisz.com/mailing-list

Return to *USA Today* bestseller Tiffany Reisz's Original Sinners series with *Winter Tales,* a collection of three fan-favorite Christmas novellas plus a novella exclusive to this anthology.

eBook, Paperback, Hardcover, and Audio

EVEN MORE WINTER TALES

MICHAEL'S
WINGS

AN ORIGINAL SINNERS COLLECTION

TIFFANY REISZ

A companion collection to *The Angel*, featuring a new novella and five previously published short stories starring the Original Sinners' Michael and Griffin.

Stories include "Griffin in Wonderland," "Gauze," "The Theory of the Moment," "A Better Distraction," the holiday story "Christmas in Suite 37A," and a new erotic novella guest-starring Mistress Nora!

eBook, Paperback, Hardcover, and Audio

9 781949 769517